# GEORGINA DEVON

# REGENCY
*Rakes &*
*Rebels*

**MILLS & BOON**

MIX
Paper from
responsible sources
FSC
www.fsc.org    FSC® C001695

Published by
Harlequin Mills & Boon
An imprint of Harlequin Enterprises (Australia) Pty
Limited (ABN 47 001 180 918), a subsidiary of
HarperCollins Publishers Australia Pty Limited
(ABN 36 009 913 517)
Level 13, 201 Elizabeth Street
SYDNEY NSW 2000 AUSTRALIA

Printed and bound in Australia by McPherson's Printing Group

# CONTENTS

## *GEORGINA DEVON*

began writing fiction in 1985 and has never looked back. Alongside her prolific writing career, she has led an interesting life. Her father was in the United States Air Force, and after Georgina received her B.A. in social sciences from California State College, she followed in her father's footsteps and joined the USAF. She met her husband, Martin, an A10 fighter pilot, while she was serving as an aircraft maintenance officer. Georgina, her husband and their young daughter now live in Tucson, Arizona.

# The Rake

# Chapter One

The morning sun barely peeked through the thick overhang of tree limbs. Green Park was still deserted at this time of morning. Not even the servants were about.

'Miss Juliet, you can no' be doing this,' Ferguson Coachman said sternly, his voice breaking the morning quiet.

Juliet Smythe-Clyde looked up between her thick cinnamon eyelashes while wiggling her toes in the too-large Hessians she had commandeered from her younger brother's wardrobe. She stamped her foot to try and better settle the heel. 'Rather this than for Papa to fight the Satanic Duke.'

The tall, spare coachman, his grey whiskers bristling about a narrow face, frowned. 'The master is a grown man. You are a slip of a girl and should no' be fighting his battles.'

'Enough,' Juliet said, slipping off the coat that fitted her brother like a second skin and herself like a too-large nightrobe. 'Take this and fold it carefully. You know Harry will have an apoplexy if it gets wrinkled.'

Ferguson snorted, but carefully laid the coat on the seat

of the dilapidated coach. Hobson, the butler, who was as round as he was majestic, presented the box holding two duelling pistols to his young mistress. Juliet reached for the one on the bottom.

That one is primed and ready to go, miss,' Hobson said. 'I saw to it myself.'

Out of perversity, Juliet took the top one.

'That too is ready,' Hobson said, allowing himself a knowing smile which quickly disappeared. 'Stop this now, Miss Ju, while there is still time.'

Ferguson came to stand beside his crony, the two having become fast comrades despite the disparity in their stations. 'Have I no' been telling her the same since this began? She will no' listen to either of us.'

'I have to do this,' Juliet said, her voice cracking as the fear she had been holding at bay threatened to spill out of control. 'Someone must protect Papa from this latest folly.'

'Someone should no' be you, lass,' Ferguson retorted, his brogue thickening with anger and anxiety. 'You did no' tell the master to marry that doxy.'

'I promised Mama to care for Papa,' she whispered, the memory of her mother's dying request tightening her stomach. Mama was dead barely a year, yet Juliet remembered as if it had happened yesterday.

Mama had lain on the daybed in the morning room, the pale sunlight giving false colour to her shrunken cheeks. The illness that had eaten at her and kept her in constant pain had shrivelled her body and made Juliet secretly glad the end was near. She could not bear to see her beloved mama suffer so.

When Mama had beckoned her closer and begged her to care for Papa—flighty, irresponsible Papa—Juliet had promised. There had been nothing else she could do. She would have done anything to ease Mama's suffering. Anything. And someone had to watch over Papa once Mama was gone. Everyone knew that.

She sighed. She had not been able to keep Papa from marrying Mrs Winters, but she could keep him from throwing his life away for the woman. Surely not even the Duke of Brabourne would shoot to kill a young man who was only taking the place of the original dueller—would he?

Besides which, the Duke was at fault. Not she or Papa. The Duke was the one who had seduced another man's wife. As the one in error, he should delope. It was the honourable thing to do.

Juliet straightened her shoulders and sighted down the barrel of the pistol. At least growing up in the country had taught her something. She could shoot with the best of them, although Brabourne was said to be as deadly with a gun as he was with a sword and just as cold-hearted with either.

The sound of horses' hooves drew her attention. Three men stopped under a large oak some distance from Juliet's little group. All were dressed in greatcoats and shiny Hessians with beaver hats perched rakishly atop their heads. She knew all by reputation and one by sight.

Dressed in man's garb, she had paid a very late-night visit to Lord Ravensford, one of Brabourne' seconds, four days before to tell him there was a change in plans. The duel needed to be moved forward. His lordship, too surprised by a puppy visiting him uninvited, had agreed to the change without argument, although his bronze brows had been raised in sardonic amusement during the entire conversation.

The other two men she had never seen. Lord Perth was

said to be a rogue who went his own way, regardless of Society's rules. She guessed him to be the one who stood beside the bronze-haired Lord Ravensford. They were much of a height. She spared them little interest for they were not the person she was here to fight.

The third man jumped to the ground with a wiry grace that spoke of strength. She had heard the Duke was not only a rake but a Corinthian of the first stare. He was tall and lean, and when he shrugged out of his greatcoat and navy jacket, she noted his shoulders were broad in their stark white shirt, and his hips were narrow in their close-fitting breeches. His hair was as black as some said his heart was. His nose was a commanding jut of authority. She had heard his eyes were a deep blue, inherited from an Irish ancestor.

A *frisson* of something akin to fear, yet much more delicious, skittered down her spine. She turned away.

She gulped a deep breath of the cold air and wiped her damp palms along the sides of her breeches. For seconds she stared sightlessly at nothing and wondered if she would survive this encounter. It was a weakness she had not allowed herself before. She did not allow it for long now, either.

Lord Ravensford headed their way.

The rising sun glinted on his hair, making it look bright as a new-minted penny. There was a twinkle in his hazel eyes and a dimple in his square chin. He was a very fine-looking man.

'Well, puppy, where is Smythe-Clyde? You said he is the one who wanted this earlier meeting.'

Juliet felt a dull flush spread up her face only to recede. 'He...' she forced strength into her voice '...he is sick. Too sick to leave his bed. But honour demands that he meet

Brabourne. So, as his second, I am taking his place.' She looked defiantly at Ravensford.

Ravensford glanced from her to the servants. A hint of disapproval tinged his words. 'Where is the other second? And where is the surgeon?'

'There is no other second, and Ferguson—' she gestured to the coachman '—is as good as any surgeon.'

'Havey-cavey.' Ravensford's gaze bored into Juliet. 'You are only a boy. There is not a chance that Brabourne will meet you. If Smythe-Clyde is too scared to follow through with this, then let him accept the dishonour.'

Juliet's hands clenched. 'I assure you, my lord, that my... that Smythe-Clyde is not afraid to meet the Duke. He is ill. Rather than draw this affair out, I am empowered to meet the Duke in Smythe-Clyde's place.'

Ravensford shook his head. 'I will pass on your words, but I doubt they will change anything.'

Without further discussion, the Earl turned away. Juliet sagged.

'Just as it should be,' Hobson said with smug satisfaction. 'Not even the greatest rakehell in all England would meet a mere boy on the field of honour. Especially when the quarrel is with another.'

Juliet had known from the beginning that the entire thing was far-fetched and likely to fail, but she'd had to try. Even now, as she saw Ravensford talk to the Duke, who looked her way, she knew she had to do something. Papa still intended to meet the Duke at the original time, two days hence. Keeping Papa from coming here then was the next hurdle Juliet intended to face—after today's duel. One thing at a time, she always told herself. Anything could be accomplished if you did it one step at a time.

Even from this distance, Juliet could see a scowl mar the Duke's dark looks. The light breeze seemed to carry his words.

'Smythe-Clyde is a coward and I refuse to meet his stand-in.'

Panic shot through Juliet as the Duke turned from Ravensford and reached for the coat he had just discarded. She grabbed up one of the duelling pistols, aimed and fired. The noise was loud in the still morning. Splinters of wood exploded from the side of the oak nearest Brabourne. Her adversary spun around to face her.

Her bravado and the closeness of the shot froze her to the ground. Not even the Duke's advance towards her released her paralysed muscles. With the only part of her mind that still seemed to function, Juliet noted the liquid power of his body as he neared her. He stopped a scant foot from her shaking body and razed her with the coldest blue eyes she had ever seen.

'You are either an excellent shot or very lucky. I don't know who you are, or why you feel compelled to stand in for Smythe-Clyde, but the meeting between you and I is now personal. Whatever happens between us will have no bearing on the other. Do you understand me?'

His voice was as hard as his look, and yet the deep timbre did something to her insides that could only be described as exciting. Surely she was not going to fall under the legendary charms of one of England's greatest rakes? She had to wound him severely enough to keep him from meeting Papa, not swoon at his feet.

Juliet raised her chin up higher. 'I understand perfectly.'

'Good. Perth is going after a surgeon. We will wait upon their return to continue.'

Panic shot through Juliet. A surgeon would be fine if the Duke were the one injured. If she were, a surgeon would be a disaster.

'We do not need a sawbones, your Grace.'

His full bottom lip curved into a smile that was anything but friendly, yet did unnameable things to Juliet's breathing. 'You will need one, be sure of that.'

She blanched. 'Th...then Ferguson will do. He is better than anyone to be found in London.'

Brabourne's gaze flicked to the servant and back to Juliet. 'Your coachman.'

She nodded.

'Then it is on your head.'

He strode away before Juliet could respond. She stared after him. He walked with a loose-limbed grace that flowed from his shoulders down to his narrow hips. She began to understand how her stepmother had succumbed to him. Even she, an innocent in spite of her three-and-twenty years, would be hard pressed to resist him if he pursued her. Not that he would. Not in a millenium. Not before today and especially not after today. Still, there was something incredibly attractive about him.

'Miss Juliet,' Hobson said, breaking into her ridiculous thoughts, 'best you use the gun I first recommended. It is bad luck to use the one already shot.'

'And I need all the luck I can get,' she murmured.

Ferguson stepped forward. 'Now, you remember what I said?'

She nodded. 'We meet, turn our backs to one another and walk twenty paces. Pivot and fire.'

She nodded again, worry gnawing at her nerves. Her jaw wanted to clench and her legs wanted to run away. Her stomach twisted into a knot and, if she had eaten anything before coming here she would be vomiting. Did men feel this way? She knew Brabourne did not.

'Now, Miss Juliet,' Hobson said softly.

Glancing at him, she saw the anxiety he felt for her. It made her hands shake more.

She did not look at the coachman, knowing she would see the same fear in his eyes. Better to walk boldly forward and meet whatever fate held for her.

The pistol at her side, Juliet moved towards the approaching Duke. His black hair was tied back in a queue a style that was no longer in fashion, but then he was a rule unto himself. One strand had broken free. He ignored it, his attention on her.

Earlier she had seen and felt only the overwhelming sense of power he exuded…now she saw details. His brows winged over eyes the shade of indigo from which tiny lines radiated out, speaking of dissipation and long nights. The late-night growth of whiskers was black against his pale skin. His jaw was a firm line that belied the relaxed set of his shoulders.

He gave her a curt nod, and she knew it was time to turn and begin pacing. One, two…nineteen, twenty.

Juliet spun around, bringing her arm up as she moved. The pistol felt heavy and awkward. In spite of all her practice and determination, she wavered. It was one thing to plan on shooting a man. It was an entirely different thing to do so.

Brabourne had no such reservations.

A shot rang out in the still, quiet air. Juliet experienced a moment of surprise, followed by excruciating pain in her right shoulder. She crumbled to the ground, her pistol falling from unresponsive fingers.

He had shot her.

She brought her left hand up to the wound. Her fingers came away sticky. The metallic tang of blood pinched her nose. She felt herself losing consciousness and wondered if she would die.

'Here, here.' Ferguson fell to his knees beside her and waved smelling salts under her nose. 'This is no' the time to be passing out.'

Juliet nodded feebly. 'No. I have never fainted in my life. I shan't do so now.'

'That's my lass,' Ferguson said, probing gently at the wound.

A jolt like lightning twisted through Juliet. 'Ahh—that hurts,' she gasped.

Ferguson grunted. 'It will hurt much more before it gets better. The ball is lodged between muscle and bone. It must come out. You will be a while getting well.'

She gazed at him, knowing what he said and what it meant, but not wanting to believe him. 'How will I keep this from Papa? I cannot stay in my room unattended even for a day. He will need me. The staff will need me.'

Hobson was on her other side. 'You should have thought of those things before starting this harebrained escapade, miss.'

'I thought he would delope,' she said softly, wincing as Ferguson probed deeper. 'He...' She gasped as fresh pain seared her. 'He is the one at fault, not Papa. Not me.'

Dark spots danced in her vision. 'The smelling salts,' she whispered.

The two servants exchanged glances. Better to let her faint. She would not feel the pain.

'Is something vital severed?' the Duke of Brabourne said from where he had stopped to watch the situation. 'If the puppy had maintained a side profile instead of squaring completely around, the ball would have grazed the flesh of his upper arm. I did not shoot to kill him.'

'Thank you for that, your Grace,' Hobson said, never taking his attention off Juliet.

'Don't thank me for something I did for myself. If the boy dies, I must flee to the Continent,' Brabourne said. 'That does not suit my plans at the moment.'

Ferguson snorted in disgust.

'You understand perfectly,' Brabourne said. 'Now, what is the prognosis?'

'He's lost a fair amount of blood, and I do no' ken if I can get the ball out here. I can stop most of the bleeding.'

Ravensford, who had come up, looked down. 'You had better get the lad home, then. We will send the surgeon to your direction.'

Juliet listened to the men talking, their words seeming to come through a long tunnel, but at the mention of going home she forced her eyes open. 'Ca…cannot go home. No surgeon. No one know.'

The effort to talk made her feel even more light-headed. She tried to sit up, but found she could not.

'Do no' fash yerself, lad,' Ferguson said. He pressed a makeshift bandage to the wound, trying to staunch the flow of blood.

'What did he mean, not go home?' Ravensford asked.

Hobson, who had gone to the carriage for the laudanum

he had packed just in case, returned and said, 'Just that, my lord. The lad cannot go home.'

Brabourne eyed the butler. 'Surely you jest. What type of family does the boy have that he cannot go home?'

Hobson stoically met the Duke's gaze. 'The young master cannot go to the London house in this condition. We will convey him to the country estate.'

Juliet tightened her grip on the butler's hand. 'I must be bandaged so none will know. I cannot stay from home long. You know that.'

Ferguson, tried beyond his patience, said, 'You will do as we tell you.'

Juliet frowned. 'I will do as I must.'

'How far away is the estate?' Brabourne asked.

'Half a day, your Grace,' Hobson said.

'That is much too far, Brabourne,' Ravensford said quietly. 'The wound does not look fatal now, but the continued loss of blood could make it so.' He met his friend's gaze. 'You cannot afford that. Only six months ago you nearly did away with Williams in a sword fight. Prinny will not be so lenient with you if this boy dies.'

Brabourne smoothed one winged brow. 'You must take the puppy to his London house. There is nothing else to be done.'

Ferguson paused in his ministrations to look up at the Duke. 'I will no' do that, your Grace. The lad is right in saying that no one must know what has happened.'

Brabourne looked hard at the servant and spoke softly. 'Are you telling me no?'

Ferguson swallowed hard. 'Yes, your Grace, that be what I'm telling you.'

'And you?' Brabourne pinned Hobson with his gaze.

The butler's ruddy complexion blanched. 'I must stand by Ferguson, your Grace.'

Brabourne looked at Ravensford. The Earl shrugged.

'What is the boy's secret?' Brabourne demanded.

The two servants looked long at one another. Hobson made the Duke a bow. 'The young master met you today without anyone knowing, except us. Lord Smythe-Clyde still plans on meeting you in two days. Master Ju was hoping that by duelling with you today you would consider it finished and not be here when his lordship comes.'

'Stupid.' Brabourne shook his head.

'Misguided,' Ravensford murmured.

Juliet groaned as much from having her plan revealed and hearing how inadequate it sounded when spoken as from pain. Everyone's attention snapped back to her.

'Enough,' Ferguson said. 'Hobson, help me carry the young master to the carriage. We must be on our way if we hope to get him to Richmond before he has lost too much blood.'

'Ravensford?' Brabourne looked at his friend.

Ravensford put one well-manicured hand up as though to ward off a blow. 'Not me, Brabourne. Nowhere does it say a second's duty is to house a wounded opponent.'

Brabourne's lips thinned before forming a small smile. 'As usual, Ravensford, you are correct. I suppose if I don't want the boy to die on me I shall have to make arrangements for his shelter. It is apparent his servants are misguided in their loyalty.' He turned to the men who were in the process of depositing the youth in the coach. 'Take the boy to my town house.' He cast a wicked glance at his friend. 'Ravensford will direct the surgeon to my address.'

Ravensford made a mocking bow. The two servants exchanged horrified looks. Their charge lay limply on the cushions, having passed out when lifted.

'Is something amiss?' Brabourne enquired at his haughtiest.

Ferguson climbed out of the coach and made the Duke a bow. 'Nothing, your Grace. If you will give me directions, we will go there immediately. But we have no need of a surgeon. A clean knife, hot water and plenty of bandages will be enough.'

'Be sure you do not need help before turning it away,' Brabourne said quietly. 'I do not intend to have the boy die.'

'Neither do I, your Grace.' Ferguson stood his ground in spite of the discomfort that had him twisting his hands.

'Then follow me,' Brabourne ordered.

Minutes later, he, Ravensford and Perth cantered from the shelter of the trees, the lumbering coach close behind.

'I hope you do not live to regret this day's work,' Ravensford said.

'So do I, my friend.' Brabourne cast one last look over his shoulder. 'So do I.'

## Chapter Two

Sebastian FitzPatrick, Duke of Brabourne, frowned down at his unwanted guest. The boy's milk-white skin was covered in cinnamon freckles. Hair the colour of a sunset tangled around the sweep of cheekbone and curve of brow. There was a tight look around the eyes, as though the youth were in pain even though he slept. He probably was. It had taken time and considerable digging to extract the ball. He had lost a fair amount of blood during the ordeal and would be weak for some time.

A chair scraped behind Sebastian. 'Can I be helpin', your Grace?'

Sebastian glanced back at the coachman whose head had been nodding seconds before. Ferguson was the man's name. 'Has your master regained consciousness?'

'No, your Grace.'

'Have you eaten or had any sleep?'

'No, your Grace.'

'Then do so.'

'Beggin' your pardon, your Grace, but I must stay with the master.'

'One of my servants will do as well. Now go.' Sebastian returned his scrutiny to the boy.

He was as frail as a willow and with a hint of lavender about him, a strange scent for a man. Full lips the colour of pomegranates gave him an effeminate air. And yet the youth had fought him in a duel. He had put his life at stake for another person. Sebastian would not do so, and was sure he did not know anyone who would, with a few exceptions—Ravensford and Perth. Perhaps that was the fascination this boy had over him, the reason he found himself in this room gazing down at a person he did not even know. He reached out to touch the boy's brow.

The servant cleared his throat.

Sebastian's hand dropped to his side. 'Haven't you gone yet?' he asked without turning around.

'I can no' be leavin' my charge...your Grace.'

Irritation chewed at Sebastian. 'I told you that one of my servants will stand watch.'

The servant made a sound very much like choking. 'Beggin' yer pardon, your Grace, but I canna trust the young master to someone unknown.'

Sebastian lowered his voice to a silky thread. 'You are stubborn and forthright for a servant.' The coachman stood his ground even though his gaze lowered deferentially. 'Then I shall stay with your charge. Surely that will meet your requirement.' In the silence that followed, Sebastian heard the man gulp.

'I must no' leave his side.'

'Are you afraid I will do something to your precious

charge? I have plenty of vices, but I assure you that molesting boys is not one of them.'

Ferguson whitened, but spoke around his obvious discomfort. 'I am well aware of your Grace's pastimes.'

His patience suddenly gone, Sebastian spun around. *'Get out now.'* Still the servant hesitated. Sebastian wondered what kind of master the boy must be to engender such loyalty in his people. 'If you do not leave, I shall have you thrown bodily from the room. When your master awakens, I wish to speak privately with him. In the meantime, I will watch him and have my housekeeper provide anything needed. I don't want him dead any more than you do.'

Still the servant stayed. Sebastian strode to the fireplace and reached for the velvet cord above the mantel.

'Ferguson...' a weak voice came from the bed '...do as his Grace says. I will be all right.'

'I'll no' be leavin' you with the likes of his Grace.'

This loyalty was vastly interesting, but Sebastian was not known for his patience. 'Get out now, before I finish what I started and have my footmen throw you out.'

The boy struggled to sit and the servant rushed to his side. 'No, you should no' be doing this.' The coachman fussed like a mother hen.

'Go,' the boy said. 'If the Duke wanted to hurt me, he would have...' He took laboured breaths, his cheeks flushing and then paling. 'He would have aimed to kill.'

'You ken why I can no' leave,' Ferguson muttered under his breath.

Sebastian had excellent hearing, but said nothing. There was something amiss here, and he was beginning to see what it might be. There was a delicacy to the youth's wrist when he lifted it to pat the servant's gnarled hand. Sebas-

tian's mouth twisted. He was a fool not to have seen it earlier, but the puppy's bravery had blinded him.

The boy whispered, 'You will only make him more suspicious by insisting.' Raising his voice, the youth said, 'Now
go. You may come back as soon as his Grace is done questioning me. Please.'

Ferguson gave the Duke a threatening look, but did as
ordered. The door closed behind the servant with a defiant snap.

Sebastian noted the dark circles under the girl's gold-
flecked hazel eyes, for girl she was. Now that he knew, it
was obvious. He was a connoisseur of women and knew
that her lashes, the colour of honey sable and just as thick
as that fine fur, would be the envy of any courtesan. As
would the lush, burnt red curls that lay like flames on the
pillow. For a moment he wondered if her temper matched
her hair and if her passion matched her determination. It
would be interesting to find out—but not now.

'Why are you impersonating a boy?' he asked without
preamble.

She paled even more, but her voice was defiant. 'You are
addled from too much dissipation, your Grace.'

He smiled slowly, his gaze running boldly over her, enjoying her bravado. 'Not at the moment. Now that I look
beyond your dress…and actions, it is obvious you are a
woman.' He ignored her snort. 'Probably with your breasts
bound and the borrowed finery of a male family member.
Since I have never had your acquaintance foisted on me,
you haven't been presented to Society, although you speak
and carry yourself like Quality. I would imagine you have
lived your life in the country and have only recently come
to town.'

She stared baldly at him. For a long moment, Sebastian thought she would continue to deny her true gender.

With a sigh of weariness, she sank back into the pillow. 'But, how…? You did not suspect before…?'

Sebastian smiled, a rare one of enjoyment that softened the hard angles of his face. He reached for the hand nearest him, realised it was on her wounded side before touching her and stretched across her instead. He caught her fingers even as she started to slide them under the covers.

Leaning over her, he brought her captured hand towards him, but not so near as to force her on to her wounded shoulder. He turned the palm up.

'Your skin is soft as velvet and unblemished. Your nails are short but well cared for. No sun has touched you to toughen or darken your complexion.' One by one, he examined her fingers. 'Long and elegant. A lady's hands. Certainly not those of a man.'

With that inherent need to charm and seduce that made him the successful rake he was, he brought her hand to his lips. She yanked back as though bitten. He let her go.

'Why did you meet me?'

She met his eyes openly even as her body sagged visibly with exhaustion. 'I had to. Someone had to stand up to you.' Her voice was weak, but a thread of determination ran through it.

Sebastian found himself taken aback by her vehemence. 'Stand up to me?'

The hand of her wounded arm lay flaccid. Her other hand clenched the fine linen sheet. 'You are a libertine and a dangerous, amoral man in a position of power that has allowed you to do as you pleased.'

A glint of admiration for her courage lit his eyes, only to

be doused by an emotion Sebastian had long ago decided would not rule him. She spoke only the truth. 'And what of it? I am not the only one of my ilk.'

'I know,' she muttered. 'But you are the only one of your kind to impact on my family.'

'Ah,' he said mildly, his reactions once more under control. 'Your family. What is Smythe-Clyde to you? An uncle, cousin, father?'

Her skin, which he had thought pale as milk, took on the translucent clarity of the moon. With the right clothing she would be a beauty; a very unusual one, but a beauty none the less. Beautiful women intrigued him—for a while.

She turned away from him. Her chest laboured. 'It is none of your business.'

'A lover, perhaps?'

Her head whipped back and there was such anger in her that he found his interest increasing. When one could have anything one wanted, a challenge was not to be ignored. Particularly one with such possibilities.

'You are perverted,' she breathed.

He pulled the nearest chair to the edge of the bed and lounged back into it. 'No, merely curious.'

He found himself fascinated by the way colour played across her cheeks, only to flee and return again later. Her lips compressed into a thin line, then opened like a fine rose when heated by the sun.

She sighed. 'It is none of your business, and I am too tired to continue arguing with you.'

He could see by the deepening of lines around her eyes and mouth that she spoke the truth. 'This is a delicious game we play, my sweet, but you are right, you have not the strength for it.'

Her face tightened. The angle of cheek and jaw sharpened. But she said nothing.

He studied her a while longer. 'I can always make enquiries about Smythe-Clyde's family. I assure you it will not take my secretary long to find out more.'

Her body stiffened. 'Why are you doing this?'

'Because you are a mystery, and mysteries beg to be solved.'

'A mystery. Something to entertain you, not a person.'

He nodded his head in curt acceptance of her hit. 'Exactly. What is Smythe-Clyde to you?'

Her chin lifted. 'My father. Now will you leave me alone?'

The answer was not what he had expected. 'For now.'

Not only was the girl foolhardy, she was reckless. As the daughter of a baron, she would be completely ruined if word of her escapade got out. Well-brought-up young ladies did not even know about duelling, let alone participate in one. Worse, if rumour reached the *ton* that she was in his house, in one of his beds, Society would try to force him to marry her. The girl had to go.

Long minutes went by as they met each other's gaze. The clock on the mantel chimed eight. A knock on the door signalled interruption.

He rose with languid grace and crossed to the closed curtains of the window before saying, 'Enter.'

Juliet sagged in relief when Ferguson entered carrying a tray. Exhaustion, pain and fear ate at her. What would Brabourne do now that he knew she was a woman? Would he denounce her to the world?

She glanced over to see him watching her with a brooding intensity that did nothing to calm her frayed nerves.

He was dressed for evening. Perhaps Almack's, although she doubted that he frequented that very respectable Marriage Mart. More likely he was headed out to one of his clubs, to be followed by dalliance with one of his many female companions. At least this time it would not be with her stepmother.

Still, he was the most handsome man she had ever seen. The perfect cut of his black coat showed broad shoulders to advantage. Black pantaloons hugged narrow hips, and white stockings revealed impeccable calves. His cravat was tied in what she assumed was the Brabourne Soirée, an arrangement her younger brother had yet to be successful duplicating, although Harry tried repeatedly. But all Brabourne's sartorial elegance was nothing compared to the man himself.

He took her breath away. Or, more probably, she told herself, it was her wound making her think air was in short supply. His unfashionably long hair waved over his collar like a raven's wing, moving with every step he took. His eyes were brilliantly blue and penetrating. Too penetrating, she thought, as a blush heated her flesh. And his mouth. She had only seen lips like his on the marble face of a Greek god. His male beauty—for there was really no other word to describe how he looked—was marred only by a look of bored dissipation that hovered around his eyes and mouth.

She was more than thankful he had no interest in her, for she did not think she could resist him if he wanted her. Better for all of them if she left immediately. Ferguson would see to it. He should have taken her to her father's country house in the first place.

'Here, young master,' Ferguson said, setting the tray down on the table near the bed.

The scent of chicken broth made Juliet's mouth water. She tried to sit up, but after a feeble attempt fell back. The exertion made her voice a thin reed. 'There is no need for the pretence, Ferguson. His Grace knows I am a woman.'

Ferguson's hand, with a spoon of broth, paused halfway between bowl and patient. He cast the Duke a fulminating look.

'Don't worry,' the Duke drawled, 'I will resist the urge to ravish her. But you had best see to it that no one else realises her deception.' His eyes gleamed wickedly. 'I cannot control everyone who works for me.'

'Yes, your Grace,' Ferguson said, frowning down at Juliet. 'I will have the lass out of here before anyone is the wiser.'

'That would be best,' her reluctant host said, going to the door. He looked back at her once, then left. The door closed softly behind him.

Tension Juliet hadn't felt rushed out, and she sank further into the softness of the feather bed. 'As soon as I've eaten we must leave.'

Ferguson nodded. 'Hobson will be back shortly to see how you do, lass. I will fetch the coach while he is here.'

Tenderly, he propped her up on the full pillows and helped her eat the broth. Juliet was glad of his help since her hand refused to be steady. When she finished her head fell back.

'I am so tired, Ferguson. I think I will sleep. Waken me when Hobson arrives.'

'Yes, lass.' He poured a generous portion of laudanum into a glass and added water to blunt the bitter taste of the medicine. 'Take this. It will help ye sleep and ease the discomfort.'

Ju smiled weakly. 'I do not need it to sleep, but it would

be nice to have less pain.' She swallowed the concoction with a grimace.

Ferguson settled her comfortably, noting that she fell asleep before he reached his chair. She was a good, brave lass. Headstrong and not much accomplished in feminine things, but a good girl.

Sebastian lifted his hand and a waiter rushed over. 'Another bottle of port.'

'Immediately, your Grace.' The servant hurried away.

'This is our sixth bottle,' Ravensford said. He tunnelled long, white fingers through his thick red hair. He had a smile and a way about him that could charm the chemise off a doxy without a penny changing hands.

'Then we are four behind,' Jason Beaumair, Earl of Perth, said. He was wickedly handsome, with the blackest eyes set in a narrow face, which was framed in equally black hair frosted at the temples and forehead. A scar ran from his right eyebrow to the corner of his mouth. It was said he had received it in a duel over another man's wife.

Sebastian gazed at his friends. If Jonathan, Marquis of Langston, were here, they would be complete. But Langston had married the famous actress, Samantha Davidson, and was an infrequent visitor to White's now.

'We need one more for whist,' Sebastian said, pouring from the newly arrived bottle of port.

A flurry of words, followed by the thud of a table hitting the floor, drew Sebastian's attention. A boy—or young man—was wrestling his way into the room. The youth had a narrow face and carrot-red hair. His hazel eyes were wild and angry. Freckles marched across his prominent nose, looking as though a cook had sprinkled nutmeg on his skin.

His gaze came to rest on Sebastian. Fierce satisfaction curled the boy's lips into a snarl. 'Release me!' he demanded, twisting out of a servant's grasp. He strode to Sebastian's table.

Sebastian took in the look of the cub and knew instantly who he was related to. In a bored tone, he said, 'A Smythe-Clyde.'

'Harold Jacob Smythe-Clyde.' The boy stood defiantly, hands on hips.

Sebastian groaned inwardly. First the chit and now this. And all because of Emily Winters. The former Mrs Winters was getting the cut direct the next time he had the misfortune to meet her, and the girl was leaving as soon as he returned home.

He propped one well-shod foot on the table and lounged back to look up at Harold Jacob Smythe-Clyde. 'You are not invited to join us,' he drawled.

The boy drew himself up. 'I did not come to game with scum such as yourself…your Grace.'

Sebastian raised one dark brow. He sensed both Ravensford and Perth tensing. To ease them he waved one languid white hand. 'Then begone. You are a bore.'

'And you, sir, are a libertine, a rake and a seducer of innocent women.' The furious words fell into a dearth of sound. Red rose up the boy's cheeks and spread to his ears. But he held his ground.

The tic at Sebastian's right eye started. He focused on the cut of his shoe. 'You tread dangerous ground,' he said softly.

'I challenge you to a duel. Weapons of your choosing.' If the boy's voice trembled, it was barely noticeable.

'I do not stoop to duel with halfwits.' Sebastian reached

for his glass and took a long drink of the strong wine. This family was becoming unacceptable.

'You, your Grace, are a bastard. I know how you—'

In one smooth movement, Sebastian rose to his feet. He planted a facer on the boy that knocked the cub to the floor. 'No one calls me a bastard,' he said quietly, dangerously. 'Now get out of here before I run you through where you stand.'

He poured out the remainder of the bottle and downed it in one long swallow. 'It is time we left,' he said, his gaze sweeping over his friends. 'White's has lost its exclusivity.'

Before the boy could get to his feet, Sebastian and his friends left. The hour was early yet, and St James's was crowded with people.

'Another puppy after your blood,' Perth said in his dark, deep voice. 'Smythe-Clyde must have been busy in his youth.'

'My understanding,' Ravensford said, swinging his gold-tipped cane nonchalantly, 'is that the baron has only one son.' He smiled at Sebastian. 'And you just laid him out with an upper cut that Jackson himself would have admired.'

Sebastian settled his beaver hat at a devilish angle. 'That is high praise coming from someone Jackson cannot defeat in the ring.' He glanced around. 'But enough. Shall we head for Annabell's? There is more to life than wine and gaming.'

'So true,' Perth drawled, falling into step. 'There is wine, gaming and women.'

'Particularly women,' Ravensford said with a devilish gleam in his eyes.

## Chapter Three

In the small hours of the morning, Sebastian strolled into the room where his unwelcome guest stayed. The two servants hovered around the bed, muttering direly. The Duke did not like the tension he sensed.

'What is the matter?' Sebastian asked, striding to the group.

Hobson looked up, his round face creased with worry. 'Miss Juliet is worse.'

Sebastian looked at the patient. Her face was flushed. The nightshirt he had loaned her lay damply against her neck and shoulder. Her hands fluttered like trapped butterflies. Irritation mingled with concern, making his brows dip inward.

'Is her wound inflamed?'

Ferguson looked up from where he was gently taking the bandage off. 'I believe so, your Grace.'

The skin where the ball had entered was swollen and red, with streaks of crimson starting to form. Her eyes opened and their sparkling gaze alighted on Sebastian.

'Brabourne,' she muttered, the words slurred but recognisable. 'A man's nemesis and a woman's heart's desire.' She giggled, only to end in a gasp of pain as Ferguson tried to clean the seeping wound. 'Blast! Must you be so clumsy?' she gasped.

They were the last coherent words she said as Hobson tipped a glass of water and laudanum down her throat.

'I need to make a poultice,' Ferguson said, laying aside the cloth he had used to sponge her shoulder. He looked at the Duke.

Sebastian almost sighed as he felt the noose of involvement tightening around his neck. It was obvious the chit could not be moved. 'And what do you expect from me?'

'You are supposed to have one of the best stables in the country, your Grace. I am sure your head groom has what I need.'

'You mean to put the same poultice on your mistress that you would use for a horse?'

Ferguson shrugged. 'It works for four-legged creatures. Why not two-legged ones?'

Sebastian had no better suggestion since they would not allow a doctor, which he thoroughly agreed with now that he knew the circumstances. 'Go and tell Jenkins that you have my permission to use whatever you need.'

The one servant left and, with a resignation that tightened his gut, Sebastian turned to the other. 'And what do you need?'

Hobson glanced up. 'More cool water would help, your Grace. Miss Juliet is raging hot; no matter how much I sponge her, she only seems to burn the more.'

Sebastian moved to the bellpull over the mantel only to stop before summoning a servant. His brooding glance settled on the girl. With her flushed cheeks and swollen lips, no one could mistake her for anything but what she was. If someone were still so unobservant as to think she was male, the swell of her breasts under the shirt and single sheet would be enough to enlighten them. One of the first things she had done after he had pierced her disguise had been to remove the binding from her breasts so she could breathe better and lie more comfortably.

This situation was becoming more and more complicated. The very last thing he needed was for word of his unwanted guest's real identity to leak out. At three and thirty, Sebastian had no intentions of marrying someone not of his choosing. Not even if some foolish chit's reputation depended upon him wedding her.

Nor did he want the world to know he had shot a woman. It was bad enough that he knew. Damn her for putting him in this dishonourable position.

He pulled the bell and moved quickly into the hall. A footman appeared instantly, impeccably dressed in the Duke's black and green colours.

'Fetch Mrs Burroughs,' Sebastian instructed.

The young man's eyes widened, but he bowed and left.

Sebastian had a rule that servants who worked during the day would not be expected to work at night. That went particularly for his housekeeper and butler, whom he knew laboured fourteen and sixteen hours a day. Never before had he summoned Mrs Burroughs from her bed. He did not intend ever to do so again.

He stepped back into the sickroom. Mrs Burroughs would knock, and he did not intend for anyone else to hear their discussion.

Juliet Smythe-Clyde looked no better. Hobson's worried

frown was deeper. 'Ferguson knows what he's about,' the butler mumbled, as though to reassure himself.

'If he does not, then we are going to have problems,' Sebastian stated. 'I have no intentions of fleeing to the Continent. Nor do I intend for anyone to discover your mistress's whereabouts.'

A discreet knock stopped the butler from saying whatever was on the tip of his tongue. Instead he turned back to his charge.

Sebastian crossed to the door and asked, 'Mrs Burroughs?'

'Yes, m'lord.'

He let her in, quickly closing the door behind her. 'We have a problem.'

She looked from him to the bed. Her iron-coloured brows shot up, wrinkling her forehead into a dozen creases. Her mouth puckered in dismay and then disapproval. ''Twould seem we do, *your Grace.*' Her emphasis on his title told him more clearly than words that she was shocked and unhappy with the situation.

He looked at the old woman who had started service with his father over thirty-two years ago. She had been his nanny. When he'd inherited the title, he had retired his parents' housekeeper and appointed Mrs Burroughs. She was not a woman who would have taken well to retirement.

'You are the only person I can trust with this information. We must nurse her until she is able to be moved. And no one must find out.'

She snorted. 'I would hope my husband can be trusted with this, your Grace. 'Twill take more than the three of us here to give the girl round-the-clock care. I have a house to run, I'm sure this gentleman here has duties, and you have all of London to carouse through.'

The disapproval in her voice when she described his activities was softened by the affection in her brown eyes. She did not like the life he led, but she cared for him.

Hobson, realising that Mrs Burroughs had a sensible head on her shoulders, moved closer. 'I am the butler to Miss Juliet's father and I cannot be gone much.'

Her knowing gaze went from Hobson to the girl. 'A secret. Well, his Grace was always one for getting into scrapes.'

Ferguson's return from the stables saved Sebastian from needing to comment. There were times he regretted making his nanny his housekeeper.

Ferguson set about applying the poultice.

Late the next afternoon, Sebastian sat at table breaking his fast. Soon he would have to take up his post with the patient. Ferguson had returned to Smythe-Clyde's house after rebandaging the shoulder. Hobson had stayed until Mrs Burroughs could find time in the late morning hours. Burroughs had been in and out. From the surreptitious glances the footman was sending his way, Sebastian knew the servants wondered what was going on.

'Your Grace.' One of the footmen bowed and presented a silver tray on which lay a white calling card with the corner bent.

Sebastian picked it up and read the name Harold Jacob Smythe-Clyde, his unwelcome charge's brother. 'I am not at home.'

'Yes, my lord.'

Minutes later, the sound of a raised voice reached Sebastian. It was followed by the closing of the front door. This family was nothing but trouble.

With a sigh, Sebastian rose. How had he let himself get into this predicament? He was a man who had always considered his own comforts first.

First it had been to keep the girl's servants from taking her into the country and possibly threatening her life. Then it had been because she was too sick to be moved.

In an unconscious gesture, he smoothed his left eyebrow with one finger. Now he allowed the chit to stay here because she needed to regain some strength before returning home. In her present condition it would not be long before someone realised she was hurt. Then the duel would come out, and her stay here. That would ruin her. Her courage intrigued him and he did not want to see her pay for it. Too few people of his acquaintance had her strength.

In spite of all that, respectable young women of the *ton* did not spend nights under any man's roof, let alone his. His reputation as a rake did not bear scrutiny. Even he, as immune as he was to Society's dictates, would be hard pressed to refuse marriage if it were ever discovered that the girl had spent several nights under his roof. She had to leave. Soon.

In the meantime, he would amuse himself at Tattersall's. There was a fine filly that had caught his eye last week. Spirited and headstrong, the horse reminded him of his unwanted guest. At least with the animal he could determine whether he wanted her in his stable.

Juliet roused from a nightmare where Papa duelled with Brabourne and was hit. Moisture beaded her brow and her night shirt clung to her skin. Why was she so hot?

Where was she?

The sound of someone lightly snoring caught her attention. A long, lithe man sprawled in one of two chairs, his legs spread out and seeming to go on for ever. A wave of dark hair shadowed his sallow cheeks and gave him a demonic cast.

Memory returned.

She rolled to one side and pushed up with her good arm. Pain shot through her bad shoulder. She gasped and squeezed her eyes shut against unwanted tears.

'What the deuce are you about?'

She turned her head and stared straight up at him. Without her hearing him he had come to the bed. His black brows were drawn and his blue eyes shot sparks.

'I am trying to sit up,' she said peevishly, wishing she did not hurt so much. 'Why else would I be twisting around?'

'Whining does not become you,' he stated baldly, the lines between his brows easing. 'Let me help you or you will undo all the good work your coachman has done.'

Without waiting for her reply, he reached down and hooked a hand under each of her arms and hauled her up on to the pillows. Another gasp of pain escaped her and once more tears welled in her eyes. She told herself that her blurred vision gave her the impression his face held contrition. There was no doubt in her mind that he found her a nuisance rather than someone he might be concerned over.

Long moments passed and his hands stayed on her. His warmth flowed into her, increasing her fever and making her pulse jump. No man had ever touched her so intimately. Juliet looked up at him and felt herself blushing.

He finally released her. 'Is that better?' he asked, his voice hoarse as though he had a cold.

She nodded. Strange sensations coursed through her

body, and for a weak moment she wished he would touch her again. She was a fool.

'Would you like some water?'

'Yes,' she muttered. 'Please. I am so hot. It is like a furnace in here.'

He poured the liquid and held it to her lips. 'You are feverish. The wound is inflamed and Ferguson has been treating it with horse poultices.'

Juliet chuckled. 'That is very like him. Has it helped?'

He set the empty glass on a stand. 'It seems so. This is the first time since last night that you have been awake and coherent at the same time.'

Her eyes widened. 'Surely you jest?'

'Not about this.' He turned away and fetched the chair he had been sprawled in. He set it near the bed and sank into its thick leather cushions.

'I suppose not,' she said, looking away from his intense perusal. 'I cannot suppose I am the kind of woman you would choose to be in one of your beds.' As soon as the words were out, she realised how provocative they were. 'I... I did not mean that the way it sounded.'

He raised one brow. 'You did not? How disappointing.'

She had thought herself warm before, but now she flamed.

A slow smile cut a line into his cheek. It was seductive in the intensity it gave to his face, as though he were truly interested in her as a woman. Part of her wanted to melt. A larger part wanted to run. He was a dangerous man for a woman to be around.

'I am sure there are many women eager to share one of your beds and that none of them would be here from wounds.' The words came out like an accusation instead of the reasonable statement of fact she had intended. He was a disturbing man.

'True, but then they would be boring. You, I'd wager, are never boring.'

She had a sense that he was flirting with her. She looked away from his unsettling scrutiny and her fingers plucked at the sheet without her being aware of what she did.

'Anyone can be boring,' she finally whispered.

'So I have generally found,' he replied drily. 'But then no other woman has ever fought me in a duel. Nor has any other woman told me she could not go home and then convinced me to let her stay in mine. Why wouldn't your family help hide your condition?'

The abrupt change of subject surprised her. It was as though he had been trying to trick her into answering him, but there was no secret. 'Harry would have. Poor Papa would have run to his new wife and expected her to handle everything. I don't trust my stepmother. Everything she does is designed to further her own ends. She would be furious.'

'Because you fought a duel or because you tried to take your father's place?'

'Both.'

'Would she have hit you?' His eyes darkened as he waited for her answer. 'Would your father?'

'No,' she squeaked, shocked that he could even think such a thing. 'Papa has never hit us. Mama was always the one to discipline us. She or our nurse, and later our governess and tutor. My stepmother would not dare.'

His mouth tightened. 'Did you see much of your mother?'

A soft smile of memory lit Juliet's face. 'Yes. Always. Mama was a curate's daughter, and she believed children were a gift to be treasured.'

'A nice fancy,' he said, bitterness making the words hard and brittle.

No emotion showed on his face. It was as though he had shut his real self behind a mask. The urge to ask him why was great, but Juliet hesitated. He was not a man who invited closeness or questions about himself.

He stood so sharply that his chair tottered on its back legs before settling down. He paced to the fireplace, grabbed the poker and jabbed viciously at the already roaring fire.

Juliet saw pain in the tense set of his shoulders. The longing to comfort him was great, but she sensed that to say something would only make him draw further into himself. Instead, she waited quietly for him to make the next overture. She did not wait long.

He put the poker back and strode to the bed, where he grabbed the chair and repositioned it in its original place. 'I will send Mrs Burroughs to help you change into a fresh shirt. But first tell me why your father's anger kept you from going home when you knew he would not punish you.'

She smiled ruefully. He would not give confidences, but he expected them of others. Still, it would do no harm. 'I could not have kept my condition hidden from Papa. When he found out, he would have been angry with me because he would have been hurt that I felt he needed to be protected. That I did not trust him to take care of himself. Although everyone will tell you that he cannot.'

'A grown man cannot take care of himself?' the Duke asked in disbelief. 'I think you exaggerate.'

'Not about Papa. He can find his way anywhere in the country, but he is forever becoming lost here in London. Just as he will misplace every one of the twelve pairs of glasses I have got for him. Or reach his hand into a lion's cage because he is curious about what the creature will do.' She gave a long-suffering sigh.

The Duke chuckled. 'A handful.'

'Always. At first I was thrilled that he was remarrying, even though it was not yet a year after Mama's death. But then...' She clamped her mouth shut on the words. In a falsely brisk voice, she stated, 'But that is neither here nor there. You are right, your Grace. A clean nightshirt would be most welcome.'

He made her a mocking bow before leaving. She had no doubt he knew exactly what she had stopped herself from saying. After all, he was the man her stepmother was having an affair with. He would know the woman. Just the thought made her chest tighten, and the wound she had nearly forgotten started to ache anew.

How long would it take her to learn to protect herself against his charm? Probably for ever, said a tiny voice she wanted to ignore.

Sebastian sprawled across the large leather wingback, his right leg indecorously thrown over the chair's arm. He swung his foot, the evening pump catching the firelight. He twirled the half-full glass of whisky before taking a long swallow. The liquor burned down his throat. He smiled grimly. The savageness of the liquid matched the emotions running through him.

'Damned uncivilised drink,' he muttered, taking another gulp. He would probably consume the entire decanter. He had got a taste for it from his friend Jonathan, Marquis of Langston, who had learned about it from his younger brother, Lord Alastair St Simon.

The chit had to go. The only thing worse than having her

continued presence in his home would be to have her die while occupying one of his beds. She had already been here two days and was on her second night. But she was out of danger, or nearly so. And she was a distraction.

He emptied his glass.

A knock caught his attention as he rose to pour more whisky. 'Who is it?' he demanded, moving to his desk and emptying the contents of the decanter into his glass.

'Your Grace,' Burroughs, the butler, intoned, entering the room and closing the door behind himself. His long, rather bulbous nose rose several inches, a pose Sebastian knew the man assumed when his sensibilities were affronted.

'There is a *person* to see you.'

Sebastian raised one black brow. 'A *person*?'

Burroughs puffed up his ample girth. 'A woman...as your Grace very well knows.'

Which one of his lady-friends would be so lost to propriety as to visit him here? Sebastian neither cared nor knew. He drank the whisky in one gulp. 'Tell her I am not at home.'

Burroughs bowed, a smile of approval making his round face glow. 'My pleasure, your Grace.'

Sebastian set the empty glass on the corner of his desk and decided it was time for bed. Most of London was asleep, and only his irritation at having his home pose a threat to his peace of mind had kept him up this late.

Sounds of a scuffle barely preceded the library door bursting open. A woman dressed in black strode into the room followed by a harassed Burroughs.

'Your Grace,' she murmured breathlessly, 'I have something of the utmost importance to discuss with you.'

Sebastian was good at remembering faces and voices. He recognised his intruder and frowned. She was the reason he was in this bramblebath. He waved away Burroughs, who hovered behind her. The only way he could evict Mrs Winters—now Lady Smythe-Clyde—would be to have her bodily carried from the room. The hair rising on the nape of his neck told him to listen to her first.

Not until Burroughs closed the door behind himself did Sebastian offer her a seat. He propped one hip on the edge of his desk and looked down at her. 'It is very late to be making a social call, Lady Smythe-Clyde.'

She pushed back the hood of her cape and untied the strings at the throat. The heavy taffeta slipped from her shoulders to billow around her lap and spill down the back of her chair. Her pale blonde curls framed a heart-shaped face with eyes the colour of a fine spring sky. Many poems had been written about the beauty of her cupid's bow mouth. Her evening dress was daringly low, even for a married woman, and showed an almost childlike figure. Sebastian knew the heart of a courtesan beat under the small bosom. But why was she here? He had already refused her overtures.

She smiled endearingly up at him. 'Please, your Grace, do call me Emily. We shall soon be well acquainted.'

'Shall we?' he murmured, wondering what her game was and knowing it boded no good for him or the girl upstairs. He knew the former Mrs Winters from old. She had been as shocking in her flaunting of conventions as she was as Lady Smythe-Clyde. The rest of their conversation would likely be just as vulgar.

She threw back her head and laughed, a tinkling sound that was her signature. Slowly, her eyes only slightly narrowed, she lowered her head and smiled at him. 'Very well indeed. Do you know where my stepdaughter is?'

Sebastian kept his gaze on her even as the warmth provided by the whisky evaporated. 'Your stepdaughter? Do you have one?'

Her lips parted in a languid smile. 'Really, your Grace, there is no need for games between us.'

Sebastian put both palms on the desk and leaned backward. 'Isn't there? There is nothing between you and I, yet you are the reason your new husband challenged me to a duel.'

She leaned forward, showing the dark valley between her breasts. 'But there could be...'

Sebastian studied her, wondering how far she would go in her pursuit of him. Women flocked to him for his wealth and power. Usually, however, they took 'no' as just that. This woman had been pursuing him for the past month.

In a mildly curious voice, he asked, 'Why are you so persistent? You have an older husband who is titled and reasonably wealthy. Isn't that enough, considering where you started life?'

An angry scowl marred her childish beauty before she smoothed her brow with an index finger. 'My husband is not the Duke of Brabourne, one of the most influential men in the realm.' She paused for effect and flicked her small pink tongue along her bottom lip. 'Nor is he renowned as the best lover in England, a man all women find irresistible—in and out of bed.'

Sebastian's gut tightened. He dipped his head to her in mocking acknowledgement of her statement.

His father had never thought of him as more than a means to pass on the title. His mother had never thought of him at all, her own lovers being legendary and all-consuming.

In an attempt to be more than a title and money, he had

taught himself to be a lover. He had made himself into a man women remembered, and if it was by giving them more pleasure than any thought possible, then so be it. They would remember him as more than a wealthy Duke, an object of advancement. They would remember him as a man.

But not this woman. He had not even kissed her, and she had already caused him more problems than any of his numerous mistresses put together.

He smiled, a cold stretching of his sensual lips. 'Lady Smythe-Clyde, I would never presume to enter a dalliance with a married woman.'

Her own smile was equally frigid. 'You would do whatever you damn well pleased, and we both know it.'

'Ah, the gloves are off,' he murmured.

'As will be more than that,' she countered, 'if you know what is good for your future.'

'Are you threatening me?' he asked, his voice silky.

She smoothed the satin of her skirt, the action drawing attention to the fine lines of her thighs, her gaze never leaving his face. 'Nothing so dramatic. Merely offering not to divulge some information my lady's maid was so obliging as to find out for me.'

He did not need an explanation. Somehow, even with all his efforts to keep Juliet Smythe-Clyde's presence in his house secret, one of the servants had found out and spread the information. Eventually the news would spread to other homes of the *ton*. And quickly.

Whether he agreed to the dalliance being proposed or refused, the result would be the same. Juliet Smythe-Clyde was ruined.

'Just why exactly are you pursuing me?' he wondered. 'There are plenty of other men who would be eager to accept what you offer. And,' he added in an aside, 'I have it on good authority that some of them are very good in bed.'

She rose and sauntered to him. Running her index finger down his shirt, she watched him through thick blonde lashes. 'But none of them are you. You are rich and powerful...and appealing. You can raise me in the eyes of the *ton*. My husband cannot. He is a mere baron, and an old, fat one at that. He has no fire.' Her eyes took on a sultry gleam. 'And I desire you.'

Sebastian's lip curled. 'If you are so quick to cheat on him, then perhaps you should not have married him.'

Her tinkling laugh rang out as she stood on tiptoe and lightly kissed him. 'Do not come the naïve with me. You, of all people, know about women marrying men and then having *cicisbeos*.'

Sebastian stiffened, her words like ice sliding down his spine. Anger immediately followed—an anger so intense it would have melted any amount of ice.

'Out.' He spoke softly, but the menace of his posture clearly conveyed itself. 'Out before I wring your very lovely neck.'

The former Mrs Winters rose abruptly. Her fingers shook as she tied her cape around her shoulders. Still, she met his unyielding gaze without flinching. 'Do not take long to make up your mind, *Brabourne*. I am not a patient woman.'

He watched her sweep from the room, the heavy scent of jasmine lingering. Yes, he knew about women who cheated on their husbands. No matter what the repercussions, he would not be the one to help her cuckold Smythe-Clyde. Dallying with married women was one vice he did not have.

# Chapter Four

Juliet woke from a laudanum-induced slumber. Her shoulder throbbed and her eyes felt gummed over. Her mouth was filled with cotton, or so it seemed.

A brace of candles flickered on the mantel, their golden light illuminating a chair and table. The Duke lounged in what she thought of as his favourite piece of furniture, one hand holding a wine glass. She must have made a noise because he turned to look at her.

'I see you are finally awake. Ferguson must have overdone the laudanum last time.'

He rose and moved to the bed. She watched him in fascination. Perhaps it was her illness, but it seemed that he became more intriguing each time she woke. No wonder women flocked to him.

He put a cool hand on her forehead, and she jerked. He gazed quizzically down at her, a small smile curving his sensual lips. He was very aware of his effect on her.

'You are not as warm as earlier. Ferguson's poultice works. A good thing. You are going home tonight.'

'Going home?' she echoed, feeling stupid, but still reacting to his touch.

He nodded. 'There has been a new development and it is best that you leave. I am sending Mrs Burroughs with you. She will keep people from bothering you and provide the perfect alibi.'

'Alibi?' It was the remnants of the drug making her sound so dull.

The cold hauteur she associated with him returned, making his eyes resemble ice. 'Yes, alibi. Ferguson will drive you up to your home this evening and you will alight from your own carriage with Mrs Burroughs. Everyone will be told you had to make an emergency trip to visit your old nanny. Ferguson says she lives close enough that the excuse is plausible.

Juliet nodded, beginning to understand. 'But I cannot return in your nightshirt or Harry's clothes.'

'Do you think we are such poor conspirators?'

'Why don't I have my own maid, then?' she asked archly.

He stared at her for a moment. 'Why indeed? Let me think.' After a pause, he added, 'She was out running an errand for you when word of your old nanny's plight reached you. You did not have time to wait for the servant's return, you were so fearful of what might happen if you delayed.'

'And I paid Mrs Burroughs out of my pin money?'

'What else?' he countered, a devastating smile playing over his lips. 'Don't tell me your Papa keeps you on a short lead, for I shan't believe it. If he did so, you would never have been able to sneak off and meet me for the duel without someone finding out.'

'True,' she muttered. 'Neither Papa nor Emily care much what I do. Harry does, but he is too intrigued by his first visit to London to pay much attention to me. And since I run the household, it is easy to do as I please.'

'Exactly,' he stated.

She shook her head, amazed at his ingenuity and correct reading of her situation, and instantly regretted it. Her ears rang and dizziness made her close her eyes.

'Are you all right?' he asked, a tinge of anxiety in his voice.

She managed a tight smile. 'Yes. I have no intention of staying here longer and causing you further trouble.' She took several deep, slow breaths before opening her eyes. 'Did Hobson manage to get some of my clothes?'

'Yes. Your servants are loyal to foolhardiness,' he said curtly, disapproval obvious in the stiffness of his shoulders.

Her smile came again, softer. 'They have always been there to help. Mama used to say she would not accomplish half of what she did if not for them. They came with her when she married Papa. Hobson was a footman then, and Ferguson a stable boy.'

'Old family retainers. That explains a lot.'

A soft knock was followed by Mrs Burroughs' appearance. 'Your Grace. Miss.' She billowed into the room, her arms full of clothing. 'Now, you must leave,' she said to Brabourne, 'while I help Miss Juliet dress. I will let you know when to return.'

The Duke made a sardonic bow and left.

Mrs Burroughs helped Juliet sit up with pillows propping her back. From then on everything was agony, and it was only stubbornness that kept Juliet from fainting. She was going home. No longer would she be beholden to the man she had tried to shoot.

Juliet woke to the scents of lavender and lilac. She had to be in her own room because she always kept bowls of the dry flowers and fresh when they were in season. She stretched and winced. Her shoulder hurt.

Everything came back in a rush. The duel, the wound, the Duke. The last thing she remembered was him kissing her hand as he helped her into the carriage. The arrival home and her getting to her room were a blur.

She forced herself to a sitting position and stopped. Her head spun, and it was all she could do not to collapse back on to the pillows. She would have to move more slowly.

After what seemed an eternity the room stopped twirling. She swallowed, her tongue feeling swollen and dry. A little water would be nice. A glance at the bedside table showed a pitcher and glass. Careful not to set off another dizzy spell, she poured the liquid and drank it down. It tasted like ambrosia.

Only now did she notice that she was dressed in her favourite nightrail. She looked around, noting the shades of lilac and lavender in drapes, carpet and bed-covering. Being in her own room provided a sense of comfort and security that she had not realised she was missing until now. It was wonderful.

A knock alerted her instants before the door opened. A short, robust lady with a grey bun and iron-straight eyebrows slipped in, quickly closing the door behind herself. Mrs Burroughs. She held a silver tray from which came the smell of hot chocolate and toast. Juliet stared as the woman set the tray on a table by the fire.

'Thank you, Mrs Burroughs. I feel as weak as a new-born pup.'

'I've just the thing, then, Miss Juliet,' the housekeeper said, a twinkle in her brown eyes. 'I see you are much better, just as Ferguson said you would be. 'tis a good thing you hired me as your lady's maid for the last several days while you went to visit your old nanny. Bless the lady's heart, being so sick and all that she needed you immediately and left you no time to notify your father. Unfortunately, your note did not arrive till today.'

The Duke had thought of everything.

She crossed to the bed and put a sturdy arm around Juliet's waist and helped her to a chair. Juliet sank like a rock on to the lavender silk cushion of her favourite chair. She was so tired.

'How long will you be staying? It seems that I am not up to snuff yet.'

Mrs Burroughs smiled gently. 'As long as needed. I have already had the devil of a time keeping your own maid out. The only thing that has saved us is the fact that you hired the girl here in London and she has no loyalty to you. Now, take some hot chocolate and toast. You need plenty of nourishment to regain your strength.' She frowned as Juliet sipped the drink. 'I would give you some laudanum, for I know your shoulder pains you a great deal, but you will need all your wits about you today.'

Juliet sighed. 'So true. Emily will very likely be here at any moment, demanding to know why I took off like I did.'

'Tut, tut, child. We will get through this.'

Juliet nibbled a triangle of toast, her dry mouth making

it difficult to swallow. 'How long exactly was I at Lord Brabourne's? I seem to remember him saying two or three days.'

'Two nights and three days.'

*Two nights and three days.* Papa. The duel. She turned an anxious gaze to the other woman. 'What about Papa? Did he meet the Duke? Did Brabourne shoot him?'

'They met,' Mrs Burroughs said softly.

'Why was I not told?' Juliet demanded, trying to push herself up and failing.

'There, there. The Duke felt it was better that you not know. He did not want the worry causing a relapse.'

'It must have been while I was drugged with laudanum.'

Mrs Burroughs rearranged the pillow behind Juliet's back. 'It was, but everything is fine now. The Duke's bullet went wide and your Papa shot into the ground. No one was hurt.'

Juliet sagged in relief and a shiver of aftershock shook her. 'Then my foolishness accomplished something.'

'More than you know, child,' Mrs Burroughs murmured, a strange look on her face. 'But you are trembling. Where do you keep your robe?' Mrs Burroughs fetched it and put it around Juliet's shoulders.

Juliet huddled into the warmth of her lilac robe as another thought erupted. 'He could have shot Papa, but did not. Why? Is he admitting that he dallied with my stepmother?'

Fierceness toughened Mrs Burroughs's features. 'His Grace saved your Papa a nasty wound. That is not admitting anything. The Duke would never become involved with a married woman. Never.'

Juliet glanced at the older woman, surprised by her vehemence. It seemed that Brabourne also commanded loyalty. Juliet took a gulp of too-hot chocolate and choked. 'Ahh!'

Mrs Burroughs was instantly solicitous, her ire of seconds before forgotten. 'Are you all right?' Juliet nodded and wiped the tears of pain away with one hand. 'Are you always so impetuous? If so, the two of you will make quite a pair.'

Juliet put the china cup down on to the saucer with such force the chocolate sloshed over the edges. She stared at the woman and wondered if her hearing had been impaired by her injury.

'Whatever are you talking about?'

'You are stubborn like him, too.'

'Are we still discussing Brabourne?' Juliet asked with an underlying chill in her voice.

Mrs Burroughs sighed. 'You do not like him. Well, that is understandable. He does not have a good reputation, and he goes his own way and the devil take the hindmost. And he is arrogant.' She moved to the bed and straightened the cover but, even with her back to Juliet her words were clear. 'He came into his title young. Much too young. And he had a disappointment that made him bitter and hard. But he's good and honourable at heart.' She sighed again, her ample bosom rising and falling like a tidal wave. 'He just needs a situation to make him act good and honourable.' She turned to face Juliet and pinned her with intense brown eyes. 'You are that situation.'

Juliet's eyes widened, and her head jerked back at the force of the other woman's look and words. 'Me? are you mad?'

'No.' She leaned down to Juliet, her face serious and her voice lowered so that Juliet had to strain to hear. 'We tried to keep your presence in his Grace's home secret. We did everything we could think of, but somehow it leaked out. We made up the story of your whereabouts for your family and we will stick to it, but the rumours of where you really were will be circulating about the *ton* before long.'

Juliet shrank into her robe, thankful for its warmth as a chill of foreboding moved through her body. 'I am ruined.'

Mrs Burroughs nodded, sympathy softening the tightness around her mouth. 'His Grace must marry you, as he will soon realise.'

Juliet stared at nothing, not paying attention to Mrs Burroughs. 'Ruined—and I have not even been presented to the *ton*. I shall never dance at Almack's or have a coming-out ball. All the things I have missed because Papa was busy in the country and then Mama was ill.'

'His Grace will see that you have all those things.'

'Well,' Juliet said, still in her own world, 'I do not need those things.' Her chin notched up and she squared her shoulders. 'They are all fripperies that mean nothing and accomplish nothing. I shall tour the cultural sights here and then return home to Wood Hall where I belong.'

'We shall see. We shall see,' Mrs Burroughs muttered. 'Now, be a good girl and eat up your toast and drink every drop of that hot chocolate. You need everything we can get into you so that you regain your strength.'

Juliet obediently finished her repast. Daintily wiping her mouth, she canted her head to better see the other woman. 'But you can forget this harebrained idea of yours concerning Brabourne. I shall never marry a man of his ilk.'

Mrs Burroughs's lips parted but, before she could speak her mind the door to the room slammed open. The former Mrs Winters, now Lady Smythe-Clyde, stormed inside. Her fair hair curled around her dainty face, and a light white muslin Empire dress flowed around her colt-like limbs. Juliet could understand why her papa had married the woman.

Lady Smythe-Clyde thrust out a clenched fist, a sheet of paper crumpled in her fingers. 'See this? This is a note to your father. Me. You. From the Duchess of Richmond, saying she is truly sorry, but she rescinds our invitation to her ball.' Her fair face was mottled in anger. 'Because of you. You. Do you hear me?' Her voice rose into a shrill demand.

'I imagine the entire household can hear you, Emily,' Juliet said drily, using the other woman's Christian name. 'You may go,' she added to Mrs Burroughs. 'And thank you.'

The housekeeper hustled out.

'All my work. All my careful planning and it is all coming to naught,' Emily fumed as she paced the floor.

'I know this is a great disappointment to you, after all your plans and hard work to present me to Society.' Juliet managed to keep a tone of sympathy in her voice, even though she knew the other woman had merely used her as a reason for her pursuit of the *ton*.

Emily stopped in her tracks and a curl of contempt marred her otherwise perfect mouth. 'Let us lay off this game-playing, Juliet, for I am prodigiously tired of it. Bringing you out was to be my introduction to Polite Society; now, through your ill-judged stay in the Duke of Brabourne's house, you have put paid to everything I have worked so hard to achieve.'

Juliet suppressed a jolt of shock. How did Emily know? Surely the rumours had not reached here yet? 'How can you say that? I have been with my old nurse.'

Emily's lips curled. 'Save that twaddle for others. I know the truth.'

Juliet eyed the other woman but said nothing, waiting to

see what would happen. There were times when she managed not to react. Few, but occasionally.

'Oh, yes.' Emily moved to the fireplace and threw the paper into the flames. 'In fact, it was I who let slip the secret of your whereabouts.'

Juliet gasped, all her careful control slipping. 'You? Why? If I am ruined, then everything you have done to enter Society is in vain.'

A cruel light hardened the other woman's eyes. 'I made the best of a bad situation. Sooner or later someone would have found out. I just speeded up the revelation.'

The words did not make sense, and Juliet wondered if she was still suffering from too much laudanum, as she had at the Duke's house. Or perhaps it was exhaustion. 'I don't understand.'

Emily gave Juliet a contemptuous once-over. 'No, you would not. Miss Prim and Proper. Always doing what is best for Papa, without a care about anything else.'

Juliet was taken aback. She knew the other woman did not like her, and she did not like her stepmother, but the venom was more pronounced than she had expected. Still, the insults fired her already edgy nerves and she spoke hastily. 'Someone has to care for Papa, for it is obvious that you do not.'

A tinkling laugh filled the room. 'I did not marry him to care for him. I married him for position and to be cared for by him.'

Juliet saw red. This woman had married Papa with no regard for anyone else. Not that she had ever doubted it, but...but there had always been a kernel of hope that she was wrong.

'If you wanted position and care, why did you not marry

a man like Brabourne instead of merely dallying with one? At least then the rest of us would not be in this mess.'

Emily gave a bark of laughter, as different from her famous trill as black was from white. 'Do you think I did not try?'

Juliet looked in horror at Emily. 'So Papa is nothing to you. Only a means to an end.'

The other woman sniffed. 'All marriages of our class are arrangements. At least your papa does not need an heir. So I am free to go my own way.'

'Which you did with Brabourne,' Juliet said, her anger simmering. The small twinge of discomfort she felt at the thought of Emily in the Duke's arms was squashed.

Emily shrugged. 'For a while.'

'You are selfish. If you had been more discreet, Papa would not have needed to challenge Brabourne to a duel, and none of this would have happened.' Juliet made her hands unclench. It was past. There was nothing she could do to change the current situation.

'So, the ever-so-dutiful and solicitous daughter has claws. Well, I never doubted it.' She turned her back to Juliet. 'If you had been less impetuous, we would not be in this situation. No one said you had to take your father's place.'

Juliet struggled to her feet, no longer willing to look up at the other woman. Dizziness made her grab the back of the chair, but she remained standing. 'Someone had to protect Papa from your folly.'

Emily sneered. 'And who will protect him from this unpleasant mess your reckless action has caused?'

'My reckless action? You are the one who let the information out, for which reason you still have not told me.' Her fingers clenched the chair until her knuckles turned white.

She was so tired, but she could not let Emily leave without finding out what was going on.

Emily took in Juliet's discomfort. 'It would seem you have returned too soon. You will need to stay in bed for some time to come.'

Juliet's chest tightened in anger. 'I will do as I see fit.'

Emily arched two perfectly cared-for blonde brows. 'Will you? We shall see what your papa has to say about your... exhaustion.'

Juliet nearly toppled over. For the first time since this argument began she realised that if Emily knew what had really happened then Papa could find out. That would hurt Papa. Something she did not want.

In a tired voice, all the fight drained from her, Juliet asked, 'Why are you doing this?'

Emily glared at her. 'Because if I cannot have Brabourne, and all that he represents in Society, I will see to it that you have him and I benefit directly from your connection to him. When the Duke decides he has to save your reputation and asks you to marry him, I expect you to accept.'

Juliet stiffened her spine, knowing she was nearly ready to collapse. 'You are crazy. He will never ask and I would never accept.'

Emily moved to the door and gave Juliet a last penetrating look. 'Do not be too sure about what either of you will do.'

Juliet stared at the door long after the other woman had left. Insanity. This was the stuff farces were made of. Brabourne would never propose. Never.

*And if he did?* a tiny voice asked. Juliet sank back into the chair and covered her eyes with a shaking hand. She would resist him, no matter how hard or how much it hurt. There was no other answer when a rake came calling.

* * *

Mrs Burroughs gave him the minimum curtsy required, and Sebastian could tell by the look on her face that she longed to box his ears. If anyone else looked at him the way she did, they would soon regret it. With her he merely sighed.

'Yes, Mrs Burroughs?'

'It has started, your Grace.'

He raised one eyebrow.

Exasperation lowered hers. 'The ostracism of the young lady. Just as I knew it would. Just as you knew it would—if you had let yourself consider it. You must stop it.'

This woman was one of the few people in his life he cared for, and the only woman. But, right now, irritation at her persistence in pushing him about something he did not want to do hardened his jaw. For the first time since becoming an adult he was curt with her.

'I am busy now, Mrs Burroughs, and have no time to discuss this matter. Nor will I ever.' He stood so that he towered above her rotund figure. 'Do I make myself clear?'

She inflated her chest and lifted her ample chin. 'Quite… your Grace.' Without asking permission to leave, she sailed out.

Sebastian watched her until she was gone, then turned to look out through the large window that let the meagre afternoon sunlight into the library. The roses were in full bloom and a few tulips lingered.

The girl was becoming an even bigger problem. Much as he did not want to become involved, he wanted to see her ostracised even less. She had spirit. And she cared about others.

He remembered her reason for dressing as a boy and

fighting him. It had all been for her father. Never once had she mentioned or seemed even to consider the repercussions to herself. He admired that trait in anyone, since it was so unusual, but in the girl he found himself more than admiring.

Making a decision, he turned and strode to the door. He went into the hall and beckoned to a nearby footman. 'Fetch Mr Wilson for me. Now.'

'Yes, your Grace.' The young man bowed and hurried off.

Sebastian returned to the library and sprawled out in the leather wingchair that was his favourite. He did not wait long for the knock.

Jeremy Wilson entered the room, his fair blond hair glinting in the light. He was a slight man. The kind that mothers wanted to nurture and women wanted to protect. Men liked him too. Sebastian trusted and depended on him.

'Jeremy, my long-suffering secretary,' Sebastian said, waving him to a seat. 'I have yet another job for you that has nothing to do with my business affairs. And hopefully, after a short while, will have nothing to do with my social life either.'

Jeremy grinned. 'Another woman, your Grace? Most men would be more than happy to be pursued at all hours and all days. You seek to get rid of them.'

Sebastian returned the smile from habit, not amusement. 'Ah, but then I am not most men. Besides, all women become bores sooner or later.'

A flash of pity filled Jeremy's green eyes, but only for a second. 'What can I do this time, your Grace?'

Sebastian straightened in the chair. 'I want you to find out the engagements of Lord Smythe-Clyde and his family.'

The secretary's eyes widened. The Duke had asked many unusual things of him, but never something like this.

'Yes,' Sebastian said drily, 'the same man who challenged me to a duel over his wife. And you may as well know, since I know you can be trusted and since the entire *ton* will shortly be a-buzz about it, the sick guest we housed for three days was Smythe-Clyde's daughter. She is the one who initially fought me. The later duel with her father was a sham.'

After a pause, Jeremy said, 'Interesting. I would warrant she would not be boring.'

The comment was too close for comfort. Sebastian ignored it. 'Let me know as soon as possible. If I do not receive invitations for the same events, see that I get them.'

Recognising dismissal, Jeremy rose. 'I should have some information by this afternoon. Oh, yes, you are invited to the Duchess of Richmond's ball. It is tonight. I understand that everyone has been asked.'

'Including the Smythe-Clydes?'

'I would assume so,' Jeremy said from the door.

Sebastian rubbed his right eyebrow. 'Her events are always overcrowded and uninteresting, but I suppose I must attend if I intend to put my plan into action.'

Jeremy waited to see if his employer would elaborate. When the Duke rose and turned to look out of the window, Jeremy understood he would learn nothing more.

Sebastian heard the door close. He wondered one last time why he was concerning himself. It had been a long time since he had done something for someone else who was not one of his cronies. It was a strange sensation.

\* \* \*

Sebastian put the final crease in his cravat, his valet looking on proudly. 'A perfect Brabourne Soirée,' the servant said reverentially.

Ravensford lounged nearby on the bed, a wicked gleam in his eyes. 'All the ladies will be in awe of your sartorial elegance.'

Sebastian cut him a fulminating glance as his valet helped him into a sleekly tailored blue jacket. A thumb-sized sapphire secured in the cravat was the final touch.

'Where is Perth?' Sebastian asked.

'Carousing in some den of iniquity. He did not tell me which one, so I'm afraid we cannot plan on joining him later.'

'More's the pity,' Sebastian said, attaching a silver fob to his waistcoat. 'he will have more fun than we.'

'Without a doubt,' Ravensford said, rising from the bed and straightening his coat. 'But we are on a mission.'

'Here, my lord,' the valet said, hurrying over to Ravensford. 'Let me brush out the wrinkles and straighten your collar and cravat.'

'No need, Roberts,' Ravensford said, fending of the servant's eager help. 'I don't mind a little mussing. I am a Corinthian, not a dandy.'

Roberts backed away, but could not keep from sighing. 'You could cut such a dashing figure, my lord, if I may be so bold as to say.'

'He already does,' Sebastian said with a mocking grin. 'He is the epitome of raffishness. All the women will swoon at his feet.'

'There is only one kind of woman I want swooning,'

Ravensford said, 'and we will not find that kind at this gathering.'

'No,' Sebastian said, opening the door. 'And more's the pity.'

An hour later, they finally entered the foyer of the Duchess of Richmond's town house. Their hostess beamed at them.

'Brabourne. Ravensford. I am so glad you could tear yourself away from your other amusements.'

Each man in turn took her offered hand.

'How could we resist?' Sebastian murmured, kissing her palm.

'Such devilish charm,' she said, smiling as he released her fingers. 'Enjoy yourselves. There are more than enough eligible women, even for the likes of you two.'

'Yes, but are they entertaining?' Sebastian said *sotto voce* as they walked away.

'Probably not,' Ravensford replied, before turning to greet the matchmaking mama of a girl just out of the schoolroom.

'See you later,' Sebastian said with a nod to the woman and a wink to his friend. He thought he heard Ravensford groan, but knew the Earl was too well-mannered to be so rude.

With practised ease and a cool smile, Sebastian circulated through the room. He ignored the speculative glances sent his way. People had been discussing him since he was old enough to realise what they were doing, and probably long before that.

There was no sign of his quarry.

Guests milled around the enormous room, spilling out on to the balconies and into the gardens. An orchestra played a waltz and couples swirled and dipped to the music. Dowagers sat in huddles, discussing anyone and everything. Several men wandered into another room where cards were being played. Everyone was here, including many he did not know. Except the Smythe-Clydes.

Irritation knitted Sebastian's brows together.

He stepped out on to the balcony for some cool air and privacy. This was the opening ball of the Season. Surely Smythe-Clyde and his family would be here if they had been invited. Emily would be.

A schoolgirl giggle wafted up from the walkway below him, and Sebastian took a step back towards the ballroom.

'Have you seen the Duke?' a girl asked.

'Oh, yes,' another girl answered. 'He looks so romantic. And dangerous.'

The first girl giggled again and lowered her voice. 'He is. Have you heard that he had Juliet Smythe-Clyde in his house for three days and three nights? Although they are saying she went to visit her old nanny.' Another giggle.

Her words stopped Sebastian. His fists clenched and he had to resist the urge to jump over the railing and put the chit in her place.

The second girl lowered her voice too. 'Oh, yes. Wouldn't you just love to be his captive?'

The first girl spoke soberly. 'Not if it ruined me as it has her. Mama said she and her family had been invited tonight, but when word of her disgrace got out the Duchess sent a note telling them they were no longer welcome.'

Sebastian had heard enough. If chits barely out of the schoolroom knew of the disaster, then it was all over town. Nor would he stay here and gratify the Duchess of Richmond by dancing with any of her eligible girls.

Never before had he been made so aware of the double standards of his world. Juliet Smythe-Clyde was not welcome while he was courted, even though she was innocent and he was anything but.

He entered the ballroom and scanned it for Ravensford. Catching the Earl's attention, he flicked his eyes towards the door. Ravensford nodded and began making his excuses.

Sebastian located the Duchess of Richmond and made his way to her. As furious as he was with the woman, he would not be so crass as to leave without saying goodbye. He was many things, but no one had ever accused him of neglecting the social niceties. That was for Perth to do.

He gave the Duchess a cool smile. 'Thank you for your hospitality, but Ravensford and I must be on our way.'

She tutted at him. 'Surely it is too early for the gaming hells, Brabourne. Stay awhile and dance with some of the chits who have been fluttering around you.'

He froze her with a look. 'I think not, your Grace. My morals are not up to your exacting standards.'

She blinked while his words sank in. Taking a step back, she returned his glare with one of her own. 'They certainly are not, but you are a Duke, and an eligible one at that. You can be forgiven many faults.'

'As others cannot,' he said softly, a hard edge underlying the words.

Ravensford arrived just then and took in the situation. He put a hand on Sebastian's shoulder and squeezed hard. Smiling at the Duchess, he said, 'We must be on our way. Thank you for your hospitality.'

She smiled warmly at him and gave him her hand to kiss. Ravensford performed his duty with grace and the two men made their escape.

Outside the evening air was like a cool caress after the stifling heat of the ballroom. Instead of entering the coach when it drove up, they opted to walk with the vehicle following behind.

'What was that about?' Ravensford asked, swinging his gold-tipped cane.

Sebastian took a deep breath and wondered why he had lost his temper. Usually there was only one thing that made him see red. A slight to a girl he barely knew was not in the same league. He told Ravensford what had happened.

The Earl whistled low. 'So, it has already begun. But not surprising.'

'Everyone will follow the Duchess's lead.'

'And there is nothing you can do about it. Why should you?'

Sebastian stopped. 'I don't know. But for some benighted reason I feel like helping this girl.'

'Oh-ho,' Ravensford said with a knowing look. 'So that's the way it is.'

'Hardly,' Sebastian said drily. 'I admire the chit; I don't love her. Or even care that much about her. I just don't want her punished for trying to protect her father. Few enough of our acquaintances would do what she did.'

'True. But what can you do about it?' Ravensford started walking again and Sebastian kept pace.

'I can bring her into fashion.'

This time Ravensford stopped. 'I hardly think so. That will only confirm in the old tabbies' minds that the rumour is correct.' He gave Sebastian a piercing look. 'The only way you can make her respectable is to marry her.'

'A little drastic, don't you think?'

'Depends on how badly you want to make her respectable.'

'Not that badly,' Sebastian said, signalling to the coach. 'Take us to Pall Mall.'

Ravensford followed Sebastian into the vehicle. 'I told you we would not be able to locate Perth.'

'But we shall enjoy ourselves trying.' Sebastian lounged back into the leather squabs, determined to put the chit from his mind for the night.

# Chapter Five

Juliet scratched absently at her shoulder before catching herself. The wound was healing nicely; she just tired easily.

Right now, she had to plan the next week's menus. Papa's new wife had no interest in running the house and had done nothing while Juliet had been gone. Nor had anything been done during the past two weeks while Juliet had claimed illness and kept to her rooms, giving her wound more time to heal. No matter that the rumour was everywhere, she stuck to the story that she had been to visit her nurse.

Much as she hated it, she owed Emily a thank-you. The other woman had not told Papa the truth, and Papa was so wrapped up in his experiments that he did not know of the rumours.

Her brother Harry strode into the room and slammed the door behind himself, focusing her attention on him. She watched him with a fond, if puzzled look. He paced the morning room of their rented house, his red hair standing up in spikes on his head. A grin tugged at her mouth.

Whenever he was agitated he ran his fingers through his hair until it resembled a hedgehog's back.

He stopped abruptly and leaned on the desk so his face was close to hers. 'Is it true?'

Her fingers tightened on the pen she held until her knuckles turned white. The urge to look away from him was strong, but she was made of sterner stuff. Carefully, she laid the pen down and forced her fingers into a relaxed clasp. Until now he had not asked her, and she could not lie to him.

'As far as it goes. Yes.'

He groaned and raked his fingers through his hair. 'Why, Ju?'

She told him about everything: the duel, her reason for going, and what had really happened during her stay. The only thing she left out was Emily's part in the mess. No one else needed to know that. Brabourne would never propose and she would never accept.

She ended with, 'I suppose I should feel shame for being in his house unchaperoned, but I don't. Nothing happened.' Or nothing of consequence, her always truthful conscience added. 'No one was supposed to find out, but somehow a servant suspected and from there it spread.'

He stood up and his mouth twisted. 'Why didn't you come to me? I would have helped.'

She saw the anguish in his eyes and knew he would be a long time forgiving her. She swallowed. 'Because I am the oldest. I am the one Mama entrusted Papa's care to. I had to do it for her.'

'I could have done it and there would have been no scandal.'

She nodded, her hands once more clenched. 'True. But I could not stand to ask you to put your life in jeopardy.'

'But you could risk yours.' Anger spotted his cheeks, making his freckles stand out like patches.

There was no way she could make him understand. She rose and went around the desk and embraced him. He remained stiff in her arms.

'I am sorry, Harry. I am so sorry. But I could not. I just could not ask you to face a man who would have had no qualms about killing you. You mean too much to me.'

He moved away from her. 'Why didn't you let Papa face Brabourne? Papa is the one who made the challenge.'

She sighed and stepped away from him. He was still too upset to want closeness. 'I told you. I had to protect Papa. To take care of him. I promised Mama on her deathbed.'

Harry shook his head, some of the colour leaving his face. 'You cannot always be taking care of him—or everyone else, for that matter. Some day you won't be here, and then what will happen?' At her stricken look, he hurried on. 'Don't look like that, Ju. Some day you will marry and leave. That's only natural. All women do it. Then Papa will have to care for himself.'

A choked laugh escaped her tight throat. 'I will never marry now. Papa's new wife may throw me out, but no man will take me in.'

His face flamed anew as he remembered the original reason he had come to see her. 'Dash it all, Ju. That ain't true. There is George at home. He loves you and will marry you no matter what.'

A sad smile tugged at her lips, and she turned away so he would not see the emotion. 'Dear George. I would never disgrace him by accepting his proposal. Not now.'

'Don't be a goose,' he said roundly. 'This is not the end of the world. All the *ton* may go to Hades. We don't need them.' His voice picked up. 'I have it. Let's go to Vauxhall tonight. We will forget all of this and enjoy ourselves. Just the two of us. There will be fireworks,' he cajoled.

She looked back at him. He had the mischievous, let's-have-fun look that had always lured her into trouble. Gone was the hangdog expression he had entered the room wearing. This was her younger brother, the boy she had also promised to look after and protect. Mama had known Papa was incapable of anything but his hunting and experimenting.

She caught his hand and squeezed it. 'What time should we leave?'

A grin split his face. 'Half past eight.'

On a much happier note, he left to prepare for their night of revelry. Juliet stayed behind and tried to finish the week's menu, but it was hard.

George's face kept coming between her and the paper. Good, kind George, who wanted to marry her. She had turned him down just before coming to London, and he had told her he would wait. She cared a great deal for him, liked him immensely, and had considered accepting him when she returned home. He would care for her and any children they might have for the rest of his life. That was a gift any woman should be glad to have.

Another visage forced its way to her attention. Hard angles and unyielding eyes made her pulse jump. Brabourne. She gave up. The menus could wait.

She rose and headed outside. The house had a small garden with a white iron bench sitting under a large elm tree. It was her favourite spot here in London. Perhaps some time spent there would ease the turmoil that threatened to tear her chest apart.

Life had been so simple before. It should be as uncomplicated now. Somehow it was not.

Juliet waited for Harry in the hall, dressed in a simple white muslin gown with green ribbons, her hair piled on her head and more green ribbon threaded through its curls. When she heard his tread on the marble floor she turned to him with a smile—and had to suppress a gasp. He was in the same coat she had worn to meet Brabourne. Visions of that horrible night threatened to close her throat.

'You look very fetching,' her brother said.

His unexpected compliment erased her tension. As her younger brother, she did not expect him even to notice her clothes.

'What is the matter, Harry? Do you have a fever?'

He grinned. 'Thought I'd start us out on the right note. Tommy says all girls like to be told they look nice.'

She chuckled. 'Coming the pretty with me? And where is the redoubtable Tommy? I am surprised he is not coming with us.'

He gave her a sheepish grin. 'He is to meet us there. He knows his way around,' he finished in a rush. 'That is why I asked him.'

'I should have known Tommy would not be far from us tonight.' She felt a twinge of disappointment that she and Harry would not be enjoying their adventure alone, but she put it aside. Young men did not like being saddled with sisters. She was fortunate to have been asked at all.

He had the grace to look embarrassed. 'Well, it was his suggestion. Thought it would show everyone that we can't be cowed.'

'I should have known. He has been on the Town longer than you,' she murmured, leading the way to the carriage.

The ride was long and boring, but when they pulled up and Juliet stepped out, a look of awestruck wonder radiated from her face. 'It is like a fairyland. There must be hundreds and hundreds of lamps.'

'Actually,' a deep voice drawled, 'there are thousands.'

She whirled around. The Duke of Brabourne, in impeccable evening wear, lounged against one of the entry pillars.

'What are you doing here?' she said, before realising it was none of her business.

He pushed away from the pillar and moved towards her. The delight of seconds before was supplanted by an edginess that increased with each step closer he took. He made her feel so vulnerable. She angled back and bumped into Harry.

Harry glared at the Duke. 'He is here to cause trouble, no doubt. Why else would one of his reputation frequent a pleasure garden?'

Brabourne raked the youth with a frigid stare. 'We meet again, puppy, and your manners are no better.'

Harry's chest puffed up and his eyes narrowed. Juliet recognised the danger signs and stepped between the two males.

'Enough,' she said, putting a hand on Harry to stay his forward momentum. 'Surely Vauxhall is big enough for all of us.'

'London isn't big—'

'Stop it. Now, Harry,' Juliet whispered, 'if you create a scene, then everyone will think the rumour confirmed. What then? Have you thought of that? Will you challenge

Brabourne to a duel to defend my smirched honour? That would only make a bad situation worse.'

'She is right, puppy,' the Duke said.

She rounded on him. 'And what are you trying to do? Make matters worse. I am trying to reason with him and you put your oar into the waters.'

Brabourne smiled, the emotion reaching his eyes. 'A firebrand to go with the hair.'

For long seconds Juliet stood, transfixed by the change in the Duke's countenance. No longer was he the cold, sardonic man who had duelled her and then kept her in his home. This was the man who had comforted her as she lay racked by fever, the man she had thought only a figment of her imagination. The realisation was unsettling.

'I'm warning you,' Harry said through gritted teeth.

'Miss Smythe-Clyde. Harry.' Tommy's light tenor cut through the animosity. 'Thought I saw you arrive.' Tommy Montmart rushed over, his gaze darting to the Duke and back to the brother and sister. He stopped between them and Brabourne.

Tommy was a slight youth with sandy hair and hazel eyes. His chin was more prominent than necessary and his nose was not large enough to balance it. While he was not good-looking, he was friendly and helpful. You could not keep from liking him.

'We must be going, your Grace,' Juliet said breathlessly, taking each youth by the arm and propelling them down the first lane they came to.

They had not gone ten steps before Harry shook himself free. 'I can walk by myself.'

She eyed him. 'Then do so. Away from the Duke.'

'She is right, you know, old chum,' Tommy said. 'Won't

do to start a fight with Brabourne. He's a prime one with his fists. Cause another scandal too. The only chance you have of weathering this one is to act as though it is all a farce.'

Harry answered with a grunt.

Juliet listened to them, but her focus was on the Duke. Why had he come up to them? Was he trying to ruin her completely?

Even now, the back of her neck tingled as though someone were watching her. Only one person had ever had that effect on her. She wrapped her paisley shawl tighter around her shoulders and forced herself to look at the sights.

Vauxhall was indeed a marvel. An orchestra played while people danced. Snatched pieces of passing conversations mentioned singing to come. Tommy and Harry talked about going to the Cascade first, a spectacle that even she, cloistered in the country, had heard of.

'Miss Smythe-Clyde.' Tommy halted and motioned Juliet to look to the right. 'It is Prinny himself.'

The Prince Regent stood in the middle of a gathering comprising both men and women. Laughter came from the group like music from a flock of gaily feathered birds. They were the élite of English society. Sudden quiet came over them as Brabourne raised his glass to the prince. Everyone toasted and the laughter began anew.

Juliet turned away.

'He comes here all the time,' Tommy said.

'Brabourne?' Juliet said before thinking.

Both Tommy and Harry frowned at her.

'No,' Tommy said. 'The Prince.'

Juliet turned quickly from their probing looks. She was behaving like a schoolgirl.

A bell chimed and Tommy said, 'We must hurry. They are about to unveil the Cascade.'

Catching their excitement, Juliet hurried after the two young men. All about them others did the same. They arrived in time to get a good position.

The curtain was drawn aside to show a landscape scene illuminated by lights. A miller's house and waterfall were near the front. The 'water', or so it seemed to be to Juliet, flowed into a mill and turned the wheel.

'Papa would love to see this,' she said to Harry. 'I wonder how it is done?'

When he did not answer, she turned and realised he was not beside her. The crowd had separated them. A man, his complexion florid and his waist ample, grinned at her. She looked away, searching for her brother.

She felt a hand on her shoulder and jolted. It was the man.

'Here by yourself?' He leered down at her.

Shivers of apprehension coursed her spine. She yanked away. 'No. My brother is near.'

He moved closer, his gaze taking in her figure. She edged back, bumping into someone else. Instead of being thrilled by the exhibition, she was fast becoming scared. There were so many people, many of whom were becoming rowdy, and she doubted any would provide help. And Harry had disappeared.

The man reached for her again, but Juliet slipped between a group of people and headed back the way she had come. She glanced behind and saw the man trying to follow. Unlike before, when the lights had delighted her and made her think of magic, they now seemed glaring. She turned left down a small lane with no lights. With luck she would be able to hide.

She twisted around another corner and skidded to a halt. A group of young bucks strolled towards her, singing a ribald song. She looked back to see the man. The singing stopped.

'Ah, what have we here?' one of the new arrivals said, moving in front of her.

A second one edged to one side of her. 'A pretty little maid out for a walk.'

The third flanked her. 'An adventurous little maid. And we can provide her with any thrill she seeks in the Lovers' Walk. Can't we, boys?'

'Yes,' they chorused, closing the circle.

Juliet's chest pounded and the roaring in her ears almost drowned out the voices. This was worse than anything. Worse than meeting the Duke. At least that had been honourable. What these men intended to do to her was anything but.

She swallowed hard past the tightness in her throat. 'Let me pass. I am not what you think.' She was thankful her voice did not shake. It was not as strong as she would have liked, but surely it would do.

They laughed.

'I think not,' the first one said, moving close enough to run a finger down her cheek.

She knocked his hand away. 'Do not touch me.'

The other two smirked.

'I don't think she is interested in you, Peter,' the one on her left said. He reached for her.

Juliet jumped away, only to be caught from behind. Two strong arms held her immobile as the others advanced on her. Fear ate at her.

She had forgotten the man who had originally followed

her. She twisted her head to look for him, only to see him gone. He must have left when these three arrived. Her jaw was caught in a vice-like grip that forced her to look back.

'Be nice to us,' the one gripping her chin said, 'and we might even pay you.'

He released her and she slapped him. The blow landed full on his cheek. He growled and swung his arm back.

Juliet was incensed beyond reason now. It no longer mattered that her knees shook so badly she was not sure she could stand up on her own. Nor would it do her any good to talk to these louts. She would fight them tooth and nail. As his arm came forward, she stared defiantly at him. His fist was a foot away from her face when she kicked him hard on the shin.

His arm dropped and he howled. The one holding her from behind snickered. Using the surprise her action had gained her, she swung the same leg back and raked her heel down her captor's instep. He gasped and his hold on her relaxed. She twisted away from him and lunged forward, flinching as her injured shoulder made itself known. The third buck caught her around the waist in a breath-snatching grip.

So close. She almost moaned aloud. The looks on the faces of the other two told her louder than words that she would not get another chance to escape. Nor would they treat her lightly now. Instead of drunkards looking for fun, they now looked for revenge.

She gulped.

'I believe you have the wrong lady,' a bored voice drawled.

Brabourne. Juliet sagged in relief. In the heat of the mêlée none of them had noticed his approach.

He came closer and, by the light of the stars and the full moon she could just make out his features. No emotion showed on his face, but there was a tension in the lithe grace of his movements that boded no good for her assailants. By his side he held a stylish black ebony cane, chased with silver that glinted like fire.

The one named Peter said, 'Go on with you. She was walking in here unchaperoned. We know the type of doxy who does that, and we intend to give her exactly what she is searching for.'

Brabourne moved closer. 'I advise you to let her go.'

'You don't scare us,' the one still holding Juliet said. 'We're three to your one. Those are the kind of odds we like.'

'I imagine you do,' Brabourne said with a sneer on his well-formed lips. 'Too bad you don't have intelligence to go with your brawn.'

Juliet had remained quiet because she was astounded at the Duke's appearance. Also, the cowardly part of her hoped he could rescue her or that they would let her go because he demanded it. Everyone else jumped to his bidding.

In one smooth, swift motion, the Duke pulled on his cane, revealing a rapier-thin blade that had been hidden in the outside case of fine black wood. Juliet felt her captor's sharp intake of breath. The three scoundrels had not expected this.

Brabourne's cold smile widened. 'I never go into dark lanes unprepared—no matter where they are. Particularly not here. It's a pity, but Vauxhall has a reputation for riff-raff such as yourselves.' He took a step closer. 'Release her.'

Still they held their ground.

A gleam of anticipation entered the Duke's intense blue

eyes. 'It has been a very dreary day. Nothing would give me more pleasure than to spit you. And I would advise you not to make the mistake of thinking I won't.'

Juliet began to tremble anew. The sense of nerves drawn taut was great enough to make her reckless. 'Oh, please, Brabourne, spit them and be done with it.'

His gaze flicked to her and he saluted her with his blade, an admiring gesture even as his eyes filled with mirth. 'You are as bloodthirsty tonight, my dear, as ever. Does the trait run in your family?'

'Brabourne,' one of the three said. 'The Duke?'

'Yes,' Juliet said. 'And he would as soon kill you as look at you. He has already killed in a duel. He could take care of you and never be penalised.'

Brabourne laughed aloud. 'She is right. The Prince will not even blink an eyelid at my dispatching filth who prey on innocent women.'

With a flick of his wrist, he marked the hand of the man holding Juliet. She was released with a push that sent her towards the Duke. He sidestepped just in time to keep her from being impaled on the point of his sword.

'That was not well done,' Sebastian growled. Before anyone knew what he was about, he moved in and flicked the cheek of the man who had held and then pushed Juliet. 'You will wear that mark for life to remind you of this night and your cowardly folly.'

The man just stood and stared while his fellows fled into the dark. 'I won't forget this.'

Brabourne looked him up and down, contempt clear in his eyes. 'I don't intend you to.'

Juliet held her breath, expecting the man to rush Brabourne. Instead he turned and seemed to melt into the darkness. Juliet, all the strength gone from her body, sank on to the pebble path. Her body shook everywhere and her shoulder throbbed from all the handling she had received.

Brabourne squatted down, still holding his sword at the ready. 'Are you able to walk? We had best get back to the lights.'

She giggled, unable to stop the release of fear. 'I...yes, just a minute.' She took a deep breath.

He stood and reached a hand down for her. She took it and he pulled her up. She stumbled and fell against his chest, fortunate that it was the side where the sword was not. He caught her round the waist and held her up.

'Steady. I cannot hold you and be prepared should they return.'

She nodded, biting her lower lip. 'I am not usually this giddy.'

'I know.' He released her and she managed to remain standing. 'Stay on my left, away from the sword, and start walking. Quickly.'

She did as he directed. Within minutes they were in the lit area again. People mingled around them, a few glancing at the sword. Brabourne quickly sheathed it.

'Come. Something to drink and eat will help restore your spirits.' He took her gently by the elbow and steered her back to the private supper boxes.

Juliet went without thinking of her reputation and how his escort must look to anyone who saw them. She was just grateful to be safe.

'Thank you. You saved me from...' she giggled again '... A fate worse than death.' She could not stop giggling.

He shook his head. 'You did not act like this when I shot you.'

She gasped for breath. 'I know. But then I anticipated the fact that I might be hurt. It never occurred to me that anyone here would accost me and...and threaten my...'

'I understand,' he murmured, his tone almost sympathetic. 'Obviously your brother and his friend failed to prepare you. Vauxhall can be entertaining, perhaps even magical, your first time here, but it is also frequented by scoundrels and thieves. You should not have been left alone,' he ended on a harder note.

She bristled at his implied criticism of Harry. 'It was an accident. We were at the Cascade and there were so many people. The next thing I knew, Harry was gone. It was my fault for not paying better attention.'

'As you wish. But next time hold on to your escort.'

'Brabourne.' A female voice intruded on their argument. 'Brabourne, I have been looking all over for you. Where have you been, you naughty boy?' She was a voluptuous woman with hair so dark it blended in with the night.

A disgusted look passed over his face, quickly replaced by cool dispassion. 'Ah, Lady Castlerock. What a pleasant surprise. I thought you were still with Prinny.'

'Of course I am. He sent me to find you, saying it is always entertaining when you are around.' She dimpled at him.

He gave her a thin smile. 'May I introduce you to Miss Smythe-Clyde? She has done me the honour of walking the promenade with me.'

Juliet smiled at the other woman.

Shocked recognition widened the other woman's eyes and pinched her mouth. 'I will see you later, Brabourne.' Then, without a word, she turned her back to Juliet and walked away. The cut was direct.

Mortification held Juliet motionless. Fury kept her from crying.

'Mary Castlerock has been rude from the first day I met her, and that was while she was still in the schoolroom,' Brabourne observed. 'She is no better today.'

His words gave Juliet time to pull herself together. The other woman's action was not unexpected. The *ton* had declared Juliet unacceptable and Lady Castlerock was definitely *ton*. It was Juliet's fault for forgetting that she should never have been seen in public—or private—with Brabourne. Still, the woman's reaction had been extreme, and Juliet was determined that she would not succumb like a whipped puppy. But it would do her no good to stay longer in the Duke's company.

She jutted her chin and squared her shoulders, ignoring the ache that radiated from her wound. She dropped the Duke a curtsy, saying, 'Thank you so much for your help. Without you, I would have been sorely hurt. But I am able to find my brother on my own.'

One eyebrow raised, he said, 'Are you going to let her treatment of you change what you intend to do? I never thought it of you.'

Goaded beyond polite manners, she said, 'That is easy for you to say. You are no better than you should be, yet no one snubs you. No one ostracises your family for your actions. Well, your Grace, I have neither your rank nor your fortune to protect me and mine from people like Lady Castlerock.' A lone tear of suppressed hurt slid down her cheek.

The tic at his right eye started. 'Here, take this.'

He thrust his hand at her and she recognised a handkerchief. 'I don't need that.'

'Take it anyway.' He grabbed her hand, pried open her fingers and stuffed the fine linen in her palm.

In a very unladylike way, she blew her nose. The ghost of a smile curved his mouth. She saw it and blushed.

'I am not very good at being dainty.'

'You are very good just the way you are.'

Her blush deepened. 'I shall have this laundered and returned to you.'

'Discreetly, I hope.'

She searched his face to see if he joked. There was a hint of something in his eyes that made her think he might. 'Most discreetly.'

She tucked the material into her reticule which, by some miracle, still hung around her wrist. Her paisley shawl was somewhere back on the dark Lovers' Lane, and she had no intention of searching for it.

Once again he took her arm. 'Shall we try this again?'

She sighed wearily. 'I am not as good at flaunting convention as you. I think it for the best if I try to find Harry on my own.'

'So, this is where you are hiding out, Brabourne.' A booming male voice made Juliet jump.

'Lady Castlerock said she had found you, but that you were occupied.'

A florid, yet handsome man who carried too much weight headed their way. She wondered if the Duke was chased everywhere he went. It certainly seemed that way.

'Sir,' Brabourne said.

Juliet closed her eyes. This was too much. First Lady Castlerock had cut her, and now the Prince Regent would do so. She sank into a hurried and graceless curtsy, head bowed as much to hide her dismay as to pay respect.

'And who is this lovely young morsel?' the Prince asked.

'May I present Miss Smythe-Clyde, sir.'

Juliet stayed down, waiting, hoping the Prince would not snub her.

'Ahh,' he said in a knowing voice. His tone turned devilish. 'I am delighted to meet Miss Smythe-Clyde. Please rise, my dear. I won't bite—at least, not yet.'

Juliet could not believe her ears. The Prince was talking to her—flirting with her? But she had heard he had a weakness for women, preferably ones old enough to be his mother.

She rose. 'Your Highness.'

'I see why your name is linked with hers, my friend. A very rare prettiness and not at all your normal prey.'

Brabourne's face betrayed nothing, but Juliet was finding it easier to read him. The straightness in his shoulders and the grip on his cane told her he was not pleased with the Prince's words.

Fireworks started going off, momentarily catching the Prince's attention. 'I must be leaving you two. You must come to Carlton House next week, Miss Smythe-Clyde. I am having a small dinner party.'

Without waiting for a response, the Prince left to rejoin his group. Juliet gaped at his back.

'I cannot go to Carlton House alone. What would people say?'

'Nothing they aren't already saying,' he said sardonically. 'But you are right. You will need an escort.'

She nervously twisted a curl that had come loose from the knot on her head, very aware of his attention bent on her. He took her hand in his and pulled it from the hair. He gently tucked the strand behind her ear.

'That will have to do,' he murmured, his voice husky. 'I am not a lady's maid.'

She could not make herself break the rapport between them. There was something magical about the way he watched her. She felt light-headed. Giddy. Ready to twirl around.

'Ju! Where in blazes have you been?' Harry said, rushing up to her and grabbing her arm.

The moment was broken and Juliet felt as though a bubble of delight had been punctured. Everything was mundane once more.

Sighing silently, she angled away from Brabourne. 'I have been looking for you, Harry. Somehow we became separated at the Cascade.'

'I know that. You need to be more careful in a place like this. It may be frequented by all the swells, but there is riffraff, too. Ain't safe for a girl alone.' He puffed like a gamecock protecting a solitary hen.

'I am well acquainted with the hazards here,' she said drily. Out of the corner of her eye, she watched Brabourne. He looked at her, and she knew he caught her understatement.

'You are.' Harry let her go and for the first time noticed the Duke. He glared at Brabourne. 'Has he been bothering you? For I won't have it.'

Juliet cut off an exasperated retort. 'No. He was merely keeping me company until you arrived.'

Brabourne made an abbreviated leg. 'I think, Miss Smythe-Clyde, that we have found your escort to Carlton House.'

She started, for it had never occurred to her that her brother might come. 'But what will the Prince say?'

'I will explain to him.'

Tommy rushed up just as the Duke moved away.

'Thank you again,' Juliet said softly, hoping Brabourne heard her. He looked over his shoulder and she knew he had.

'What is this all about?' Harry demanded.

'Been cosying up to Brabourne?' Tommy said. 'Not good. Not good at all, Miss Smythe-Clyde, if I may be so bold as to say.'

Juliet shook her head, finding that she was shorter on patience than usual. Normally she could let Harry and Tommy ramble on and rant and rave without any bother. Tonight she was suddenly tired. As calmly as possible, she told both young men about the meeting with Prinny and the invitation.

Tommy's eyes popped. 'Invited to dinner with the Prince Regent? That is an honour. You must go. No doubt about it. Can't refuse. Isn't done.'

'Exactly,' Juliet stated firmly. She took Harry's arm and steered him towards the entrance. 'I am tired and would like to go home. I am still not totally recovered.'

'But we have not eaten yet,' Harry complained. 'The ham is famous throughout England.'

'Thin enough to read through,' Tommy added.

Juliet managed to smile at them. 'I know—Harry, you get the coach to take me home. I shall send it back for both of you.'

The two youths gave each other long-suffering looks. Harry said, 'I shall go with you, Ju. Ain't proper for a young lady to go alone.'

She suppressed a tiny smile. They were so like schoolboys. 'No, you shan't, Harry. I am old enough to take care of myself. Why, I am a spinster. No one will think twice about my going by myself—and no one need even know.'

The two boys exchanged another look, relief replacing the former resignation. 'Capital idea,' Harry said.

They chatted on, while Juliet stood silent waiting for the carriage. The last thing she had expected tonight was to meet Brabourne. And to have him rescue her and then introduce her to the Prince—that was the stuff of any young woman's dreams. But it left her uncomfortable. One dinner at Carlton House would not restore her good name. It would only give more people more opportunities to snub her. Also, it would put her near Brabourne, something else she did not need. She was already too susceptible to him for her own good.

She would have to feign illness the night of the dinner. The tightness in her stomach eased as she thought of this excuse. She absolutely could not go.

## Chapter Six

'What is the meaning of this?' Emily demanded, storming into Juliet's bedchamber.

Juliet looked up from her lending-library novel to see a cream vellum sheet clenched in her stepmother's fingers. 'Whatever are you talking about?'

'This!' Emily thrust the sheet up to Juliet's face.

Juliet drew back to be able to focus. The Prince of Wales's crest jumped out at her. Reading quickly, she realised this was the invitation to Carlton House. Only Harry and she were invited.

Juliet opened her mouth to speak, but nothing came out. There was nothing she could say.

'How do you know his Royal Highness?' Emily hovered over Juliet.

'Um…' Juliet rose and twisted around the other woman. 'Now that I can breathe again.'

'Don't be smart with me. Answer my question.'

Juliet moved to the fireplace to give herself some time.

Carefully she laid the book on the mantel and arranged it so that the spine met and ran along the marble edge.

She turned to face Emily. 'I met him at Vauxhall. A mutual acquaintance introduced us.' She waved her hand as though to dismiss the acquaintance. 'The Prince seemed to like me and asked me to dinner at Carlton House. I needed a chaperon so he added Harry.'

Emily glared, her blue eyes flashing. 'A *mutual acquaintance*? I don't believe it. Nor can Harry chaperon you. I am the person to do that. I will go in Harry's place.'

Juliet clamped her mouth shut on words better left unsaid. Harry would like going to Carlton House for all of five minutes. Then the social posturing would make him restless, while the rich foods she had heard the Prince served would not be to her brother's liking—Harry was a beefsteak eater.

'You are right, Stepmama. You will make a much better chaperon. I am sure Harry won't mind.'

The other woman flounced to the door. One hand on the knob, she said, 'It does not matter what Harry minds. I am going. If you wish to argue this, you may do so with your father.'

Juliet flinched. Emily had Papa obedient to her slightest wish. Everyone in the household knew that, and no one crossed her because of it.

Thinking of Papa made her want to see him. She glanced at the small silver mantel clock. It was two in the afternoon. He was probably in the cellar, which he had made into a temporary laboratory for his experiments. Only his new wife's importuning had brought him to London in the first place.

She grabbed a shawl to ward off the damp cold that was always present in the underground room. She did not know how Papa could stay there all day and not catch an inflammation of the lungs, but he did.

Minutes later, she pushed open the heavy oak door and peeked around the corner. 'Papa?'

'Come in, come in,' his distracted voice said.

She slid quietly into the room. Papa was in the middle of something, and he hated to be disturbed when he was concentrating. His work table was littered with papers and scientific instruments. He fiddled with something that looked like a stack of metal plates. An arc of light that Papa said was electricity shot out. He jumped back, a huge grin on his face.

'That is more like it,' he said proudly. Dusting his hands off on a leather apron he wore tied around his ample waist, he looked over at Juliet. 'What brings you here, miss? Come to see my latest work?'

She always found his hobby fascinating, but never understood what he told her. 'Yes, please.'

'Come over here, then.'

His square spectacles perched precariously on the end of his bulbous nose. 'This is a Voltaic pile, the first electrical battery. I am trying to make a smaller and more powerful one.'

She nodded, understanding that much. But when he launched into the scientific jargon and started pulling out all sorts of machines and pieces of metal, she was lost. Still, she continued to nod and say, 'oh, yes.'

After a while, he ran down. Peering at her over his spectacles, he asked, 'What is the real reason you came down?'

'To see you,' she said, meaning every word. 'It has been days since you have come to dinner or been at breakfast.'

He puttered with his instruments in a futile attempt to

clean his table. 'I am so close. I hate to take time away even to eat. But, bless her heart, Emily has food sent down to me. I don't know what I ever did without her.' A besotted look eased the line between his grey brows.

Juliet nearly groaned. She was the one who ordered the trays prepared. Emily took advantage of the opportunity and came down with the servant when the food was delivered, thus making it appear to be her idea. Still, seeing Papa's happiness, she did not tell him the truth. It would hurt him to think his new bride did not take care of his comforts.

'Shall I send one of the maids to dust and pick things up?'

His gaze sharpened. 'Absolutely not. She would misplace everything and break my most important equipment.'

That was his standard answer. Later, when he was out for his daily ride, Juliet would come back and straighten everything. She had done so since she was a small child, and he had never realised. She was very careful to put everything back where he had it, but she managed to dust and pick up any broken pieces.

'While you are here, what's this I hear about your being invited to Carlton House? The Prince runs with a rakish lot and I am not sure I want you moving in that crowd. Brabourne is one of his special cronies.'

He took her by surprise. Normally he did not involve himself in her whereabouts. It was obvious from his question that he was unaware she was already ostracised by most of their peers.

'Everything will be fine, Papa. Stepmama has agreed to chaperon me. Surely you cannot think anything improper will happen with her there to guide me?'

'Ah, yes.' He patted her hand, his thoughts already drifting back to his experiments as his gaze shifted back to the

Voltaic pile. 'That will be perfect. I shall have more time to myself for my work.'

Juliet slipped away, Papa having forgotten she was in the room. Sadness at his lack of interest in her flitted through her mind, to be pushed aside. Papa had always been like this and always would be. She had to accept that he was the one who needed care. Still, a little voice insisted, it would be nice if once in a while he would talk to her about what she was doing.

The night of the Carlton House dinner was upon Juliet before she realised it. She wore a simple pink gown caught under the bust by silver ribbons. A matching cluster of roses and ribbon nestled in her hair. Pearls gleamed around her slender throat and dropped like tears from her earlobes. Long white gloves completed her toilette.

Her maid—Mrs Burroughs having returned to the Duke's house—handed her a silver gauze shawl. It would be no protection from the weather, but it was a charming addition. Juliet smiled her thanks and left to meet Emily in the hall.

Her stepmother was more than half an hour late, time Juliet occupied by fetching a book from the library and reading.

The other woman was ravishing, her child-like figure shown to advantage by a daringly risqué dress of royal blue silk. There was no ornamentation. She needed none because of the multi-strand diamond and sapphire necklace draping her neck. It was worth a sultan's ransom. Matching earrings dripped from her ears. Her wrists were coated in bracelets, each one enough for many families to live on comfortably their entire lives. Even with the lavish jewels, there was an innocence about her that Juliet knew to be false.

'Here you are, Juliet,' Emily said, as though Juliet were the one who had been late. 'We must hurry. I am sure this will be a sad crush.'

Juliet nearly rolled her eyes. The woman was desperate to go, yet acting as though it were a hardship.

They entered the carriage and travelled in silence. Upon arriving, they were ushered into one of the most ornate and cluttered residences in the world. Everywhere were candles and chandeliers. Nooks and crannies held priceless art. Gilt covered anything that did not move. The brilliance was mesmerising.

Juliet had heard many descriptions of Carlton House, but they had not prepared her for the reality. She stopped and blinked.

The footman paused as well, as though he was used to guests being overwhelmed. Emily continued on through the entry and into the drawing room, not bothering to see if Juliet followed.

People continued to arrive, some glancing at Juliet as they walked by. Many ignored her in their haste to reach the activities.

'You must be blasé,' a too familiar voice said softly. 'Although Prinny will be thrilled with your reaction. He likes nothing more than to know he has impressed someone.'

She turned to him, noting the elegance which did nothing to blunt his masculinity. 'Were you impressed your first time?'

She knew he had not been, but it was conversation, and her tongue was otherwise tied and her mind blank of anything but his presence. Reacting to him on an instinctual level was the worst thing she could do for her own emotional safety. She knew that. It did not matter. He made her pulse jump.

'Ah, but I watched him redesign everything. I knew beforehand what it would look like finished. Familiarity breeds…shall we say, less excitement?'

'Of course.'

'May I escort you in?' He extended his arm.

Her fingers twitched with the need to touch him. She resisted, ignoring her thumping heart. 'Thank you, but I don't think that would be wise.'

'Usually the best way to combat rumour is to flaunt it.'

She shook her head. 'I am not so brave as you.'

His arm dropped, but his gaze stayed on her as though he were searching for something he could not quite find. 'I know better than that.'

'You flatter me,' she managed to utter around the breathlessness his scrutiny created.

'Where is your brother? Since you will not have me, you should stay with him until you have been presented to the Prince and introduced to several people.'

A wry smile curled her lips. 'My stepmother is my chaperon tonight, and she was in too much of a hurry to wait while I gaped.'

His face lost all expression. 'I see. Wait here and I will send someone back for you.'

She bristled. 'I am perfectly able to fend for myself.'

'Yes, you are. But trust me in this. It will be better if someone takes you in. More proper. Less flaunting of convention.' She frowned and he added, 'Or you can reconsider and accept me.'

She accepted defeat as graciously as her competitive nature would allow. 'I will wait here.'

'A pity, but not surprising.' With a slight dip of his head, he sauntered off.

Juliet occupied herself studying each piece of art individually, the footman still hovering nearby.

'There you are, Miss Smythe-Clyde,' a booming voice said.

She turned and instantly sank into a deep curtsy. 'Your Royal Highness.'

'No, no,' he said, reaching a hand down for her. 'I don't stand on such formality. Ask anyone.'

'Such as the Duke of Brabourne?' she asked, accepting his help up.

The Prince Regent beamed at her. 'He did mention that your chaperon had gone on without you because you took too long admiring my handiwork.'

Trust Brabourne to take the truth and twist it into something infinitely palatable. 'I have never seen anything nearly as impressive, Your Highness.'

He tucked her hand into his arm. 'You should see my pavilion in Brighton. In fact, I insist that you visit me there.'

Things were going much too fast. Juliet felt caught in an undertow of dangerous currents. 'Thank you, Your Highness. You are far too generous.'

'Nothing of the kind.' He patted her hand and led her back the way he had come.

The strains of music reached them long before they entered the room where the orchestra played. The wittiest, most glamourous and hard-living of London Society filled the vast area. Lord Holland, Lord Alvanley, and Lady Jersey to name only a few. Everyone looked their way. Juliet wanted to sink into the floor.

Brabourne sauntered up to them and, in a move unsurpassed for audacity, asked, 'Sir, please be so kind as to introduce me to your companion.'

It took everything Juliet had not to laugh out loud at his boldness. Some of her tension drained away.

'And if I do,' the Prince said, a gleam of mirth in his eyes, 'you must promise not to steal a march on me, Brabourne. For I know your reputation with the fairer sex.'

Brabourne put a hand over his heart and looked pained. 'Sir, you misjudge me.'

'Not you, but you plead so nicely that I find myself weakening.' The prince took Juliet's hand from the crook of his elbow and extended it to the Duke. 'Miss Smythe-Clyde, may I recommend the Duke of Brabourne to you?'

Juliet made a short curtsy. 'Your Grace.'

He bowed over her hand, raising it for his kiss. His eyes held hers as his lips touched her skin. Chills, followed by heat, followed by shivers raced up Juliet's arm.

'Your servant.'

He released her and she snatched her hand back to safety. Her face felt hot with embarrassment at the marked attentions the men paid her. Never had she been the centre of any group of males, and never had she thought in her wildest dreams to be the focus of two of the most sought-after men in England. Some women would have found the experience heady. Juliet found it nerve-racking and wished it over. But she could not leave the Prince's presence without first being dismissed by him, and he and Brabourne were having too much fun bantering for Prinny to remember to release her.

For the first time since she had met Brabourne, he looked as though he were enjoying himself. Despite all the Prince's faults—and Juliet thought they were many—Brabourne seemed to like the man. The *bon mots* flew between them.

Some referred to people and places Juliet could not place, but the men knew exactly what each was saying.

The music stopped, and one of the women who had been dancing left her partner. 'Your Highness,' she said, interrupting the talk, 'we have a bet. Maria Sefton says there are one hundred candles in your chandelier. I say there are three. We need you to tell us who has won.'

He laughed in pleasure. 'Lady Jersey, you are always entertaining. But before I come with you I want to present you to my latest guest. Lady Jersey, may I introduce Miss Smythe-Clyde?'

Sally Jersey smiled, albeit a small one. 'How do you do? I have heard much of you.'

The Prince frowned. 'I think the young lady should come to Almack's. Don't you, Lady Jersey?'

She looked at her Prince, then at Brabourne. In a flat tone she said, 'I shall send the vouchers round tomorrow.'

Prinny broke into a smile. 'Very good of you, Sally.'

She ignored Juliet. 'Now, will you come and tell us who wins the bet, Your Highness?'

He caught her hand. 'I am yours to command. Until later, Miss Smythe-Clyde. Brabourne.'

'Your Highness,' Juliet said. At the same time Brabourne said, 'Sir.'

Juliet started to sink into another curtsy, but the Duke's hand under her elbow stopped her. 'Not now,' he said softly. 'He is very informal at these gatherings. You would look gauche. Not at all the thing, and after he has tried so hard to bring you into fashion.'

'Is that what he was doing?'

He angled a questioning look at her. 'What did you think he was doing?'

She shook her head. 'I did not know. I am not used to this kind of attention.'

'We shall have to fill that void,' he said, propelling her towards a mixed group.

Ravensford and Perth were the only two she recognised. Brabourne introduced her to them as though she had never met them. Ravensford welcomed her with a teasing smile. Perth gave her an ironic nod. Everyone else in the circle was coolly civil, their gazes going from her to the Duke. She knew they would talk about this later. Much as Brabourne had tried to maneouvre, it was not working.

One lady asked, 'Are you here alone, Miss Smythe-Clyde?'

The barely disguised disapproval made Juliet raise her head defiantly. 'No, my stepmother is here.'

'Really?' another woman said.

Juliet was beginning to feel like a mouse being toyed with—not a pleasant feeling.

'Here you are, you naughty child,' Lady Smythe-Clyde said, gliding into the group and stopping between Juliet and Brabourne. 'I saw you with the Prince, but then lost you.' She gave the assemblage a brilliant smile.

The two women who had been quizzing Juliet made their excuses. None of the men did.

Juliet watched as her stepmother proceeded to charm the males. Much to her dismay, Brabourne made his adieux shortly. She felt bereft, not a good emotion to have because the Duke had left. Without any trouble, she faded away herself, finding a secluded area and being thankful for it. She did not belong here. Even if her name was on the tongue of every rumourmonger in London, she was still not up to snuff enough for this collection of the *ton's* most rakish and wild habitués.

Several women, lavishly clothed and jewelled, strolled by. Their eyes met Juliet's and then slid past. Words drifted behind them.

'Brabourne is a devil. The nerve of him to bring his unmarried mistress here. It is just not done.'

The second woman sniffed. 'Flaunting, more like. And she nothing out of the ordinary, with that carrot-red hair and all those ugly freckles.'

They were quickly past, but Juliet imagined that their conversation continued. She bit her lip on the pain that flared to anger. The hypocrites. She might be naïve, but she had heard the envy in the women's voices. It was not done for an honourable man to take an unmarried woman as his mistress, but either of them could have filled the position as long as both parties were discreet. And she was not even the Duke's *chère amie*.

Her stomach churned at the unfairness of it. Her feelings felt raw. She would find the Prince and beg his leave to depart before dinner. Food was the last thing she needed if she was to keep from being sick with overwrought emotion.

Sebastian watched Juliet from an alcove. She looked distraught. When she started walking purposefully in the direction where Prinny held court, he began to worry.

'No sense in following her,' Perth's pragmatic voice said.

Sebastian glanced at his friend. The candlelight flickered on the other man's face, shading the side with no scar and highlighting the one with the imperfection. The slash gave Perth a hard edge that was echoed in the man himself.

'Don't be a hypocrite,' Sebastian said. 'If the roles were reversed, you would pursue.'

A slow grin eased some of the tightness from Perth's mouth. 'I would never have got into this mess to begin with. And never with a virgin.'

'*Touché,*' Sebastian muttered. 'I must have been out of my head ever to let her into my house.'

'You were unwilling to take the chance that she would die and make it necessary for you to flee to the Continent.'

'Oh, yes,' Sebastian muttered ironically. 'Now I remember the story of it. Remind me in future to have all my duelling opponents checked for their sex before I fight them.'

Perth chuckled.

Juliet reached the Prince, who took one of her hands and drew her into the group surrounding him. She flushed, then paled, but stood her ground bravely.

'She's a game one,' Perth said. 'But if I were you I'd leave her alone for the rest of the night. It does neither of you any good for you to seem to pursue her.'

'You are right, as usual,' Sebastian said, his attention not wavering.

'You had best marry her,' Perth said quietly. 'It will solve a lot of problems. You need an heir, and she needs respectability.'

The Duke jerked as though he had been shot. Perth was the third person, after Mrs Burroughs and Ravensford, to say that to him. As with Mrs Burroughs, he could not be cutting. Instead, he drawled, 'Are you ready for Bedlam? I am not in the marriage mart.'

'No, my friend, but there are times when one stumbles into it against one's better judgement. I believe, for you, that this is one of those times.'

Sebastian picked up his quizzing glass and surveyed the room with a bored expression. 'I think not.'

Before Perth could say more, the Duke sauntered off in the direction of a group preparing to go into dinner. Even though he no longer watched Juliet, he was aware of her still standing beside Prinny. There was something about the chit that tugged at him, but nothing that he could not ignore.

The Prince Regent continued to hold Juliet's fingers even though he had tucked them into the bend of his arm. She was flustered and embarrassed by his continuing attention. Surreptitious and not-so-surreptitious glances followed them as they walked the perimeter of the room. The others who had been with him when she had arrived were gone, seeing that he had no interest except in her.

'Your Highness,' she said, her fingers clutching spasmodically at his elaborate coat, 'if it is possible, I should like to be excused. I… I am not feeling my best.'

'My dear Miss Smythe-Clyde, I am so sorry. Let me have my own physician attend you.'

She gulped, and would have bolted if his hold on her had not been so tight, or so she told herself. 'It is nothing much, Your Highness. Just an irritation of the stomach.'

He tutted and they continued their walk as she tried to persuade him to let her leave. Finally, when they had circled the room once and were back at the door where she had originally entered, he released her enough to bring her fingers to his lips.

'If you are truly sick, I could not be such a beast as to keep you here. But you must promise me to come another time.'

Juliet had never stammered in her life, but she did now. 'I—I…th-thank you, Your H-highness. I should be d-delighted.'

He released her and she sank into a grateful curtsy, forgetting Brabourne's admonition not to.

'Now, none of that,' the Prince said. 'You are not at court.'

She rose, her face blushing fierily. All she wanted was
to escape this awful situation. Others might pray to receive
this type of attention, but she was severely uncomfortable.

The Prince signalled to a footman while she tried to think
of something to say—anything that would ease the discomfort she felt. Nothing came.

The footman bowed to her and indicated she was to precede him. She made her farewells to the Prince, and left
with alacrity. It was some time before her coach arrived at
the door. When it did, she rushed down the steps and clam-
bered into its safety. Even Ferguson's raised brow failed to
elicit any response that might slow down their departure.

If she never went to Carlton House again in her life, it
would be too soon.


Sebastian watched Juliet's hasty departure. She would not
even blend well into his world. She was a country bumpkin.

A small hand crept between his arm and his side. 'Introduce *me* to the Prince.'

He looked dispassionately down at Lady Smythe-Clyde.
Her jasmine scent engulfed him. He always sneezed around
the jasmine plant and it was all he could do to keep from
doing so now.

'Importuning, as usual?'

Her eyes narrowed and her nails scratched along his arm
before he removed them. 'I saw what you did for Juliet. Do
the same for me and I will do what I can to scotch the rumour about the two of you.'

'You should be doing so already. She is your stepdaughter.'

'And I am already tarred by the same brush that blackens her. No one was home today when I went calling. Previous invitations have been rescinded.'

'There you are,' he said. 'You have stated all the reasons you should be trying to protect her reputation. Whether I introduce you to Prinny should have nothing to do with your course of action.'

'Ah, but it does.' She looked up at him through thick blonde lashes, her head barely reaching his shoulder. 'If he is seen to enjoy my company, then all those old biddies who have snubbed me will have to cosy up to me. It is the way of our world.'

He looked down at her, noting the angelic curve of her brow and the sweet fullness of her lips. Her looks belied the calculating coldness of her heart. His mother had been much like this woman.

A darkness entered his eyes, and Emily edged away from the barely controlled danger that seemed to lurk around him like a shadow. But nothing could still her tongue. 'Otherwise you would not have gone to all the trouble to introduce Juliet to the Prince.'

'Brabourne.' Prinny's voice broke between them. 'Come speak with me.' His attention moved to Emily. 'After you have introduced me to this lovely lady.'

Sebastian did the honours, a sardonic curl to his mouth as he watched Lady Smythe-Clyde simper and the Prince puff up like a peacock. They made a very unusual pair. If one were not the heir apparent, they would be said to be an amusing pair, so different in size. He easily made six of her.

It took long minutes of flirtatious badinage before the Prince remembered his original intent. 'Come, Brabourne, we must talk and have a chat.'

Sebastian bowed his head in acknowledgement. Both took their leave of Lady Smythe-Clyde.

They had barely reached a position of relative privacy when Prinny said, 'You will have to marry the chit. I have done my best to bring her into fashion, and Sally's vouchers for Almack's will help prodigiously, but neither will be enough. We are becoming a prudish lot.' His gaze swept over the gathering.

Sebastian controlled his retort. 'I don't think marriage would be good for either of us, sir.'

Prinny looked at his companion. ''Fraid it will clip your wings? Don't worry. Women don't expect fidelity from a husband, just financial support and social position. She won't care what you do as long as you keep it quiet.'

Sebastian snorted. There was no other acceptable answer other than yes, and he was not going to say that.

Accepting that Sebastian's answer would be yes, Prinny sauntered off. Sebastian turned away. He would not be forced into a situation not of his choosing.

No matter how sorry he felt for the chit.

## Chapter Seven

The vouchers for Almack's came the next afternoon. There was no note or anything to indicate who had sent them. If Juliet had not known Lady Jersey was supposed to do so, she would have never found out. The woman had done as her Prince told her, but in a way that made it unmistakable that she did not want to do so. Juliet had heard that Almack's patronesses would not bow to anyone. Perhaps Lady Jersey was currying favour for some private reason.

Juliet shook her head. She was not normally this suspicious. She usually took everyone and everything at face value.

Well, she did not have to go to Almack's. She tossed the vouchers into the wastepaper basket in the morning room. She had household accounts to go over and no time to worry about Almack's or the Prince or Brabourne. Particularly Brabourne.

Later that evening, as she read in her room, Harry burst in upon her.

'What brings you here this late? I thought you and Tommy were going to Drury Lane to ogle the actresses,' she teased.

'Isn't that just like a sister?' he said, hands on hips, indignation making his hair seem to stand on end. 'I've come to warn you that the fat is in the fire and you act flippantly.'

With a sigh of resignation, Juliet folded and set down her book. Perhaps she would get to read it later. Perhaps not. Harry could be as impulsive as she, and something had aroused him.

'Emily found those Almack's vouchers in the morning room, and she's fit to string you up by the neck until dead and leave your body to rot.'

Juliet snorted in an effort to cover her laugh. This was no laughing matter and Harry would not appreciate her levity. 'You are too colourful, although I am sure it is an apt description.'

'She is in Papa's laboratory right now, screaming and crying like a spoilt child.'

'Which is exactly what she is.' But Juliet knew there would be trouble. She should have burned the vouchers.

The door to Juliet's room crashed open. She was getting very tired of this. With dry resignation, she asked, 'Don't you ever knock? It is quite rude to enter without permission.'

Emily stormed into the room, dragging Papa behind her. His face was crimson and his glasses sat at a precarious angle on his nose. The leather apron he wore while experimenting still rode his ample girth. He looked flustered.

Emily was scarlet from anger, her eyes ice chips. 'What do you mean by throwing these away?' Her voice rose an octave as she waved the vouchers at Juliet. 'These are like gold, you stupid girl.'

Juliet bristled and said the first words that came to her tongue. 'Only to a social toady.'

Shocked silence filled the room.

Papa stepped forward and puffed his chest, a trait he had just before giving an ultimatum. 'Ahem... Juliet, that is no way to talk to your stepmama. She only has your best interests in mind. You will listen to her.'

'You are such a pillar of strength, dearest Oliver,' Emily said, her complexion easing back to its normal English rose. 'I knew you would support me in this.'

Juliet averted her face so Papa would not see her grimace. She saw Harry turn away in disgust. But no matter how sickened she was, she was trapped. She never defied Papa. Never. Mama had raised both her and Harry to do exactly as Papa wished. Things had gone much more smoothly that way. It was a habit Juliet was not sure she could break.

She took a deep breath and spoke as calmly as possible. 'But I do not wish to go to Almack's. If I had known Stepmama wanted to attend then I would have been glad to give her the vouchers.'

Emily glared at her. 'They are for you and your chaperon. I shall take you next Wednesday.'

Juliet clamped her mouth shut on the defiant words bubbling up inside her. She looked imploringly at Papa, but he stood beside Emily with a complacent smile. In his mind everything was settled.

She looked at Harry. He shrugged and mouthed, What can it hurt?

He was right. She should not have made such a big issue of this. 'Perhaps Harry can go with us, Stepmama.'

His eyes popped, but he stood manfully. 'I shall escort both of you. Unless Papa wants to do the pretty.'

'No, no. I don't wish to take away your fun,' Papa said. Before anyone could pursue that topic, he left the room, muttering that he had been away from his batteries too long as it was.

With him safely gone, Juliet said, 'Are you satisfied now?'

'Immensely,' Emily said. 'This should be a good lesson for both of you on respect—to me.'

Juliet was so furious she could think of nothing scathing to say. With a satisfied smirk, Emily left.

Harry and Juliet looked at each other. Neither one wanted the signal honour of Almack's, but both were going. It did no good knowing that dozens of young ladies would give their fortunes for the opportunity to drink lemonade and dance to country tunes and, if they were lucky, be allowed to waltz.

Juliet did not want to go. It was just another opportunity for the *ton* to snub her. But she was backed into a corner.

At least she did not have to worry about seeing Brabourne there. Rakes of his ilk never went to such dry and boring gatherings.

Wednesday came much too soon, and once more Juliet found herself in the hall, waiting for her stepmother to make an appearance. Harry, never patient, paced along the black and white tiles like a caged animal.

'That will not help,' Juliet said with a smile.

He grimaced. 'It helps me.'

She was tempted to grab his arm and make him stop. 'You are getting on my nerves. At least stop for five minutes.'

He groaned, but complied. 'You look bang up to the nines in that brown stuff.'

She made him a shallow, playful curtsy. 'Thank you, kind sir.'

He flushed. 'I was just trying to practise.'

She grinned. 'Yes. For your information, this gown is made of bronze silk. My hair is threaded with gold ribbon.'

'I am sure I will need that at some time,' he said sarcastically.

'You never can tell.'

'Is the carriage ready?' Emily's demand stopped their banter. 'We don't want to be too late.'

They looked at each other and rolled their eyes. 'Ferguson has been waiting for the last twenty minutes,' Juliet said. 'And you know how he dislikes keeping the horses still. It is not good for them.'

Emily flitted by. 'It is not Ferguson's place to fret. He will do as he is told.'

Juliet's lips tightened, but she told herself not to let Emily ruin the night. Too many hours lay before them for her to let anger fester.

Hobson put a brown velvet cape trimmed in bronze satin around Juliet's shoulders. She smiled at him. He put an ice-blue satin cape around Lady Smythe-Clyde. She ignored him.

Tonight Emily wore a silver gown trimmed in pale blue ribbons. Around her neck hung a single large sapphire. Matching earrings dangled below her jaw, drawing the eye to her slender neck and elegant shoulders.

Juliet looked away, a pang twisting her stomach. The last time she had seen those jewels her mama had been wearing them on the way to a ball at the Squire's. She had thought mama looked beautiful in the magnificent sapphires. It hurt to see that the jewels looked better on Emily.

Deliberately she blanked her mind.

No one said a thing as they made their way through the London streets. Fog was drifting in from the Thames and the few street lamps were golden hazes that illuminated nothing. The clop-clop of hooves on cobbles echoed eerily.

Juliet was glad when they reached their destination.

They entered Almack's with another group, affording them some anonymity. Juliet paused to look around. Nothing was as she had expected. It was just a plain large room with no embellishments, yet this was the most famous room in London. Some of the most advantageous marriages owed their start to the weekly assemblies here. Disappointment was something Juliet had not expected.

As soon as they were in, Emily left them.

'So much for a chaperon,' Harry said. 'Good thing I am with you.'

'She did it at Carlton House, too. But I am glad of it.'

Across the room, the Earl of Perth approached the Countess Lieven. 'Madam,' he said, making her a perfect leg and giving her a wicked smile, 'would it be too much to request that you introduce me to Miss Smythe-Clyde as a waltz partner?'

She turned sharply to him. 'You are always in the thick of trouble, Perth. Will you start first off tonight?'

'I fear I must, dear lady. The redhead has caught my interest and I would like to know her better.' His black eyes snapped with life.

She sighed. 'You always were an irresistible rogue. Come along.'

They met Juliet and Harry coming off the floor after a country dance.

'Miss Smythe-Clyde?' Countess Lieven asked.

'Yes.'

'I am Countess Lieven, and I would like to introduce the Earl of Perth and recommend him as a waltzing partner.'

Juliet blinked, then quickly dropped a curtsy. 'I would be delighted.'

'I thought so,' Countess Lieven said drily, and left.

'She does not approve of me,' Perth said.

'You are too kind, sir. I am sure my reputation is the cause of her curtness.'

'That too,' he said, surprising her by his bluntness.

Harry interrupted to say, 'I shall wait here, Juliet.'

She nodded and followed the Earl to the floor. He put one arm around her waist and took her left hand with his right. It felt strange to be this close to a man she did not know. He held her lightly and guided her with sureness.

'I am glad Harry and I spent time learning this. Otherwise I should be tripping all over your feet right now.'

Instead of flirting with her, as he had Countess Lieven, he looked down at her solemnly. The flickering candles cast his face into shadow and then in the next twirl shone directly on his scar. Juliet found him disconcerting.

'I wanted to speak with you,' he finally said. 'I believe you are the only female to ever fight a duel in England.'

Her hands went clammy, and she looked away from his intense stare. 'Why are you discussing that here?' she managed to whisper, fearful that someone might hear. That was the last thing she needed for people to find out.

'I never see you at my regular haunts, and since the incident I've been curious about what kind of female would do such a thing.' He spoke as softly as she. Anyone watching them would think they were flirting and did not want to be overheard.

'An impulsive one,' she muttered.

'A troublesome trait,' he said.

'Sometimes,' she answered with a rueful grin.

The dance ended quickly, and before Juliet quite realised it they were taking their leave of one another. She turned to speak with Harry, to tell him how exhilarating the waltz was with someone you did not know, and came face to face with Brabourne. The breath caught in her throat and her hand went involuntarily to her throat.

'Oh, you startled me.'

'Would you care to dance?'

It was the last thing she expected from him. Shyness overwhelmed her. She would rather dance with anyone but him. No, that was not true. But it should be true. He was trouble. He was dangerous. To her. To all women. He was temptation, and she was unable to resist.

'Yes,' she murmured, dimly aware of Harry fiercely frowning at her. She gave her brother a vacuous smile and allowed Brabourne to lead her to the floor.

He did not hold her any closer than Perth had, yet it seemed as if she was pressed to the length of him. She would swear she could feel the heat of his body and the curve of his chest against hers. She tried to ease away but he held her firmly, his arm burning a swathe across the small of her back. She shuddered.

'Bronze silk is very becoming on you,' he said quietly. 'Few women wear it successfully.'

His voice glided along her nerves, making them tingle. She was so immersed in the physical reaction he evoked that she nearly missed the meaning of his words. When they sank in, they broke his spell on her and she choked back a chuckle.

'You are so accomplished. Poor Harry told me this "brown stuff" looked well on me.'

'I am a rake,' he drawled. 'Harry is but a youth fresh to life's adventures.'

'That is one way of putting it,' she muttered.

'A truthful one.'

She cocked her head to one side and studied him. He was as handsome as ever. His black hair was still longer than fashionable, his eyes bluer than blue, his mouth a sensual slash. Yet...his former cool disdain seemed muted. Almost as though he were letting her closer?

'Am I a an object of curiosity, or is there another reason you are looking so intently at me?'

She dropped her gaze and focused on the sapphire in his cravat. It was the exact colour of his eyes. He must have purposely chosen it. 'It is a bad habit of mine. Staring, that is.'

'But endearing, and not nearly so hazardous as your impetuosity.'

She could not believe this was the cynical, cold Brabourne with whom she had duelled. He was flirting with her, exuding all the charm that made him such a successful libertine. He must realised how dazed she was.

'I am not being fair. For me, our dalliance is just another incident in a string of such incidents. It is my attempt to make you smile and look less as if you have been stunned by a knock to the head.'

Cold water could not have distanced her more quickly. 'Of course. I knew that.'

'I am sure you did,' he murmured smoothly, turning her into a dipping swirl.

The dance ended then and he deposited her next to Harry with a perfunctory bow. She watched his broad back disappear into the throng, feeling as though she had lost her bearings.

Harry snapped his fingers under her nose. 'Are you in a trance?'

She blinked and focused on him. 'Brabourne has a powerful presence,' she said, wondering why her hand still throbbed and her back still felt as though he held her. She was not a schoolgirl experiencing her first dance. She definitely belonged in Bedlam.

'No doubt,' Harry said, disgust dripping from his words. 'I can see the effect he has on you, and you had best get hold of yourself. He will only break your heart if you allow him. For that matter, why is he dallying after you? You ain't in his normal style, to say nothing of how you met and the rumours flying about the two of you.'

Juliet chewed her lip. 'I think he is trying to bring me into fashion, against all the efforts of the rest of the *ton* who are trying to ostracise me. I just don't know why he should care.'

The next thing she knew, Ravensford begged her company for a country dance. Her following partner was introduced by an unsmiling Lady Jersey, who had obviously been coerced into it.

'Miss Smythe-Clyde, may I introduce Lord Alastair St Simon?'

Juliet recognised St Simon as the family name for the powerful Duke of Rundell as she curtsied. She had not risen before Lady Jersey sailed away. She murmured her acceptance and wondered why all these men, who were high in the levels of Society, were asking her to dance.

Lord St Simon smiled down at her. He was a tall man with black hair silvered at the temples and warm grey eyes.

'Would you care to dance or stroll around and talk? My wife would like to meet you.'

'Your wife? I don't understand.'

Although she had a sneaking suspicion, it was one she found hard to believe. Brabourne had said he never went out of his way for anyone. Surely he was not responsible for all these introductions? Yet she did not know anyone else who could accomplish this.

He took her hand and tucked it into his arm. 'Brabourne has said nothing to you. That is typical. He has asked the help of all his friends to bring you into respectable fashion.'

'Very kind of him, I am sure.'

'But not what you want.'

She looked up at him. The friendliness in his eyes eased some of her discomfort. 'This is very trying. I know he is doing what he considers best, but all I want is to go home to Wood Hall and leave London and all its disapproval behind.'

'It is hard to weather the ostracism of our peers, but it can be done. My brother Langston's wife was an actress before they married. She has never been totally accepted by the highest sticklers, but she has enough friends and interests that it does not bother her. You can do the same with time.'

'Thank you for the information and concern. I shall keep it in mind.'

'But not use it.'

They stopped near a woman nearly as tall as he. Her hair was the colour of a roaring flame, and her eyes were like slanted marquise-cut turquoises in the oval of her face. She was stunning.

'Liza, this is the lady Brabourne has asked us to befriend. Miss Smythe-Clyde, my wife Lizabeth, Lady Worth in her own right.'

He looked with such pride and love at the woman that for the first time in her life Juliet found herself envious of another female. The two were very much involved in one another. Most marriages among her kind were for convenience. Watching them, she wished she could marry for love. It was something she had thought about upon occasion, but never particularly longed for. They were amusing and witty. Harry soon joined them and they treated him with a casual acceptance that won Juliet over.

A sudden hush filled the room so that one of Liza's laughs sounded like a shout. Juliet looked around to see what was happening.

Her heart skipped a beat.

Brabourne was talking to her stepmother. Emily's hand was on his arm, and her smiling face was turned up to his impassive one. How dared Emily? Hadn't she fought Brabourne in a duel because of this behaviour?

She took a step towards them. A hand clamped over her arm and held her like a vice. Frowning, she looked to see who held her.

St Simon said softly, 'Don't. It will only make the situation worse if you intrude.'

She glared at him. 'Worse? How could it be worse?'

Lady St Simon flanked her other side. 'Things such as this are better ignored. If you make it into a large scene, it will become tomorrow's tea-time entertainment. If you do nothing, it might fade away.' She smiled gently. 'Give Brabourne a chance. He was never interested or involved with your stepmother. She is the one doing the chasing.'

Juliet digested this information. They were experienced in the ways of their world. She would do better for all involved to give way. With a sigh she accepted their advice.

Harry grumbled but, when Juliet shook her head at him he half-turned half away from the couple. Even so, she knew that, like her, he was keeping them in sight.

Sebastian watched Lady Smythe-Clyde with a jaundiced eye. The woman was a bore, not to mention a troublemaker. He removed his arm from her grip.

'What is it you want this time?' he asked coldly.

Her smile widened, showing white, sharp little teeth. She looked like a hungry cat. 'The next waltz.'

'No,' he said bluntly, taking a step away.

Her hand gripped his sleeve again. This time her nails dug in deeply. 'You danced with Juliet; you can dance with me.'

His gut tightened. He did not like having any woman clutch at him as she was doing. He set out to put an end to her machinations. 'Not only are you vulgar, but you are stupid. After your husband challenged me to a duel, the last thing we need to do is dance together. Furthermore, you complain that no one invites you anywhere because of Juliet. Do not anger me, for I am the only reason you are here tonight. I can see that you do not attend again—or anywhere else, for that matter.'

Her eyes glinted maliciously, but she managed to keep her lips in a rictus of a smile. 'How dare you? I shall see that the little hussy suffers for your treatment of me.'

She dropped her hand and walked gracefully away, a sway to her hips that he knew was intentional. It added fuel to the fury she had fanned. He'd be damned if he would allow her to make things worse for Juliet. He had not gone to all this trouble to have that witch ruin it.

He caught himself immediately. What was he thinking? He had done everything he could and more than could be expected. Irritated with himself, he glanced coolly at the object of his thoughts.

Juliet and her brother moved towards the door, obviously planning on leaving. As they approached a group of dowagers the older women looked them up and down with haughty disdain and then turned their backs on the couple.

Cold fury filled Sebastian.

'Easy,' Ravensford said, having come up to Brabourne without the Duke being aware. 'Anything you do now will only make matters worse than they already are.'

'As usual, you speak sense.'

'But it does not make it easier when you feel responsible for the treatment the chit is receiving.'

'I am not responsible for that silly girl's predicament,' he said, more harshly than he had intended. 'I am merely sorry for her. Nothing more.'

'Of course,' Ravensford murmured.

Sebastian looked at him. 'Sarcasm does not enhance your reputation for easy charm.'

'Nor does anger over the treatment of a mere female strengthen your reputation for cool indifference towards that sex.'

'*Touché.*'

'Let's get out of here before anything else happens,' Ravensford said. 'White's will probably have something interesting going on. If nothing else, we can get something decent to eat and drink.'

'Agreed,' Sebastian said, leading the way. But he did not feel any less furious over the night's happenings; he just hid his emotions as he always had. His father had taught him that lesson.

Sebastian sauntered into White's, his demeanour at odds with the anger coursing through him. He looked around the heavily panelled room, taking in the regulars: Alvanley, Holland, and others. Slowly the relaxed atmosphere sank into him.

'That is much better,' Ravensford said. 'For a while I thought you were going to explode like one of Vauxhall's fireworks.'

'Those old crows and their simpering daughters are more than I can take at times.'

'Stifling,' Ravensford agreed.

The two men moved to a table where whist was being played and port consumed with a determination that was hard to match. One of the players glanced up. A worried look came over his face when he saw Sebastian.

'What's bothering you, Durkin, losing again?' Ravensford asked with a grin.

Durkin shook his head and gulped down the ruby wine in his glass, poured another and gulped that too. 'Nothing so harmless.'

Sebastian gazed down at the man whose sandy hair and blue eyes seemed to glint in the candlelight. The two of them had gone to school together and, while they were not the best of cronies, they still liked each other. Durkin's edginess meant something was not right.

'What do you know that we don't, Durk?' he asked, using their old school name for the other man.

Durkin ran long fingers through his already mussed hair and glanced warily at his partner, who nodded back at him.

'Best tell him now,' Salter said, his brown eyes looking as worried as Durkin's. 'The devil will be in the fat no matter what.'

Sebastian stiffened. There was only one topic that had ever made him lose his temper to the degree that his friends were indicating would happen here. His mother and her infidelities.

'What is it?' he demanded, his voice harsh.

'The betting book. Best look at it.'

Sebastian looked from one to the other and nodded curtly. In two strides he had the infamous book. He flipped it to the last page with writing and read the content. *When will a particular Duke tire of the lovely Miss S-C so that someone else may have a go with her?*

He slammed the book shut. His eyes narrowed to slits of blue fire as he looked slowly around the room. Most of the occupants met his gaze, a few looked away. Without a word he left, Ravensford rushing to keep up with him.

Enraged, Sebastian was glad he had sent his coach home. He needed to walk. The cool summer night air felt good.

'Bad business, that,' Ravensford said, keeping pace.

'It will be a deadly business if I learn who wrote it,' Sebastian vowed.

Ravensford glanced curiously at his friend. 'The chit is nothing to you that you need fight a duel over her honour.'

Sebastian blew out a breath and stopped. He turned to look at the other man. 'Not right now.'

Ravensford quirked one bronze brow but said nothing, waiting patiently.

'I have resisted the inevitable. Prinny ordered me to marry the girl. You even said I should do the honourable, even though it was none of my doing that brought her into my home. I resisted both of you because I don't wish to be leg-shackled. Nor do I care about flaunting Society's petty prejudices.'

He started walking again, his long legs covering distance like a thoroughbred horse racing to the finish line. Ravensford, a smile starting in his eyes, followed.

'But you can't let them vilify her, can you?'

'No.'

The curt word, with all its implications, cut through the night.

'I knew you would do the honourable thing,' Ravensford said.

Sebastian gave his friend a sardonic look. 'You did. Even I did not know I would go against my better interests because of someone else.'

Ravensford shook his head. 'You are too hard on yourself. I know plenty of people you would help at your own cost.'

'But none of them a chit from the country whom I barely know.' Self-derision dripped from each word.

'You know the old saying,' Ravensford said. 'There's a first time for everything. If there weren't we would not have the saying.'

Sebastian snorted and kept walking. What kind of hold did the chit have over him? Yes, he admired her guts and determination. He liked the way she cared for others before herself. He was even attracted to her physically, something he would not have thought. She was not the seasoned widow or courtesan he normally kept. But none of those reasons were enough to marry her.

It must be something else, but he was damned if he knew what.

# *Chapter Eight*

❦

'I don't want to marry Brabourne.' Juliet jumped up from her seat. The dainty yellow-striped silk chair tottered on its back legs before settling back down.

'*You* don't have a choice,' Lady Smythe-Clyde said, venom dripping from every word.

Juliet paced the room. 'Why isn't Papa here to tell me?'

The other woman's tinkling laugh filled the air. 'Don't be absurd. You know he is immersed in his experiments. Count yourself lucky he even bothered to see Brabourne. Particularly after their past.'

Juliet scowled. 'I am surprised Papa did so.'

'Ah, well, you have me to thank for that.' Emily patted her yellow curls and a complacent smile curled her lips. But only momentarily. 'Considering the state your reputation is in, you should be thrilled by this offer.'

'Well, I am not.' Juliet ground to a halt in front of the window. Outside carriages passed and people walked. A nanny and her charges trundled by like a loaded mail coach.

'If you had behaved yourself in the first place, none of this would have happened.'

Emily surged to her feet. 'Don't you dare talk to me like that.'

Juliet swung around. She was well and truly angry. Her reputation had been ruined because of this woman, and now she was to be handed off to the Duke like a piece of furniture. She was beyond calmness.

'I will talk to you any way I please. We were all fine until you came along with your London airs and little-girl looks.' She lifted her chin. 'Besides, Papa needs me.'

Emily stalked up to Juliet, her head reaching Juliet's nose. 'Don't delude yourself. Your papa is happy now, and that is all that matters. As long as he has me he has no need of you.'

Juliet frowned down at her, all the fight gone like a balloon that had been pricked. Every word the other spoke was true. Papa was besotted with her. She could do no wrong. Everything good in his life he attributed to this woman.

A pang of hurt tightened Juliet's chest. Papa had seen Brabourne because this woman insisted, but he could not be bothered to tell Juliet about the proposal of marriage. Her fists clenched and she pushed back the pain. That was just Papa. He was always like this and it had never mattered before. Except that before Mama had always been there to act as a buffer against Papa's indifference.

Mama. She had promised Mama to care for Papa. She could not do that married to the Duke. She looked at Emily. This woman would not care for her father.

A little part of her hurt seeped out. 'You don't even love Papa. You no more consider his needs than you do mine.'

Emily stepped away, having won the battle. 'In my own way I am quite fond of him. And we are married, a very permanent arrangement while both of us live.'

The supercilious tone told Juliet everything. If she left, Papa would be on his own, or very nearly so. Hobson would try, but it would not be the same.

Nor did she want to marry Brabourne. He was arrogant and cold and…and a rake. A rake of the worst sort. He would marry her, bed her and put his child in her, but he would see other women. His kind always did. 'Faithful' was not a word in his vocabulary.

He would treat her worse than Papa, only it would hurt more because he was not absentminded and focused on experiments. Brabourne's indifference would be true indifference, a cold void without emotion.

'I would rather marry a slug than the Duke.' She stalked past Emily and slammed the door behind herself. Emily's laughter tagged behind Juliet.

A good long walk in the park was what she needed. Since coming to London she did not get enough exercise. Sometimes her emotions built up to exploding point and she wanted to destroy something, anything. This had seldom happened to her in the country.

She called for her pelisse and set off towards Hyde Park. What if she was without a maid or chaperon? People already thought the worst of her; that was why Brabourne had offered. He was allowed every indiscretion imaginable. She was allowed none. Her blood boiled at the unfairness of it and what it had done to her.

When Ferguson pulled the carriage around to the front, she ignored him and continued marching down the walk. He fell in some distance behind and patiently followed.

\* \* \*

Sebastian guided his big black gelding around a group of walkers. Ravensford rode beside him on a spirited chestnut mare. They were making the daily pilgrimage around Hyde Park, the Serpentine glinting dully in the summer sunshine.

'So you did it,' Ravensford said when they were safely past listening ears.

Sebastian grunted. 'I could not very well *not* after last night.'

Ravensford shook his head. 'Bad business, that. Sally Jersey gave her the vouchers, we all danced with her, and still some of the pinch-faced prudes cut her. And the bet.'

'When she is the Duchess of Brabourne they will all grovel at her feet. They grovelled at my mother's no matter what she did.'

Ravensford looked over at his friend's tight face. The bitterness in Sebastian's tone was unsettling. 'That was a while ago, and things have changed in the last fifteen to twenty years. If those old biddies defied Prinny, they won't think twice about doing so to you.'

'Perhaps. Perhaps not.' He turned ice-hard blue eyes to his friend. 'I protect what is mine.'

Ravensford looked away, uncertain whether to groan or laugh. 'It is time for me to return home. I have a meeting with Gentleman Jackson that I don't want to miss. Last time I was late he took someone else and made me rebook my appointment.'

Sebastian calmed down somewhat and nearly smiled. 'He is an impudent man for all that he was born a nobody.'

'He is a talented man who knows his own worth.' Ravensford slanted Brabourne a sardonic glance. 'Much like someone else I know.'

Sebastian laughed. 'Yes, but some of us deserve our sense of importance.'

Chuckling lightly, they exited the gate and headed for home. Minutes later, Sebastian saw Juliet storming down the street—alone. No maid or chaperon tailed her, as was proper. She was the most irritating and independent woman it had ever been his misfortune to meet. And he was going to marry her. He shook his head, stopped his horse, and dismounted.

'What are you doing here alone?' he demanded.

She jerked to a halt and stared defiantly at him. 'That is none of your concern. Besides, Ferguson is with me.'

He glanced at the man who had stopped the carriage and stayed put, his attention focused on the two of them. 'He is not a chaperon. Not here,' he added for good measure.

She flushed, and he knew she was remembering her time in his home, in one of his beds. 'He is sufficient. Besides, my reputation is already beyond repair—what is a little more to gossip about?'

'You are the most infuriating woman,' he said coldly. 'I am doing everything I can, and you are undoing it as fast as I try.'

She tossed her head, her magnificent red hair flaring out in an arch of curls under the brim of her chip-straw hat. 'You have gone too far this time, Brabourne. I will not marry you. That is why I am out like this, trying to burn off some of my anger at your audacity in approaching my father. After everything that has happened, I would have thought you would be too embarrassed to even talk to him, let alone ask for my hand.'

Sebastian's lip curled, but he was not amused. 'I am never embarrassed. That is something you will learn with time.

As to approaching your father, I had no choice. Something has to be done. Marrying me is the only way to restore your good name. No one, and I mean no one, would dare snub the Duchess of Brabourne.'

'Really?' she said. 'You think you are that influential and powerful?'

'I know I am,' he said quietly. 'I watched my mother flaunt every convention and still be accepted by all.'

He knew from the surprise on her face that some of his bitterness must have slipped out. He did not care. Sooner or later she would hear all the sordid details. Someone would make sure of that.

'Well, that is interesting, but I don't intend to follow in your mother's footsteps.' She swept the skirt of her periwinkle gown aside. 'If you will excuse me, I find I am tired of walking.'

Sebastian watched her stalk regally to her carriage, head up, shoulders straight. He did not mount his horse until she was safely ensconced. And then he waited with Ravensford until her vehicle drove off.

'She will be a handful,' Ravensford said, a glint of appreciation in his hazel eyes.

Sebastian watched him speculatively. 'Perhaps you should marry her.'

Ravensford laughed. 'Not me. My name ain't enough to protect her. Remember? Only you can do that.'

Sebastian snorted, but took the teasing easily. What bothered him was the tiny twist in his gut when he'd suggested that Ravensford marry her. He must be getting ill or be hungry.

'Let's go back to my house. I am sure Mrs Burroughs can find us a beefsteak and ale.'

'You set such an elegant table,' Ravensford said as they set off. 'My French chef is still at Brabourne Abbey. He will be up here in time for my wedding.'

Together they set off, Sebastian putting from his mind any pang of loss connected with Juliet Smythe-Clyde. They would be married in four weeks. Time enough to ponder what to do with her.

Juliet slammed down *The Gazette*. Brabourne had posted the announcement of their marriage. How dared he? She had told him she would not marry him and she meant it. This was one instance when she would defy Papa. This was her future happiness at stake. And Papa's, although he did not realise it.

She surged to her feet and stomped to the wardrobe. She was not going to sit idly by while everything went from bad to worse. She dragged out a black cape, swung it around her shoulders and pulled the hood up to completely cover her hair.

Brabourne needed a come-uppance and she was going to give it to him.

Minutes later she was in the stable, ordering a boy to wake Ferguson. When she and the coachman were alone, she said, 'I need to go to Brabourne's house.'

He rolled his eyes. 'Lass, have ye got maggots in yer head? We are still reelin' from yer last visit.'

She tapped her foot. 'This is of vital importance. Either you can drive me in the carriage and put down a street away so no one will see the crest, or I will hire a hackney. But I am going.'

He groaned, took off his hat and wiped his brow. ''Twould

be best if we both took the hackney. I will wait in the kitchen, or wherever Mrs Burroughs can hide me.'

'You are making this complicated.'

'I am trying to protect ye from yerself, lass. You're overly rash at times.'

'This is the only way. I have to stop this preposterous marriage now. I cannot wait until I happen to stumble on Brabourne at some function. It would never happen. I am not invited anywhere.'

'Aye, he will no' be makin' ye a good husband. He is too high in the instep for the likes of you.'

'Exactly. Among other things.' At last he was beginning to understand her desperation.

'A gently reared lass like yerself should no' be matched to a rake.'

'That is what I think.'

Even though her voice was firm and brisk, a small part of her—a very small part of her—sighed. There was something about Brabourne that drew her; it had started the instant she had seen him dismount from his horse at the duelling field. Whatever it was had grown stronger each time she saw him. If she were honest, it had peaked at Almack's, when she'd realised all the trouble he was going to in order to give her back her good name. His not dancing with Emily had solidified it.

She turned away from Ferguson's penetrating gaze so he would not see the distress she knew showed on her face. Over her shoulder she said, 'If you are coming, let us go now.'

Almost an hour later Ferguson was hidden in Mrs Burroughs's private sitting room and Juliet had been smuggled into the library. She hoped no one had seen them. If word got out about this visit not even marriage to Brabourne would make her respectable in the eyes of the *ton*.

Her teeth chattered in the cold room, and she wondered irritably if the Duke was even coming home. It was nearly midnight. She was rarely out this late, even though she understood that in London it was fashionable to be out much later.

Impatience ate at her. She started prowling the room, taking out a book here, another there. Brabourne had a very well-stocked library. Her irritation peaked and she decided, in a fit of uncharitable spite, that he did not spend time reading. He was not at all the type she would consider bookish.

She found a copy of Byron's *The Bride of Abydos*, and a smile of pure delight lit her face. She had always wanted to read this book, but first Mama and then later Papa, when he accidentally caught her with it in one of his rare appearances in the sitting room, had forbade her. It was not as famous as *Childe Harold*, but she did not care.

She moved a branch of candles to a small pie table set beside a large, comfortable-looking leather chair. With a sigh of satisfaction, she sank into the cushions and tucked her feet up under her. In minutes she was lost.

The mantel clock chimed four.

Juliet set the book on her lap and yawned. She was so tired. She would close her eyes for a few minutes. She hoped Ferguson was doing the same. He had to be up early.

Sebastian arrived home close to five in the morning, his mood better than when he'd left. He had won at whist, drunk three bottles of excellent port, and enjoyed the company. He could not remember when he had last spent a more enjoyable evening. It had to be some time before that *chit* had come to town.

He let himself in with the key he always kept on his watch chain. There was nothing he disliked more than coming home half-foxed and having servants fuss about him. Even his valet should be in bed.

He turned around from securing the door and nearly walked into Burroughs. 'What the...?'

'Begging your pardon, your Grace, but there is a young lady in the library.' The always-impeccable butler looked flustered. His gaze darted to and fro, as though he was afraid of being overheard.

'Tell her to go home. Or, better yet, kick her out.' Sebastian was in no mood for games and frolic.

Burroughs stepped closer and said in an undertone, 'It is Miss Smythe-Clyde, your Grace. I told her she should not be here, and definitely could not wait for you to return.' He sniffed and looked affronted. 'But she said she would march boldly in if I did not help her sneak in. I could not let her do that. Not when she will soon be your Duchess.' He pulled himself up. '*And* her coachman is in Mrs Burroughs's sitting room.'

Sebastian's mouth thinned. 'Thank you, Burroughs.' He handed over his beaver hat and cane. 'You have gone far beyond the call of your duties.' His greatcoat came off. 'I shall handle this now. See that Ferguson is prepared to leave.'

'Yes, your Grace,' Burroughs said, relief the predominant emotion in his voice. 'Gladly.'

With a militant click of his heels on the polished parquet floor, Sebastian went to the library. He would make short shrift of this idiotic situation. The tic by his eye started. No woman should be in a single man's house unchaperoned, and a coachman did not count. She knew that, and yet here she was.

He did not see her immediately. The room was cold and the only light came from a brace of candles near the fireplace. Closer inspection showed a figure in his favourite chair. He moved closer.

A book lay on the carpeted floor. He picked it up and a slight smile eased the harshness of his face. *The Bride of Abydos.* Interesting reading. He laid it on the table.

She lay curled into the embracing cushions of the chair, her legs tucked under her so that the toes of her half-boots peeked out from the folds of her dress. Crimson lashes swept like fire across her cheeks. She looked young and innocent. And foolish, he thought, his anger at her actions resurfacing in a rush.

He gripped her shoulders and shook her more gently than he wanted. Her eyes popped open and she stared at him. He watched confusion play in their green depths, followed by memory and then by an emotion he had seen in many women's eyes. Desire.

Her reaction took him aback. It also excited him.

Still holding her, he hauled her to her feet. 'What in blazes are you still doing here?'

Her face coloured, then paled, accentuating the freckles marching across the bridge of her nose. She pushed against his chest. 'Let me go and I will tell you.'

'Tell me and then maybe I will let you go.' It was a provoking statement, but he was in the mood to nettle her and more.

Her palms flattened against him, their shape penetrating the several layers of his coat and shirt. The urge to teach her a lesson she would not soon forget entangled with the need to feel her lips on his.

'I came to tell you I will not marry you.' The words left her in a rush. Her bosom moved up and down in feathery motions as she watched for his reaction.

A hardness entered him. 'Of course you will marry me. The statement was in yesterday's *Gazette*. Not to mention that as far as the sticklers of Society are concerned you are ruined—by me. I don't usually sacrifice myself for others, but unfortunately for me I still have enough honour left to know I must marry you.'

Her eyes widened at his cruel words. 'Don't do me any favours, your Grace,' she said, her voice dripping loathing. 'I am more than capable of living without your powerful name.'

'Are you? We shall see,' he muttered, fed up with this game of words they played. He wanted to play another game with her.

His eyes holding hers, he pulled her tight. Her fingers flexed against his coat as she tried to keep distance between their bodies. Desire coiled in him, waiting to escape in a rush of pleasure and satisfaction. Not since his first time with a woman had he felt a reaction this intense.

She licked her lips and he groaned in anticipation. But she was inexperienced, so he needed to go gently with her. Taking a deep breath, to ease some of the tension holding him tight, he lowered his head.

Softly he touched his lips to hers. She clenched her mouth and stiffened like an iron poker. Her forearms pressed against his ribs as she tried to get loose. He wanted them around his waist, pressing him close, as close as two people could be. He shuddered from the control needed to keep from lowering her to the floor and throwing caution and propriety out of the window.

'I am only going to kiss you,' he whispered against her mouth, meaning every word. 'It is acceptable for an engaged couple.'

She gasped and drew her head back. 'We are not engaged.'

His smile was feral. He traced a string of kisses from her earlobe to the top of her shoulder. She jerked against him. He pulled far enough away to see the shock on her face. Her mouth was a round O. He cradled the back of her head with one hand and, with an alacrity he refused to analyse, kissed her.

His lips moved against hers and his tongue teased her into letting it in. Tentatively she opened for him and he slipped inside her waiting warmth. Her entire body responded. He had to deepen their joining. He had to give her the unsettling pleasure she was giving him.

'Relax,' he murmured. 'I won't hurt you.'

She renewed her efforts to escape. He sighed and released her. She skittered away. He was too experienced with women to press her further. She wanted him, but was scared. He watched her through narrowed eyes. She was flushed, her lips plump and red, her chest pounding. Her hands fluttered to her neck.

'You are drunk,' she finally said after her breathing slowed. 'I could...' She edged further away from him. 'I could taste it.'

His dangerous smile returned as he narrowed the distance between them. 'No, merely enjoying myself.'

Disbelief radiated from her. She moved until the back

of her knees hit the chair. 'I must go. I have accomplished what I set out to do. I will send a retraction to the paper.'

Fury hit him. He grabbed her arm and dragged her near. 'You are the most stubborn woman. What must I do to make you understand that we are marrying? Seduce you here and now?'

Fright followed immediately by innocent speculation deepened her eyes, only to end with determination. She twisted. 'I won't send anything to the paper if you release me.'

He did and stepped away. 'Bargaining already? I will meet you halfway this time. But don't try my good intentions too far.'

She nodded and warily skirted around him towards the door. 'I must get Ferguson and be gone.'

He picked up the book and held it out to her. 'Don't forget this.'

She looked longingly at it. 'I cannot take it. Papa says it is too *risqué* for me to read.'

He laughed. 'Then you shall finish it after we are wed.'

Instead of arguing with him, she fled.

Sebastian stood for long moments after she left. Her nearness and her reaction to him had left him too aroused for sleep. He might not want this marriage emotionally, but his body wanted it. Badly.

The hackney coach ride home was much too long with Ferguson sitting across from her frowning. If possible, he was even more disapproving than when he had agreed to accompany her.

'Don't say a word,' she ordered him. 'Your attitude says it all.'

He grunted and folded his arms across his chest.

She looked away, watching the London streets drift by. Soon it would be light. They had to reach home before then. So far no one had seen her—she needed to keep it that way.

Strange sensations flooded her body, making her feel heavy and lethargic. Her mouth tingled and she reached up to touch it lightly with a finger. It did not feel any different. Her neck felt branded by his kisses. She wondered if a scarlet line trailed from her earlobe to the base of her neck. She would not be surprised. She dropped her hand.

She was lucky he had stopped. She should be glad. Somehow she felt empty, not fortunate. He had opened a whole new experience to her, and for a fleeting moment, as his lips had touched her, she had wanted to explore what he offered. She had wanted it so badly that it frightened her, this power he had over her senses.

She could never marry him. He would seduce her body and then her mind. Before long she would love him—and it would break her heart, for he would never love her.

# *Chapter Nine*

Juliet stepped into the hall, her wet cape dripping on the black and white tiles. Her arms overflowed with roses she had just cut from the garden behind the house. Their smell filled the room.

'Miss Juliet,' Hobson said, 'you have a visitor in the morning room.'

There was an edge of excitement in his normally non-committal voice. What was going on? 'It isn't Brabourne, is it? she demanded. 'For I will not see him.'

'No,' Hobson said, taking the mass of flowers, 'you have always liked this visitor.'

Curious, she started off without removing her cape. Hobson made it sound as though someone from home was there. She hurried into the room. A man with a familiar stocky figure and brown hair stood looking out of the window.

'George,' she said, breaking into a run. 'What are you doing here? It does not matter,' she said before he could answer, 'I am so glad to see you.'

He had turned at the first sound of her voice and held his hands out to her. She took them and he squeezed.

'I came as soon as I heard, Ju.'

She saw the anxiety and hurt in his brown eyes and knew immediately what he referred to. 'It is not my choice. I have told both Papa and the Duke that I will not marry.'

Confusion knit his sandy brows. 'Then why was the announcement in the paper?'

She made a very unladylike snort and pulled her fingers from his still-tight hold. 'Because Brabourne is stubborn and arrogant and high in the instep and anything else you can think of that is derogatory.'

George's eyes widened. 'That bad, and your father is still making you marry him? That does not sound like Lord Smythe-Clyde. He is usually too engrossed in his experiments to force you to do anything, let alone something you so definitely dislike.'

'I know,' she said, wringing her hands. 'It is his new bride. She wants to be related to Brabourne to further her standing in Society. She is forcing Papa to force me.'

'What about Brabourne?' George asked, obviously confused.

'Him?' For some reason he feels he must marry me and protect me from the *ton's* disapproval.' She shrugged. 'Silly, but there it is. Once the announcement was in the paper, his pride came into play. No one refuses the great and powerful Duke of Brabourne, whether he really wants to marry one or not.'

'I am more in the dark than ever,' George said. 'Perhaps we could sit down and have a bit to eat and drink?'

'Oh, dear, I am so sorry. Of course. I was so excited to see a familiar and friendly face that I have forgotten my manners.' She moved to the pull near the fireplace and had just gripped it when the door opened and the butler entered, bearing a loaded tray. 'Hobson, you have the manners I lack. What would I do without you?'

The butler said nothing, but he straightened up at the praise. Setting the tray down, he asked, 'Will there be anything else, miss?'

'No, thank you. You have provided generous proportions of everything we may need.'

He bowed. 'I know from the past how Mr Thomas likes his food and drink.'

George beamed as he took in all the refreshment. 'That you do, Hobson.'

The butler left the room with a very satisfied air about him. Juliet sat in a gold embroidered chair across from George and began serving. She asked no questions about his preferences because she knew them all. They had practically grown up together. He was like a brother to her, which was why she had been unable to accept his marriage proposal. Unlike Brabourne, George had been sad, but had also accepted her decision.

'I owe Hobson more than I can ever say,' Juliet murmured.

'How's that?' George said around a mouthful of ham.

She told her old friend everything, omitting nothing that had happened since she arrived in London except Brabourne's mind-numbing and body-electrifying kiss. That was still too fresh and too raw and much too personal.

George chewed a mouthful of biscuit and washed it down with well-sugared tea. 'You have been busy. No wonder the Duke offered for you. It is the only honourable thing he could do.'

She nearly choked on her tea and ended up coughing until tears ran from her eyes. 'How can you say such a thing?'

He took another portion of ham and mixed it with potato. 'Because it is the truth.'

She set her cup down and crossed her arms. 'I don't wish to marry him. I won't.'

He looked up from his plate, hope sparking in his eyes. 'Then marry me. I have asked before and I still mean it.'

She leaned forward and put her hand on his arm. 'Thank you, George. You are the best friend a person could have.'

He patted her and sighed. 'I suppose that means no.'

'I love you like a brother, not a husband. It would not be fair to you.'

For the first time since his father had refused to buy him an exorbitantly expensive mare Juliet saw anger in his eyes, his most expressive feature. He was normally quite placid.

'How do you think I feel, knowing that another man will be your husband? I would rather you wed me and love me like a brother than that you go to another man. I will wait for you to learn to love me as a wife should love her husband. Will Brabourne? From what I have heard of him, I doubt it.'

His bold talk made her blush. 'Would you really rather wed me, knowing you would not be a husband in truth for some time?'

'Yes.'

His simple answer moved her more than any protestation ever could. She began to think it might be the best solution.

'What...?' She paused and took a calming breath. 'What if I never love you that way?'

Some of the hope left his eyes. 'It would still be better than having you marry someone else.'

'Oh, George, I don't want to take the chance of hurting you.'

He sat straighter. 'Then respect me enough to let me be the judge of what will hurt me. I've always known you don't love me as I love you, but I have never met another woman I am as comfortable with as I am with you. That means a great deal to me.' He gave her a lopsided grin. 'You know how I don't like to stir myself.'

'All too well,' she answered, grinning back at him.

'I won't mind how much time you spend with your father.' The look on his face told her he knew exactly what he was offering. 'And you won't have to marry Brabourne. Even he won't dare make you a widow or a bigamist.'

Uncertainty flickered through her mind and she turned away so George would not see her expression. Much as she rebelled against marrying the Duke, much as she told herself she did not want to wed him, there was still that tiny part of her that found him exciting and dangerous. That same part acknowledged that there were times when he could be kind. Chagrin at her weakness tightened her hands into fists.

Without further thought, without allowing herself to feel, she said, 'I will.'

'What?' George dropped the biscuit he was eating. It hit the carpet and spilt.

Juliet nearly smiled. 'I will marry you. The sooner the better.'

Stunned was the only way to describe George. For a second, Juliet wondered if he really wanted to marry her. Perhaps he had proposed because he felt safe doing it, knowing she would not accept. Only she had.

'Ah. Good,' he said, bending over to pick up the crumbs. When he sat back up, his round face was red.

'I will make all the arrangements,' she said.

Relief flooded his countenance. 'Very good of you. We can take my carriage.'

'I will see to food and clothing. We must start immediately, before anyone knows you are here.'

'Oh, yes, yes,' he said, gulping down the remains of his tea. 'Where are we going?'

She stopped in mid-stride and turned back to him. He looked genuinely puzzled. She shook her head. Brabourne would know exactly where they were going and he would take care of all the arrangements too. No, she scolded herself. *George is not the Duke. That is why I am marrying him.*

'We are going to Gretna Green, just over the Scottish border.'

'I know where it is,' he said defensively. 'I just thought that you meant to procure a special licence so we could be married here in England.'

'George,' she said patiently, wondering if she was really doing the right thing and immediately telling herself she had no other choice, 'I am a woman. I cannot get a special licence. If we were going to do that, you would have to do it. Besides, it would take too long.'

Hastily, he said, 'I will have my carriage brought round.'

She headed back to the door. 'I will be down shortly.'

'Not too long, Ju. It don't do the horses good to be kept waiting.'

'I know, George. You have told me repeatedly.'

Sebastian brought his greys to a halt in front of Lord Smythe-Clyde's townhouse. He had never been here before, but thought it best if he was seen around London with Juliet. It would make their engagement more believable.

The note he had sent her this morning asking her to go driving had elicited no answer. Never patient, he was here to bodily lift her into his phaeton if needed. The chit would not snub him.

He leapt down and strode to the door. Imperiously he banged the knocker. The door opened just as he pulled his hand away. Hobson stood in the doorway, looking down his nose.

Sebastian smothered a smile. The butler would not appreciate being found amusing.

'I am here to take Miss Smythe-Clyde driving.'

Hobson did not usher the Duke inside. 'Does Miss Juliet know you are coming?'

Sebastian frowned. 'She should. I sent round a note this morning.'

The butler looked flustered, but he maintained his ground. 'She is not available.' He moved to close the door.

Anger spurred Sebastian. He put his palm against the heavy oak and pushed. 'I will not be turned away. Show me to a place to wait and tell her I am here.'

By strength alone, Sebastian made his way inside. This was the last time the chit would treat him so cavalierly. Not waiting for Hobson to escort him, Sebastian strode across the hall and opened the first door he came to. It was the drawing room. He went in and sat down in the only comfortable-looking chair.

Minutes passed and no one came. He rose, determination hardening his jaw. No one had ever treated him this poorly. He would find where she was and drag her out. She needed to be taught a lesson.

His hand was on the doorknob when the door moved inward. He backed away. Harry stood in the archway, looking apprehensive.

'So she sent you,' Sebastian drawled, keeping his anger in check. 'I had not thought her a coward.'

Harry slid inside, keeping his face turned towards the Duke. 'Umm...she don't want to see you.'

'Do you always state the obvious?' Sebastian asked, wanting to draw blood.

Harry turned beet-red. Even his ears glowed. 'Ripping up at me won't do any good. *I* cannot make her do what she don't want. Nor can you,' he added for good measure.

'Your tongue is as sharp as hers.'

Tired of the verbal battle that was getting him nowhere, Sebastian went to the door and opened it. He walked into the entry and headed for the stairs.

'Hey,' Harry yelped, rushing after the Duke. 'What are you doing?'

Sebastian started up the steps. 'Use your brain. I am going after her.'

'You can't!' Harry pounded up the stairs and grabbed the Duke's arm.

Sebastian stopped and looked down at the youth. 'Take your hand off me,' he said, his voice deadly.

Harry blanched. His hand fell away. 'She ain't here,' he said, his voice barely audible.

Sebastian's eyes narrowed. He did not like the way this was going. 'Where is she?'

Harry looked around. Several servants were moving around in the hall. 'If you come back to the drawing room, I will tell you.'

Cold premonition stiffened Sebastian's spine. The chit

had done something truly reprehensible this time. He just knew it.

Back in the privacy of the drawing room, he stared at Harry. 'Out with it.'

Harry paced the room, his fingers raking through his hair in time to his feet. He would not meet the Duke's fierce look. 'She's left.'

'I know that,' Sebastian said, his patience at an end.

'She went with George.'

'Who is George? And make it quick and thorough. I am done putting up with your delaying tactics. Your sister has gone too far this time.'

'Don't I just know that,' Harry mumbled, his feet still moving. He took a deep breath and let it all out at once. 'She eloped.'

'She did what?' Sebastian said, his voice low.

Harry was not fooled. He knew the Duke was ready to throttle him, and heaven only knew what he would do to Ju if he got hold of her. 'Eloped. Gretna Green.'

'Bloody…' Sebastian ground his teeth together. 'And you did nothing?'

Harry swallowed, his Adam's apple bobbing convulsively. 'George will not hurt her. He left a message to be delivered to me. Seems he did not want anyone to get worried.'

Disgust flared Sebastian's nostrils. 'And that makes it all right?'

'Yes. I mean, no. That is, George is an old friend. We grew up with him. He is like a brother.'

Sebastian could not believe the naïveté. 'You do realise, don't you, that after what is being said about your sister now an elopement will be the *coup de grâce*. She will never be accepted anywhere, country or town. I imagine she will even be shunned by your neighbours.'

Harry's eyes widened. 'Surely not.'

Sebastian shrugged. 'Perhaps. However, I do not intend to let your sister succeed in this harebrained scheme. She is too impetuous for her own good.'

'You are going to chase her?'

'Someone has to,' Sebastian said, wondering why he continued to put himself through this hell. If he had an ounce of self-preservation, he would send a retraction to the papers. He might be called a cad, but he had been called worse.

'Can I go with you? I won't be any trouble and I'm her brother. I should be there to protect her.' Harry's excitement made his hair seem to stand on end. 'Not from you... That is...'

Sebastian looked the youth up and down. He would be a complication, but he did have a point. There was enough impropriety in this mess which his inclusion might help blunt.

'We are riding horses. Quicker. I shall leave in half an hour. If you are not at my house, I will go without you. Is that clear?'

'Yes, sir...your Grace.'

Sebastian wasted no time getting home and to his chamber.

'A change of shirt and linen,' he told Roberts. 'I am leaving in fifteen minutes.'

'Shall I pack a portmanteau, your Grace?' the valet said, already pulling out the luggage.

'No, thank you. I shall be on horseback.'

'What?' A horrified expression filled the servant's face. 'Surely you jest. What will people say? You have a reputation to maintain. You are one of the best-dressed men in all of England.'

'Calm yourself, Roberts. No one of importance is going to see me. I am going into the country.'

'Yes, your Grace,' the valet said in a despondent tone. 'I shall have my own bag packed in a trice.'

'You are not coming.'

'What?'

'Close your mouth, Roberts, you look like a beached fish. I am travelling alone.'

The valet clamped his teeth so hard they clicked and he winced. Not a further word escaped him as he watched the Duke leave. But his head drooped.

Juliet sat across from George, the inn's best cherrywood table between them, and watched him eat and eat and eat. At the speed he was going they would be here until it was too dark to travel and the inn's larder was empty. She had finished long ago. She muffled an irritated sigh with her napkin.

He looked up from his mutton. 'Are you all right? We can stop the night here if you would like.'

She felt as if they were barely out of London and all its environs. The last thing she wanted was to stay here. 'No, I think it best that we continue on. You could have them pack that up for you,' she ended on a hopeful note.

'Capital idea. Should have thought of that myself.' He rang the little brass bell the innkeeper had left with them.

Soon they were on the road again. Juliet took a breath of the cool evening air and wished she were somewhere else. Anywhere except eloping. But there was no help for it.

George sat on the opposite side of the carriage, snoring.

He had finished everything the innkeeper had wrapped and then promptly fallen asleep. At least she did not have to worry about poor dear George trying to seduce her or in any way embarrassing her with his overtures. She was not sure he had an amorous bone in his body, for which she was heartily glad.

How different it would be if Brabourne sat across from her. First, he would not be on the other seat, he would be beside her. She had no doubt that his sensuality would overwhelm any protests she might have. He was...he was...

She sighed and looked away from her companion. The Duke was everything George was not.

That, she told herself harshly, is why you will do better with good stolid George. He will let you run things the way you wish and not bother you. Brabourne would devour you and then bed other women. Infidelity is in his nature.

This was better by far. It had to be—this was her future.

Energy coursed through Sebastian as he urged his mount onwards. 'We are not far behind,' he said, the passing wind catching his words and flinging them back to Harry.

Harry lagged behind. Even the best horse-flesh Lord Smythe-Clyde had was no match for the Duke's.

Sebastian thought he saw a glimmer of light in the distance. It flickered and disappeared, only to reappear again. He was sure it belonged to a carriage.

Wait until he got his hands on the minx. He would teach her a lesson she would never forget. He would curb her impetuosity. No woman was going to leave him after the banns had been posted and the announcement put in the paper. He had declared his intentions to the world, and his pride and heritage demanded that she wed no one else. Especially not some country bumpkin.

They closed quickly on the vehicle. In the twilight, Sebastian could see the back of the coachman's head. There were no outriders. Stupid. They would pass through stretches where robberies occurred on a daily basis, sometimes multiple ones within twenty-four hours.

'By Jove,' Harry's voice rang out, 'that looks like George's old coach.'

Sebastian drew even with the first carriage horse and shouted to the coachman to stop. The servant slowed down, but before he could bring the vehicle to a complete stop Juliet popped her head out of the window.

She gasped. 'Brabourne! Coachman, don't stop. Speed up. This is the man we are running from.'

The servant only faltered for seconds. He knew whom he took his orders from. With a flick of the whip, he urged the four horses on. The carriage, old and large, lumbered behind the panting animals like an overfed cow.

Sebastian cursed under his breath. He was not afraid of losing them. He just wanted to put an end to this charade.

The carriage took a wide turn. One of its wheels hit a large rock. The coach tottered.

Sebastian heard a loud snap and the wheel that had hit the rock cracked. The vehicle skidded on the remaining three wheels until coming to an abrupt stop toppled to one side.

'Harry,' Sebastian yelled, jumping from his horse, 'go to their heads. They are panicking.'

To Sebastian's relief, the youth did as he was told without comment. While Harry tried to calm the horses Sebastian rushed to the carriage door and yanked it open.

Pandemonium reigned.

Juliet scrambled to regain her feet, only to fall down on to the lopsided cushion. Her companion looked dazed, as though he had hit his head. Several blankets littered the floor, which was now the other side of the coach. A wicker basket, with the lid open, lay at the door. The smell of baked chicken and fresh bread filled the interior. Chicken bones were sprinkled throughout as though a giant hand had deposited them.

Sebastian's gaze locked on to Juliet. 'Give me your hand and I will help you out.'

She shook her head.

'Now,' he said, his volume low, but with an underlining of iron.

She glanced at George, who merely looked confused. Seeing there was no help there, she grabbed the strap above the door and used it to pull herself to the opening. Sebastian caught her around the waist and swung her down before she could protest.

'I could have done it myself,' she said irritably, smoothing down the brown wool of her skirt. 'I am not helpless.'

She was stubborn and belligerent. Sebastian would have smiled under different circumstances, but the anger that had driven him to pursue her still held him.

'You,' he said coldly to the coachman, 'had best help your master. He looks as if he took a hit to the head.'

'Oh, dear,' Juliet said, edging past Sebastian and leaning her upper body inside the carriage. 'Are you all right, George? You were sleeping when the wheel broke.'

'Yes, yes,' he muttered. 'Just a bit confused.'

'Where is my reticule?' she said, starting to climb back into the vehicle. 'I have smelling slats. They will help.'

She had just put her left knee on the top of the carriage

when Sebastian wrapped her arm around her and hauled her out. 'He will be fine without your ministrations. You are not going back in there. No telling what will happen next. This is a relic and should never have been on the road, let alone racing.'

Together with the coachman, Sebastian helped George out. The country squire sank to the ground. One glance at the poor man told Sebastian this was no love match.

Juliet grabbed a blanket from the vehicle and wrapped it around George. 'Is that better?'

He nodded.

Harry had the horses calmed and unharnessed. They were munching on grass by the side of the road. He came up to them and said, 'I think he needs a doctor.'

Sebastian ignored him and spoke to George. 'This is going to hurt, old man, but I want to feel around your head and find out where you bumped yourself.'

George groaned, then gasped sharply. 'Damme, that hurts.'

'Shine the carriage lamp on this,' Sebastian ordered. The coachman found an extra candle and lit it, then put it close enough for Sebastian to see. 'You've got a nasty bruise forming, but it is not bleeding much. You will have a knot the size of Prinny's waist by tomorrow.'

'I… I think I'm…going…' George did not finish.

Sebastian stepped away just in time. Juliet stared and managed to suppress her own sympathetic gag. Harry turned green.

'A wet cloth will do wonders,' Sebastian said laconically.

Juliet hastened to wet one of her handkerchiefs from the jug of water. She knelt by George and gingerly wiped his forehead.

'Not there,' Sebastian said. 'On his bump.'

She glared at him, but did as he directed.

Harry sidled up to Sebastian. 'How do you know so much?'

'Had my share of over-indulgence. Head wounds too.' Sebastian motioned to the coachman. 'I want you and Mr Smythe-Clyde to stay here with your master. Miss Smythe-Clyde and I are returning to the last inn to find a doctor and send help.'

Juliet jumped up, dropping the damp cloth. 'I will not go with you. I will stay here. George needs me.'

Sebastian looked from her face to the now dirty cloth. 'I doubt that.'

'You do, don't you, George?' she asked.

'I do,' George mumbled obediently.

Sebastian took hold of her arm and steered her towards his horse. 'You are coming with me, either in front of me on my horse or on Harry's mount. Which will it be?'

She stared stubbornly at him.

'As you wish.'

He gripped her around the waist and tossed her up. She landed with a bone-jarring thud in his saddle.

'You will have to ride astride so you don't fall off,' he said. 'Unless you promise to co-operate and let me balance you against my chest without fighting; then you may ride side-saddle.'

'You know I cannot ride astride,' she hissed.

He eyed her narrow skirt. 'I can remedy that. Coachman, do you have a knife?'

She gasped. 'You would not dare.'

He met her angry gaze with his cool one. This was almost worth the chase, he thought. She might be a hazard, and too impulsive for her or anyone else's own good, but she had spirit.

'Try me,' he said calmly, taking the knife from the servant.

'Harry,' she said, 'are you going to let him bully me like this?'

For the first time in his life, her brother did nothing to help. 'Deuced stupid thing you did, eloping and all. Even if I don't think his Grace is the husband for you, I don't think a flight to Gretna Green just days before your wedding is the thing either.'

She frowned at him. 'Should I have stood Brabourne up at the chapel? For I would have.'

Harry shook his head. 'I still think you could have talked Papa around.'

She looked away from him, and Sebastian would have sworn he saw a tear slide down her cheek in the dim glow of the lantern. He almost felt sorry for her. But she had gone too far this time.

'You win,' she said softly.

He handed the knife back to the coachman and mounted behind her. Taking the reins in one hand, he wrapped his other arm around her waist.

'It should not be above an hour,' he told the three men.

Juliet shivered as Brabourne set the horse in motion. The evening was cool and her pelisse was more fashionable than practical.

Brabourne held her pinned to his chest as though he expected her to try and get away. Not much chance of that. She recognised defeat when it sat behind her.

The heat from his body penetrated the clothing separating them. It felt good. Too good. She stiffened and tried to put distance between them.

He hauled her back.

'You are cold,' he said. 'Staying close will help.'

'I don't want your help,' she said.

'Just as you don't want my name and title,' he said harshly.

'Exactly.'

His grip tightened painfully, squeezing the air out of her lungs. Then he loosened his hold. She sensed that his reaction had been automatic. She did not think he would intentionally hurt her, not physically.

'You will have both,' he said. 'The banns have been read, the announcement is in the paper, the church is reserved, your dress is made and the invitations are out. There is no turning back. Nor are you going to botch it all by running off with some squire's stolid son.'

Anger and the urge to hurt him as she knew he would eventually hurt her drove her. 'He is twice the man you are. Ten times. A hundred times,' she said defiantly, her voice rising. 'You are nothing but a rake and a libertine who has wealth and position. I despise you for what you are.'

He reined the horse to an abrupt halt that would have sent her tumbling to the ground if not for his hold on her. He slid down and pulled her with him so that their bodies bonded.

She felt everything about him. The silver buttons on his coat scraped against her belly and then her breast, sending sensations skittering down her spine. His arms banded her waist and back like iron, and his chest crushed hers. He held her body immobile against the length of his. It was wickedly thrilling and frighteningly comfortable, as though she were meant to be this close to him.

She was going crazy.

'Let me go.'

'Not yet,' he replied, gripping the back of her head with one hand.

She stared up at him, anxiety twisting her stomach. It had to be anxiety, she told herself as his face lowered to hers. She did not want him to kiss her. Never again.

'You are an infuriating minx,' he said, just before his lips met hers.

The kiss was hard and punishing, not gentle and coaxing like the first. This one seared.

His mouth slanted across hers, and when she would not grant his tongue entry he nipped her bottom lip so that she gasped. He took instant advantage. He plundered her, swamping her senses with his sensual onslaught.

She reeled, and would have collapsed if not for his support.

'When I am done,' he vowed, 'you won't want that man you say is worth a hundred of me.'

His kiss gentled just before he broke away to nuzzle the hollow at the base of her throat. His tongue flicked against her skin. The hand that had held her head slid down and pushed the collar of her pelisse aside to give him better access.

She gasped when his hand cupped her breast through her clothing. Even with the barrier, she felt as though he touched her bare skin. Her mind reeled.

'Stop,' she gasped.

He looked down at her, the light from the moon and stars more than enough for her to see him clearly. His eyes were a brilliant blue, seemingly lit from within. His mouth was sensual in its hardness.

She gazed at him and saw hunger in every line of his

face. She exulted in her power to arouse him like that, even as she feared what he would do to her. He would make her want him.

His lips found hers again. His hand caressed her breast, making her nipple peak. His arm pressed her tightly against his hips so that she felt every hard angle of him.

She was doomed.

She felt his fingers on the button running down the back of her dress and a traitorous disappointment filled her. He would never be able to undo them. Not now. Not like this.

One. Two. Three… They opened under his fingers. The only thing keeping the garment from sliding down her shoulders was the pelisse she still wore. Soon she felt the heat of his palms moving inside the shoulders of her pelisse and edging it down her arms. All the while he held her captive with the power of his kiss.

The pelisse fell to the ground and the cool night air moved across her exposed back. Then the bodice slipped from her shoulders and Brabourne took his mouth from hers and placed it at the swell just above her bosom.

She shuddered at the moist warmth of his lips. One of his hands cupped her breast, easing it out of her chemise. His thumb flicked the aroused nipple as he raised his head and watched her reaction. She licked her lips and heard him groan.

Her head dropped back to be supported by his arm around her shoulders. He bent his head until his tongue replaced his thumb. She moaned, shock and pleasure twinning into a knot centred in her abdomen. She arched against him.

He was destroying all her resistance as though it was nothing.

Her bodice hung around her hips, followed by the top of

her chemise. She was bare to his perusal, allowing him to plunder from her head to her waist. He cupped her breasts with his hands and took turns nuzzling and sucking them with his mouth until she no longer knew where she ended and he began.

The world swirled around her.

It was a cold shock when he once more raised up to look at her. 'You are more beautiful than I imagined,' he said, his voice raspy, as though too long unused.

She gazed up at him, no longer caring what else he did to her. It would all be mind-and body-exploding.

She sucked in air, more aware of him than she had ever been of anything in her life. She clung to him, her fingers tangled in the folds of his coat.

'You are more skilful than I ever imagined,' she managed to say between lips swollen from his kisses. 'I never thought seduction would feel this way. No wonder Emily wants you.'

He released her so quickly she stumbled and fell to the hard ground. He turned from her and walked away to stand head resting on the trunk of a nearby tree. Stunned, she sat still for long moments.

'What did I do?' she finally managed to say, her voice coming out small and unsure. Belatedly, she realised she sounded like a timid little mouse.

He kept his back to her. 'Do not ever again mention your stepmother to me. I did not seduce her.' He turned back and strode to her, towering above. 'Do you understand?'

His anger was like a slap in the face. She scrambled to her feet, reality returning with a vengeance. What a weak fool she had been.

She stuffed her arms back into the chemise and yanked

it up over her breasts, trying to make it reach her chin. She shoved her arms into the sleeves of her bodice and contorted like an acrobat in a futile attempt to button the back. Tears of frustration and shame blurred her vision. She angled away so he would not see her weakness.

Stupid, stupid, stupid. She had been a complete fool. He had done nothing to her that he had not done to a million other women, and she had let him. No, she had revelled in his ardour.

He touched her shoulder and she jumped away. 'Don't come near me,' she ordered.

She heard him sigh, but when he spoke his voice was stripped of emotion. 'You will never be able to do up your bodice by yourself.'

'I shall do the best I can, for you shan't touch me again. I promise you that.'

His voice hardened. 'Don't make promises you cannot keep.'

'Where is my pelisse?' she muttered, looking around. The brown wool made the garment hard to see against the dirt. 'Ah.' She pounced on it and yanked it on, hoping it was long enough to cover most of the exposed skin of her back.

'You look unkempt,' his hateful voice said. 'As though you have been ravished and enjoyed every minute of it.'

She scowled, her resentment of her weakness and his skill rising to uncontrollable heights. She rounded on him. 'And you are a philanderer. A seducer of innocent women. A rakehell.'

He sneered. 'I have heard "rake" from your lips more than I like. Is your vocabulary so limited that you can think of nothing else?'

She lunged for him, her open palm connecting with his

cheek. The instant her flesh met his, she knew he had let her hit him. The knowledge was in his bitter eyes.

The fury left her. 'I am sorry. I lost control, something I never do.'

His laugh was cynical. 'You do it all the time. Whenever you act impulsively you are losing control.'

Much to her dismay, he was right. It was her greatest weakness. Mama had told her so often enough. And now it had landed her in this bumblebroth from which she finally acknowledged to herself there was no escape.

'You are right,' she said in a tiny voice. 'I should never have fought you in that duel. Look where it has taken us, what it has done to us. I should have found another way to protect Papa.'

'You should have let him fight his own battle.'

'Oh, no, I could never do that. I promised Mama that I would care for him. And I shall.'

'What nonsense,' he said.

'It is a promise. I keep my promises.'

He studied her. 'And will you keep your promises on our wedding day?'

She blanched. 'You are a cunning devil, turning my words against me.'

He shrugged. 'Enough, minx. I am tired, and I venture so are you. We still have to reach that inn and send someone back for the others.'

She had forgotten all else in the wonder of his lovemaking. Disgust at herself gave her energy. Briskly, she said. 'You are right.'

This time she co-operated with him when he mounted and pulled her up in front of him. She felt the tension in him when her shoulder touched his chest, but she told herself to ignore it. Just as she had to ignore her reaction to him.

She was, beyond question, a fool. Soon to be a hurt one.

# Chapter Ten

For the second time since coming to London, Juliet returned home from Brabourne's protection. This time, however, Harry accompanied her and they arrived in George's carriage, which had been repaired speedily because of the Duke's intervention.

She was glad Brabourne had not come with them. After what had happened between them she never wanted to see him again. A forlorn wish. He had made it plain that he intended their wedding to take place and would brook no further evasions on her part. Nor would she get the chance for another. Her papa would have her watched, or rather Emily would. Papa never stayed focused on anything for long except his experiments.

George left them at the door and went on to his rented lodgings. No words were said between any of them.

She and Harry were met inside by Emily and Papa and marched into the library. Anger at the other woman's obvious influence mixed with Juliet's sense of guilt over having been the cause of discomfort for Papa. Her job was to care for him, not upset him.

Harry looked at her and rolled his eyes. She nearly smiled at him, but remembered she was still angry. It was his fault Brabourne had caught her. She turned away, prepared to face the consequences without his help.

'How dare you, you ungrateful brat?' Emily started. Papa put a restraining hand on his wife's arm which she shook off. 'No, Oliver, I won't be denied my say. She has completely undone everything I have accomplished. She was about to marry Brabourne. Brabourne, the most sought-after man in all the realm. And she runs away. Not only is she ungrateful, she is stupid.'

Juliet stood stoically, but her stomach churned. The only thing that kept her standing was the knowledge that she had tried to do what was right for her. Brabourne was not the man for her, no matter how much her body responded to his and her weak emotions desired his nearness.

Emily continued her tirade.

Papa just shook his head, as though the entire situation bewildered him. It probably did. Finally he asked, 'Why, Juliet?'

'I don't want to marry him, Papa. He will make me miserable.'

'Then why didn't you say something instead of running away with poor George? It is not done. His father will be furious with him.'

She blinked rapidly, hoping no one saw the moisture in her eyes. This was so hard. Not even knowing she had been wrong eased the ache. 'I tried, Papa. You would not listen to me.'

'Of course I did, but you were wrong. Emily is right when

she says this is for the best. You are ruined otherwise. No man will marry you.'

Juliet's stomach twisted again. 'George would have. Still will.'

She longed to tell Papa everything, particularly Emily's part, but for once controlled her tongue. It would do no good and only hurt Papa.

'You are too young and inexperienced,' Emily said in a condescending voice.

Juliet glared at her. 'I am three and twenty, nearly as old as you. And I may be inexperienced in the ways of the *ton,* but I am not ignorant of people.'

Emily raised on elegant blonde brow. 'Is that so? You have an odd way of showing it.'

Juliet sighed and looked away. There was nothing else to say. But it hurt just the same. If Mama were alive, none of this would be happening. But she was not.

'Go to your room,' Emily ordered. 'And be assured that you will not get a second opportunity to so disgrace us. Fortunately for you no one realises what really happened.'

Juliet cast one last imploring glance at Papa, who looked bewildered as he shook his head. She turned and left the room. Harry followed, the tread of his boots loud in the stilled house. He stayed behind her.

Reaching her door, she turned to him. 'Please go away. I know all you want to do is agree with *her.*'

He ran his fingers through his red hair. 'I'm sorry, Ju. I didn't mean for it to be this bad. Just…you just cannot run away with someone to avoid someone else. It isn't done.'

'Some of the most high-ranking people in the aristocracy have eloped,' she hissed. 'And I don't care. George and I would never even have come to London.'

He sighed. 'Those runaway marriages were mostly in our grandparents' time, Ju. People don't do it so much now. At least, not respectable ones.'

His words piled more pain on. 'But you forget,' she said sarcastically, 'I am no longer respectable.'

Her neck ached from stiffness and tension. Soon she would have a raging headache. She rubbed the stiff muscles.

'Please, Harry, just go away. I need time to myself.'

She could see his uncertainty, but he did as she asked. With feet that dragged, she entered her room and crossed to the bed. She crawled on to the large mattress and curled up, staring at nothing.

She was trapped now. No other chance to escape Brabourne would present itself. Emily would gain admittance to the select of Society. She would see some doors open and others remain closed. She might even become an intimate of Prinny. She did not care.

She rolled on to her back.

Then there was Brabourne. She did not want to marry him. Not really. Or so she told herself. He would break her heart. Perhaps he already had, if the pain in her chest was any indication.

She rolled to her other side and squeezed her eyes shut against the tears she had managed to hold in until now. They soaked her pillow.

When had it happened? How could it have happened?

There had been times when he had been kind to her. He had not shot Papa in the duel, even though he could have. That alone had endeared him to her against her better judgement. Then he had rescued her from the thugs in Vauxhall. But those events should not have captured her heart.

Yes, he made her body throb with pleasure and sensations she had never known existed. But that should not have been enough either.

Mama had once said that love was never logical and never comfortable. Perhaps she had been right. Look what it had done to Papa.

To her.

A week later, Juliet stepped down from the travelling carriage Brabourne had sent for her family. Brabourne Abbey, the seat of the Dukes of Brabourne, was stupendous. A large, rambling abbey in the Gothic style, acquired when Henry VIII had dissolved the monasteries, it had been in the family ever since. The grey rock blended in with the cliff on which it perched, the English Channel visible from all the south-and east-facing rooms.

To Juliet's mind it suited Brabourne perfectly. Dark and arrogant.

She had not taken three steps from the carriage before footmen in the Duke's green and black livery were there to assist. Brabourne was right behind them.

'Welcome to my home, Juliet,' he said, taking the hand she had not offered. Watching her the entire time, he kissed her fingers.

Even though she wore gloves, the feel of his lips was distinct and unsettling. Memories flooded back of their minutes in the dark night. Her pulse raced and her heart pounded. She could not look away from his knowing eyes.

'I believe Prinny was right. You will set a new fashion for freckles, my dear,' he said *sotto voce*.

The spell broke and she snatched her hand back. 'I seriously doubt that. No one likes freckles. They are too much like blemishes.'

Before he could further discompose her, she turned away. Emily and Papa exited the coach with Harry close behind. The carriage that carried their luggage drew up and more servants converged on it. It was organised mayhem.

Brabourne welcomed her papa. 'Come this way, Smythe-Clyde. My butler and housekeeper will show you to your accommodations.'

'Yes, yes,' Papa said, his gaze darting all around. 'Nice place you have here, Brabourne. If it were mine, I should never go to the city.'

Emily rolled her eyes. 'Oliver, don't be ridiculous.'

The small group headed to the marble steps that led to the front door. Juliet lagged behind, marvelling that Papa was acting as though he had never challenged the Duke to a duel. Men were so strange. Or Papa was.

She was not surprised to see Burroughs waiting for them. Not even with the blink of an eye did he reveal that he knew her. He assigned a footman to show Harry to his room and took Papa and Emily to theirs himself. Juliet was left standing in the entry with Brabourne.

Old muskets adorned the walls in circles like radiating suns. Many-antlered deer gazed down at them with sightless eyes. The Brabourne crest and motto, a jousting knight and the words *Never Fear*, were emblazoned above the entryway. Soon they would be hers too.

'Not nearly so ornate as Carlton House,' the Duke said drily.

'Not enough gilt,' she managed to remark with a slight smile.

'I will take you to your chamber,' he said abruptly. 'Come with me.' He held out his arm.

The ease that had started to slow her pulse ended. She

glanced apprehensively up at him. He stood implacably, waiting. Juliet knew when she was up against a wall. With ill grace, she accepted his escort.

The muscles of his lower arm were sinewy and strong beneath her fingers. She knew their power from his rescue and his lovemaking, thoughts she did not want to have at this moment.

They progressed up a flight of stairs wide enough for three ladies to walk three abreast while wearing the wide skirts of a generation ago. Gleaming marble overlaid with a fine red carpet stretched ahead. Periodically they passed a footman, who bowed until they were past. It was overdone and overwhelming.

'You are like a potentate here,' Juliet said, hard pressed to keep the distaste from her voice.

'Do I detect displeasure? You will have to get used to this. Anything less would not be fitting for my station.'

Was there bitterness in his last words? She looked at him as they walked. His face, as usual, was unrevealing.

They stopped in front of two double doors with the Brabourne crest and motto carved across them. She got a strange feeling in her stomach.

With his free hand, Brabourne opened the doors. Juliet gazed into a room big enough to be a ballroom in many houses.

He ushered her in, leaving the doors open. 'This is your sitting room. Beyond is the sleeping chamber and a room for your maid.'

Done in shades of pale green and black, the Brabourne colours, it was enough to take her breath away. A settee and several chairs grouped around a table where tea had been laid out. A large secretary and several bookcases took up part of one wall. The wood floor was covered in carpet. Many-paned windows, with green brocade curtains with black trim pulled back, presented the view of a stormy English Channel. She imagined that during a storm she would hear the waves pound the shore.

'Magnificent,' she breathed.

'It is the suite of rooms traditionally occupied by the Duchess. My rooms are connected through a door in your sleeping chamber.'

She was not surprised. Even a house as grand as this could not have many rooms this fantastic. Still, he was bucking respectability by putting her here before their marriage.

He must have known her thoughts. 'By tomorrow it will no longer matter. I am tired of being dictated to by narrow minds.'

There was nothing she could say. She was not yet mistress here. Besides, a large part of her agreed with him. She was heartily tired of having her life tossed about because of what others expected.

'I will leave you now,' he said, releasing her. 'We keep country hours here, in spite of Prinny's presence, but we do dress. The dinner bell will ring at five.'

'Prinny is here?' She had known he was close to Brabourne, and that he intended to attend the wedding, but she had thought he would arrive tomorrow.

'He came several days ago. He likes the hunting.'

The Duke's voice was non-committal and Juliet wondered what else the Prince liked. But it was none of her business.

'We will be twenty for dinner,' he added as he left.

Juliet stood looking at the closed doors long after he had gone. Twenty might be small for him, but to her it was too many. The day had been long and the preceding weeks even longer. Tomorrow was her wedding day, the ceremony to be held in the estate chapel. She really did not want to spend the evening trying to appear excited and eager.

A knock on the door signalled the arrival of her trunks. More would follow over the next week or so. Striding into her sleeping chamber and seeing the massive wardrobe and tallboy, and a separate room specially designed for her gowns, Juliet began to wonder if she had enough clothing for the life she was entering into. She would worry about that later. Right now she needed to direct the unpacking and find a gown suitable for tonight's activities. Pleading sick on the eve of her wedding was not the thing to do.

Several hours later, she studied herself in the large bevelled mirror. She wore the same bronze silk gown she had worn to Almack's, with the same single strand of pearls. Gold ribbon threaded through the curls her maid had let fall like autumn leaves on to her shoulders from a gold clasp on top of her head. Something was missing.

She looked like a schoolgirl. The last thing she wanted. It had not bothered her before, but now she felt gauche in these magnificent surroundings. Out of her depth.

And, a small part of her acknowledged, she wanted to stand out so that Brabourne would notice her and admire her. As much as she told herself she did not want to marry him, she still wanted him to be proud of her. For what reason, she could not, would not admit to herself. The need was just there, nestled in her chest and demanding satisfaction.

She sighed and stood. This was silly.

The smooth sound of wood sliding on wood alerted her.

The door to Brabourne's room opened. He stood in the entryway, watching her, a velvet box in one hand.

He was magnificent, everything she had ever dreamed a man should be. There was a powerful grace about him when he moved, showing his lean body to advantage. His longish hair brushed his shoulders, its darkness nearly lost in the midnight colour of his coat. Black breeches moulded to him.

She gulped and looked away.

'I have something for you,' he said, stopping too close for her comfort.

He flicked open the box and held it out to her. On a bed of black velvet lay a necklace that caught the candlelight and split it into many shades of yellow, orange and red. It was a choker made up of three strands with a large, canary-yellow oval stone in the centre. Around it was a circle of red stones with an orange tinge. More yellow stones made up the three strands. It was stunning. Matching earrings and bracelets lay beside it.

'I have never seen anything so…so striking,' she said.

'They are the Brabourne diamonds. The centre stone is one of the largest yellow diamonds in existence. They will look good on you.'

She looked from the jewels to him. 'I cannot wear them. What if I lost them?'

'You are impossible. I had them cleaned and the catch strengthened. The settings are also good.' He took the necklace out and set the box on a table. 'You will not lose them unless you get into a skirmish with someone, which I don't expect tonight.' A slight smile curved his lips. 'To my knowledge, there are no thugs present.'

She returned his smile with a grimace. 'One never knows.'

'True. You are prone to finding trouble. Now, turn around so I can hook this.'

She looked at him, noting the implacable gaze he bent on her. No argument would sway him. That much she had learned about him. With a reluctant sigh, she did as he ordered.

His fingers brushed the nape of her neck just seconds before her pearls slid down so that one end came to rest where the fabric of her bodice ended. The smooth feel of pearl slid along her skin as he pulled them free. The breath she had not realised she held slipped through her parted lips.

She had barely regained her composure when his fingers once more touched her. A *frisson* shot down her spine. The cool kiss of diamonds and gold rested against the heated flush of her reaction to him.

For a fleeting instant she thought she felt his lips against her neck and across her exposed shoulder. Shivers joined the *frisson* that continued to move through her. Then he stepped away.

'Turn around so that I may see you,' he said, his voice a harsh sound in the utter silence.

She did as she was told, unable to do otherwise. His voice held the same sound it had the night he had nearly ravished her. When she saw him, the hunger in his gaze took her aback.

He reached out and with one finger traced the line of the necklace. Where his flesh met hers fire erupted. He bent forward and kissed the base of her throat, just below the centre diamond. She moaned in shocked surprise and delight, her fingers reaching out to grasp something so she would not fall. Her nails dug into the fabric covering of the chair behind her.

He raised his head and stared down at her. Her chest rose and fell in small panting gasps.

'They become you,' he murmured. 'I knew they would.'

She stared at him, her eyes wide with reaction while his were slumberous. If he crooked his finger, she would fall willingly into his arms. It was a shameful admission, but she knew it for the truth.

She was his—body and soul.

Instead, he stepped further away. 'We must go down. Our guests are waiting.'

Disappointment made its insidious way through her emotions. She caught herself up short with a shake of the head. Would she never learn?

'You are right,' she said, her voice remarkably level for the turmoil her thoughts were in.

Holding her head high, she preceded him through the door. After his bestowal of the jewels, anything else would be anti-climactic.

She was right.

The next morning, Juliet stood across the altar from her groom in the small chapel situated on the Brabourne estate. This was not her choice of place, but Brabourne had thought it best after her attempted elopement. Behind them stood her family, Prinny and Perth. Ravenswood stood as groomsman to Brabourne. She had no bridesmaid.

George had not been invited.

In half an hour all the rich and powerful who were not already here would be arriving for the wedding breakfast.

Right now, she had to turn to the Duke and allow him to kiss her. Her hands shook, so she hid them in the folds of her white silk and silver lace gown. Please let it be chaste.

She did not want to succumb to him in front of these people. She never wanted to melt against him again.

He touched his lips to her cheek before holding his arm out for her hand. Relief flooded her. She laid her fingers lightly on him and hoped he did not feel her shivers.

He graciously accepted congratulations, even smiling at his friends and the Prince. She managed to keep her lips parted in what she hoped looked like a smile. It was the best she could do.

'Beautiful bride, you lucky devil,' Prinny said with a wink.

Before Juliet realised what the prince intended, he planted his mouth full on hers. She gasped, but managed to keep from jumping back. She could not stop the blush.

'Thank you, Your Highness,' she said, grateful her voice did not tremble.

'Oh, Your Highness,' Emily cooed, having come up beside him, 'you are such a charming rogue.'

He took her hand and beamed down at her. Together they left the chapel. Juliet glanced at her papa, who stood to one side watching.

'Why don't you ask him to go in with us?' Brabourne said quietly.

Juliet gave her new husband a speaking look, torn equally between gratitude for his kindness and irritation that he was so thoughtful, which weakened her resolve to dislike him. She could not control her heart, but she was determined to control her mind.

She rushed to Papa, only to have Harry get there first. 'Come with us,' she said to both of them.

Harry grinned and shook his head. 'We will follow. This is your moment—and your husband's.'

She frowned at him, but knew from the stubborn light in his eyes that he would not change his mind. With ill grace, she returned to the Duke, who once more held out his arm.

'You can do better than that,' he chided, his face once more masked by his cool reserve. 'After all the trouble we have gone to, there is no sense in defeating our purpose by having the tongues wagging that our marriage is a sham.'

'Why should they think anything else?' she hissed. 'Everyone knows you only married me to save my reputation.'

He shrugged. 'That does not mean you have to confirm their suspicions. They can just as easily believe it is a love match. After all, I compromised you. Let them guess.'

She gave an unladylike snort.

They entered the large ballroom that Brabourne had had made into a bower of flowers. Through the many french windows she saw white silk tents set up on the acres of lawn. Beneath them were more tables laden with food. Her husband had spared no expense.

People were everywhere, dressed in the height of fashionable morning dress. She had to endure the next couple hours and into the evening. Many of the important guests had arrived last night and stayed over.

Brabourne led her to the largest table, where a many-layered bride's cake reposed. His French chef had been working on it for days. Crystal, china and silver sparkled like constellations around it. With luck, she could spend the rest of the morning and early afternoon cutting the cake.

Then there was the night.

# Chapter Eleven

Juliet could stand the waiting no longer. With a huff of ire, she jumped out of the massive four-poster bed and marched to the mantel. She grabbed a brass poker from the stand and attacked the coals. Heat jumped out at her from the reinvigorated fire. It was small satisfaction.

This was her wedding night and she had come to bed hours ago, or so it seemed to her heightened nerves. Many of the guests had left that afternoon. The only ones remaining were her family, Prinny, Perth and Ravensford. She had left Brabourne drinking with his cronies, thinking he would soon follow.

She was a fool.

She returned the poker to its stand and went to the large window. Pulling the curtains back, she peered out at the night. Clouds scuttled across the sky, obscuring the stars. The moon was only a sliver. If she listened hard enough, she could hear the waves hitting the rocky shores. This was a primitive, vital land, like its owner.

She let the curtain close. Some hot chocolate would be nice, and might help her to sleep, but she did not want to let anyone know of her shame. Her husband was not interested enough in her to come and do his duty. She must have been mistaken when she'd thought she saw hunger on his face after he had fastened the diamonds around her throat.

Her temples began to throb.

Everyone had gasped the night before when they had entered the salon. Emily had turned green. The large gilt mirror over the mantel had shown her the necklace sparkling like a miniature sun around her neck. She had been beautiful, if only because of the jewels. She had even felt beautiful for the first time in her life.

Now, the diamonds were back in their case on her dressing stand. She was back to her normal self.

She returned to the bed, crawled in and burrowed under the covers. It might be summer, but being so close to water kept the abbey too cool for comfort. She turned into the embrace of the fluffy pillows and told herself she was better off without Brabourne in her bed. He was too expert at what he did to leave her unscathed.

Sebastian paused at the door separating his room from Juliet's. He had drunk everyone under the table and now felt a cool detachment about his new wife. The desire that had driven him lurked beneath the haze caused by good French wine. Yet he knew that if he crossed the wooden barrier separating them, all his good intentions would be for naught. He would have her to wife and be damned to anything else.

The cynical part of him said do it. He would ensure her first child was his.

The side of himself he showed only to those few people close to him said wait. For her first time with a man she deserved to have someone who was sober enough to give her pleasure and to care about how she felt. Right now he was not that person.

He should not have drunk so much, trying to exorcise the spectre of his mother and her infidelity to the man the world had known as his father. His marriage had opened wide the already-weeping wound of his bastardy. Telling himself Juliet was not his mother did no good. Juliet was a woman, and he did not trust women.

Hands clenched, shoulders tight, he turned and went to his bed. He snuffed the single candle he carried and set it on the side table, then undid the sash of his navy robe and let the silk slither to the floor. Naked, he got under the cold covers.

It was going to be a long night.

The next morning Juliet rose before the maid came to her room and made her bed. Raised in the country, she knew the first servant in to tidy the room would realise she and Brabourne had not consummated their marriage. She had never thought herself prideful, but having people know her husband could not bring himself to make love to her on their wedding night was more than she could bear.

She pulled the bell; when a footman came, she told him she wanted Mrs Burroughs. It was not so strange a request for a new bride. Brabourne had introduced her to the staff yesterday after their marriage. It was plausible that she intended to speak to the housekeeper about the running of the abbey...what if it was a little too early? She was eccentric.

Mrs Burroughs arrived promptly, making a curtsy to Juliet. 'Your Grace?'

'Please, Mrs Burroughs, don't treat me that way. I am not used to it.'

The housekeeper smiled warmly. 'Used to it or not, you are a Duchess now and must learn to accept what comes with it.'

Juliet wrung her hands and paced the floor of her chamber. How did one go about asking for help to hide this sort of thing? If only Ferguson or Hobson were here.

Reaching the sticking point, she stopped short and blurted, 'Mrs Burroughs, I need your help. The Duke did not visit me last night.' Embarrassment was like a flame that burned her face.

The old woman's round cheeks turned ruddy even as sympathy softened the lines around her eyes. 'Oh, dear. I knew he would have problems, but I was so sure he was attracted to you enough that he would... Well, anyway. We must get you dressed, and you need to go to the Long Gallery to see the pictures. That will tell you. Meanwhile, I will tidy your room. No one must know what did not happen last night. Least of all your stepmother.'

Relief eased the constriction in Juliet's chest. She had found an ally. She dressed in a pale lavender morning dress, with a white paisley shawl around her shoulders to ward off the morning chill. Mrs Burroughs gave her directions to the Long Gallery and she set off, wondering what she was supposed to learn that Mrs Burroughs did not want to tell her.

She got lost twice, and finally asked a footman to show her the way. The young man made her a very impressive bow, which made her more uncomfortable. She was going to have trouble getting used to her new rank. At her destination he bowed again.

'Please,' she said, then stopped herself. She could not tell him to stop bowing. 'Thank you.'

He raised one eyebrow, but otherwise managed to keep an impassive face as he took his leave. Her impetuosity had nearly got her into trouble again. Being a Duchess was going to be hard work.

Drawing the shawl close, she started slowly walking the length of the room and studying the portraits as she went. The style of clothing changed with each painting, as did the women. Each Duchess differed from the one before or after her. Blonde, brown or black hair, and blue, brown or grey eyes, graced the women randomly. Some were plump and others thin. Some were tall and others short.

The men never seemed to change. Their clothes reflected the time period, but their features and bearing never altered. All the Dukes had blond hair and heavily lidded pale blue eyes. Their noses were arrogant hooks that turned down at the tip. Their lips were thin. Even the last Duke, Brabourne's father, looked like all those who had gone before him.

She stopped at the end of the gallery and studied the portraits of the last Duke and Duchess. The Duchess looked like Brabourne, the same raven-black hair and piercing blue eyes. Her lips were full and sensual like her son's. Her nose was straight and well defined and, like her son's, had no hook. She was willowy and he was lean. Brabourne had a squarer jaw, but that was the only major difference.

Juliet felt a presence and turned to see her husband. He stopped beside her and looked up at the picture of his mother.

'We are much alike.'

There was a harshness to his voice and an intensity to his body that told Juliet he was disturbed. He glanced down at her and his eyes were hard.

'I don't look anything like the last Duke.'

'Your father,' she said, before realisation hit her. She had been so stupid.

He stiffened. 'The man the world calls my father.'

Instinctively she reached for him. He moved as though to look somewhere else and managed to avoid her touch. She drew back, hurt.

'I have his name and title, but I am really a bastard,' he said softly.

She did not know what to say, but had to do something. The gulf between them was widening. 'You cannot know that for sure.'

'He told me.'

'Oh.'

'I was ten. It was my birthday. He never forgave my mother for doing it to him, and he never forgave me for living. I never forgave her either.' His voice was void of emotion, as though he spoke of someone else.

Juliet was appalled by the pain the last Duchess had wrought. She longed to comfort Brabourne, but did not think he would let her.

'I am so sorry,' she whispered, knowing the words were inadequate.

He turned back to her. 'Don't be. It is in the past.'

'But not forgotten or overcome.' Even as she said the words she knew she spoke the truth. When he said he had never forgiven his mother, he also meant he did not trust women. 'I will not do that to you, to our children.'

He looked at her for long minutes, then walked away

without saying a word. Her heart ached for him as she watched his proud back disappear around a corner. Her heart ached for herself. She had known her marriage was far from perfect, but she had never imagined there was so much past pain that had to be put to rest before they could start to make the best of their life together.

One step at a time, she told herself. He would never love her, but she would make him trust her. She could live with that. She would have to.

For dinner that night she wore the palest of lavender. Brabourne sent her a magnificent set of amethyst and diamond jewellery. Her maid fastened the necklace. Juliet missed the electrifying sensuality of her husband's touch even as she wondered what maggot had taken up residence in her brain. She should be glad he was keeping his distance. It was what she had wanted from the beginning.

The Prince was still with them. During the meat course, he announced, 'I will be returning to London tomorrow, Brabourne. I hope to see you there after your wedding trip.'

'Within the week,' Brabourne answered without looking at Juliet.

No one said a word about there not being a trip.

'Really?' Emily said, 'Oliver and I were just talking about when we were returning to town. We have decided to go tomorrow as well.'

Juliet watched her papa, noting the look of confusion on his face.

Harry said, 'That is news to me. The hunting here is excellent, and Papa likes hunting above everything except his experiments.'

'Don't be ridiculous,' Emily said quickly. 'Oliver wants to get back to his experiments, don't you?'

'Yes, yes. Quite, m'dear.' He returned his attention to his meal.

Juliet watched her stepmother and wondered just what the other woman was up to. She had used Juliet's connections to Brabourne to better her position in Society. Was she now going to use her budding acquaintance with the Prince to further boost her position? Was Prinny aware?

Prinny smiled warmly at Emily. 'Delightful to have you coming back so soon, Lady Smythe-Clyde. The two of you must come to Carlton House.'

Juliet glanced at her husband. Brabourne was watching the exchange with a jaundiced air. He obviously knew something was going on between the Prince and Emily and did not approve. Papa seemed oblivious, his food holding all his attention.

What a mess, Juliet decided, grateful dinner was essentially over. She signalled for herself and Emily to leave the men with their port.

Her relief at escaping the quickly deteriorating dinner was short-lived.

With an insinuating tone, Emily asked, 'Was last night everything you thought it would be? Brabourne is reputed to be the best lover in England.'

Juliet's hated blush came in full force. Pulling herself together, she gave Emily a supercilious stare. 'How unladylike a question.'

Emily's eyes narrowed. 'High in the instep, now that you are a Duchess.' She moved nearer and said in a venomous whisper, 'But don't expect him every night. He has a reputation. No woman has ever held him exclusively.' Her tinkling laugh filled the room as she went to the sideboard and poured herself a glass of sherry.

Juliet left while the other woman's back was turned. She would not stay and hear Emily's bold words and hurtful insinuations. The truth in them was something she did not want to face tonight.

In her own rooms, she quickly dressed for bed. Her last request to her maid was for a cup of hot chocolate. She intended to sleep.

An hour later she sighed and threw the covers off. She got out of bed and lit the candle left near. By its golden glow she found her lavender wool robe and donned it, tying the sash tightly. She should have known oblivion would evade her.

A chill hung in the room. She crossed to the fireplace and stirred the banked coals. Sparks jumped up and rode the air currents like fairies. She smiled, remembering the tales of little people her nanny used to regale her and Harry with before bed.

A click and the smooth slide of a door across carpet froze her, poker in right hand. Very careful not to appear startled, she put the tool back, then pivoted around.

She swallowed hard.

Brabourne was a dark figure in the entry, the glow of the fire barely reaching him. He stood there, watching her for long moments before stepping into the room. The door slid shut behind him.

Juliet's heart pounded.

In one hand he held a bottle of wine, in the other a velvet box. He set them down on the table nearest the bed, then continued towards her, not stopping until he was close enough so that she could see every nuance of his face and feel the warmth from his body. Much too close.

Her stomach knotted and butterflies seemed to fly up her throat. This was the moment she had been dreading as much as she had been longing for it. He was finally going to consummate their marriage.

'Juliet,' he said softly, taking her hands in his, 'it is time.'

She nodded, allowing him to lead her back to the bed. He released her and poured them each a glass of golden wine. She took hers and sipped. It was champagne. The bubbles floated up her throat. A surprised smile eased some of her discomfort.

He watched her with an intensity that brought back her sense of impending disaster. Intuitively she knew that when he was finished with her nothing would ever be the same. She swallowed down the wine in one long gulp.

He shook his head. 'Fine wine is for sipping, not quenching your thirst.' Still, he poured her more.

This time she sipped, allowing the effervescence to cascade down her throat as she wondered what he was going to do next. Anticipation was a delicious tingle in her toes. None the less, it was a shock when he undid the belt on his robe and allowed the silk to fall to the floor.

He stood naked before her, his magnificent body glowing in the light from the fire. She gaped, taking in his splendour before squeezing her eyes shut. Her cheeks flamed. The empty glass would have fallen from her nerveless fingers if he had not rescued it.

'Get into bed,' he murmured.

Without opening her eyes, she backed away until her knees hit the mattress. His hands gripped her waist and lifted. He held her against him so she could feel his arousal pressing into her. She gasped and put her hands on his shoulders and pressed, trying to put some distance between them.

'Don't,' he ordered. 'This is only the beginning.'

The beginning of the end, she told herself. He would take her and make her his. She licked her dry lips. He laid her on the bed.

'Here,' he said, handing her another glass of champagne. 'It will help relax you.'

She opened one eye and took the wine. She needed a lot of relaxing. He grinned indulgently at her as she gulped down the contents.

'Remind me not to waste good wine on you again,' he said, taking the empty glass and setting it on the table.

She began to feel a little giddy and drowsy. It would be so nice to sink into the comfort of the feather bed and sleep.

'You cannot go to sleep yet,' he said, untying the sash of her robe. 'I have things to show you.'

It was an effort to open her eyes, but she managed. He loomed over her, his face golden on one side where the fire-light hit it. Overwhelming curiosity drew her gaze downward. Dark hairs scattered across his chest, swirling around his nipples. The temptation to touch was great.

'Go ahead,' he murmured, his voice husky. 'Feel me.'

'How did you know?' she asked, her words only slightly slurred.

'Your face. Every thought you have shows on it.'

When she did nothing, he caught one of her hands and placed it on his chest. The invitation was irresistible. With wonder, she explored the textures of his upper body.

His skin was firm, not as soft as hers, but not coarse either. The dark hairs that had beckoned her twined around her fingers, their wiry toughness so much like him. Firm muscles twitched. When she finally found his nipple, it hardened with an alacrity that enthralled her. She swirled her thumb over the nub until he groaned.

'For a beginner you do very well.'

She smiled, hearing the need in his voice. 'I am a fast learner.'

But she knew it was bravado. She had no idea where they were going or how to get there. He was the one who would control their joining.

With infinite skill, he eased the robe off her shoulders. She shivered as the cool air caressed her exposed skin.

'How can you stand being naked?' she asked.

'Anticipation.'

'Ah,' she murmured, memories of his caresses returning. 'I can understand that.'

'Can you? Then help me get your nightrail off.'

That stopped her. 'Can you not do it with me dressed?'

'I could,' he said, leaning down and catching her nipple in his mouth through the fine linen. He sucked and nibbled until she shivered with delight. He raised his head to watch the wonder moving over her face. 'But it is not nearly so nice.'

'If it were any more so, I would not be able to stand it,' she murmured.

'Oh, you will,' he promised, easing the material over her head.

He dropped the clothing on the floor with his robe, the two garments entwining as he imagined their bodies soon would. His heart hammered with desire. It was all he could do not to enter her now.

She flinched, but did nothing to stop his hand from cupping her breast. His warmth felt good, adding another layer

to the sensations he gave her. This time when he took her
into his mouth his tongue slid smoothly over her flesh.

'Oh,' she whispered. 'I see what you meant. This is much
better.'

He chuckled. For an innocent she was certainly hedonistic. All the better. Her arousal would intensify his reaction.

He reached across her for his half-full glass of champagne. With a tilt of his wrist, he poured some on to her
flat abdomen. She flinched, pushing her breasts up against
his chest.

'What are you doing?' she asked, raising her head so
she could see.

'Patience,' he said, lowering his head to her belly.

With flicks of his tongue he licked up the wine. Her muscles spasmed at each touch.

Juliet had never known such pleasure. She caught his
hair in her fingers and held him to her. He chuckled and
his warm breath on her skin was like torture. Divine torture that she knew was only the beginning.

Some of the champagne slipped down to the secret place
between her legs. He followed it.

Juliet stiffened and tried to pull his head up. 'Please, no.'

He looked up at her, his face implacable. 'Yes.'

She shook her head.

He smiled and slipped his hand where his mouth wanted
to go.

She gasped, her eyes wide. 'What are you doing?'

'Making love to you,' he murmured, watching carefully
as his fingers slid along the moist warmth of her skin. When
he slid one into her, she tightened, and a groan of anticipation escaped him.

Juliet licked dry lips and stared up at the ceiling. She

could not watch what he was doing. It was too intimate, too depraved. But it felt so good. She moaned.

'Relax,' he crooned. 'This night is for pleasure.'

Still unable to look at him, she murmured, 'This is so... so unladylike. I never imagined it would be so—'

'Delightful?'

'That too.' She gasped as he found a particularly sensitive spot.

He chuckled, and in her moment of weakness moved her legs apart and touched her with his tongue. Juliet cringed, only to have shivers rack her body with each caress he gave her. Her stomach clenched.

'What is happening?' she gasped.

He raised up on his elbows to better see her face. 'You are becoming aroused.'

She gulped as his fingers replaced his mouth. 'Oh.'

It was a small sound and all she could make. Her world was spiralling down to the way he made her feel. Nothing else mattered any more. Not the indignity of her position or the crudity of what he was doing. Only the way he made her feel.

Sebastian watched her, his own need mounting. She responded with such sweet intensity he did not know how much longer he could put off entering her completely. He felt her muscles contract and knew she was close.

Never taking his fingers from her, he slid up until he lay in the valley between her legs. Her whimpers drew him on.

In one smooth motion, he pulled out his fingers and inserted himself. He slid in with only a slight hitch.

'Ohh! That hurt.' Her eyes opened and she stared up at him where he lay above her.

He clenched his teeth. 'I... I took your maidenhood.'

She said nothing.

Driven nearly beyond his celebrated control, Sebastian kissed her. He kissed her as if there was no stopping them. Only when she started to kiss him back did he start slowly moving.

She gasped.

He grinned, not knowing it was nearly a grimace. 'Move with me,' he murmured. 'Match my rhythm.'

'I cannot,' she whispered, eyes wide in shock at the knowledge he was inside her. Yet it felt good. Terribly good.

'Yes, you can,' he said, catching her face between his hand and taking her mouth again.

His tongue slipped into her mouth and teased hers. His body slid over hers, his belly meeting hers in shivering pleasure. He moved faster.

Juliet gave in to the demands of his desire. Her hips met his and withdrew in response to his. Her back arched and her breasts pressed tightly against his chest. Sensations drenched her nerves. Her nails raked down his back until her hands clutched his buttocks and urged him on.

Her gasps matched his.

'Now, now,' he moaned.

She thrust up and exploded. Spasms of pleasure tore her apart. She could hardly breathe.

His mouth still covered hers when he lost control. His shout filled her lungs as he bucked into her.

It was a long time before either could move. She lay beneath him her legs still wrapped around his hips, her eyes slumberous jewels that watched him with satisfaction.

'You are very, very good,' she murmured, running her fingers along his spine. 'I never imagined it could be like that.'

He grinned, enjoying her feather touch on his back. 'Not a fate worse than death after all?'

She smiled and tightened her legs, making him wonder if he would soon be able to repeat what had brought the glow to her body. He certainly wanted to.

Soon he was moving in her again as she moaned and thrashed beneath him. He began to wonder if he would survive the night. If not, he could not think of a better way to end.

## Chapter Twelve

Juliet woke up the next day with a sense of wellbeing. She sighed and tried to roll over. A heavy arm held her pinned to the bed. Soft snores gently blew the curls from her face. Brabourne had stayed the night with her.

She smiled, remembering all they had done to and with each other. Never in her wildest imagination would she have created the things he had done to her. Not even *The Bride of Abydos* had prepared her for the bliss of making love. She flushed as desire quickened her blood.

His eyes opened and she wondered if she had spoken aloud. He gave her a slow, sensual smile, and before she knew it she had straddled him. She lowered herself until he filled her.

'Do your duty, wife,' he said, his voice a hoarse growl.

Feeling her power over him in this position, she took her time, drawing it out until he begged. When she felt him jerk and his eyes close, she knew he had taken his pleasure.

After his breathing returned to normal, he opened his eyes and said, 'Now it is your turn.'

She squealed as he flipped her over and began doing things to her that she remembered only too well. They had not slept much the night before.

He teased her with mouth, tongue and hands until she was hot and ready. Then he slipped into her.

She watched him with eyes glazed by passion, waiting for him to start the rhythm that ended in such delight. He began slowly so that her tension mounted.

'Brabourne,' she pleaded, her hands on his hips urging him to greater speed.

'Sebastian,' he said.

'Yes, yes,' she muttered. 'Faster, please, I am so—'

'Sebastian.'

She gazed up at him, not knowing what he wanted. She wiggled her hips, hoping to entice him into doing what she needed so desperately.

'Call me Sebastian,' he said, holding back so his face was a grimace caused by the effort it took not to ram into her and take them both to the top.

'Brabourne. Sebastian,' she said, wriggling beneath him. 'They are both your names.'

'Sebastian,' he gritted. 'That is my Christian name.' He panted as he held back. 'Call me Sebastian and I will end this torture.'

'What's in a name?' she muttered. 'Sebastian.'

He released a pent-up sigh and thrust deep. She arched up to meet him, their bodies straining.

Some time later she woke to find him gone. The bed seemed too large and very cold without him. She rose and wrapped her robe tight before going to the window. Pulling the curtains back, she saw it was dusk. She had spent the entire day in bed. She never did that. But, then, she had never made love to a man all night and day either.

When she finally went downstairs, Burroughs met her in the foyer. 'His Grace is waiting in the library, your Grace.'

She glanced at him to see if he had kept a straight face while sprinkling all those 'Graces' in one sentence. He was the perfect butler, his countenance betraying nothing, not even the ridiculousness of the situation.

'Thank you,' she said, and headed off in the direction he indicated.

She knocked and waited for permission to enter. Once it was given, she opened the door and walked through.

Bra—Sebastian stood by the window looking out, his back to her. He was casually dressed, like a country squire, only on him the simplicity was actually striking. Juliet sighed. He was a magnificent man.

He turned and smiled, the emotion actually reaching his eyes. 'Come here. I want to show you something before it is completely dark.'

She moved to him until they stood side by side. He slipped an arm around her shoulders.

'Look out there,' he directed.

An expanse of grass stretched to the horizon. Every imaginable tree dotted the earth. Manicured gardens of roses, nasturtiums, honeysuckle and much more tempted the beholder to walk through them. A lake in the distance reflected the red rays of the dying sun. Further still were cultivated fields and the smoke from tenants' cottages.

'It is impressive,' she said, not knowing what his point was.

'Yes. And it is mine.' His voice firmed. 'And it will pass to the first male child you bear.'

She stiffened.

He turned her to face him, but she refused to look at him. He caught her chin and made her eyes meet his.

'I know you were a virgin last night, so I know you are not carrying another man's child. Don't betray me as my mother did my father.'

She gazed at the flat blue of his eyes. She now understood that his feelings on this subject were so strong he hid them behind a blank surface. Still, his assumption that she might be unfaithful hurt.

She took a deep breath before speaking. 'I am not your mother. I have already told you I will honour my vows. Obviously you did not believe me.'

He stared down at her, his countenance still inscrutable. 'Ours was not a love match—I don't expect fidelity. Just wait until after I have an heir.'

She slapped him, her reaction instinctual. 'How dare you accuse me of your sins? When I said I honour my vows, I meant I honour them for my lifetime.'

She wrenched from his loosened embrace and stormed to the door and through it.

Sebastian watched her go before turning back to the view. He was sorry to have hurt her, but she had to understand. He would not brook raising another man's bastard as his heir. He would divorce her and disown the child first.

Still, he wished it could have been different. A part of him wished he could have trusted her. But trust was something he had never learned to have for women.

That night he came to her and she let him make love to her, knowing he would visit her every night until she conceived his heir. It was bitter-sweet knowledge as she dissolved under his caresses.

* * *

The next morning Juliet woke to an empty bed, the warmth and intimacy of their first night together gone. The loss brought tears she could not stem. For a while she had allowed herself to enjoy her husband's attentions without feeling the future press down on her.

The door between hers and Sebastian's rooms opened. He entered, dressed for riding.

'I am touring the estate today. Would you like to come along?'

'Why?' she asked without thinking, concerned only with concealing the fact that she had been crying. She swiped at her cheeks.

He flinched before his cool hauteur returned. 'I deserved that. I would like to show you around and introduce you to some of the people. This is your home now, and will be so for the children you bear.'

Her stomach churned. The children she bore, not *their* children. 'Any children I have will belong here.'

He nodded. 'Are you coming?'

He was implacable. She was tempted to throw his invitation back in his face, but she was also curious. As he had pointed out, she would spend a large part of her life here.

'Give me a few minutes to dress.'

'I will be in the library.'

She made a fast toilet and descended the stairs in her leaf-green riding habit. A jaunty black hat with a lone peacock feather tilted rakishly on her auburn curls. She looked her best and knew it. Somehow she did not think it would make any difference. Sebastian had his pick of beautiful women and trusted none of them. Beauty would not win him, but it gave her courage to know he would not be embarrassed to introduce her as his Duchess.

They wasted no time.

Juliet rode a placid gelding while Sebastian rode a spirited mare. He led the way down a dirt road.

Rich fields spread out around them. She could see people working the earth. Up ahead was a cottage with a woman and child standing outside.

Sebastian reined in. 'How are you, Mrs Smith?'

The woman bobbed a curtsy. 'Well, your Grace. The harvest will be large this year.'

'We can use it,' Sebastian said. 'I have brought my bride. You will be seeing a lot of her.'

The woman made another curtsy. 'Your Grace.'

Juliet smiled. 'How old is your child and what is his name?'

'He be eight. We call him Tom after his pa.'

Juliet smiled at the boy who stood bravely beside his mother, taking in the novelty of the lord and lady speaking with them. He raised his hand to a lock of hair and tugged it.

'We must be going,' Sebastian said. 'Let my steward know if there is anything you need.'

At the next house a young girl met them. She bobbed respectfully. 'Your Grace.'

Sebastian nodded and introduced Juliet. After the acknowledgments, he asked, 'Where are your parents?'

'In the village getting provisions.'

'Tell them someone will be out within the week with materials to repair your roof.' And they were off again.

By the end of the afternoon Juliet felt as though she had met more people in the past few hours than in the last year.

All of them were well fed and seemed contented. Sebastian was a good landlord. She was not surprised.

That night she fell into bed, tired and aching. It had been a while since she had spent so much time in the saddle. Not even a hot bath had helped. Her eyes were drowsily shutting when the door opened. She suppressed a groan of pure exhaustion.

Without asking permission, Sebastian got under the covers of her bed and snuffed the candle he carried and set it on the table. He reached for her.

Juliet scooted back. 'Please, not tonight. I ache in all the wrong places.'

'Ah. Too long on horseback.'

She rolled over on her back. 'Yes. I have not ridden like that since before Mama died. Coupled with the soreness from our activities, I feel I am splitting apart.'

He chuckled. 'Poor Juliet. Come here and let me rub your back and legs.'

She snorted. 'I know where that will lead.'

'I promise.'

She knew he would keep a promise. And it did sound divine.

'Just for a little bit.'

'Of course,' he murmured.

She rolled onto her stomach and let him do as he would. His fingers dug into the sore muscles of her lower back and thighs. At first it hurt, but soon she loosened as his massage continued. Shortly she purred contentment.

'Glad now?' he asked, his voice husky as his fingers moved down from the small of her back.

Little jolts of pleasure shot through her as he rubbed. 'You are very good,' she murmured.

Instead of answering, he turned her on her side and cuddled her close. 'I will leave you alone tonight,' he said, wrapping his arm around her waist so that his hand cupped her breast.

'You have a very unusual way of doing that,' she muttered, wiggling into him.

'And you have a very tempting way of getting comfortable.'

She stopped all movement. As much as she enjoyed his lovemaking, she was truly sore and tired. With a sigh she closed her eyes and tried not to let hope flare in her heart. He was staying only because he was determined she would have *his* child. Sadness filled her instead as she drifted to sleep.

The next morning Juliet drifted awake, feeling warm and cosy. She snuggled into the source of her delight.

'Time to wake up,' Sebastian murmured, his lips skimming along her face.

She opened her eyes and looked straight into his. Their blue depths were filled with desire and she knew there would be no denying him this time. Nor did she want to.

Two days later, she sat in the Duke of Brabourne's travelling carriage, the Brabourne crest emblazoned on the glossy black paint outside. The thick gold velvet seats were the most comfortable she had ever ridden in. Sebastian rode his favourite horse.

Brabourne Abbey disappeared from sight and Juliet leaned back into the cushions. They were going to London. She had not wanted to leave, thinking that with time and no other distractions she might win her husband's trust, if not his love. He had not given her that time.

She sighed and forced herself to read the book she had brought along. The journey would be too short.

Juliet could have done without dinner at Carlton House, but Brabourne—no, Sebastian—was still one of Prinny's intimates regardless of being married now. She supposed she should consider herself lucky she had also been invited.

Resigned, she took another bite of salmon and smiled at her dinner partner, Lord Appleby. He was tall and slim, an elegant man with blond hair and a dimple when he smiled. He was also a witty talker and a wicked flirt. Innuendoes fell from his lips like water from an icicle.

Sebastian was further up the table near Prinny. So was her stepmother, but that did not bother her much. What ate at her was the woman beside her husband. She was beautiful and endowed in ways Juliet never would be. She also constantly touched Sebastian, and he enjoyed it if his sultry smile was anything to go by. Watching them was like twisting a knife in her heart. If she could, she would leave. She could not.

She took another bite and looked away. There was nothing she could do, no matter how much it hurt. She would worry about something else, such as the way Papa was watching Emily flirt with the Prince. He had the same gleam in his eye that had been there the night she had overheard him tell Hobson about challenging Sebastian. He absolutely could not challenge the Prince. That was treason.

'Lady Brabourne,' Lord Appleby said, breaking into her thoughts, 'you have not heard a word I have been saying and now dinner is over. You owe me the pleasure of your company for a walk.'

She turned and blinked at him. She owed him? She pulled herself together and glanced at her husband, only to see him still flirting with the same woman. Perhaps she did owe Appleby after all. He rose and she allowed him to take her hand.

Sebastian watched his bride walk off with one of the most notorious womanisers in London. Michael Appleby had been chasing skirts since their days at Eton. Appleby left his own wife in the country while he pursued his pleasures in town.

A spurt of anger caught Sebastian unawares. He did not want Juliet consorting with the likes of Appleby, not after all he had done to improve her reputation. With a murmured excuse, he extricated himself from his companion's clutches.

The couple sauntered ahead. Sebastian knew exactly where their roundabout walk was taking them. He had entertained his share of women there, too.

Juliet allowed Appleby to guide her down ornately decorated halls where footmen stood around doing nothing. All the while he kept up a witty monologue. He stopped at a door that was indistinguishable from the others, but he seemed to know where they were.

Smiling down at her, he said, 'There is an Italian picture in here that I would like your opinion on.'

She studied him in the light provided by wall sconces. His hazel eyes dared her, and his dimple teased her. She wondered how many women he had charmed with those two assets.

'An Italian picture?' She grinned at him. She was married to Brabourne and knew what a rake looked like when he was bent on conquest. 'That sounds perilously close to a walk in a darkened garden.'

His smile widened. 'You are too astute for me. Brabourne must have taught you well.'

She shrugged. The last thing she intended to discuss was her husband.

With a mock sigh, he extended his arm once more. 'Let me escort you back to the salon.'

'That will not be necessary,' Sebastian said, coming round the corner where he had stopped to see what Juliet would do.

Appleby frowned before stepping away graciously. 'Overprotective, ain't you?'

Sebastian gave him a feral parting of lips. 'I know you too well, my friend.'

Appleby's gaze went from Sebastian to Juliet and back. 'I once thought the same of you. But things seem to have changed.'

'Precisely.'

Juliet watched the two men and wondered what they were really saying to each other. With a mock bow, Appleby sauntered off. Sebastian turned his attention to her.

'What was that all about?' she asked. When he did not answer, she narrowed her eyes. 'Don't look at me like that. I did not do anything wrong.'

'I know,' he said solemnly. 'But you need to know I am not my father, my dear. I will not share.'

She clenched her teeth and glared at him. 'Neither will I. So you had better remember that!'

The corner of his mouth twitched. 'What is good for the goose is good for the gander?'

'Absolutely,' she huffed.

Head high, she skirted past him, resisting the urge to stay close. It was a battle she fought every time he was near. But this time she was not going to weaken. How dared he tell her to be faithful when he was not? And then to be amused when she told him he had to be equally true to her. More amazing than anything was that she had told him anything. He was not a man one gave ultimatums to, and she had told herself she would never do so. She would do her best to accept his infidelities.

She shook her head at her bravado. A giggle of nervous reaction bubbled to her lips which she smothered with a hand.

She rounded a corner well ahead of Sebastian and came to a dead halt. Down the long hall, in plain sight for anyone to see, the Prince stood kissing and embracing her stepmother. All thought of her bold words to Sebastian evaporated in the anger that gripped her. Her hands fisted. More than anything she wanted to hurt Emily. How dared she do this to Papa?

'I would be careful about what I do. Attacking the Prince could be construed as treason,' Sebastian said in a sardonic whisper.

Juliet shot him a fulminating glance. Keeping her voice as low as his, she hissed, 'It is Emily I wish to kill.'

Sebastian took her arm and steered her back around the corner and out of sight, shaking his head the entire time. 'I shall be careful not to anger you for I am looking forward to a long life.'

He was teasing her, and at a time like this. She rounded on him, hands on hips. 'This is awful. What will Papa say if he finds out? It will break his heart.'

Sebastian moved his hands to her shoulders and scowled.

'You cannot protect him from everything. You certainly cannot fight a duel with Prinny. It isn't done.'

'Then what am I supposed to do? Stand by and let that… that *woman* hurt Papa? I do not think so.'

He shook her. 'Don't be ridiculous. Your father is a grown man. He can and should take care of his own problems.'

Her face scrunched up and it was all she could do not to shout in her frustration. 'I promised Mama. I have to take care of him.'

'No, you don't, Juliet. What she made you promise was unfair. You were hurting and under duress. You must let it go.'

She twisted in his hold, but he tightened his grip. Part of her knew he was right, but a larger part could not release her from her promise. Not yet.

'Remove your hands, please,' she said hoarsely. 'I need to find Papa and make sure he does not come this way.'

Sebastian did as she asked, but stayed close, blocking her from an easy exit. 'You are the most stubborn woman it has ever been my misfortune to meet. Your father is a grown man. Let him solve his own problems, especially since he seems to make all of them. No other man in his right mind would have married Emily Winters. Forget the past.'

She lashed out at him. 'Then what about you? Instead of carrying your hatred of your mother around like a mountain on your shoulder, why don't you forget? Do as you order me to do.'

He stepped away and all emotion fled from his face. 'You hit below the belt, madam.'

'So do you,' she muttered.

Not meeting his burning gaze, she started edging around him. Fortunately, the walls were as wide as they were opulently decorated. The Prince Regent skimped on nothing. She looked up just in time to see Papa rounding the nearest corner. She groaned.

Sebastian heard her and pivoted to find out what was the matter. He put a hand on Juliet's arm. 'Don't interfere.'

Ignoring him, she stepped in front of her parent. 'Papa, are you lost? Let me show you the way back to the drawing room.'

He did not even glance at her, only swerved to miss her and continued down the hallway. She shook off Sebastian's hand and ran after him. Papa turned the corner and halted so quickly the tails of his coat were still visible to her. She reached him and wrapped both hands around his right arm.

'I am sure there is a reason for this,' she spouted, without thinking how inane her words sounded.

He stared at his Prince and his wife. As though sensing they were no longer alone, the couple slowly separated and looked towards where Juliet and her father stood. The Prince had the grace to flush, the colour heightened by his ruddy complexion. Emily gasped and moved further away from her royal conquest.

Juliet dug her nails deeper into Papa's arm. He seemed impervious to anything she did or said, his focus completely on the couple.

'You cannot challenge *him* to a duel,' a dry voice said. 'It's considered treason.'

Juliet breathed a sigh of relief. Even though she knew Sebastian would not interfere, having him close gave her a sense of strength. If nothing else, he might keep Papa from doing something rash.

'Just showing Lady Smythe-Clyde around,' the Prince said, moving away from Emily as he walked towards the trio.

Emily loosed her tinkling laugh. For the first time since
Juliet had met the woman, the noise sounded strained.

'Oliver, darling, Prinny has been so kind as to point out
his works of art to me and tell me where they are from.' She
stopped by her husband and linked her arm in his.

Juliet watched everything, eyes wide, ready to jump between everyone if that seemed necessary. Sebastian's light
touch at her waist would not stop her.

Lord Smythe-Clyde stared down at his wife for a long
time. His jaw worked and the hand of his free arm clenched
and unclenched. Juliet held her breath.

With no warning, her father gave the Prince a curt bow.
'Your Highness, we must leave.' Nor did he wait for permission. He moved off so quickly that Emily stumbled and
would have fallen if Smythe-Clyde had not had a death grip
on her arm.

Juliet released her pent-up breath, nearly sagging in the
process. Sebastian's arm slid completely around her waist
and held her. His solid strength and warmth felt good.

Sebastian shook his head. 'That was not well done, my
liege. You know Smythe-Clyde's propensity for violent ret-
ribution.'

Prinny shuddered. 'Yes, but he could not challenge me.'
He watched until the other couple were gone from sight. 'I
almost feel sorry for her.'

'I don't,' Juliet retorted. 'She needs a come-uppance.'
She gave the Prince a jaundiced look that said she thought
he did as well. Once more he flushed.

'Well, I must be getting back to my other guests,' he
blustered.

After sufficient time had passed, Sebastian turned Juliet

in the circle of his arms so that she faced him. 'That was not so hard, was it?'

After a second's resistance, she allowed herself to sink into the comfort of his strength. Now that the crisis was past, she began to shake. He held her closer. When the short reaction had run its course, she pushed away from him. He let her move several inches so they could see each other's face.

'It was certainly not easy. I thought for a moment Papa would either challenge him or hit him.'

She closed her eyes on the picture of mayhem that would have ensued. Sebastian's lips on her forehead brought her back.

'He handled it on his own. I doubt Emily will be quite so free with her favours in the future.'

'Papa has never done that before,' she said in wonder.

He raised one brow. 'I doubt you or your mother ever let him before.'

He had a point, and rather than argue she said, 'We must return or people will begin to wonder.'

The slow, sensual smile that made her stomach flutter parted his lips. She gulped, but could not look away from the deep blue of his eyes.

'Let them. We are married. Remember?'

His voice was deep and caught on the last word. She knew what that meant.

'We cannot,' she said, panic rising. 'We are not at home.'

His smile turned sardonic. 'There are plenty of places here, believe me.'

Pain flared, squeezing her chest, at this reminder of how experienced he was. She twisted in his arms. 'Thank you, but I don't wish to have that experience.'

His grip tightened. One hand caught her jaw and forced her to meet his gaze. 'Juliet, I have been a rake. You knew that when we wed. Nothing can ever change that.'

'Yes,' she whispered. 'That is why I did not want to marry you.'

His eyes darkened as though she had hurt him. 'But because of that I am skilled and you enjoy my lovemaking.' Memory lit fires in his body. 'You like it a lot.'

She closed her eyes, not wanting to see the hunger in his, not wanting to be drawn into the passion he did nothing to control. 'Yes, but not here. Please.'

It was an eternity before he released her. She had begun to despair that he would listen to her plea. With cold formality, he offered his arm. With the best face she could summon, she laid her fingers on his coat, barely touching him.

That night he came to her bed and made fierce love to her as though demons drove him. She lost herself in his passion and was glad for it. Nothing else mattered.

# Chapter Thirteen

Juliet laughed from sheer pleasure. The veil of her riding hat billowed out behind her as her mare flew along the bridle path in Green Park. She heard the pounding hooves of Sebastian's gelding gaining on her. She urged her mount on.

Out of the corner of her eye, she saw Sebastian's horse edge closer until it was even with her. Sebastian reached out and grabbed her mare's bridle. Juliet grinned at him.

Rather than risk either of them or their horses being hurt when it was not necessary, she pulled in on the reins. Her mare slowed until she walked. Sebastian did the same. They continued to walk their horses while the animals cooled down.

After a time, they meandered to the early-morning shade provided by a huge oak tree. Sebastian dismounted, then went to Juliet and grabbed her waist. She put her hands on his shoulders and slid down the length of him. Excitement curled in her stomach.

He held her a long time.

'Why are you staring?' she asked, her brows furrowed. 'You have seen me look a mess before.'

He tucked several tendrils of hair behind her ear, a gesture she had come to expect from him when she was dishevelled. Then he righted her riding hat so that it sat at an angle on her head and the ostrich feathers tickled her cheek.

'You are so vibrant,' he said. 'I have never met a woman before with your enthusiasm for life, and not just in bed.'

This was so unlike him that she became embarrassed. 'I am sure you exaggerate.'

'No.' He abruptly released her and turned away.

She reached for him, wanting the security of feeling his body. Something was very wrong this morning. He did not draw away from her touch, but neither did he cup his hand over hers as he usually did.

'What is the matter?'

'Nothing,' he said curtly. Before she could remonstrate with him, he asked, 'Do you recognise this tree?'

Nonplussed, she stepped back and looked at the tree. It was obvious Sebastian was not going to tell her what troubled him. Absent-mindedly she studied the oak. Then it came to her.

'This is where we duelled. It seems like an eternity ago.'

He nodded, his mouth curling sardonically. 'It certainly seems that. So many things in our lives were changed by that one act.'

Dismay swamped her. She knew he would not have married her without being forced, but she had fooled herself into thinking he was at least contented with their union. He definitely seemed that way in bed. But then he was a man and a rake. Lovemaking was his forte. All the pleasure of the morning and the ride evaporated. She wanted to go home.

'We should be leaving. There are so many things to do today. I have to return Maria Sefton's visit, and I must write to Papa.' Sebastian raised an eyebrow in disbelief. 'I know he very likely does not read my letters, but it gives me comfort to tell him how things are going in London. Since he forced Emily to return to the country, I find I miss them. Silly, but Papa has always been a large part of my life.'

She stopped. She was rambling on in an attempt to cover the hurt his mood had brought on. Better to be quiet.

'Thank goodness they are gone, and good riddance. Heaven only knows what you would have done next in your misguided efforts to protect him from the world. I don't like to think of it.'

She hoped he was trying to be amusing, but there was no glint of humour in his eyes. He was deadly serious. The knowledge added to her discomfort. Just a week ago she would have argued with him, but not now. Not here.

'Please help me to mount. If we don't get home soon, I shall not have time to change for my visit.'

He did so and they cantered home, neither saying anything.

At the townhouse a groom helped Juliet dismount. She thanked him and went inside. She smiled at Burroughs and a nearby footman. Burroughs gave her a disapproving look while the footman smiled shyly.

'Your Grace,' the butler said, taking her riding crop. 'I hope you enjoyed yourself.'

'Oh, yes. Since we returned to London I have missed riding more than anything.'

'You ride,' Sebastian said, entering behind her and handing Burroughs his hat and crop.

'In Rotten Row,' she said derisively. 'That is meandering.'

He flicked her cheek. 'I must finish some work. I will see you later.'

She watched him go, wondering how long she would be able to stand the sham of their marriage. She knew everyone married for convenience, as had they, but her feelings had gone beyond that. She loved him.

Sebastian went up the stairs and she watched him avidly. She wanted so much for him to love her as well as desire her. It was an ache in her heart.

'Ahem.' Burroughs interrupted her thoughts. 'Mrs Burroughs has the week's menus ready when you have time, your Grace.'

'Thank you. I will meet with her later.'

Burroughs bowed and left to perform his other duties.

Juliet turned to see if any notes, invitations or messages were on the silver tray by the door.

Only one envelope lay on the salver. There was no visible writing so she picked it up and turned it over. An overly ornate feminine hand had written 'Sebastian'. That was all, except for the heavy scent of tuberose.

Juliet licked suddenly dry lips. Her hand began to shake so that it was a supreme effort to return the note to the tray without dropping it. She stared at nothing, wondering why having the truth staring her in the face was so much worse than just thinking about it. Sebastian had never promised to be faithful.

'Your Grace?' Burroughs asked, louder than normal.

'Yes,' she said, her voice a croak.

'Are you all right? Should I send a footman for the doctor?'

He must have returned while she stood numbly. She turned to him, still dazed from the heartache eating away at her chest. 'A doctor?' Could a doctor mend a broken heart? She was ready to cry. 'No, thank you.'

Before he could ask something else, she walked past him towards the back of the house and went out into the garden. She needed to be alone. She had Sebastian's name and as much of his lovemaking as any woman could want. They were not enough. She wanted his love.

She wandered down the path leading to a white gazebo where roses climbed towards the sun. The peace and scent of fresh roses always made her feel better. Perhaps they would help. She sank on to her favourite bench and cupped a blossom in her palm, inhaled the wonderful fragrance. It was lovely, but, as she had known, it was not enough. Nothing would ever be enough to dull the pain of her husband's infidelities. Nothing.

Hands clasped in her lap, she closed her eyes and let the tears fall.

Sebastian found her half an hour later, his forehead creased in worry. Burroughs had come to his rooms and told him her Grace was not feeling well. From the butler's tone, Sebastian knew he wondered if Juliet was pregnant. Sebastian wondered himself. Part of him hoped so.

She looked pale and tired. He should not have talked to her this morning the way he had, but he had not known exactly what was happening to him. He still did not know. The oak tree had brought back the memory of their duel and for an instant he had been glad she had fought it. Which was preposterous. She had entered his life and nothing was the same. He did not even visit his former lady-friends.

He sat beside her and took her hand. 'Are you sick? Is your shoulder still paining you?'

She opened her eyes and looked at him. Their green depths sparkled with unshed tears. 'No, I am fine.

He traced the path of one tear with his finger. 'Then why have you been crying?'

She turned away and her voice came out barely audible. 'I am tired, that is all.'

'Are you in the family way?' He caught her chin and gently drew her face back so he could watch for her reaction.

She shook her head. 'No. I don't think so.'

'Ah.' Disappointment he had not thought he would experience shafted through him. There is plenty of time for that, he told himself. 'Then it must be too many late nights and too much of your husband's attentions,' he added with a lecherous smile.

She gazed dully at him. 'Perhaps. I think I should lie down.' She stood and looked down at him. 'Alone.'

He rose and took one of her hands in his. 'Are you sure?'

'Yes.'

He released her and stepped away. He had seen people look as she did, usually when they had lost everything. It made no sense for her to feel that way. He had given her their world.

Maybe questioning Burroughs more thoroughly would bring something to light.

That night at dinner she looked no better for her rest. Sebastian watched her pick at her food, moving it around on her plate and cutting it into small pieces she did not eat. Nor did she drink any wine.

She looked up from her activity and caught him watching her. The circles under her eyes accentuated her high cheekbones. 'Will you be staying in tonight?'

She had never asked him that before. He pondered her question before answering. Did she know about his summons and who it was from? He did not think so.

'No. I am to meet Ravensford and Perth at White's,' he lied with smooth proficiency.

'I see,' she mumbled. 'If you will excuse me?' She pushed back her chair before the footman could help and left the room without glancing back.

Sebastian rose, his only thought to follow and comfort her. He got three steps and stopped. This was not the time. Something was upsetting her and he could not spare the time to find out what.

His mother waited.

Juliet pulled the hood of her black cape more securely around her face. Her fingers clenched the heavy wool so tightly her nails went through, and she had to blink rapidly to rid her eyes of the moisture blurring her vision. Ahead of her, Sebastian moved quickly through the early evening shadows. He was going to another woman.

Thankful it was dusk and the shadows were settling, she edged into the doorway of a closed shop. A few people still milled around, some with purpose, others aimlessly. They helped keep her hidden as well. Not that Sebastian would look. He thought she was safely at home reading a book while he cavorted.

She knew she was making a mistake. A wife did not follow her husband to his mistress's abode. It was very improper. It also hurt as nothing else she had ever experienced—except, perhaps, finding out about the infidelity.

He was heading towards Piccadilly. She hastened to keep up, his height the only thing that allowed her to keep him

in sight. Without once looking back or around, so she knew
that he did not know she was following him, he entered the
Pulteney. It was where the Tsar and his sister had stayed
when they'd visited London in 1814.

She was surprised. She had thought his mistress would
be set up in a house somewhere. Still, if she was a member
of Society, she might meet him here. However blasé her
husband might be, he would not want his wife meeting another man in their own home. Even Juliet understood that
much about dalliances.

She could not follow him into the hotel without drawing attention she did not want. No one must know what she
was doing. With a sigh, she settled into a shadowed alcove
across the street to wait, thankful she had remembered to
bring the little one-shot pistol Harry had given her a num-
ber of years before. No matter how decent an area might
be, a woman alone was at risk. She had learned that lesson
well in Vauxhall.

Sebastian strode through the lobby of the Pulteney towards the stairs and the room the note had indicated. This
was the last place he wanted to be. His jaw twitched and
the tic at his right eye was a constant irritant. But he had
no choice.

Reaching the door, he stood and did nothing. Many years
had passed since he had last seen his mother. He did not
want to see her now, but neither did he want her setting up
house in England. He had given her plenty of money to
move to Italy. He still gave her a very generous quarterly
allowance.

Girding himself for the encounter, he knocked sharply.
Her imperious 'Come in' filtered through the door, mak-

ing her voice soft like a young girl's. Sebastian grimaced and entered.

She sat straight-backed in a chair pulled close to the fire. Her once-black hair was streaked with silver. It was the most obvious change in her.

'Have a seat,' she said, motioning with her hand to another chair. 'I have much to say to you and would prefer not to look up. It puts a crick in my neck that later gives me a headache.'

That was just like her, Sebastian thought, doing as she said. Even knowing it was crazy, he acknowledged that his mother had a hold over him. First it had been the love of a child for the parent. Later it had been disgust at her stream of lovers, and later than that it had been hatred when he had learned he was not the son of the Duke of Brabourne. Her hold on him now was curiosity. He needed to learn why she had returned and speed her removal back to Italy, preferably without her meeting Juliet.

'Would you care for some wine?' she asked.

'No, thank you.'

He crossed one booted leg over the opposite thigh and studied her. In spite of the greying hair, she had aged well. There were lines around her blue eyes and crinkles near her mouth but her skin was still a creamy white with no age spots. Her bearing was regal and her figure slim. She wore a very stylish gown, its simplicity drawing attention to her magnificent bosom and small waist. A multiple strand choker of pearls circled her neck; he assumed it was to hide the wrinkles that were inevitable on that part of the body. Her vanity would make that a necessity.

'Why have you come back?' he asked, determined to finish this quickly.

'You always were brash and disrespectful.'

'Not always,' he murmured.

She cocked her head to one side. 'No, I suppose not. When you were young you were loving and eager to do anything asked of you. You changed.'

He was surprised to hear regret in her words. He had not thought her capable of anything but self-interest. 'I changed because of what you did.'

She sighed and her gaze dropped to her folded hands. Her black lashes hid any emotion that might show in her eyes. 'I did what was necessary. I am sorry if it hurt you.'

A sharp bark of laughter escaped the tightness in his throat. 'Sorry? You should have thought of that while you were busy sleeping with every man in England.'

Her laugh was bitter. 'I was not talking about that. I meant marrying Brabourne, even though he was not your father.'

'You married him while you were carrying me? Did he know it?'

'No,' she murmured. 'I told him you were early. At first he believed me, but the nurses talked and he heard them. They said you were too big for a premature baby.'

'Why did you do it?' He could barely believe what she was saying. Not only was the man he had considered his father for years not, but he had been tricked into marrying a woman he did not know was pregnant.

She twisted a large pearl and diamond ring she wore on her wedding finger. As soon as the late Duke had passed on, she had returned the heirloom engagement ring Juliet now wore. Sebastian had not had to ask for it back.

'It was the only way. I would have been ostracised. You would have been a bastard. I could not let any of that happen.' For the first time since they had started talking she sounded anxious.

He stared at her. 'You tricked him. The least you could have done was tell him and let him make the choice.'

She shook her head. 'No. He would not have married me. He was a proud man. Much as you are. I could not have had you out of wedlock. I could not do that to you or myself.'

She was right. He would never marry a woman who carried another man's child, no matter what the circumstances. Except...perhaps Juliet. No, he quickly told himself. Not even Juliet.

'What about my real father? Why didn't he marry you?'

She looked back up at him and he thought he saw moisture in her eyes. He had to be mistaken. Never in his entire time with her had he seen her display this much emotion. He did not expect it now.

'He was already married. He said he would leave her and we would go to the Continent. I loved him. I believed him.' She sighed sadly. 'I was a fool.'

Appalled, Sebastian sat like a statue. 'But the other men?'

'You have never been in a loveless relationship. I did not love Brabourne and he never loved me. Ours was a marriage of convenience. Once he realised you were not his, he did not even maintain a semblance of civility to me. He insulted me in front of everyone—our friends and family and the servants. He made my life a living hell.' Anger sparked from her eyes, making her resemble her old self for the first time since her confession had started. 'I hated him, and openly sleeping with other men was the only way I could hurt him. His pride and arrogance could not withstand the public humiliation.'

Sebastian felt the first glimmer of sympathy for her, this

woman he had hated all of his adult life. As a child he had not been in his parents' company much, which was normal for the nobility. He had known there was something uncomfortable between them, but he had never understood exactly what it was. Then he had learned of his own background and of his mother's infidelities. After that, nothing had been able to penetrate the wall he put around himself for protection from emotional pain.

'Is this why you came back, to tell me these things?'

She nodded. 'When I heard you were married I felt you needed to know the truth behind my actions. I have always known you hated me. I did not want you to take that hate out on your wife, who is innocent of anything I did.'

Nobility of character in a woman he had always considered to have none—it tugged at the part of him that worried about honour.

It was hard, but he finally managed to say, 'Thank you. I know this could not have been easy.'

She gave him a weak smile. 'No, but I had to do it. I owed you that much. If you hold your wife at arm's length because of what I did, you will forge yourself a miserable life. Even if you did not marry for love, marriage can give you children to love and raise together and bring companionship for your older years.'

For the first time he realised how lonely she must be, exiled to Italy and away from her family. He had not thought of it before, and if he had, he would not have cared. Now it mattered.

He stood and paced the floor, unsure of what he was going to say and how to say it. But he felt impelled to do something. Juliet would certainly expect it of him if she knew about this. He found he expected it of himself.

He stopped and made a conscious effort to ease the knotting of his shoulder muscles. 'I think my wife would like to meet you. If you have the time.'

She looked up at him and the tears he had imagined before became real. 'I would like that very much.'

Sebastian had never felt so awkward in his life. It was not a pleasant experience. 'Then I will send my carriage round for you tomorrow,' he said gruffly. 'Now I must take my leave and let Juliet know to expect you.'

'Of course,' she said, some of her earlier strength returning. 'Until tomorrow.'

She held out her hand, which he took. He raised it to his lips and brushed her knuckles with his mouth. With her, kissing her fingers was an old-fashioned, courtly action, a gesture from her youth.

He took his leave, wondering where all this would end. The things she had told him eased some of the old hatred, but anger still lingered in the back of his mind. There was too much hurt and not enough time to resolve it. Not yet.

As to how it related to his marriage, he just did not know. Trusting was not easy for him. Trusting a woman was the hardest of all.

Juliet saw him exit the Pulteney. He had been there barely thirty minutes. She knew from their own lovemaking that half an hour was not nearly enough for Sebastian. At least not with her.

Hope rose. Perhaps she had been mistaken. But who could have sent the note and when would he meet with her?

He headed back the way he had come.

It was starting to rain. She huddled into her cape and glanced around, looking for a way to watch him and still keep out of the wet. With a sigh of regret she realised there was no way to avoid the moisture. She would be as soaked as he by the time they got home.

One more look around and she started out.

Something moved in her peripheral vision. A man dressed in black moved along the side of the buildings. If she did not know better, she would think he followed Sebastian. Still, she watched the dark figure for a while. There was something elusively familiar about the way he walked and the tilt of his head. She did not know what exactly, but it was there, teasing at her memory.

A hint of something wrong made her follow behind him as he kept some distance from Sebastian. She edged closer to the man.

'Brabourne,' the man said, his voice carrying in the damp night.

Sebastian turned to see a pistol aimed at his heart. His pulse speeded up and his senses sharpened. This was not the time for him to die. He had too much to do and all of it centred around Juliet.

'Ah, it is you,' he drawled, hoping to keep the man off guard. 'I see your cheek has healed nicely. The scar becomes you.'

The thug from Vauxhall stepped closer, his face a furious mask. 'You will not be so smug when I have finished with you.'

Under the guise of a bored yawn, Sebastian looked around for some means of distraction. All he needed was to divert the man's attention for a moment. The figure sneaking up on them would do. He was sorry to draw the other person in, but he did not think the thug had the skills to kill both of them. With luck, no one would even be hurt except the would-be killer.

'Don't look now,' Sebastian said drily, 'but there is some-one behind you.'

'I don't believe you,' the other growled.

Sebastian shrugged. 'It is your party.'

Doubt flitted across the other man's face, which was a pale oval in the light from a street flambeau. Though not many people were around, this part of Piccadilly was well lit. Soon, however, the light would be gutted by the water coming down.

The rain had soaked Sebastian's hair and made his great-coat heavy. The man holding him up looked worse, as though he had been waiting in the wet for some time. Se-bastian hoped the thug would slip on the cobbles.

The man edged around, keeping the pistol aimed at Se-bastian but looking over his shoulder to see if Sebastian spoke the truth. The figure that had been following them stopped. For the first time Sebastian saw that the innocent he had dragged into this wore a cape. A woman.

'Blast,' he cursed, lunging forward. He could not put a female in danger. No matter what.

He heard a bang and saw a flash of light from the barrel pointed his way. He jerked his torso around so that the ball entered his shoulder instead of the centre of his chest. Pain raked through him.

Another shot rang out.

The figure in front of Sebastian bucked just as Sebastian tackled him. Ignoring the fire radiating out from his shoul-der, Sebastian straddled the thug and punched his jaw. The man's head jerked.

'Sebastian. Sebastian, is that you? Are you all right?'

Sebastian could not believe his ears. His head came up just as he landed the thug another facer. 'Juliet? What in blazes are you doing here?'

She fell to her knees beside him. 'I…oh, I cannot tell you. But I am so glad I did. This villain has been following you.'

'Ah, yes.' Sebastian looked down at the man he still straddled. Blood flowed freely from a wound on the thug's right side, soaking through his coat. 'I think he is completely incapacitated.'

'Will he die?' Juliet asked. 'He deserves to, for that is what he intended to happen to you.'

'You are the most bloodthirsty woman I have ever met,' he said, catching the back of her head with one hand and pulling her to him for a long, hungry kiss. 'But I am glad to see you. I think he might have killed me otherwise, instead of just injuring me.'

She blinked water from her eyes. 'Injured! Where? We must get you home. You will catch an inflammation out here.'

He smiled at her, feeling his energy of minutes before seeping out. 'First we must take care of this fellow.'

'Leave him for the night watch, Sebastian. You are more important.'

He staggered to his feet and offered her a hand. She took it and he pulled her up. 'Remind me not to anger you.'

She glared at him. 'Your levity is out of place.'

Ignoring her, he pulled out his handkerchief from inside his coat and wadded it into a ball. With a grimace, he pushed it inside his clothing and pressed it hard to his wound. It was not much, but it was the best he could do under the circumstances.

His teeth started chattering and he noticed her lips were

blue. Both of them needed a warm fire and a hot drink, but first he had to take care of this villain. For good this time.

'Juliet, go to the Pulteney and tell them to send out several servants to help us. I do not intend for this scum to get away.'

She clamped her mouth shut on what he was sure was another reprimand. With a sweep of her soaked cape, she stalked off. His wife had more spirit and courage than ten men. But why had she been following him, for that was the only explanation for her presence? He would find out soon enough.

## *Chapter Fourteen*

Sebastian relaxed into the chair, grateful for the warmth of the nearby fire. A tumbler of whisky and a full decanter sat on the table beside him. The doctor had just left. He had a flesh wound, more painful than serious.

They had taken care of the scoundrel who had shot him and come straight home. Juliet fussed around him, plumping the pillows on the bed and getting his robe.

'You must be cold with just your breeches on,' she said, bringing the fine woollen garment to him.

He leaned forward and allowed her to wrap it around his shoulders. She was careful not to touch his bandage.

'Thank you.' He took a big swallow of whisky, enjoying the warm sensation all the way down his throat. 'Why did you follow me?'

'Why did you go there when you were supposed to be with Perth and Ravensford?' she countered, meeting his gaze without any hint of remorse.

He swirled the burnt brown liquid and sniffed the woodsy aroma. 'I had to meet someone.'

'Your mistress?' She moved away from him.

He could tell by the tightness around her mouth and eyes what the question had cost her. She had not taken the time to change out of her wet clothing and she looked exhausted, worse than this afternoon.

'No. Before we discuss this, and we need to, will you please get out of that wet dress and into something dry? I don't want you getting an inflammation of the lungs when I need you to nurse me.'

Her face turned mutinous. 'I am tired of you telling me what to do all the time. I will change when I am good and ready. As for getting sick, it would serve you right if I did and Burroughs had to take care of you—or Roberts.'

He sighed. 'You are the most stubborn woman. At least come over here, where I can see you better and the warmth from the fire can reach you.'

She edged closer.

He finished the whisky and poured another glass. Dutch courage. What he had to say to her was not going to be easy. He had never said this sort of thing to a woman. He hoped it was not too late.

'I went to see my mother.' He waited for her reaction, dreading that she might feel disgust for the woman who had birthed him.

'Your mother? I thought you hated her.'

'I thought I did. I don't know any more.' He stood and went to her. Putting his hands on her shoulders, he asked, 'Are you happy with me?'

'What kind of question is that?'

She looked wary, as though she expected him to say something that would hurt her. He knew he had made her feel that way by his actions. He had kept her at a distance.

'This is not easy.' He released one of her shoulders and held his hand out. 'See, I am shaking.'

'That is very likely from your wound and all the whisky you have consumed,' she said drily.

His mouth twisted. 'You are not being very helpful.'

'I did not know I was supposed to be.'

'It would help.'

She eyed him speculatively. 'I don't think I want to help you. Remember, you did not help me when Papa caught Emily and Prinny.'

'That was between your father and stepmother. This is between us. And you are not happy with me anyway,' he finished for her. 'You thought I was unfaithful.'

Juliet nodded. A sense of dread weighted her down and her stomach was a tight knot. Was he going to tell he had a mistress, as she suspected? How cruel.

'Don't say anything else,' she said hastily. 'I don't want to hear any more.'

He caught her chin and made her look at him. 'I have never been unfaithful to you,' he said solemnly. 'I have not been with another woman since you burst into my life on the duelling field.'

Juliet stared at him, not sure she had heard correctly. She swallowed the lump that had lodged in her throat. 'I... I—'

'Don't believe me,' he said bitterly. 'I never thought I would regret my past, but you are fast making me do so.'

He abruptly released her and went to the window, his back to her. She staggered before catching her balance.

'I don't understand,' she said, her voice barely above a whisper.

'Neither do I,' he said, sounding as though the words were dragged out of him. 'I thought I had everything under control. You are a woman, and women cannot be trusted. I was going to stay faithful until I got you with child, then I was going to go my own way and let you do the same.' He turned to face her, a haunted look in his eyes. 'But I can't. The thought of you with another man tears me to pieces.'

Her mouth dropped.

He gave her a wry smile. 'Amazing, isn't it?'

'What are you saying?' She held her breath, hoping against hope.

'My mother told me everything tonight. About her being pregnant with me when she married the Duke. How he hated her for it and treated her badly. Everything. It gave me a lot to think about. Especially about us.'

She took a step towards him, but stopped. She did not know what he was really saying.

His smile disappeared. 'Come here.'

'Why?'

She knew that if she went to him and made everything easy he would never finish what he had started. Or so she told herself when she held back. She wanted him more than anything. But she would not be hurt by him again. She could not go through that.

'You don't trust me,' he said.

'You are the one without trust,' she said sadly. 'You made that clear from the beginning. You told me that you have no mistress. I find that hard to believe, but I am willing to do so because you tell me it is so.' In her heart she added that she was willing to believe because she wanted so badly for him to belong only to her.

'I know. And I am still not sure. Not completely.'

She bit her lip to keep from saying something she would regret later. 'Then perhaps it would be better if I left for a while.'

Leaving him would be the hardest thing she had ever done but if it would give him a chance to decide what he wanted she would do it. More than anything she wanted their marriage to work. Having him love and trust her would be heaven, but if he could not do that she would settle for his companionship. She loved him that much.

He came to her and wrapped her in his arms. 'No. I want you to stay with me. I am just not sure that I can give you everything you deserve.'

She kept her head lowered, not wanting him to see the need in her. His words, that said so much but not enough, left a bone-deep ache in her chest.

He stroked her hair, tucking a loose strand behind her ear. 'I have not trusted a woman in a long time…since I was ten and learned what my mother had done. Yet she came back to explain everything to me, things I had not been willing to listen to before. She told me not to take my bitterness and distrust out on you. She made me think.'

Juliet began to shake.

'Don't,' he said, stroking her back. 'I don't want to cause you pain.'

She nodded, her head rubbing up and down on his chest. She still refused to look at him.

'I wanted you from the beginning. At first it was physical and…curiosity. I had never met a woman like you. Then it was more. I could not stand the thought of you being hurt.'

He took a deep breath. 'After we were married, it was more. I wanted to make love to you all the time, and when we were apart I wanted you by me, just to be near.'

Tears started to seep from Juliet's closed eyes. She was so anxious about what he was saying, what he was going to decide.

'I want you to stay with me, Juliet. I don't know for sure if I love you, but I want you. I am not sure that the two are not the same.'

She slowly slipped her arms around his waist. It felt as if she had longed to hear those words from him all her life. 'I love you so much, Sebastian, it is a constant ache.'

'Then look at me,' he said. 'Tell me to my face.'

Taking her courage and determination in both hands, she angled her head back. 'I love you. I think I always have.'

'Ah, Juliet,' he murmured, bending down and kissing her.

It was a sweet melding of flesh. Desire was there, but it was like a banked fire waiting to flare to life later. They could wait. Right now they were committing themselves to one another.

When the kiss was over, she gave him a tremulous smile. Tears still seeped occasionally from her eyes. Only one thing remained. As much as she did not want to ask, she had to know about trust. Without it their love would not last. That much she knew.

'What about trust, Sebastian? Do you trust me? Can you?'

He groaned. 'You cannot leave well enough alone, can you?'

She shook her head. 'No. If you don't trust me, then what will happen to us? You will forever torture yourself, and consequently me, with your doubts about me and about our children.'

His arms tightened around her. 'I know. That is what I have wrestled with all night, and I cannot answer you for sure. Trust is too new. I want to trust you, but I fear there will be times when I slip. When I hurt you with my lack of faith.'

'Oh, Sebastian,' she whispered.

'But I want to try. If you will give me the chance.'

She heard the doubt and longing in his voice. 'I don't think I can live without you. I am willing to try with you to make this work. I know it will not be easy, but I want to be with you.'

'Juliet, my love,' he vowed.

# *Epilogue*

*Twelve months later...*

'Sebastian,' Juliet called, 'what are you and Timmy doing? Your mother will be here any minute, and you know how she dislikes not seeing Timmy.'

The Duke and a baby with a head of peach down came out from the dining room, where they had been for the last hour. Sebastian handed the boy over. 'I think he needs changing.'

'Oh, no,' Juliet said, crossing her arms. 'You can take him to Nurse as easily as I can. And you had better hurry.'

'I will call Mrs Burroughs,' Sebastian said with a wicked gleam in his eyes.

'No, you will not,' Juliet said, humour tipping up her mouth.

Sebastian gathered a gurgling Timothy close with one arm and pulled his wife in with the other. 'You are a stubborn woman, my love.'

She grinned up at him. 'And you are a scoundrel, always trying to foist the unpleasant aspects of parenthood off on me.'

He returned her grin. 'The boy is the spitting image of you, therefore you should be the one to do the nasty things.'

The smile left her face and she paled. 'He is your son, too.'

Sebastian's eyes darkened and Timmy squirmed. 'I am sorry. I told you it would not be easy, but that was a year ago. I know these past months have not always been the bliss we could have wished, but I don't doubt Timothy's parentage. He is mine and yours. No one else had a part in his creation, and I believe no one else will have a part in the begetting of our next children.'

'I would not trade them for the world. But are you sure?' she asked, doubt still a tiny kernel lodged in her heart.

'Yes,' he said. 'Now and for ever.'

Joy replaced the disquiet. She clung to her family with an intensity that she knew would increase with time.

'I love you, Sebastian.'

'And I you, my love.'

Timothy, caught in the middle of his hugging parents, laughed in sheer delight.

* * * * *

# The Rebel

# *Chapter One*

Andrew Dominic Wentworth, Earl of Ravensford, paused in the act of bringing a glass of Irish whiskey to his mouth. The door to the library where he lounged had opened with a vengeance and then slammed shut. The delicate scent of lavender filled the room.

'I am tired of dancing to your tune,' a husky female voice stated.

A smile tugged at Ravensford's lips. A wife or mistress. In his experience, they were the only women who occasionally danced to a man's tune, and then only for something in return. Mothers and sisters did whatever they wanted regardless of what they were told or what was involved.

'You will do exactly as I tell you,' a man's light tenor replied.

A low, feminine growl followed the arrogantly superior words. 'What if I don't? What if I tell you no?'

The man chuckled low in his throat. 'Then I will be

forced to do something you won't like, and we both know what that is.'

The woman groaned, her husky voice ending in a sob. 'What do you want?'

She sounded completely defeated. The man must have a powerful hold over her. For some strange reason, Ravensford felt disappointment. He had wanted her to win their contest.

'That is more like the dutiful miss I know you to be.' Sarcasm and gloating filled each word.

'Only because you have something I value highly.' The woman's rich, nerve-tingling voice caught on the last word.

Her voice was incredible. The deep, almost growling tone demanded attention at the same time as it created an image of a sleek feline. Ravensford found himself entranced. Never had a sound aroused him so, not even his former mistress's voice when she was in the throes of passion.

He was a connoisseur of women, often finding himself embroiled with a second before he was free of the first. Why hadn't he seen this woman—or heard her? For if he had, he would have remembered her voice. He had never heard one so sensual and arousing. Just sitting here listening to her made him want to experience her in other ways.

With very little enticement he could be enthralled. He imagined the woman to be small and supple like the cat her low, raspy tone brought to his mind. For a brief instant he wondered if she would purr like a contented feline when a man stroked her. It was an errant thought and one he had no business thinking where a respectable woman was concerned. And respectable she must be or she would not be in his mother's establishment.

The Countess was fanatical about other people's morals,

an unusual trait in someone of her generation. More often than not, he had found others of his mother's age to be more risqué than most people closer to his age.

However, it was time he made his presence known. He took another sip of the liquor and started to rise.

'I want you to stay close to the old Countess. I have need of some of her possessions.' The last word was said with a repulsive snicker.

Ravensford decided not to stand. Something was afoot. Something unsavory from the man's words, and something that involved his mother.

'Haven't I been doing exactly that?' Exasperation and perhaps remorse tinged every word the woman spoke.

Ravensford's curiosity increased. The urge to reveal his presence was strong, but he resisted. It was his experience that when one avenue was cut off a person would find another. Words were not enough for him to have the couple arrested. Nor did he want to. The woman was reluctant and he found himself unwilling to harm her when he did not even know her. His best course was to tell his mother that someone in her household intended to rob her, even though he doubted it would do any good.

As for him confronting the two now, that would not do either. He had no evidence but their words and, even with his rank, he could do nothing without more substantial evidence. Nor would he want to. He had spent his life championing those not as fortunate as himself. The game laws, Corn Laws, all of those were biased for the wealthy. As were the criminal laws. No, he would not do anything until he actually caught the pair in the act of stealing.

He had arrived at his mother's Irish estate early this morning. Derry House and the surrounding farms had been part of her dower, and she returned to them on a regular basis. This time, she had summoned him to attend her. Never a good omen.

'You have been a good little girl so far,' the man said, focussing Ravensford's thoughts back on the couple. 'See that you remain such.' His light tenor was at odds with his implied threat. 'Best you go before someone notices us.'

There was a sharp inhalation. 'Until you command my presence again,' the woman finished bitterly.

She definitely did not like dancing to the man's tune. Ravensford wondered if she disliked the job or the man or both. And what was his hold over her?

The sound of footsteps followed by the opening and closing of the door told Ravensford he was alone once more. The large centre log in the fireplace cracked and split, sending sparks scattering through the room. The servant who had started the fire had forgotten to put the screen in front. He rose and stomped out any little flames before they could do damage to the Aubusson rug.

While the thought of someone stealing from his mother was unpleasant, he found himself intrigued by the turn of events. Perhaps a dull, but comfortable and mandatory visit to his parent would become an entertaining proposition.

If nothing else, he had a mystery to occupy his mind. He did not recognise the man's voice and was not sure he would notice if he were to hear it again in ordinary circumstances, for it was not remarkable. The woman was another story. He would remember her deep-throated purr in his dreams. Whatever she did in his mother's household, he would soon find out. Then the game would begin.

A wry grin twisted his well-shaped lips. With the luck he had been having lately, she would be a drab tabby and married.

He finished the whiskey and strode from the room. Action was always preferable to inactivity. It was a maxim he had put to frequent good use in the House of Lords. He was sure it would be so here.

Ravensford propped one Hessian-shod foot on his knee, careful not to rub dirt on his beige pantaloons. He was as casual in his dress as his mother was meticulous, but casual did not mean dirty. Then there was his valet, who would make him miserable for several long minutes if he returned messed up after so short an absence.

Across a small space, his mother reclined on a gold-lined chaise-lounge, looking frail to the point of ethereal. Her silver hair was cut fashionably short, an ideal foil for the oval perfection of her creamy complexion. She was a handsome woman and had been the toast of the *ton* in her first Season. A pale lavender afternoon dress, trimmed lavishly with Brussels lace, accentuated the slim curves of a young girl. All in all, she was very well preserved.

Ravensford wished her mind were as tidy as her person. She was, to put it generously, scatterbrained. He did not relish the task of telling her about the proposed robbery. Still, he had to do his duty.

There was no sense waiting. 'Mother, I overheard a conversation today between a man and woman. They plan to rob you.'

'Nonsense, Andrew.' She dismissed his warning with a wave of her elegant hand. 'You always were an imaginative child. I had thought you beyond that.'

His jaw clenched before he forcibly relaxed it. This was nothing he had not expected. 'I am, Mother.'

'Well, I cannot believe that anyone in my employ would be so ungrateful as to do what you suggest.'

'Is there someone new who might be in need of money?'

She scowled at him. 'There is Mary Margaret, but her brother-in-law is the curate. She grew up here. Her father was one of my tenants. No, it is not her.'

'Someone else?' he asked, even though his suspicions now lay with the mysterious Mary Margaret. He did not know his mother's tenants, having spent very little time here.

'No, Andrew, there is not.' Exasperation tinged every word. 'But if you insist on this, I shall line up all the servants and demand the guilty party to step forward.'

This was no more than he had expected. He should have known better than to tell his mother. Still, an irritation he rarely allowed himself to feel toward his parent made his next words harsh.

'That would be the worst thing you could do. The thief would be on his guard after that and we would never catch him.'

'Then be done with this nonsense. No one in my employ would do so despicable a thing.' She waved a languid hand, the wrist drooping like a wilted flower. 'I did not summon you here to be told such foolishness.'

Ravensford knew when a subject was ended. To continue pushing her would only make her do up as she threatened. He had not expected her to give credence to his words; she rarely did. He would have to bide his time and catch the pair in the actual act of stealing. Then he would not need his mother's belief or cooperation.

'Now, Andrew,' she continued, her voice light and musical, 'I asked you to visit for a very specific reason.'

He put the other matter aside for the moment and made himself smile indulgently at her. 'I surmised as much, Mother, and I am at your service. What exactly is it that you wish me to do?'

'My goddaughter, Annabell Winston, needs to have a Season.' She reached for the teapot. 'Do you still take your tea plain?'

'Yes, please.'

In spite of the foreboding edging up his spine, he waited patiently while she poured him a steaming cup of tea. There was no sense prodding her. That route only caused discord without accomplishing any increase in speed or comprehension.

'Now, we shall be arriving in London in early May to give the child plenty of time to assemble an appropriate wardrobe. I expect you to make sure everything is in order.'

He took a swallow of scalding tea and realised that somewhere along his parent's thought processes he had missed something important. 'What exactly do you expect me to do?'

'Really, Andrew, don't be so dense. It isn't like you.' She sipped daintily at her cream-and-sugar-laden drink. 'You are to have the town house properly opened and prepared for us. The ballroom floor very likely needs to be refinished if we are to have a successful coming-out ball for Annabell.'

It was an effort not to groan. The idea of protesting passed through his mind, only to be discarded. His mother had that light in her blue eyes that preceded intense activity—by him.

'And what else am I to do?' he asked, knowing he would not like any part of the answer. His comfortable bachelor life was about to be turned topsy-turvy.

'Oh, very good, Andrew. I knew you would get into the spirit of things once I explained them.' She beamed at him, the charm of her smile identical to his own. 'Vouchers for Almack's are a must. As are invitations to all the private events. The child will likely want to attend Astley's Amphitheatre and all those disgustingly plebian entertainments. Of course, we mustn't forget Covent Garden and Vauxhall.'

Ravensford finished a pastry in one gulp, dreading the answer to his next question. 'And who will be escorting Annabell about since you are not capable of getting out much?'

Her smile widened. 'Why, you, of course. I know how much you enjoy her company and she adores you. Why, the two of you make a perfect couple. It would be delightful if this visit brought about a closer union between you. Your father often said so.'

A twinge of sadness tightened his chest at the mention of his sire, but no matter what his parents had wished, he was not going to marry a miss barely out of the schoolroom. Others might do so, but not he. He preferred women with experience.

'I am not in the market for a wife,' he stated baldly, knowing that nothing short of bluntness got through to his parent and too often not even that.

'So you say.' She leaned gracefully back into the pale yellow silk cushions of her seat, only to bounce forward again. 'I nearly forgot. My companion will help chaperon since it would not be proper for you to escort Annabell alone.'

'Your companion? I thought Miss Mabel left to care for her father.'

'She did, she did. I already told you that I have hired a new companion, Mary Margaret O'Brien.'

Ravensford resisted the urge to shake his head. His

mother had mentioned hiring the chit, but not making her a companion. It was the perfect position for a thief. He put the suspicion aside as his mother continued blithely on.

'Quite proper and all, but not of the Quality. Still, a very obliging young woman. She shan't bother you. She is quiet as a mouse.' A complacent smile curved the Countess's lips as she once more leaned back into the plump cushions. 'And her looks are too unusual to be considered attractive. She won't cause you any problems.'

Ravensford narrowed his eyes. In his experience, whenever his mother considered something to be unimportant it ended up being a nightmare. He vividly remembered the litter of puppies she had foisted on him just six months ago. They were supposed to be a *bagatelle*, nothing more. They had ruined his stable and very nearly cost him his head groom. After much cajoling, he had managed to place every pup but one with a good owner. Wizzard ruled Ravensford's country estate with a benign paw. But that was neither here nor there. Right now he had to keep his mother from creating another disaster.

'You do plan on accompanying Annabell whenever possible, don't you?' he asked drily.

'Don't be a goose, Andrew. Of course I do. What kind of godmother would I be otherwise?'

There was no polite answer, so Ravensford made none. Thankfully a tap on the door saved him from his mother's habit of pursuing an answer to her questions.

'Come in,' the Countess said.

Ravensford heard the door open seconds before the faint scent of lavender wafted through the room. Could this be the woman from the library? His pulse quickened. Still, he did not turn his head to look. Better that he appear completely uninterested.

'My lady,' the newcomer said.

It was she. Her voice purred like that of a contented cat. His gut tightened pleasurably.

Ravensford caught movement from the corner of his eye. Seconds later she was in his line of sight. His entire body responded.

She wore a plain olive-coloured wool gown that hugged the ample curves of her bosom before slipping gracefully past a tiny waist and narrow hips. In profile, her nose was slightly turned up at the tip and her lips were plump and very pink. The watery sun coming through the many-paned window shot blue highlights through her ebony hair which was long, parted in the middle and caught in a severe chignon at the nape of an elegant white neck.

'Mary Margaret,' the Dowager said, 'I asked you here to meet my son, Lord Ravensford. You and he will be spending a great deal of time together in London while you chaperon my goddaughter. My son shall provide the cachet for you to be accepted into the homes of the *ton*.'

Ravensford kept himself from wincing. His mother was not known for her tact. That discomfort faded as the young woman turned to face him.

His mother was right. The chit was not a traditional beauty. She was an exotic temptress.

Her hair lay like a smooth satin cap against her head. He would have likened her to a Madonna because of the demure style and calm scrutiny in her eyes, but there was too much of the unusual in her looks. Her face was heart shaped with winged brows and high cheekbones. Her chin was pointed and with a dainty cleft. But it was her eyes that held him captive. They were green as the finest emeralds and tilted at the corners like a cat's. Her features intensified his impression of her voice, as did her movements when she took a step closer. She was lithe and graceful, flowing like a feline that glides along the ground intent on its own world.

She was amazing. Too bad she was also untrustworthy.

'My lord,' Mary Margaret murmured, making a shallow curtsy.

He rose. 'Please be seated, Miss O'Brien.'

'Thank you.' She took the chair closest to her and sat ramrod straight, yet gracefully as a cat positioning itself to watch the world.

He eased back down and waited to see what more his mother intended and how the woman would react. Much could be told about a person by watching them. It was a trait he had cultivated and which made him very successful in getting some of his less than popular bills through the House of Lords.

'Mary Margaret, we will be staying with my son in London. You will be in charge of completing anything my son has not finished so that the house is ready for us to entertain.'

The woman nodded her head, keeping her huge eyes turned to the Countess. Ravensford found himself wanting to provoke her to speak. He wanted to hear her voice now that he could watch her body and face at the same time. She fascinated him.

'Will you be sending Miss O'Brien ahead, Mother? That would be best if you intend her to make sure that everything is in order.'

It was a provocative idea, and his mother's answer would tell him much about where the Countess placed the woman socially. That she did not think the chit a person of Quality did not mean she thought the girl should be alone with a man. Propriety was propriety.

'Why, that is an excellent suggestion,' his mother said. 'I should have thought of it sooner.' She turned her attention to the other woman. 'I believe you should go ahead. Andrew, arrange for Mary Margaret to depart immediately. With luck and good weather, she should be in London within two weeks. That will give her plenty of time.'

Ravensford thought that some colour mounted Miss O'Brien's high cheeks, but she was so composed he could not be sure. She might be his mother's new companion, but his parent did not consider her of consequence. Inexplicably, Ravensford found himself irritated with his mother. She was often oblivious to the feelings of others, and he had thought himself inured to it. It seemed he was not.

'It would be better if I escorted Miss O'Brien. A woman travelling alone is fair game for anyone.'

No respectable woman travelled with a man unchaperoned, but Mary Margaret O'Brien was considered a servant and therefore had no reputation to lose. Even though part of him rose in anger at this lack of regard for the woman, another part of him looked coldly on. She intended to steal from his mother. The trip would allow him to watch her.

The fact that his gut tightened in anticipation was nothing. He must put aside the very physical reminder that she was an enticing woman and remember only that she was a woman out to steal from his mother. That was where his focus should be.

Mary Margaret O'Brien glanced at him, her expression unreadable. She would be a good card player.

Or a good thief.

His mother frowned. 'I really don't see that your presence is necessary. Several outriders will do just as well.'

Ravensford looked blandly at his mother. 'I disagree. It's obvious that Miss O'Brien is gently reared or you would not have her for a companion. The trip to London is long and not always safe. I must insist on accompanying her.'

His mother's frown turned to a glare. It was not often that he refused to do her bidding.

'If you insist,' she said ungraciously. She stood up and moved to the fireplace where the bell pull was, casting Ravensford a you-will-pay look. 'The two of you should not linger here. There is much too much to be done. I will order the travelling carriage to be readied for departure tomorrow morning.'

Ravensford groaned. He should have known that, once he insisted on thwarting her, she would make the result as unpleasant as possible. That was her way of seeing that he did not refuse her in the future. She had used that method on him all his life and it usually worked.

He remembered the time shortly after his father died when he had suggested they have Raven Abbey modernised. She had not wanted anything changed. To her Raven Abbey was a symbol of her life with her husband. But Ravensford had insisted. Before he had even had time enough to determine whom the architect should be and what should be done, the Countess had hired Nash and determined the entire structure should be redone in the Egyptian mode so popular at the time. He still had difficulty visiting his country seat.

During the entire exchange, Miss O'Brien had looked straight ahead. Never once had she so much as glanced at the two people who were deciding her immediate future.

He would have felt like chattel. Part of him rebelled at what they were doing to her.

'You are dismissed, Mary Margaret,' the Countess said haughtily. 'I am sure you have much to do before you leave.'

Miss O'Brien rose quickly and curtsied to the Countess. 'My lady. I shall be ready whenever you wish.' Then as though reluctant, she turned to him and dipped down. 'My lord.'

He rose quickly. 'I will send a maid to help you pack.'

Her incredible eyes widened momentarily. 'That won't be necessary, my lord. I have little to take and nothing I cannot pack myself.'

He met her calm gaze. 'Someone will help you.'

'Really, Andrew, don't be importunate,' his mother said, only barely covering her disapproval with disdain.

Ravensford ignored his parent.

Miss O'Brien bowed her head in acceptance even though Ravensford sensed that the chit was far from compliant. 'Thank you, my lord.'

'You may go, Mary Margaret,' the Countess said coldly.

A flash of what might have been anger entered the younger woman's eyes, but was gone so quickly that Ravensford decided he had been mistaken. He would not have blamed her had she taken offense at his mother's words and tone.

He watched her leave the room, intrigued by her walk. Tall and regal, she held herself as though a book balanced on the top of her head. She was magnificent. Too bad she was employed by his parent. Otherwise he would offer a *carte blanche* and the devil take the results.

No woman had ever made him react this strongly. Try as he might, the idea of her in his arms and in his bed created an unquenchable fire in his loins.

'Andrew!'

He turned his attention back to his mother. 'Yes?' he asked, pretending that he saw nothing unusual in her command.

'The girl is nobody. She does not need your attentions or your help. Leave her alone.'

Irritation tightened the corners of his mouth. His mother was used to having her way. 'I do not intend to do her harm.'

'See that it remains that way.' The Countess chopped her normally languid hand. 'Now be gone. I must rest.'

Ravensford made an ironic bow and left. He would arrange for a maid to help Miss O'Brien, a loyal servant who had been in his mother's employ for years, despite what his mother and the girl wanted. Perhaps his mother's personal maid, Jane. She would know if anything in Miss O'Brien's possessions really belonged to his mother, and she would come to him immediately if that were the case.

## Chapter Two

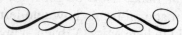

Mary Margaret left the drawing room as sedately as her thumping heart would let her. Behind her the Countess and Earl talked as though they were alone. To them, she was a servant, and the aristocracy talked in front of their servants as though they did not exist.

She carefully closed the heavy door. The butler stood nearby, waiting for orders. She smiled at him before turning and hurrying down the hall toward the servants' stairs and the back entrance.

She had to tell Thomas immediately. He would be furious. Nor did she want to go to London. This was home and she had never been farther than the nearby village of Cashel.

And there were Emily and Annie to take care of.

She rushed out the door, not bothering with a cape, and sped down the path that led to the trail through the pastures. As curate, Thomas had a small cottage near the church. She hoped he would be there and if not, then at the church.

She was out of breath when she got there. She pounded

impatiently on the door. After what seemed an eternity, Annie answered.

Her niece was small for her age, with large green eyes, a pointed chin and a wealth of black hair. She had been crying.

Mary Margaret fell to her knees and gathered the child in her arms. She stroked back the long hair, dread filling her. 'What is the matter, sweetheart?'

'Hiccup.' Annie squirmed away and rubbed at her eyes. 'Daddy...was angry.'

Mary Margaret closed her own eyes, wishing she could blot out the misery in her niece's and knowing she could not. 'Where is your mama?'

Annie jerked her head toward the bedroom.

'Stay here, sweetheart,' Mary Margaret said calmly, even though she was far from calm. The last thing she wanted was to upset Annie further.

As curate, Thomas had a modest cottage. The large rectory was occupied by the parish minister. Thomas had spent many afternoons and Sundays trying to ingratiate himself into the Countess's good graces in the hope that she would provide him with his own living. So far, he was unsuccessful. That was just one of the reasons Thomas wanted her to steal for him.

She knocked before entering the room. Her only sister sat hunched on the bed, one hand cradling her cheek. Mary Margaret rushed to her.

'Oh, Emily. Let me see.' She pulled Emily's hand away and frowned. 'You will have a bruise.'

'I walked into the door.'

Mary Margaret moved away to the water basin where

she wet a cloth. Taking it back to her sister, she said, 'No, you did not. Thomas hit you. But why?'

Emily refused to meet Mary Margaret's eyes. Compassion and anger warred in Mary Margaret. Emily had been a beauty, her hair dark as a raven's wing and her eyes blue as the sky. Now she was worn beyond her twenty-six years. Mary Margaret hated Thomas Fox, hated him with a passion that, in her calmer moments, shamed her.

Emily shrugged. 'Who knows?'

Mary Margaret was afraid she did. He had not liked her defiance. What would he do now?

'Emily, leave him. Come away with me. We will take Annie.'

'And go where? Neither of us has money to even feed ourselves for one day, let alone care for a child.' Bitterness tinged every word. 'No, I must stay. At least Annie is fed and clothed and has a roof over her head.'

'Come to the big house with me.'

'Ha! The Countess cares less than nothing for the likes of us.'

'But the Earl is here. They say he is compassionate, and so he seemed.'

A slight gleam of interest entered Emily's dull eyes. 'The Earl is here? Perhaps that is why Thomas was angry. He might fear that the Earl will take his mother away and just when Thomas is getting close enough to ask her for a better living.'

She had not thought of that and her fear mounted. He would be furious when he found out that they were all leaving for London shortly. Unconsciously she started wringing her hands.

'Oh, dear, Emily.' She fell to her knees in front of her sister and grasped Emily's hands. 'Please, please come away with me now. Please.'

'Why?'

'We are all leaving. The Earl, the Countess, and…me. Going to London.' She rushed on. 'I have a little put aside. I will send you more when I get my first quarterly salary.'

Emily sagged. 'I have nowhere to go.'

Desperate as she was, Mary Margaret knew Emily was right. There was nowhere to go. No one would believe that the saintly, wonderful Mr Fox beat his wife. Not even the vicar. Nor could she go to the Countess. As Emily had said, the woman would not care.

Wearily she stood. 'Where is Thomas? I must tell him.'

Emily sighed. 'At the church.'

Feeling more defeated than when her parents had both suddenly died of influenza and she had had to shoulder the burden of caring for her younger sister, Mary Margaret trudged from the room. The church was only a five-minute walk away.

She entered the darkened sanctuary and had to give her eyes several moments to adjust. Thomas was at the front talking to Mrs Smith, one of the farmers' wives. Mary Margaret sat on the nearest wooden bench to wait.

When Thomas finally headed her way, she could tell by his walk that he was furious. She gulped back her fear and resisted the urge to flee. Unpleasant as her news was, she had to tell him.

He stopped short of her, arms akimbo. He looked like a golden god towering above her. With his blue eyes, sun-bright hair, perfect physique and immaculate grooming, he looked to be everything a woman could want and everything a parish could desire in their spiritual leader. How false.

Unbidden, the image of the Earl formed. He was not breathtakingly handsome as Thomas was. Ravensford was rugged, more earthlike in his masculine appeal, with auburn hair and piercing green eyes. He was also more powerfully built, giving a sense of protection to those around him—or so she had felt. He was oddly disturbing to her.

'Why are you here?'

Thomas's demand effectively ended Mary Margaret's thoughts. She stood, not willing to have him lord it over her.

Taking a deep breath, she rushed the words. 'The Countess, the Earl and I are leaving for London immediately.'

'What?' His voice filled the tiny church, echoing off the centuries-old stone walls.

It was all Mary Margaret could do not to cringe. She had learned to fear Thomas's anger.

'The Countess is taking her goddaughter to London for a Season. I am to go ahead with the Earl to prepare the town house.'

Thomas's hand moved as though he meant to slap her. Mary Margaret stepped back. How could they have ever thought him the answer to Emily's prayers? How his charm and seeming devotion to her sister had fooled them.

'When?'

'Tomorrow. The Countess is to follow.'

He paced away, his boots ringing on the stone floor. Coming back, he ordered, 'Do as the Countess wishes. There are bound to be more opportunities in London for you to steal from her.'

Mary Margaret blanched. She had secretly hoped he would tell her to quit, that London was too far away and did him no good.

When she spoke she was glad her voice did not quaver.

'But how shall I get home? Even if I do manage to get her jewels, I don't know how to get back from London.'

His fine mouth sneered. 'That is your problem, one you will solve since Emily and Annie will be here.'

His implied threat was only what she had expected. He knew she would manage somehow to keep him from hurting them more. He was ordering her to do an immoral and illegal act. Even though she hoped to thwart him and still save her sister and niece, the anger toward him that she usually held in check burst out.

'If you harm them, if you so much as lay a finger on Annie or hit Emily again, I shall turn myself into the authorities and I shall tell them all about you.'

He laughed. 'Very noble. But no one will believe your story about me. I am the younger son of Viscount Fox. It would be your word against mine—and you are nobody.'

The sense of defeat gnawed at her. She fought it off. 'They might not believe me, but it would do your reputation no good to have the accusation made public.'

His narrowed eyes told her she had finally succeeded in getting past his armour. 'Do so and I will make you rue the instant you opened your mouth.'

She never doubted him. Her hands clenched in the folds of her gown.

'Now, get out of here. I will be waiting for your first report and your final return.'

His cold words washed over her nerves like a scratch on a blackboard. She was defeated. Again.

She retraced her steps to Derry House. She came even with the Gothic folly the Countess had built last summer. Honeysuckle mingled with climbing roses, acting like curtains for the structure's windows. Soon they would bloom and their scents would fill the air. A brook raced along behind. Birds cavorted overhead and roosted in the eaves. It was a haven she had frequently gone to during her short time with the Countess.

Her feet took her toward it now.

She reached the door just as a rustle caught her attention, followed by a shadow disengaging from an interior wall. Her heart thumped and her left hand rose to her throat.

'Miss O'Brien,' a male baritone said.

She recognised the Earl's voice instantly. The deep tone slid like velvet along her senses. Even in the dim, filtered light she could see the glint of his copper hair. His teeth were a bared white slash.

She forced herself to relax. Her hand fell to her side and her breathing evened out. 'My lord.'

He advanced on her until he was close enough that she imagined she could feel the heat from his body. Awareness of him rose within her like a tidal wave reaching for the full moon. She shivered.

'Do you come here often?' His tone was conversational, yet she thought she detected an underlying current of interest. But why?

'When I feel the need for privacy.' She answered him bluntly and boldly, knowing she should be more respectful, yet needing that privacy very much. He was too disturbing, increasing her discomfort.

Instead of finding solace in her hidey-hole, she was finding a very disquieting part of her nature. Since watching her sister fall in love with a man like Thomas Fox, Mary Margaret had made herself impervious to men. The Earl was slipping past her barrier. Even his voice aroused her senses. What would it be like if he touched her?

Shocked at her own forwardness in even thinking such a thing, she drew herself straight. Proper ladies did not have such thoughts, not even ladies born of yeoman farmers.

'And you wish me at the devil instead of invading your solitude,' he murmured, a hint of amusement making his voice rich and creamy.

'I had hoped to be alone,' she said, keeping her tone even in spite of the tremors shifting through her body.

She was never this bold, but desperation drove her. He disturbed her too much, and she needed time to think through what she was going to do. Relief flooded her when he moved forward, as though to pass her and go out the door that was behind her. The relief was short lived.

He stopped beside her, close enough that she could feel his warm breath. She had never been this close to a man who was not family. She licked suddenly dry lips.

'You look upset, Miss O'Brien. Is there anything I can do?'

Her eyes widened. He sounded genuinely concerned. For a moment, but not longer, she found herself tempted to pour out her problem. He was a powerful man. He could help her, help her sister and niece, if he chose. Then the moment was gone.

She had heard many things about this man standing too close to her. The young female servants said he was known for his mistresses and his charm. The men admired his abilities in sports. He was what the fashionable called a Corinthian. She had even heard that he was a champion of the downtrodden.

All she could think of was that he was the Countess's son, and the Countess cared nothing for those beneath her.

No, no matter how tempting the Earl made his question

sound, she would not answer. She had too much to lose and, as far as she knew, nothing to gain by confiding in him.

'Thank you for your concern, my lord, but I am fine. I am a solitary person, that is all.'

His eyes met and held hers for a long time. She realised with a thrill of apprehension that she could not make herself look away. For her, he was more dangerous than Thomas.

'Then I shall leave you.' He nodded before sauntering from the building.

Mary Margaret barely made it to one of several chairs positioned around the folly before her legs gave out. She gripped the arms until her knuckles turned white and she lost feeling in her fingers. If she reacted this strongly to him after such a brief exposure, how was she going to survive the trip to London in his company? This was madness.

And yet...was this how Emily had felt the first time she saw Thomas? She had never understood Emily's immediate attraction to Thomas, and when they had wed after only knowing each other a month she had been shocked. Perhaps now she could understand.

But none of this solved her problem. Even with the threat to Emily and Annie, she was not sure she could bring herself to steal from the Countess. In the back of her mind, she had hoped to devise a plan that would outsmart Thomas. So far, she had not.

She chewed her bottom lip.

This trip to London might be better than she had thought. It would give her time to formulate something without having Thomas constantly coming upon her and demanding that she act immediately or he would hurt her sister. Not even Thomas could be so impatient as not to realise how much more time it would take to gain access to the Countess's jewels now that she was going to London. It was her only hope.

She rose with a sigh. Tired as she was, she still had to pack her meagre belongings. The day was nearly over and tomorrow would be here all too soon.

She made her way to the manor's back entrance. From there, she climbed the servants' stairs to the third floor. Wearily, she pushed open the door to her room and froze.

'What are you doing here?'

Jane, the Countess's personal maid, looked over her plump shoulder. She was a round woman, her apple-red face as full as the rest. Iron-grey hair worn tightly back made her look like a dumpling. She was not the merry character her person resembled.

'What are you gaping at, girl?' Jane demanded.

Mary Margaret tamped down on the anger brought about by this invasion of privacy. 'Who let you in?'

'Don't be daft. I let myself in.' Jane straightened out and turned to face Mary Margaret.

'I told the Earl that I don't require help to pack.'

Jane snorted, her full mouth and button nose prominent. 'His lordship does as he pleases. He ordered me here even though waiting on you is beneath me.' She cast an unfriendly look at Mary Margaret. 'Don't be thinking you're better than you are. The Earl is in a hurry to do his mother's bidding, missy.'

She turned her back on Mary Margaret and marched to the plain oak dresser. She pulled out the few neatly folded clothes and eyed them with a jaundiced look. 'Least they are clean.'

Mary Margaret had done her best to tolerate this invasion, but this last was too much. 'They are more than clean.

They are decent and come by honestly. More than some can say.' She stalked to the other woman and took the maligned clothing from Jane's plump fingers. 'I do not need your disparaging comments or your help. Please leave.'

Jane's brown eyes narrowed and her lips thinned. 'Don't be getting above yourself, missy.'

Seeing that she was only making matters worse, Mary Margaret tried another track. 'I know my place very well, and I am far beneath your notice. You are a busy woman and have other things to do. My meagre packing should not detain you.'

'True,' Jane said with a haughty sniff. 'But if I don't help, his lordship won't be happy.'

Mary Margaret considered the Earl for a minute. He was the source of quite a bit of her uneasiness, and she liked him less by the instant. 'He will live. Surely I am not the first person during his lifetime to refuse his bidding.'

'That's as may be. *I* have never gone against his lordship's orders unless my lady has bid me differently.'

'I have no doubt of it,' Mary Margaret murmured, weary of the confrontation and the conversation. They went in circles. 'Perhaps it would be enough for you to see my few belongings.'

Jane looked down her tiny nose as Mary Margaret took out the remainder of her belongings and spread them on the narrow bed. A travelling dress, two day dresses, boots, pattens, one pair of slippers, a nightdress with a plain robe, and underclothes completed her wardrobe.

'What about jewellery?'

Mary Margaret pulled a simple gold locket from beneath the collar of her dress. Inside were tiny pictures of her parents. 'Only this.'

Jane looked disdainfully at the unadorned piece. 'Anything else?'

Mary Margaret curled her fingers protectively around the locket. It was all she had left of her parents. The farm her father had worked had passed to someone upon his death, the furniture and personal items going to pay debts and hers and Emily's education with the vicar where Emily had met Thomas. She pushed away the painful memories of loss and regret.

'No, I have nothing else,' Mary Margaret said. 'Except my portmanteau. Would you care to examine it? Or watch while I pack?'

Jane took the only chair, her ample dimensions flowing over the sides. 'I will watch.'

Mary Margaret bit back a sharp retort and started folding clothes. The sooner she was done the sooner she would be alone. Minutes later, she stuffed the last item into the now full portmanteau.

'Harumph! You will never get the wrinkles out,' Jane stated, standing.

'I will manage. I am, after all, merely a servant, and not even an important one.'

'True.'

Without another word, Jane left, her ample form squeezing through the sides of the door. Mary Margaret released a sigh.

Why did the Earl care about her packing? It seemed such a small and silly thing for him to be concerned about.

He was very disconcerting, as was her reaction to him. If he told her to do something, she would be hard pressed to refuse him simply because she found him so mesmerising. Hopefully she would see very little of him. Most gentlemen did not like travelling in a carriage, so he would probably ride most of the trip. In London he would be too busy to pay attention to her.

She rose and went to the single window. Using her handkerchief, she rubbed a spot clean and gazed out at the immaculately groomed garden. Green speckled with other colours met her eye. Above, clouds scudded across a pale blue sky. This evening would bring rain. Nothing unusual in Ireland. Spring was her favourite time of the year, a time of new beginnings and birth.

How she wished Emily would run away with her and start anew. But so far she refused. And because of that, Mary Margaret had to do as Thomas ordered. When she had initially refused his orders, he had threatened to do more than blacken Emily's eye or Annie's jaw. So she had agreed. But somehow she would thwart him and get Emily and Annie from him. No matter that the law said a wife was her husband's property and a daughter the same until given to another man in marriage.

A robin flew by the window, its little chest covered by a red vest, and alighted on the nearby tree. His colourful feathers reminded her once more of the Earl of Ravensford.

He was a ruggedly handsome man, not at all classical in looks. His eyes sparkled with something deeper than humour that was more compelling than mere charm, although she was sure that he had more than his fair share of that attribute. Then there was his mouth that hinted at passions she could only guess about. When he had spoken to her, she had been hard pressed not to lose herself in the fantasy of his lips on hers. A silly thought and totally impossible.

She sighed at her own weakness, her finger tracing a

pattern in the glass. Before she quite realised what she had done, there was a man's profile etched in the window.

With the strong, patrician nose, the picture could only be of Ravensford. He was a forceful man, used to having his own way. She also knew he could be dangerous for her.

She put her palm to the glass and smeared out the image. If only she could as easily banish him from her mind. Everything seemed to lead back to him.

With a sigh, she turned away. These melancholy thoughts helped no one, and tomorrow she began her long journey to London with the Earl as her protector.

A shiver chased down her spine. From fear or anticipation, she knew not, only that she felt alive as never before.

## Chapter Three

Stone-grey clouds scuttled across the early morning sky. Damp, cold wind rippled through the trees and whipped Mary Margaret's cape into a frenzy about her legs.

She started down the first marble step, wondering when the Countess would appear and order her to return inside the house and go out the servants' entrance. The Countess had done that Mary Margaret's first day. The butler and footmen had watched impassively, but one of the young female servants had snickered. Mary Margaret had not made that mistake again—until today. It was nerves.

The travelling carriage, with whatever the Earl and his mother had thought necessary, waited on the gravel outside the front entry, scant yards from her. The horses champed at the bit and pawed the ground, their breath mist on the rising wind. It would storm soon, spring forgotten in winter's dying hand. Travel would be hard.

In her hurry, she tripped in her skirts. Her feet skidded on the slick stone, and she pitched forward. The hard marble raced toward her face. She flung a hand up to break her fall, dropping her portmanteau.

An arm like a band of iron wrapped around her waist. A firm hand caught her elbow and helped steady her. In seconds she was pressed against an unyielding chest.

She took a breath to still her beating heart, knowing she had been saved from a nasty accident. Thinking herself once more in charge of her emotions, she tried to move away from the man who held her. The grip tightened so that she twisted in the no longer needed embrace, intending to set the importunate person in his place. She might not be a lady of Quality, but she was a lady and no lady was held so intimately by a man who was not her father, brother or husband.

Eyes the colour of newly scythed grass met hers. A mouth she had thought sensual yesterday curved into a wicked smile, showing a dimple in the left cheek that threatened to weaken her knees. Still, the Earl's grip on her waist did not loosen. If anything, it tightened.

The look he bent on her took another turn, becoming slumberous and intense. Awareness of his body pressed so tightly to hers shivered along her every nerve.

After an eternity, his arm slid away, gliding along the curve of her waist and skirting the swell of her hips. It was nearly a caress and she felt it through all the layers of her dress, pelisse and cape. Heat threatened to engulf her entire being.

She forced her eyes to look away from his and her knees to bend in a curtsy. 'Thank you, my lord,' she murmured, not sure what she thanked him for. Part of her mind knew he had saved her from a disastrous fall, yet another part of her mind understood that he had awakened something in her that had been dormant. 'Thank you for stopping my fall,' she said at last.

'You are welcome,' he said, his voice low and husky as though he had an inflammation of the lungs. He had not sounded this way yesterday.

'Are you unwell, my lord?' she blurted.

His smile became rueful. 'Nothing so mundane. Let me help you down the rest of these steps. They are treacherous in weather such as this, and it would not suit my mother to have you injured and forced to remain here.'

He spoke the truth, yet she sensed more beneath his words. Instantly she scolded herself. His hand still held her elbow and it made reasonable thinking hard. Her reaction to him scared her. Scared her as nothing else ever had.

'Thank you, my lord,' she murmured once again. 'But I am on my guard now and able to care for myself.'

She bent to retrieve her portmanteau. His hand was before hers.

'I can carry it.'

'I am sure you can, but I shall do so.'

He gave her a mocking half-bow that brought the blush of embarrassment to her cheeks. What would the other servants say about this? What would his mother say when she heard the gossip? The Countess would not be pleased. Perhaps it was just as well that she was leaving.

From beneath her lashes, she watched Ravensford hand her portmanteau to a footman. His shoulders appeared broader than yesterday, the many capes of his coat accentuating them. His hair sparkled like copper even in the dull light coming through the clouds. She shook herself in an effort to dispel his draw.

He turned at that moment. 'You are cold. Get inside the

coach. There are blankets and heated stones. A bottle full of hot water as well. Another full of hot chocolate.'

'Are you travelling in the carriage, my lord?' All those comforts could not be for her.

'Later. Perhaps.'

He helped her into the carriage, his hand lingering. Her gaze went to his touch before rising to his face. The look he gave her was one she did not understand, but knew instinctively meant danger to her.

He released her. 'Drink all the hot chocolate. It will help keep you warm until we stop for lunch.'

She looked at him. 'Surely it is for you.'

'I think not.' He chuckled. 'Too sweet for my tastes. I like a drink that burns its way down and keeps me warm.'

Almost she thought he meant something besides what his words said. In her fancy, she could think he spoke a special language just for her. This would not do.

She fell back on the security of protocol. 'Thank you, my lord.'

He gave her a quizzical look before turning away. She breathed a sigh of relief. His regard was too disturbing.

Ravensford made his way to his mount. Could a woman with a voice and looks such as hers truly be the innocent she portrayed? Or was this all part of her plan to steal from his mother? Both were questions he could not answer yet, but he would eventually, no matter what he had to do.

Ravensford mounted, and with a wave of his hand to the groom holding the horse's reins, he set out. It would be a long journey.

He glanced back once, wondering if his mother was up and watching. No pale face looked out from a window. The Countess was still abed, as he had expected.

The weather rapidly worsened, and Ravensford considered riding in the carriage—a big lumbering vehicle designed to carry luggage, not people who were in a hurry. And they were in a hurry. There was much to be done to his town house in order to bring it up to his mother's standards and very little time to do it in.

Riding his horse and getting drenched to the bone would accomplish nothing, while if he rode inside he would be able to question Miss O'Brien about herself and her future. Not to mention take in his fill of her exotic features. The last was a consideration he pushed from his mind. His duty was to learn enough to outfox her, not to become entangled with her.

He signalled the coachman and outriders to stop. His mount was tied to the back of the vehicle and the ancient steps let down. Ravensford entered in time to see the woman hurriedly stuff something under the neck of her gown, as though she did not wish him to see whatever it was. He wondered if it was something to do with her mission.

Mary Margaret saw the Earl's gaze on her neck. Homesick already, she had been gazing at the pictures of her parents in her locket. The moment was too personal to share with someone she did not know, so when she had heard the coach door open, she had put the locket back.

Warily, she watched the Earl take the seat opposite her, back to the horses, and make himself comfortable. She had not thought he would join her, no matter how awful the weather became.

'I thought gentlemen preferred to ride,' she said. 'Nor should you be the one to sit facing away from the horses.'

His right eyebrow rose, a burnt slash across his broad brow. 'Gentlemen do as they please, and it pleases me to get inside away from the wind and rain and to sit where I am. 'Tis too bad the others cannot do the same. I would call a halt if I thought this storm would let up soon. Unfortunately, it looks to follow us to the coast.'

Mary Margaret felt her mouth drop in surprise. 'You care about their discomfort?'

Ravensford frowned. 'They are human beings, are they not?'

She nodded, clamping her teeth shut. She had already more than overstepped the gap between an earl and a tenant farmer's daughter. She did not need to compound her error with more inane comments.

Silence fell, but she was intensely, painfully aware of his nearness. She could hear him breathing and cast him fleeting glances from beneath her lashes. He lounged at his leisure, or as much as was possible with the carriage swaying from side to side and jolting with every numerous hole in the road. His right hand gripped the leather strap for stability. He had long fingers, covered by riding gloves.

She saw his muscles bunch beneath the folds of his coat. Confusion spread through her as she remembered the strength in his circling arm when he had caught her up. No man had ever held her so close, yet it had felt right—and exciting.

She turned her head sharply, hoping to forget the sensation of his touch by looking anywhere but at him. He was a disturbing man. More so because of what she had to do—unless she could outwit her brother-in-law.

'What do you see in the rain that is so interesting?'

His voice was deep with the refined tones of the British aristocracy. Yet there was more to it than that. There was a warmth that seemed to stroke her nerves, heightening her senses.

She shook her head at her fancifulness. This had to stop. He was so far above her as to be as unattainable as the sun. Not that she wanted him. She was not so susceptible nor so stupid as to let her imagination run that wild.

He probably treated his women poorly. He certainly would never marry such as herself, and she would never be a man's mistress—not that he had asked or even intended to do so. So, there it was. She was being overly silly and all because he was handsome and had a voice that made her insides feel like warm pudding.

She said the first safe thing that popped into her head. 'We shall have to stop soon if this rain continues. The road is becoming a morass.'

'True.'

He leaned forward to look out the window, moving so close to her that she felt stifled. She wondered if he did so on purpose, if he knew how his proximity affected her. She drew back, putting as much distance between them as the confines would allow. He shot her a glance that in her mind seemed to say he knew how disturbing his nearness was.

'I am hoping to reach a small inn on the outskirts of the next town. At least there we can stable the horses and all get warm food and a place to sleep.'

Instead of shifting back to his place, he stayed watching out the window. The dim carriage lamp showed his profile, his arrogant nose a-jut and his jaw a firm statement of strength. Golden stubble dotted his face, surprising her. She had thought he would grow a red beard because of his hair. She was wrong.

After her heart had raced itself to a near stop in sheer exhaustion, he finally sat back. He slanted her a speculative glance. She met his study with as much aplomb as she could dredge up. She had never been uncomfortable around men, but she was with him. Her skin prickled and her imagination ran amok, neither one being a condition she enjoyed, or so she told herself.

'I hope you won't find the lack of comforts at this place too much of a hardship, Miss O'Brien.'

That was the last thing she had expected him to be concerned about. 'Me? I should think your lordship will have a greater problem than me.'

A bitter smile twisted his fine mouth. 'I bivouacked in the Peninsula. I am used to Spartan accommodations. It is you I am concerned for.'

Was he baiting her? And if so, why should he think this would do so? 'I am sure you are, my lord. However, I too am used to not being coddled.'

'Really? Where did you live before coming to stay with my mother?'

His voice showed only mild interest, yet Mary Margaret was instantly on her guard. There was no reason a man of his standing should be interested in her past. But once the question was asked, there was no reason to lie. She would tell him her life's story, except for Thomas's treatment of Emily, and the Earl would quickly find himself bored.

'I am the oldest daughter of one of your mother's tenant farmers. My parents are gone and my sister is married.'

He picked up the earthenware container of hot chocolate. 'Would you care for some, Miss O'Brien?'

The abrupt change in conversation nonplussed her. 'Please.'

Somehow he managed to pour her a cup without spilling the liquid. She took it, startled by the shock when her fingers accidentally brushed his. The jolt felt like the spark caused when her feet brushed along a carpet and then she touched something.

'You are very well-spoken for a tenant farmer's daughter,' he said while she took a sip of the hot chocolate.

She wondered if he always jumped from topic to topic. It was very disconcerting.

'My mother's father was a vicar. She…married beneath her. She taught us diction and everything she knew. When her knowledge ran out, she did chores for Reverend Hopkins in exchange for lessons in Greek and Latin for us.'

'Who is us?'

'My sister Emily and myself.'

'You are very well educated. Most women of my acquaintance are only barely conversant in those languages. Many can't even speak French fluently.'

His praise embarrassed her. She was not used to compliments in any form, let alone from someone of his position. His mother certainly had not thought her accomplishments worth much.

By the time her first quarter with the Countess was over, she would have barely enough to keep herself and Emily for a year and that was if they lived as frugally as their upbringing had taught them and did small chores in exchange for food. Still, they would manage. They had to.

Thankfully, the carriage lurched because she had no answer to his praise. The liquid in her cup sloshed over the rim and on to her lap. She bounced forward as the vehicle stopped.

For the second time in one day, she found herself in the Earl's arms. If it were not so disturbing to her peace of mind and calmness of body, she would find it amusing. As it was, she could barely breathe. His face was too close, his arms too tight, and his lips too enticing.

'Catching you seems to be my job today,' he murmured, continuing to hold her.

She stared up at him, a distant part of her awareness wondering why he did not release her. The majority of her awareness thrilled to his touch.

She watched as his gaze travelled from her eyes to her mouth. Hunger, or some other strong emotion she could not name, drew harsh lines in his cheeks. If she didn't know better, she would think he intended to kiss her. She was being silly.

His face lowered until his warm breath caressed her skin. The scent of lemons and musk filled her senses. She knew she should struggle. She was not the type of woman men kissed unless their intentions were less than honourable. She had nothing to offer and no family to defend her.

His mouth skimmed hers and she melted against him, knowing even as she did so that she was making a terrible mistake.

'My lord,' a male voice said from outside the coach.

Ravensford thrust her away so quickly Mary Margaret's head swam. She blinked several times in a vain attempt to clear her senses.

'My lord, we are stuck solid in the mud.'

'Damnation, I was afraid of that,' the Earl said, opening the carriage door and jumping out without a backward glance at Mary Margaret.

Unconsciously, the trembling fingers of one hand went to her mouth. He had nearly kissed her. His lips had brushed hers. She still felt weak as a kitten. He had such power over her without even trying.

Taking a deep breath, she composed herself as best she could. She pulled a handkerchief from her reticule and dabbed half-heartedly at the spill of chocolate that had started the whole episode.

From the open door came the sounds of men cursing. She edged to the door and looked out. The back wheel on her side was sunk up to the axle in mud. The two outriders, the groom and coachman were all trying to lever the wheel out of the hole. She knew her weight was not making their effort any easier.

Gathering her cape close around her neck, Mary Margaret leapt from the carriage to what had once been the dirt road. She landed with a splat and sank several inches. Rain pelted her. Thank goodness the wind had stopped or the weather would be truly beastly. As it was, she was a country girl and could stand in this rain for hours if need be.

'What do you think you are doing?' the Earl demanded, stalking toward her. He stopped barely a foot from her, his face a mask of irritation.

His angry voice surprised her. 'I am getting out of the carriage to lighten the load,' she said in a voice that implied that her action was self-evident. Still, she backed away.

'Get back in.'

'When they are done,' she said calmly, hoping the quiver she felt didn't sound in her voice.

'Get back in or I shall be forced to throw you in.'

She edged back, the mud sucking at her feet and making movement difficult. 'I am used to weather like this. Besides, without my weight the work will go quicker. This is better for everyone. I should feel badly if my staying dry in the carriage meant everyone else had to work harder and longer than necessary.'

'Very noble,' he said sarcastically. 'But I meant what I said. There is no reason for you to suffer like this.'

While he spoke, he stripped off his great coat and then his inner coat until he stood in his shirt. The rain instantly plastered the fine linen to his body.

Try as she would, Mary Margaret could not keep from looking at his chest. Muscles rippled beneath the soaked material, and his shoulders looked broad enough to bear the weight of the coach without help from anyone else.

'Miss O'Brien,' Ravensford said dangerously. He took several steps toward her.

The sound of her name grabbed her attention and she looked up at his face. His eyes seemed to spark in the grey light. Had he seen where her attention had been focussed? She hoped not. She would be too humiliated if he had.

He loomed over her. Dimly she perceived that the other men were watching them, waiting to see what would happen. Her hair had loosened in sodden ropes and she pushed them off her face. The Earl's hair dripped water down his face. They were both being ridiculously stubborn and doing no one any good.

She knew defeat when he stood scowling down at her. She turned and scampered back into the carriage as best she could with mud clinging to her boots like a lover clings to his fleeing mistress. A fanciful thought if she had ever had one, she decided, once she was safely inside the vehicle and away from the Earl's menacing presence.

The rain beat on the roof in rhythm to the men rocking the carriage. Mary Margaret clenched her teeth and hands, hoping they would succeed soon. Everyone was going to be cold, wet and dirty.

A sudden jolt and lurch accompanied by a loud sucking sound told her they were free. She relaxed against the squabs, only belatedly realising her soaked clothing would ruin the velvet cloth. She pealed off her cape and spread it on the seat beside her. The Earl would be joining her soon and they would continue on their way.

The coach moved slowly forward.

Seconds dragged into long minutes and Ravensford did not appear. She looked out the window and saw him mounted on his horse, his coats on once more. His beaver hat provided his face a modicum of protection from the steady downpour.

She relaxed back on to the seat with a sigh, torn between irritation that he was riding in the awful weather and relief that he was not sitting in the carriage with her. She sat engrossed in her confused thoughts until the carriage finally rumbled to a halt.

She quickly realised they must be at the inn that was the Earl's destination. Ravensford himself opened the door and extended his hand to help her out. Reluctantly, she put her fingers into his and met his eyes. His anger sparked at her, and she realised that a confrontation with the Earl lay ahead. And all because she had tried to help.

# Chapter Four

The rain pelted her face as she looked defiantly up at Ravensford. His hair dripped water beneath the brim of his beaver hat. Lines radiated from his eyes. On most men of his station the creases would be the results of too many long nights spent gaming, wenching and drinking. She doubted he was any different. The knowledge was small comfort.

When she hesitated, he nearly yanked her from the coach. She gasped and put her free arm on his chest to keep herself from tumbling.

'When I tell you to do something, Miss O'Brien, I mean exactly that.'

'Yes, my lord,' she muttered, twisting her arm in a vain attempt to free it.

'Here,' he said, releasing her while using his one hand to unclasp his great coat. He shrugged out of it and swung it around her.

'I cannot.'

She reached to pluck it from her shoulders, but his hands gripped hers. His eyes blazed down at her.

'What did I just say?'

'I have forgotten,' she said in a spurt of unusual rebellion.

'No, you have not.'

He fastened the top button before grabbing her again and urging her toward the inn's door. The dried dirt on her hem and shoes quickly became mud again. She noticed that his Hessians were coated.

The door opened before the Earl could grasp the handle and a round, squat man stood before them and tisked.

'My lord, I was not expecting you,' the proprietor said, his hands wiping futilely at his pristine white apron.

'I am sorry to discommode you, Littleton. I had hoped to make the coast this evening and therefore not need your services. This storm put paid to that.'

The innkeeper nodded before turning and leading them down a narrow hall. 'My parlour is unoccupied, my lord.'

At the Earl's prodding, Mary Margaret followed the owner to a small room where a fire blazed. Heat engulfed her. Warm, welcome heat that made her garments steam and smell of wet wool.

'Please, my lord, I will send a girl to fetch your coat for cleaning. And soon—'

'Whiskey for me and tea for the lady,' Ravensford said, interrupting. 'And whatever you are cooking. See that my servants are cared for as well.'

'Yes, my lord. Mutton and potatoes. Ale as well for the others.'

'Plenty of it, Littleton.'

'Yes, my lord.'

The landlord was barely out of the door when Ravensford turned on her. 'Take the coat off, Miss O'Brien. The last thing I need is for you to get an inflammation of the lungs.'

'I am much hardier than that...my lord,' she added.

'And stop "my lording" me. Call me Ravensford.' He slanted her a cool smile. 'All my acquaintances do.'

Instead of responding, she gingerly slid his coat off. It dripped water and mud on the floor.

A knock preceded the door opening and a serving woman entering. 'The landlord sent me to fetch your coat, my lord.'

'Thank you,' he said. 'And please send someone to get Miss O'Brien's cape from the coach. It will never dry there and will need cleaning.'

'Yes, my lord,' the woman said, taking the coat from Mary Margaret's hands and bundling it up. 'I will be right back to mop up this mess.'

'If you will bring the mop I will do it,' Mary Margaret volunteered, feeling badly about the puddle.

The woman gaped at her. Ravensford scowled.

'That is... I am used to cleaning up.' She knew she was making matters worse, but the words continued to tumble from her mouth.

'Why don't you show Miss O'Brien to her room? Her portmanteau should be there by now and she can change.'

The servant cast him a grateful glance. Mary Margaret realised her offer to mop the floor had made the woman feel awkward. Chagrined, she clamped down on any other words and followed the maid up a narrow flight of stairs to a small corner room. It was neat and clean with a single bed and wash stand. Her portmanteau was on the bed.

The woman left before Mary Margaret could thank her. Just as well. She would not have known what to say.

\* \* \*

Half an hour later, she had struggled out of her wet clothing and donned dry ones. The lukewarm water in the wash bowl was brown from dirt, but she felt much better. Hunger rumbled in her stomach. Indecision kept her stationary.

Surely she was not supposed to join the Earl for supper. Which left the public room. The idea of going down among a group of men she did not know was daunting. But not so much as the thought of spending her small hoard of coins. The money was only for an emergency. She did not have enough to spend on anything else if she was going to take Emily away at the end of the quarter.

She sighed. Hungry as she was, she had been hungrier before and lived. She crossed to the bed and sat down. Exhaustion moved through her.

A knock on the door startled her.

The servant stuck her head in and said, 'His lordship be waitin' for you.'

Hunger warred with caution. Hunger won.

Minutes later, Mary Margaret entered the private room and was assailed by the smell of mutton and gravy. Her stomach growled.

'Not a second too soon,' Ravensford said with a grin. 'Have a seat, Miss O'Brien. We will eat and then we will discuss your habit of disobeying me.'

Her pleasure died. She turned to leave, knowing that eating would only make her uncomfortable now.

'I believe I told you to sit down,' Ravensford said in a dangerously calm voice.

Mary Margaret looked back at him. His mouth was a thin line. His hands paused in the act of carving the leg of mutton. Things were going from bad to worse.

'Thank you, my lord, but I am not as hungry as I thought.' Her stomach chose that moment to put the lie to her words.

'And I am not accustomed to people disregarding my instructions, Miss O'Brien. That is the crux of this situation.'

She straightened her shoulders.

He placed a large slice of mutton on a plate that would have been hers and followed it with vegetables and gravy. Her mouth watered.

'When I tell you to do something,' he said, fixing his own plate, 'I mean for you to do exactly that. This afternoon when I told you to get back in the coach, I did so for a reason.' He took his seat, pointing toward hers with his fork. 'You got out with good intentions. I am sure you meant to lighten the load. What you really did was make the other men feel embarrassed. It is their job to take care of such situations and having a female expose herself to weather such as that made them feel even worse than they already did that the coach had hit a hole. Particularly John Coachman, and he already felt bad enough. It was much kinder for you to remain in the carriage.'

Her attention left the food and focussed on him. 'I had not thought of it that way. I had only meant to help.'

'So, when I tell you to do something, Miss O'Brien, believe that I know best.'

His autocratic manner was irritating, but she recognised the validity of his words.

'Now, please be seated. The food is getting cold.'

She did as he bade. She had thought herself no longer hungry, but the instant the food touched her tongue she was ravenous. She was nearly through when he offered her tea.

'Thank you, my lord,' she murmured, realising too late that he intended to pour for her. 'I should be doing that.'

'So you should.' He shifted the teapot, cream and sugar to her side. 'And I believe I told you to call me Ravensford.'

She stopped putting cream into her tea. 'I know, but your mother would be scandalised.'

He grinned, looking like a small boy who has pulled a prank. She could see the charm he was famous for glinting in his green eyes.

'Yes, she would be, but she isn't here.'

A picture of an irate Countess formed in Mary Margaret's mind. She smiled. 'I will try, my—Ravensford.'

'That's the way.'

He poured himself a drink and lounged back in his chair. He watched her over the rim of the glass. Mary Margaret felt like a bug pinned to a mat for someone's pleasure.

'I am very tired, m— Ravensford. And I am sure that tomorrow will be an early day. Do you mind if I go to bed?'

His scrutiny intensified. The angle of his cheek and jaw sharpened. 'Yes, I would mind, Miss O'Brien, but I will allow it. The last thing I want is for you to become exhausted before we even reach London.'

Feeling like the fox fleeing the hounds, Mary Margaret jumped up, nearly spilling her half-drunk tea. 'Thank you.'

She scurried to the door, only to find the Earl there. His large frame blocked her exit. She gazed up at him, trying to ignore the blood pounding in her ears.

He caught her chin in his well-shaped hand and rubbed his thumb back and forth over the tiny cleft below her bottom lip. She was unable to look away. He could do anything to her and she doubted that she would be able or even willing to say him nay. She gulped hard, her eyes wide.

'You are tired,' he murmured. 'I hope your bed is soft

and to your satisfaction. If not, I will have you given another room.'

She did not know what to say. His solicitousness was unexpected and inappropriate. Yet a glow of warmth started in her stomach and spread. No one since her parents had cared for her like this.

'I will be fine, my lord,' she managed to mumble.

He stroked her chin one last time and let her go. Stepping away, he said, 'Ravensford. And remember, if the bed keeps you awake, I will see that something is done.'

She nodded and backed out of the door, never once taking her attention off him. Any second she half expected him to take her in his arms. They would both regret that later. So she watched him until the door closed behind her.

Only once she was safe in her room did she berate herself for over-dramatising the situation. The Earl was only interested in her comfort. If she arrived in London too tired to do what must be done to the house, then the burden would fall to him. Naturally he did not want that to happen.

But there was the caress.

She shivered beneath the thick covers. Why had he touched her and looked at her as though he wanted to devour her? He could not be attracted to her. Surely not.

Her fingers plucked at the bedcover, finding a feather and pulling it out. What if he were interested in her? She could never be a man's mistress and he would never offer marriage. A hollowness settled in her chest.

She fell asleep, telling herself the Earl was only being considerate. She could not, would not let herself think his behaviour was for any other reason. To do so would be insane.

* * *

Downstairs Ravensford finished his drink. He wondered
what hold the man in the library had over Miss O'Brien.
She was a very attractive woman and well educated. While
he had been angry at her leaving the carriage earlier, he
had also admired her desire to be helpful. Most—no, *all*
the women of his acquaintance would have stayed huddled
warm and dry in the vehicle, never thinking about the servants outside in the cold and wet. She had qualities that he
valued.

He templed his fingers and gazed unseeing at the fire as
he brought his focus back to the problem. It did not matter that he was beginning to like her. His goal was to find
out who her accomplice was and to keep them from being
successful.

If seeing to her comfort did not win her trust, he could
seduce her. Women always talked to their lovers. A drastic measure, but so was her plan to steal from his parent.

The idea was instantly gratifying, something he would
not have thought possible. Never in his entire life had he
set out to cold-bloodedly seduce a woman. He hoped he
would not have to do so now—or so he told himself. It did
not sit well with his idea of honour, even as the idea made
his blood pool in areas best ignored.

They started early. The sun shone brightly, already drying some of the smaller puddles on the road. Mary Margaret had not slept well. She refused to breakfast with the
Earl. She was not hungry and it was not proper. She had
done so last night, but that did not mean she intended to
continue doing so.

A brisk breeze swept across the coaching yard as she

made her way to the carriage, carefully stepping around mud puddles. She was glad to have her cape back, clean and dry.

Reaching the carriage, her gaze still on the ground, she saw a pair of shining Hessians. She licked suddenly dry lips and looked up to meet Ravensford's gaze.

'Are you thirsty, Miss O'Brien? There is lemonade and hot chocolate in the carriage.' A smile tugged at one corner of his mouth.

'No, thank you. Whatever gave you that idea?'

His smile widened to a wolfish grin. 'The way you licked your lips. And you did not join me for breakfast.'

Did she detect a trace of irritation in his voice? He still smiled at her, but the showing of teeth resembled that of a large predator.

'No, I am not hungry, either.'

She looked away and started up the carriage steps. His hand caught her elbow and she halted, one foot still on the ground.

'I took the liberty of having the proprietor pack biscuits and ham for you to have later.'

She looked over her shoulder at him. Why was he doing this? She was nobody to him. He should be ignoring her.

'Thank you,' she muttered.

Hastily, before he could say or do anything else, she scampered into the coach. His hand fell away from her elbow and she breathed a sigh of relief, or so she told herself. As yesterday, she found blankets and hot stones. He was doing everything to make this journey as comfortable for her as possible. She did not understand any of this. Nor did she want it. She might have to steal from his mother if she could find no other way to save Emily and Annie.

Nervous melancholy gripped her. Somehow she had to outsmart Thomas. To escape her thoughts, she settled herself in the blankets and tried to sleep. She was exhausted and soon drifted off.

She woke with a start when the carriage jolted to a stop. Strands of hair had come loose from her chignon and she pushed them behind her ears, curious to find out what had made them stop. Peering out the window, she saw the outriders digging dirt and placing it in a large hole directly in front of the carriage.

Ravensford came over. 'They are filling any areas that might cause us to break an axle or become stuck. The last thing we need is a repeat of yesterday.'

'How clever.'

Ravensford gave her a scrutinising look. 'Have you never travelled?'

She shook her head. 'People of my station do not go far from home, my lord.'

He had the grace to look nonplussed. 'Forgive me. I didn't think.' He glanced at the men who still worked. 'Are you finding everything to your satisfaction?'

She was grateful he had changed the subject although this new one was not much more comfortable for her. 'You do too much, my lord. I don't need all of these luxuries.'

She could feel his gaze on her, giving her the sensation that the sun burned down on her exposed skin. Never had a man made her this aware of her senses.

'I already explained why you must arrive in London ready to work.'

'Yes, you did. I don't need all of this to do so. I come of hardy farmer stock.'

'You don't look it,' he murmured, his voice low and caressing and creamy. 'You look as fragile as an orchid and just as exotic.'

She gaped at him, not able to look away any longer. The intensity of his perusal seared to her toes. Confusion held her still. What was he doing?

She jumped to the first conclusion that came to mind and blurted, 'I won't become your mistress.' Instantly embarrassment overwhelmed her. 'That is—oh, dear. I didn't... I don't...'

He watched her, a gleam in his eye. 'Don't worry, Miss O'Brien, I have not asked you.'

The blush that had mounted her cheeks turned to flames. Not even a cool breeze could ease the heat that consumed her. Without considering how rude it would seem, she fell back into the coach and pulled the curtain over the window. She heard Ravensford chuckle softly.

Mortification made her stomach churn. She was such a fool.

Thankfully he did not join her for the rest of the journey. If he had, she would have had to jump out the other side of the carriage. His presence would have been too much to bear. What was she going to do for the rest of the journey? She would not be able to avoid him unless he wanted her to.

Agitation still held her when the carriage finally stopped and the scent of salt water greeted her. Impatient and not wanting Ravensford to open the door for her as he had got into the habit of doing, she opened the door herself and jumped out. She narrowly missed a puddle.

They were at a quay. At the end of the pier floated a sleek ship, probably Ravensford's. He probably called it a yacht.

'We'll be boarding immediately,' Ravensford said, coming up behind her and putting his hand to her elbow.

She had not heard him and it was all she could do not to jump. Her embarrassment rushed back so that she barely felt his fingers on her sleeve.

'I've never sailed before,' she said, not wanting to come anywhere near their last exchange of words.

He smiled down at her. 'You'll enjoy it.'

She let go a sigh of relief. He seemed focussed on sailing. She looked up at him, noting the sparkle in his eyes. 'You must like it.'

'I do.'

His valet came up. 'My lord, be careful. The mud will dirty your Hessians.'

'I shall endeavor to be careful,' Ravensford replied with a look on his face that Mary Margaret was sure hid amused resignation.

With that reassurance, the valet continued on his way, ordering the servant carrying the Earl's trunk to tread cautiously. 'Don't, whatever you do, Tom, drop that in water. That trunk is made of the finest leather.'

Mary Margaret watched the procession, amazed that someone could spend his entire life focussing on another person's clothes.

'Why so glum?' Ravensford asked.

She answered without thinking. 'That poor man is obsessed with your clothing. How boring his life must be.'

'Why do you think that?'

She glanced at him to see if he was having fun with her, but he seemed to be seriously waiting for her reply. 'Because there is so much more to life, and so much of it more important than what one wears.'

'Have you heard of Beau Brummel?'

'Who has not? I find his fixation with fashion to be very shallow.'

As they talked, the Earl continued to steer her toward the end of the pier. Up close the yacht was impressive. A gangplank connected it to land, bobbing with each wave. Mary Margaret gulped. She was not sure this was a safe means of travel. Still, at Ravensford's urging, she stepped forward.

It was worse than she had imagined. Her feet seemed to move without her volition and she was sure that if Ravensford released her elbow she would pitch over the side and into the water.

'Captain, please show Miss O'Brien to the guest cabin and see that she had everything she needs.'

'Yes, my lord.'

Mary Margaret turned to Ravensford. 'Thank you.'

He smiled at her, his eyes dancing in his unfashionably tanned face. The sun buffed his hair into strands of copper.

'I will expect to see you for lunch. It will be served on the deck under that canopy.' He pointed to a bright red and white covering that shaded a small table and several cushions.

Joining him for anything was the last thing she wanted when her knees threatened to melt under her every time he looked at her. But she had no polite refusal.

'As you wish,' she murmured.

Two hours later, she lay prostrate in the double-sized bed of her cabin. Sweat beaded her forehead and upper lip and her stomach buckled with each rise of the boat. Mary Margaret thought she had never felt worse.

'Miss.' The cabin boy's voice penetrated the closed door. 'His lordship requests your presence.'

She mumbled something.

'Pardon?'

'I... I cannot,' Mary Margaret managed to get out. 'I... am not...feeling...well.'

What seemed like an eternity later, the door opened. It was all she could do to force her eyes open. Ravensford entered without permission. He took one look at her and went to the wash basin where he dipped a cloth into the tepid water.

'Why did you not tell someone?' he demanded, squatting down by the bunk and wiping her forehead.

'I...did.' He raised one bronzed brow. She took a deep breath and stated defiantly, 'I told the...boy who...knocked. Ask him.'

Indignation at his refusal to believe gave her the strength to grab the cloth from his hand. She wadded it up and pressed it to her mouth.

He frowned. 'Why didn't you tell me you get seasick?'

She squeezed the cloth until her knuckles turned white. 'If I had known I would have said something. Besides—' she fought the nausea down '—how else would I get to England?'

'True.' He rose on legs long accustomed to ships. 'I will be back in a moment.'

Mary Margaret stifled a moan. The last thing she wanted was to have him near her. She knew she was not a pretty woman and being sick did nothing to enhance what looks she had. Nor did she want him being around if she lost control of her stomach. She could think of nothing more humiliating.

With a groan she rolled to her side, facing the wall, and curled into a tight knot. Surely she could survive until they reached land.

The ship lurched, or so it seemed to her heightened nerves, and she wrapped her arms around her middle. At the same time, the door opened.

'Here, I've brought something for your nausea.'

The Earl's deep voice would have been arresting any other time. She turned her head just enough to look balefully up at him.

'Unless it is poison,' she muttered, closing her eyes so as not to see the rocking cabin, 'there is nothing you can do to help.'

'Keep your eyes open and focus on something.'

Instead of answering, she curled up tighter, wishing he would go away. His hand on her shoulder shocked and angered her.

'For pity's sake, go away and let me suffer in private.' She heard him chuckle, and her wrath grew. 'How would you like to have someone bothering you when you wanted to die?'

'I tried to shoot my benefactor,' he said, all the humour gone.

'What?' She rolled on to her back to see his face.

His smile was twisted. 'It was after Salamanca.' His eyes took on a faraway look, but only for a moment. 'Now, drink this. Stevens prepared it. He claims it has ginger root and will do wonders.'

'Ginger root.' She reached with trembling hands for the mug. 'My mother would give us ginger root in warm water when we had stomach aches. It always worked.'

'Good.'

He kept hold of the mug, his fingers warm against her own. Part of her was glad. She shook so badly that without his help she would likely spill the contents. Still, some of the contents dribbled down her chin.

'You should be sitting up more.'

He took the cup from her, set it down on a table with rails to keep the cup from sliding off, and turned back to her. While he did that, she manoeuvred herself into a semi-sitting position.

'I would have helped,' he said.

Which was the last thing she wanted. Even as sick as she felt, his touch still disturbed her in ways she did not want to experience.

'Thank you, but I can manage on my own. It should not be long before the ginger settles my stomach.'

He studied her dispassionately.

Mary Margaret felt even more dishevelled and grimy than before. Unconsciously she raised one hand to smooth her tangled hair back from her face. Large strands had worked loose from her chignon. She had to look a fright.

His gaze intensified. 'Drink your ginger root tea and after I will brush your hair.'

Heat mounted her cheeks, receded and came back. The idea of him stroking her hair was exciting and tempting. She told herself that having her chignon in place would make her feel almost well. That was the reason she was so tempted to let him care for her. Nothing else. She resisted.

'After I finish the drink I will be more than able to care for myself.'

'You are as weak as a kitten.'

He put the mug to her lips and tipped it so that she had to swallow. He had moved so quickly and she had been thinking about his fingers in her hair that she was caught unawares and more of the liquid dribbled down her chin. He kept the mug to her mouth until she finished. After he laid the empty container down he took the cloth from her unresisting hand and gently wiped the tea from her chin.

'Since you don't want me to brush your hair, I will take you on deck. Some fresh air will make all the difference.'

'I do not think I am up to being moved,' she mumbled.

'You look better already, and you will be glad you did,' he said, reaching down.

Before she knew what he was about, he had lifted her to his chest. She gasped. 'What are you doing?'

He shook his head as though she were a dense child and smiled down at her. 'What does it feel like, Miss O'Brien? I am taking you up on deck. The sea is calm and the fresh air will make the ginger work much faster.'

'But…but…'

Her mouth worked but nothing more came out. His arms were comforting and strong. His heart beat steadily against her cheek. This was awful.

Ravensford strode to the door of her cabin and out.

# Chapter Five

The cabin boy stood outside the door. When he saw the couple his mouth dropped open. Mary Margaret gave him a hesitant smile and wished herself anywhere but here.

'Put me down,' she hissed, her nausea abated by shock. 'This is not appropriate.'

Ravensford shrugged. 'This is my yacht and I shall do as I please. Right now it pleases me to take you on deck.'

'What if I lose control and…and…?'

'Vomit on me? You shan't be the first.'

He was insufferable.

The Captain was coming down the stairs when he saw them. He stopped in his tracks. 'My lord? May I be of assistance?'

Ravensford grinned at him. 'Make sure no one is coming down as I am going up.'

'Yes, sir.' The Captain retraced his steps. 'All clear, my lord.'

'Thank you.' Ravensford started up.

Mary Margaret was appalled. She should have never come on this journey, no matter what Thomas threatened. Never. She would not be able to look at anyone on this boat knowing they had seen this débâcle. They would think there was more between herself and Ravensford than that of servant and master.

She groaned and buried her face against Ravensford's chest. His heartbeat was oddly reassuring. He was a large man and held her easily, his arms surrounding her comfortably. She felt protected. She belonged in Bedlam.

'Here you are,' he murmured, setting her down.

Her feet hit the deck and she swayed. Immediately his arm was back around her waist, holding her tightly to his side. What had seemed protective just seconds before was now something entirely different. The breath caught in Mary Margaret's throat as the heat of his body penetrated their clothing. She did not know which was worse, being held in his arms or being held to the length of his body.

'I am perfectly able to stand on my own,' she finally managed to say, pushing against his chest.

He looked down at her. 'Are you sure?'

His concern took her aback. 'Yes. Quite.'

He released her. She stumbled backward and tripped over a chair that had been placed beside a table that was laden with food. She twisted around, reaching for something to hold on to. Her left ankle twisted.

'Oh,' she moaned as her left leg went out from under her.

Ravensford grabbed for her.

The last thing she wanted was for him to hold her. She had had more than she could tolerate already. She scooted away. Her hand caught something cold and hard. She realised it was the ship's railing just instants before she tumbled over it.

She hit the water with an icy splash. She sank down, her skirts pulling her deeper. Fear galvanised her. She struggled to the surface and gasped for air. She did not know how to swim. Her legs tangled in her skirts. Her arms flailed.

Ravensford watched in horror as Mary Margaret disappeared over the side of the yacht. Without even thinking, he shed his coat and boots and dived into the water. He surfaced several feet from her just in time to see her sink beneath the surface for a second time.

He dived again, kicking with all his strength. The salt water burned his eyes, but he had to keep her in sight. Mercifully he caught her. He circled her waist with one arm and thrust upward with his legs and free arm.

He thought his lungs would burst, but he had to get them to the surface. Her skirts twisted around his legs, making it next to impossible to get any power, and added to her weight. Without a second thought, he ripped the woollen fabric from her body. The loss of weight made her seem nearly buoyant. He kicked hard, sending them upward.

They popped into the air and both breathed deeply. Ravensford trod water, one hand under Mary Margaret's shoulders and the other moving in circles to help keep them afloat.

'Stay calm, sweetings,' he murmured. 'Everything is fine. They will get us.'

Her large, scared eyes clung to his. She nodded, her lips trembling.

'Breathe,' he commanded. 'Breathe.'

It was only minutes before the yacht lowered a boat. To Ravensford, watching Mary Margaret's pale face, it seemed like an eternity.

He felt the heat seep from his own body and knew Mary Margaret was in worse shape. She had been in the water longer and was slimmer. He had to get her out of here.

'Hold on to my neck,' he ordered, rolling to his side. Her teeth chattered and her lips were blue, but she nodded and did as he said. 'That's my girl.'

Her wide, frightened eyes stared into his. He forced a smile and started kicking. They moved slowly toward the oncoming boat. Hands reached for them not a minute too soon.

Ravensford thrust Mary Margaret into the arms of the first seaman and pushed her into the small vessel. When she was safely on board, he followed.

She huddled on the wooden seat, a tiny, bedraggled ball. Her shoulders shook. He slid next to her and gathered her close. Using his hands, he chafed her arms.

'Are there no blankets?' he demanded, his voice harsh with worry.

'No, milord,' one of the two seamen answered, never stopping in his rowing.

Disgusted, Ravensford pulled her on to his lap. Anything to warm her chill skin. She did not protest. She did not say a thing. That, more than anything else, scared him.

'Come on, sweetings, rail at me,' he ordered, rubbing her back and arms.

Instead of speaking, she burrowed deeper into the warmth of his body. He groaned.

Finally they reached the yacht and a rope stair was lowered. There was no way he could climb it and carry Mary Margaret.

'You have to let go of me,' he murmured, stroking the hair from her face. 'You have to climb that rope.'

She looked from him to the ladder. Her jaw clenched, and he felt her tremble. But she rose from his lap and gripped the rope. Slowly, she climbed.

He followed closely behind, ready to catch her if she slipped. Only now that she was nearly safe did Ravensford notice her clothing. He had ripped her skirts away so that only her pantaloons remained. They were translucent.

He swallowed hard.

Her derrière swelled enticingly against the white fabric. Her hips flared out into shapely thighs.

He climbed up behind her, noticing that the Captain was trying to keep his gaze averted from Mary Margaret's near nakedness. Ravensford smiled wryly. The Captain was a better man than he. He had completely given up on looking away. But that did not mean he would leave her exposed like this for everyone to see.

He grabbed his coat from the deck and wrapped it around her before lifting her and striding to the stairs. Her head fell back on his shoulder. Her face was white and her breath came in little sobs. All he wanted was to comfort her.

Minutes later, he shouldered open her cabin door and entered, closing it behind them. He laid her gently on the bed.

Her eyes opened. 'I have never been more scared in my life,' she whispered, her lips still blue.

'And all my fault,' he said, smoothing her loose hair back from her forehead.

She smiled wanly. 'No. I am the one whose clumsiness sent me pitching over the side.'

He took his coat from her and quickly wrapped a blanket around her, careful to keep his gaze averted. 'If I had notinsisted on taking you on deck, it would have never happened.'

Her eyes closed and she sank back into the pillow.

He gazed at her, unable to resist the memory of her nearly naked in his arms. Her full, rounded breasts pressed against his chest, their tips rosy and taut from cold as they strained against the thin fabric of her chemise. Her rounded hips and slender thighs snuggled into his loins. His body tightened painfully. He closed his eyes, knowing that he could not stop himself from picturing her naked and in his bed.

Her hand on his arm drew his awareness. He took a deep breath and looked at her.

Her black brows were drawn in worry. 'Are you getting sick, my lord? You look in pain.'

He groaned. Seducing her and getting her to tell him everything about the plan to steal from his mother was supposed to be a last resort if he could not win her trust. Picturing her naked in his bed was not going to accomplish his goal.

He forced himself to speak clearly instead of rasping like someone pushed to his physical limit. 'I am fine, Miss O'Brien. You are the one who is not feeling well.'

He straightened and moved away. Still, the outline of her body under the blanket did things to him that made his skin-hugging wet pantaloons even tighter.

'I am not seasick any more,' she said, a hint of amusement in her voice.

The deep purr of her voice slid along his nerves, adding to his discomfort. He had to get out of here or he would ravish her—immediately, without any regard for what she wanted.

'I will get Stevens, Miss O'Brien. He will have just the thing to keep you from getting a fever.'

He strode from the room, shutting the cabin door firmly behind himself. For long moments he stood with his back to the wall, taking deep breaths and trying to tame his body.

It was no use. Every time he saw her he was going to see the way she looked lying in that bed, her luscious figure as good as bare.

'My lord,' Stevens said, coming up the tiny hallway, 'are you ill?'

He released a bark of laughter. Ill with desire and there was only one cure for that. 'No, Stevens, but I fear Miss O'Brien might become so if she is not given one of your possets.'

The valet became brisk. 'Tut, tut. We cannot have that, my lord. The Countess's maid told me the responsibility Miss O'Brien will have in London. There is no time for the young woman to be sick.'

'Right you are,' Ravensford managed. 'No time at all.'

'You go change, my lord.' Stevens gave his master an appalled look. 'That is—'

'I can take my own clothes off and put others on,' Ravensford said. 'The results won't be as polished as when you assist me, but I will be decent.'

His thoughts flicked again to Mary Margaret. What would it be like to have her undress him? He could not think of that right now.

'Of course, my lord. Then I shall take care of Miss O'Brien. Do not worry about a thing.'

Only my sanity, Ravensford thought, as he watched Stevens enter Miss O'Brien's cabin. No woman had ever aroused him this quickly and completely. His reaction was as disconcerting as it was pleasurable.

Nor had any woman aroused his protective instincts as she had. He could tell himself all he wanted that he was concerned because her brush with death had been his fault, but he knew that was only part of it. Mary Margaret O'Brien was beginning to matter to him.

Mary Margaret tugged at her hair with a brush. They were docking any moment now and her hair was still damp. If she put it in a chignon, it would never dry. If she wore it loose, she would look like a doxy.

And her dress. She wore her second-best dress. Her travelling outfit was at the bottom of the sea. Her chemise and pantaloons were stiff from salt and would have to wait until they stopped for the night before she could properly wash them. Everything was a mess.

But she was not seasick. That was a great comfort.

A knock on her door preceded the Earl's voice. 'Miss O'Brien, we are docked and will be unloading immediately. We have a ways to go before we reach tonight's inn.'

She jumped up, twisting her hair into a knot. Heat suffused her entire body. Only when she had changed clothes had she realised that her pantaloons and chemise might as well not have existed for all the cover they had given her. Ravensford had seen every inch of her as though she had been naked. And so had the crew. The last thing she wanted was the Earl in this cabin.

'I am ready, my lord,' she said hurriedly, breathlessly. 'I will be out.'

'Good. I will meet you on deck in five minutes.'

'Yes, my lord.'

'Ravensford.'

She heard him move away. What had he thought about her dishabille? Had it disgusted him that she had not even realised her exposure and so had not shown any modesty? She moaned. Nor had she thanked him for saving her life.

With a groan she realised that one hand still held her hair twisted into a knot on her neck. She quickly jabbed several pins into the thick tresses until they were secure. She would worry about drying her hair later. As it was, the strands smelled of sea water and salt. She would have to wash it when they got to the inn. Until then, there was nothing else she could do.

This trip was horrible. Her only consolation was that it could not possibly get worse.

She was wrong. Having the gaze of every crew member watching her walk the gangplank was excruciating. The only thing that got her through the gauntlet was pride. Ravensford waited for her.

His eyes smouldered as she approached him. His gaze swept over her. She remembered all too clearly how she had looked when she rose from the bunk to change and caught sight of herself in the mirror. He had seen her all but naked.

Embarrassment flooded her cheeks.

'You look none the worse for your ducking,' he said, extending his arm.

She sighed and considered walking past him, but that would only add to the speculation so rampant in the faces of the men watching them. She stopped and laid her fingers lightly on his arm, nearly wincing from the heat he radiated.

'I owe you a great debt, my lord.'

He frowned. 'You are a stubborn woman. How many times must I order you to call me Ravensford?'

She quirked one brow at him, and instantly regretted it. His smile could charm the chemise off a lady of Quality, let alone someone as susceptible to him as she was.

'I would berate you over not using my name,' he murmured so no one else could hear, 'but it would do no good.'

She did not answer, thinking herself lucky they were in public and the heat in his gaze could not be directed at her in a more physical manner. She was weak enough to succumb.

'Let me help you up,' he said, stopping and putting his large, strong hands around her waist.

Totally immersed in what she imaged his kiss would be like, Mary Margaret was taken by surprise. 'Wha…what are you doing?' she babbled.

He smiled down at her. 'Lifting you into my phaeton.'

She looked up and gulped. He was too close and the contraption he wanted to put her into was too high. She gripped one of his forearms with each hand and pushed him until he released her. She stepped back.

Raised in the country, Mary Margaret had never seen a carriage like the one before her. It was high off the ground, with room for two only. The finish was a glossy hunter green with thin black lines outlining the curves. Two prancing chestnuts stood impatiently in the traces, a young boy in the Earl's livery holding them in place. Altogether a dangerous means of transportation.

'What kind of vehicle is this?'

He laughed. 'This is a high-perch phaeton. The fastest carriage on the roads.'

'And the most deadly,' she said flatly.

He sobered instantly. 'Not with the right driver.'

She stepped away, not wanting to be any closer to the thing than she had to be. 'Isn't there another carriage I can ride in? The baggage must be somewhere. I will go with it. 'Tis only proper.'

He caught her as she turned away. 'I am considered a fair hand with the ribbons, Miss O'Brien. I won't tip you into a ditch.'

"Is lordship be a prime member o' the Four-in-'and Club, miss,' the young boy said proudly.

Ravensford smiled at the lad. 'Thank you, Peter.'

'Whatever the Four-in-Hand Club is,' Mary Margaret muttered.

Scandalised, the youth spoke up again. 'It be a group of swells what knows how to 'andle the ribbons like no others. 'Is lordship is the best.'

'Thank you again, Peter,' Ravensford said. 'I think I can deal with this on my own now.'

The lad flushed.

'I can get you to the inn much quicker this way, Miss O'Brien. You can eat and be in bed by the time the baggage carriage reaches the inn. Think about how nice it will be to have a full stomach and a nice soft bed that does not move.'

She eyed him. He had a point. Exhaustion ate at her and her stomach fussed at her. She looked back at the phaeton.

'I promise not to spill you,' Ravensford said as though reading her mind.

'Well...'

'Up with you, then,' he said.

Before she realised what he intended, his hands were around her waist and lifting her up. It was either step into the carriage or continue to be held aloft by him. Entering the phaeton was more dignified and less intimate than his hands wrapped around her waist.

She sat down gingerly, feeling the carriage sway slightly. When Ravensford climbed in, the vehicle bounced on well-sprung wheels. The breath caught in her throat. Then he sat beside her, and she scooted to the very edge of the seat, only to look down. The ground seemed a long way away.

She sighed.

'I won't bite,' he said, a wicked grin belying his words.

Before she could think of a suitable reply, Stevens hurried up with a blanket. 'This is for Miss O'Brien,' he said, handing it to her. 'It would not do for you to catch an inflammation, miss, after your ducking.'

She took the warm wool covering. 'Thank you, Stevens. This will be very nice.'

Ravensford took the blanket from her without asking and spread it over her lap and legs. His gloved fingers moved over her thighs with a sureness that made the breath catch in her throat. Seconds before she had worried about falling out and breaking her neck. Now she knew the greater danger was sitting so closely to the Earl.

They could travel as fast as the wind and it would still be too slow for her peace of mind and body.

# Chapter Six

The carriage came to a sudden halt and Mary Margaret jolted awake, her cheek bumping against something hard and unyielding. Dazed, she pummelled whatever her head had been resting on.

'That is my shoulder, if you don't mind,' a deep voice drawled.

Memory came back in a mortifying rush. She was in the Earl's high-perch phaeton which he had stored here in England while he had been in Ireland. The baggage carriage he had hired was somewhere behind them.

'Pardon me, my lord.' She sat up and straightened her bonnet, which had fallen to one side of her head.

'Let me do that.' He angled around after handing the reins to his tiger.

'Thank you, but I can manage.' The last thing she wanted was for him to touch her. He had already had his hands on her more than enough these last twenty-four hours.

He ignored her—as usual.

He carefully set the bonnet to rights, leaning back to get a better look. He shifted it slightly to one side. She glared at him. He smiled lazily. His eyes held hers captive as his fingers dropped to the ribbons tied under her chin. He undid the knotted bow and retied the silk into a rakish bow just under her right ear.

'There. A lady's maid could not have done better.'

The urge to say something scathing nearly overwhelmed her good sense. But she managed not to make a difficult moment more so.

'Thank you again,' she muttered, trying hard to keep her resentment from coming out.

He jumped abruptly from the carriage and held an imperious hand up to her. Another touch. She sighed. The only way to stop this was to grit her teeth and do what was necessary so that she could get to her room.

He smiled up at her, the emotion reaching his eyes and making the corners crinkle. Somehow he knew his touch bothered her. She never had been good at hiding her feelings.

'Come along. You need some food and rest.'

Her gaze skittered away from his. His voice had been deep and dark, hinting at things she only barely understood and definitely did not want to delve into. Still, her heart pounded and her skin tingled when she put her fingers in his. He helped her down, continuing to hold her hand longer than was necessary.

'Thank you,' she murmured. Then added with some asperity, 'I can walk on my own, just not on a boat.'

Even to her own ears her words had been breathy and disturbed. No wonder he continued to gaze at her, his fingers wrapped firmly around her skin. Was it her imagination, or was his face closer? Her heart skipped a beat.

He laughed. 'I hope never to have such an experience again. You scared ten years off my life.'

A strange fluttering started in her stomach. 'Well, I can assure you that the ducking did not prolong mine any.'

Belatedly, she realised that he still held her hand. She pulled but, instead of releasing her, he tucked her fingers into the crook of his elbow. His attentions were too marked. She caught one of the outriders watching with a smirk on his face. She looked away.

'I have bespoken dinner and rooms. There should be no delays before you seek your bed.'

She started shivering. He took off his many-caped great coat and wrapped it around her.

'Come,' he said, leading her to the front door.

She followed without protest, too shocked by his behaviour to do anything else. He treated her as though she was a lady of Quality and someone whose comfort he cared about. He made her feel safe.

She stumbled inside, Ravensford's arm supporting her. The landlord stood eyeing them. His gaze went from her to the Earl.

'My lord,' the owner said, rushing forward. 'Your rooms are ready and supper will be served immediately. I kept the parlour for you.'

Ravensford nodded his head. 'Thank you, John. Please show Miss O'Brien to her room so she can change into dry clothes.'

The landlord nodded, casting a scandalised look at Mary Margaret. 'Will your man be bringing in the luggage, my lord?'

Ravensford nodded. 'I will wait for you, Miss O'Brien, before starting supper.'

Mary Margaret felt dazed. Too much too fast. With fingers numb from nerves, she pulled the Earl's coat off and handed it to him.

'I would be happy with toast and butter and a pot of hot tea in my room.'

'I have bespoken dinner, Miss O'Brien, and I would like your company.'

Aware of the landlord watching them, she nodded. 'As you wish, my lord.'

'I will expect you as soon as you have freshened up.'

He turned and strode back to the coach yard. He had not been this high-handed with his mother. When she had requested something, he had agreed. Did he treat all other women this way, or only her?

'This way, miss,' the landlord said, breaking into her thoughts.

She followed him up a flight of stairs. He paused and opened a door.

'His lordship's room is across the hall.'

She glanced sharply at the man, wondering if there was more to his words. His countenance was bland.

'Thank you.'

'Dinner will be served downstairs, in the room next to the commons.'

'Thank you,' she said again as she slipped inside.

She shut the door slowly, giving the landlord time to back away. Immediately there was a knock. This time it was one of the Earl's servants, delivering her portmanteau.

'Thank you,' she said once again, smiling at the man.

When she was finally alone, she turned to view her

room—and froze. This had to be one of the best, if not the best, available. A large four-poster bed took pride of place with a massive wardrobe and elaborate nightstand grouped around it. The fire was ablaze with two chairs pulled cosily close. Flowers in muted colours rioted beneath her feet.

She shook her head in amazement.

Another knock brought a sigh of exasperation. Who was it this time? She opened the door to a bobbing maid.

'His lordship ordered a bath.'

Another maid appeared, lugging a hip tub. Before Mary Margaret could protest, everything was arranged and the maids were gone. She was cold and grimy and the steaming water was an invitation she could not resist. It felt so good to get the salt out of her hair.

She was clean, warm in her second-best dress and half-asleep when the summons came. The maid who had brought the tub said, 'His lordship sent me to escort you to his private dining room, miss.'

Mary Margaret's first inclination was to plead exhaustion. She could not be so rude. Ravensford had taken every care for her comfort, the least she could do was go down and thank him. She did not have to stay. With that self-deluding thought, she followed the maid.

The maid left her at the door.

Mary Margaret took a deep breath and told herself that the tightness in her chest was due to the soaking she had taken earlier. The same for her shaking fingers. Resolutely, she knocked. His deep baritone bid her enter and the air went out of her lungs.

She chided herself for overreacting. He was her employer.

If he ever found out that the sound of his voice made her stomach feel like lightning was striking it, he would laugh.

In one fluid motion she turned the handle and entered. He stood near the fire, one forearm resting on the mantel, one booted foot propped on the andiron. His brown jacket fit his lean form loosely. The collar of his white shirt was open. His casualness accentuated the rugged lines of his face.

Her pulse jumped.

To hide the delight she felt, Mary Margaret bobbed a curtsy and averted her face so that she talked to the fire. 'Thank you for everything, my lord. You have been more than kind. I must return to my room now.'

His low chuckle was like velvet stroking her skin, but his voice was firm. 'It's Ravensford and you will eat something first.'

'I'm not hungry.' She backed up. The room was suddenly overly hot.

He smiled and a dimple peeked out of his left cheek, softening the harsh lines of his jaw. She wondered if he knew how devastating his smile was. Probably.

'Truly, I am more tired than hungry. But I thank you for offering.'

He lifted one brow. 'Another argument over dinner, Miss O'Brien? This becomes boring.'

She lifted her chin. 'Then you will not wish my company, my lord.'

He laughed. 'Very good, but not good enough. Sit down and be done with this.'

He moved to the table placed just in front of the fire and lifted the cover off one of the dishes. The aroma of roast beef filled the room, making her stomach growl. Lunch had been a long time ago. She blushed at the indelicacy.

He eyed her knowingly. 'Come, eat some of this and then I promise to let you go.'

He was right, she needed to eat. She sank into the chair he had indicated.

He carved a large piece of beef and set it on a plate, added some potatoes and peas, and set it all in front of her. Next he handed her the tea and let her lace it with cream and sugar. He poured himself an amber-coloured liquid with a smoky scent.

He sat after loading his plate with twice what he had put on hers. Neither spoke much for a while.

Ravensford watched her eat with dainty dispatch. He could almost image delicate whiskers twitching. When her pointed pink tongue darted out to lick a drop of tea from her lip his gut clenched. Pictures of her lying practically naked in the bunk raged through his mind. Blood pounded in his ears. He took a deep breath. He wondered if she knew how arousing she was. Perhaps not.

She looked up and caught him looking at her. He smiled. 'You eat like a cat, delicately and focussed,' he said.

She laid her fork and knife down. He watched her magnificent bosom swell as she watched him. He knew she wanted to say something, probably not complimentary, but was restraining herself.

After a long pause, she said, 'My lord, why are you treating me like this? I am not Quality, nor am I your responsibility.'

He leaned back in his chair, finished with his food even though half of it still remained on his plate. He sipped his whiskey and eyed her over the glass rim. Why was he treating her this way?

He had set out to gain her trust, but that did not mean he

had to treat her like a prized companion or force his presence on her when she did not want it. Nor did he have to be the one to dive in to save her. Any one of his sailors could have done so. Just as Stevens could have nursed her through her seasickness from the beginning.

Why was he doing this?

The answer was startling, although he instantly realised it should not be. His reaction to her was stronger than he'd had to any other woman. His body was like an adolescent around her, aroused and aching all the time.

'Be my mistress. I will pay you well and you will no longer have to endure my mother's slights.'

She dropped the cup of tea she had just lifted to her lips. It hit the table with a thump, sending scalding tea all over the cloth. Neither one paid it any mind.

'You jest, and very cruelly,' she said.

Amazed at his bluntness, Ravensford shook his head slowly. 'No, I don't believe I do, Miss O'Brien—Mary Margaret. In fact, I have never been so serious about asking a woman to become my mistress as I am now.'

Her bosom heaved in agitation and her eyes flashed anger. Even knowing she was about to refuse him, he enjoyed the show. She was not a traditional beauty, but she appealed very much to him.

She licked her lips and his loins tightened. He downed the whiskey, wondering if it would numb his nether parts. He could only try, for it was obvious she was not going to help him in that area.

She stormed to her feet. 'I am not…not a loose woman. I might not be your equal, my lord, but that does not make me someone you can take advantage of so cavalierly.'

He stood, admiring the way fury put colour into her

high cheeks and brought a flutter to her breasts. How he wanted her.

'My apologies, Miss O'Brien. It was my baser self speaking.' He gave her a roguish grin. 'But should you change your mind, don't hesitate to tell me.'

She stalked to the door. Turning, she asked, 'May I be excused?'

Sarcasm was something he had not heard in her throaty voice before. He did not like hearing it now, but he deserved it. He had overstepped the bounds of propriety.

He bowed her from the room, wondering how he was going to survive the rest of the journey in such close proximity to her.

It was just as well that she had refused him. She was a potential thief, not a potential mistress—no matter what his body said.


Mary Margaret woke before the sun was up. She sat up, only to fall back on to the pillows. Her head felt like a herd of sheep pounded through it. Her throat hurt. Her heart ached.

She moaned.

She did not know which felt worse, her body or her spirit. Just moving was an effort, but remembering last night was a nightmare. Ravensford had asked her to be his mistress and she had turned him down. Shame warred with anger and regret with relief.

She rolled to her side, ignoring the tightness in her chest, and buried her face in the pillow. The linens were still damp from her tears of last night. Exhaustion was the only reason she had been able to sleep, and even then her dreams had been full of loss and longing.

How could she face him today? With luck, she would die of consumption and not have to. She was being a coward. Ravensford was the one who should be ashamed, not she. He was the one who had acted improperly, not she.

She flipped on to her back, fists clenched, jaw clamped. Her head protested with a sharp pain at the temples. No matter how she felt, she needed to get up. They were leaving at dawn.

She managed to dress herself. Determination held her upright when she swayed on her feet. She had survived worse. She would live through this. However, a cup of tea laced with honey and cream would be very nice.

When the maid knocked, she was ready. Carrying her portmanteau, she followed the woman downstairs. Ravensford sat in the common room and chose that moment to look up from his ham and ale.

He rose and walked to Mary Margaret, his stride loose-hipped and easy. To her jaundiced eye, he looked like nothing had occurred between them.

'Please join me,' he said, stopping just short of her, his fresh citrus scent filling her senses.

She studied him through narrowed eyes. 'No, thank you,' she said, her voice a painful rasp in her throat.

He frowned. 'You are sick. Come and have some tea and toast. I will send for Stevens to fix you another one of his possets.'

She shook her head and winced. 'I don't want anything to eat and would prefer to have my tea in the carriage.'

He took her by the arm and propelled her toward his table. She resisted the urge to dig her heels in. When they reached the seats, she forced a false smile to her lips.

'You must not have heard me, my lord, but I prefer to take tea in the carriage.'

Ravensford gave her a tight stretch of lips. 'I know what you would prefer, but you and I have some things to discuss.'

She blanched.

'My lord,' the proprietor said, coming in through the door from the kitchen with a laden tray. 'The lady's tea is ready.'

Ravensford resumed his seat and the landlord set out the teapot, cream, sugar, cup and saucer, and a plate of scones with butter and marmalade. In spite of her sore throat, the smell of warm bread and steaming tea drew her. When the proprietor looked expectantly at her, she gave in.

'Please bring some honey,' Ravensford said, 'and see if someone can find my valet.'

The landlord hurried out on his errands.

Mary Margaret felt Ravensford's gaze as she fixed a cup of tea and a scone. When she glanced up at him, his attention was on her fingers as she broke off a piece of the pastry. His gaze followed her fingers and the scone to her mouth. A dark hunger entered his eyes, making them appear hunter green in the dim light of the room. She shivered.

His eyes met hers. 'I want you.'

His voice was deep and husky. His mouth was a grim curve of sensualness. Her stomach churned as her body went from cold to hot. The scone dropped from nerveless fingers.

'I... I told you last night, my lord,' she said, her voice a harsh whisper.

'That was last night. Tell me again,' he demanded, his gaze never leaving her face.

Her chest constricted and she felt as though she was suffocating. The room was unbearably warm. One hand fluttered to the high neckline of her dress.

'I am not that kind of woman.' She took a deep breath. 'Please stop asking me.'

His lips thinned, but he leaned back in his chair. 'My apologies,' he finally said, his voice nearly normal. 'I have never wanted a woman as I want you. I find it harder than I would have thought to take no for an answer.'

She gulped, more uncomfortable than she could remember being in a long time. Turning her face away from the intensity of his, she started to rise. One of his large, strong hands caught her wrist, keeping her sitting.

'Please don't go,' he said. 'You need the food and tea. I will leave.'

She nodded, unable to reply.

But instead of standing, he said, 'We will put this behind us—for now. You are under my protection and it was ungentlemanly of me. However...' he gave her a rueful grin '... I think it would be best if you make the rest of the journey in the baggage carriage with Stevens. You are sick and the exposure of the phaeton would not be good for you, and I am not at my best around you.'

He stood abruptly, bowed and left her.

She stared after him, nonplussed. Everything had happened so quickly and her head felt like it was packed with cotton. At least she did not have to continue travelling in the Earl's company. He was as much a temptation to her as he claimed she was to him.

Stevens said from behind her, 'Miss O'Brien, do you know where his lordship has gone? He sent for me.'

Still dazed, she turned to look at the valet. 'I don't know.'

'You have a cold,' the valet said. 'I will fix you another posset.'

Even as she murmured her thanks, he left, moving swiftly and purposefully. She knew that in a short time the posset would arrive. She wished her heart could be cured as easily as Stevens's posset intended to cure her inflammation. Right now she felt as though her world would never be the same again.

With a sigh, she drank the now-lukewarm tea.

Ravensford watched Mary Margaret climb into the baggage carriage. Even though she was bundled up as though she expected a snow storm, he could still make out the line of her hips. He shook his head in exasperation. He was like a boy still wet behind the ears where she was concerned.

Besides, he had not arranged this trip so he could seduce her—not originally. His plan was to gain her trust and get her to tell him about the plan to rob his mother. Now he would be lucky if she even spoke to him again.

He sighed and turned away from the inn window. Stevens stood patiently by the door, waiting for instructions.

'See that Miss O'Brien has every comfort,' Ravensford said, taking a full purse from his bed and giving it to the valet. 'I shall be travelling on ahead. With good weather and no problems, I can be in London within the week. You will be much slower.'

'Yes, my lord,' Stevens said, taking the money.

'I know I can count on you.'

A smile of genuine pleasure lit the valet's face before he left. Ravensford turned back to the window. He had not planned on travelling ahead, but even as he had said the words he had known they were for the best.

Mary Margaret had refused his offer of protection; the last thing she or he needed was for him to continue importuning her. Much as he desired her, his actions disgusted him. He did not believe in taking advantage of others, particularly those less fortunate than him.

So why was he so determined to have her? He did not know, but he was going to stop this stupidity once and for all. A separation was the best thing for him.

Unfortunately, she very likely agreed.

## Chapter Seven

Excitement held Mary Margaret spellbound as they reached the London outskirts. Not even Steven's severe countenance could dampen her spirits. He was frowning at her because she insisted on opening the window so she could see everything better. He did not want her to have a relapse from the cool spring air.

She had not seen the Earl since he passed them on the road their first day out from the inn. She told herself it was better this way, but no amount of reasoning eased the ache in her heart. She would have never thought it possible to care for someone she barely knew, but against all logic she did.

So what if there was no excitement to her day and each hour dragged by? She was used to life's easy flow. If she was bored, then it was her own fault as her mother had so often said. When they reached the Earl's town house she would use some of her precious money to send Emily a letter. Her sister would love to hear all about London.

In order to have plenty to write about, Mary Margaret

concentrated on the outside. There were people everywhere, dressed in all manner of styles. Vendors crowded the streets.

The coach slowed and she noticed that while there were still plenty of pedestrians, they were more stylish. The men resembled the Earl, the women the Countess. More phaetons and curricles passed them, all drawn by prime horseflesh. The houses were larger and more ornately decorated.

Shortly, the carriage stopped. Stevens got out without giving her a glance. She told herself that was as it should be. Still, a rebellious part of her missed the Earl's attentions.

She chided herself. Not only was she silly, she was wicked. The Earl had made his intentions clear and they were not honourable.

Gathering the skirts of her only presentable dress into one hand, she jumped out. Before her stood a house more grand than the Countess's estate in Ireland. She craned her neck to see up to the roof. Four stories, all with elegantly carved windows and cornices. The house fit her impression of Ravensford—powerful and magnificent.

Belatedly, she realised they were at the servants' entrance. She could not image what the front looked like. An open door emitted delicious smells so she entered and found herself in the kitchen. A man speaking French and waving around a butcher's knife could only be the chef. Young boys scrambled to do his bidding, whether they understood him or not. Several girls scrubbed big copper pots.

She stood in the middle of the jumble, not knowing what to do or where to go. She had just decided to go back outside and fetch her portmanteau when a short woman stopped in front of her.

'You must be Miss O'Brien. I am Mrs Brewster, the housekeeper. Come along, now. No sense dawdling in the

Frenchie's domain. Gaston fixes the best meals in London, but his temperament is volatile.' She shook her head and started off without glancing back to see if Mary Margaret followed.

Mary Margaret trailed the housekeeper's tiny, black-clad figure from the kitchen. Just past the green baize door were a narrow set of stairs. Mrs Brewster started up them. Two flights up, the housekeeper took a turn and came out on a wide landing. Delicate carpeting muffled their steps. Silver sconces with wax candles flooded the area with light. They were in the family portion of the house.

Three doors down, the housekeeper turned to face Mary Margaret. The older woman's face was narrow and lined at the mouth and eyes. Her brown hair was thick and braided tightly to her head. A delicate white cap perched properly on her crown. Her hazel eyes looked Mary Margaret over. She must have liked what she saw because she smiled.

'His lordship told me to put you here. If there is anything you'll be needing, let me know. A boy will bring your luggage up shortly. I will have a tray sent up. I am sure you are hungry and thirsty.'

Mary Margaret smiled in relief. She had been afraid that Mrs Brewster would somehow know the Earl had asked her to become his mistress. If the housekeeper did know, she was still treating Mary Margaret like a respectable lady.

'Thank you, Mrs Brewster. Thank you so much.'

The older woman smiled gently. 'I know how strange it can be your first time in London. And I know what a large task you have ahead of you. I'll do my best to help you.'

Mary Margaret blinked back tears. She was exhausted. Mrs Brewster opened the door and Mary Margaret entered, hearing it close behind her. She stood transfixed by the grandeur of the room. Surely there was some mistake.

She yanked open the door and, seeing Mrs Brewster's figure just disappearing around the corner, ran after her. 'Madam, Mrs Brewster,' she gasped when she caught up with the other woman, 'there must be some mistake. I am the Countess's companion, not a guest.'

Mrs Brewster shook her head. 'No, miss, there is not. His lordship picked the room himself.'

Mary Margaret took a step back. Oh, dear. Even after her refusal, Ravensford had continued to get her the best rooms available in the inns they stopped at, but she had thought that was just consideration and that things would return to a more normal aspect once they reached London.

'Thank you, Mrs Brewster.' She continued backing away, watching the other woman for any hint of what she felt. There was none. 'I am sorry I bothered you.'

'Quite all right, miss. I thought you might be surprised.'

There was nothing to say to that. Mary Margaret nodded and turned around. She needed privacy to come to grips with this most recent incident.

But first she had to become accustomed to her room.

It was nearly the size of her sister Emily's entire house. No wonder Thomas was so bitter if he grew up like this. He had fallen far.

Shamrock-green silk curtains were pulled back to admit the late afternoon sun. The ceiling-to-floor windows looked out on the back of the house and an Elizabethan garden and maze. A wrought-iron gazebo snuggled in one corner. She would have to explore it as soon as possible.

Under her feet was the thickest and most luxurious carpet she had ever seen. Vines and ivy dotted with delicate pink roses spread like a verdant jungle. Two Chippendale chairs, upholstered in pink-striped silk and green trim were grouped cosily around a mahogany pie table with inlaid sandalwood designs.

And then there was the huge four-poster bed with its green and pink curtains and mountainous pillows. She would be lost in it. But the Earl would not.

She flushed and buried her face in her hands. How could she think such a thing? The memory of his smouldering gaze while he waited for her reply gave her the answer. She might not want to be his mistress, but she wanted to be more to him than his mother's companion.

She took a deep breath and regained her composure. He was far above her, and she was supposed to steal from his mother.

She shook her head to clear it of the troubling thoughts and strode across the room to another door. It was a dressing room. She laughed, not a happy sound. She had three dresses to her name and a ruined cape, one pair of boots that the constant rain and mud had taken a toll on and a pair of leather slippers. She did not need this room in the least.

She shut the door with a firm hand. Still, Ravensford had been more than generous with her. She would have so much to tell Emily, and even a desk to write on, she noted. The light, fully stocked lady's desk nestled between the two windows. She sat at it and took a sheet of the Earl's embossed stationery. She dipped the quill in the ink and began.

It was dusk when she finished. A knock on the door caught her attention. Her dinner waited, as did a bath when she was finished eating. Life with the Countess had not been anything near like this.

\* \* \*

Three weeks later, Mary Margaret wiped her brow before finishing the arrangement of a large bouquet of lilacs from the Earl's garden. The vase, overflowing with the lavender blooms, sat in the salon between two floor-to-ceiling windows that faced the front street. The town house was as ready as she could make it with the help of the entire staff. When she had been in doubt about something, the Earl's secretary had provided the needed information. Even Ravensford's valet, Stevens, approved.

The Countess and Annabell Winston were to arrive today. She waited in apprehension, hoping the Countess would be pleased but knowing that she would find fault with something. That was how it had been in Ireland; she did not expect it to be any different here. But that was all right. She had done her best, and she had a sense of satisfaction.

'Well done, Miss O'Brien.'

She jumped. The Earl's butterscotch baritone sent shivers down her spine.

'I didn't mean to startle you.'

'I did not hear you, my lord. And thank you.' She made her hands relax at her side. 'I could not have done it without the staff and your secretary. Mr Kartchner has been invaluable.'

'I find him so. And my staff is the best in London. I am glad they could be of assistance.'

Silence fell between them. A long, awkward silence that made Mary Margaret search her brain for something, anything to say. Nothing came to mind.

'How do you find your room, Miss O'Brien?'

For some reason that was the last thing she had expected. 'Lovely. I have never seen anything so beautiful, let alone lived in something so magnificent.' She laughed nervously. 'I pinch myself every morning to make sure I am not dreaming it. I am sure that I should be on the fourth floor with the other servants.'

He frowned. 'I don't care how my mother treats you, I will treat you as you deserve.'

'Thank you, my lord.' Her voice was tight. He always made her feel awkward.

'And stop thanking me and calling me "my lord". I told you to call me Ravensford.' His eyes darkened. 'Or have you forgotten?'

She had forgotten nothing—not his order to call him Ravensford or his offer of *carte blanche*. 'Yes, m...' She caught herself. It was better to humour him. 'Ravensford.'

'Better.'

He pivoted on his heel and strode from the room, taking her by surprise. It was as though he had suddenly lost interest in their conversation. What a ninny she was to have been so totally caught up in their interaction. It was obvious that he did not regret her turning down his offer to become his mistress. That knowledge, as much as she hated to admit even to herself, was a disappointment. Against her better judgement, she had secretly hoped that he was avoiding her because he did not want to lose control and ask her again.

Not that she wanted to be his mistress—because she did not. But it would be nice to know that he still found her desirable. She shook her head in bewilderment at her conflicting emotions. She had to stop this.

Sounds of commotion penetrated the salon door. Her heart jolted. The Countess must have arrived. Hastily wiping her hands on her skirts and wishing she had had time to clean up and change to a clean dress, she rushed into the hall and on to the foyer.

Boxes and trunks were strewn around with more coming in. The Countess stood in the middle of everything and presented her cheek for Ravensford to kiss, which he dutifully did.

Beside the Countess stood a young girl who looked barely out of the schoolroom. Her bright blonde hair was cut short and fashionably frizzed around her elfin face. Her blue eyes sparkled with curiosity, and her feet danced. She was as excited as a person could be and not explode.

Mary Margaret smiled. The child would be a delight.

The Countess caught sight of her. 'Miss O'Brien, I want you to meet my goddaughter, Miss Annabell Winston.'

Annabell turned her dazzling smile on Mary Margaret. 'I am so pleased to meet you, Miss O'Brien. Godmother has told me about everything you have been doing.'

'Don't gush so,' the Countess said.

The girl quieted, but nothing could dim her exuberance.

'Miss O'Brien has worked diligently and accomplished a great deal,' Ravensford said.

'I shall be inspecting everything once I have rested,' the Countess said, sweeping up the stairs. 'Is my room prepared?'

'Yes, my lady,' Jones, the butler said, following in the Countess's wake.

Mary Margaret followed more slowly, trailing the Earl and Annabell. She had overseen the final preparations, arranging the flowers and ensuring that the fire was properly laid.

The Countess entered her rooms in a swathe of servants and family and stopped. Her gaze swept the immaculate blue drapes and bedspread. She took in the rich carpet underfoot.

'Whoever brought those flowers in here should be let go, Andrew. You know I loathe lilacs.'

Mary Margaret paled and wanted to sink into the floor, but she could not let the Countess think someone else was responsible. If anyone suffered, it should be she.

'My lady, I am truly sorry. I did not know you disliked the flowers when I brought them in.'

The Countess turned on her. 'I should have known. Next time check before you do anything.'

'Yes, my lady.' Mary Margaret bowed her head in submission even though she railed at the Countess's high-handed treatment. This was nothing different from when she had been in Ireland.

'You are dismissed,' the Countess said, unfastening her cape and letting it fall to the rug where it was quickly picked up by her maid, Jane.

Mary Margaret breathed a sigh of relief and made her escape. Things did not look good for her stay in London. Thank goodness her quarterly salary was due soon. Somehow she would return to Ireland then and convince Emily to leave Thomas and come live with her. She would not let herself think anything else.

Ravensford waited for the door to close behind Mary Margaret before turning to his mother. 'That was unnecessary, Mother. She has worked harder than anyone to ensure the house is ready.'

The Countess eyed him narrowly. 'I will not be spoken to like that by you, Andrew.' She turned away from him. 'Annabell, you will be in the Green Room. Jones will see that your luggage is taken there.'

Always the perfect butler, Jones managed to keep his face blank, but his gaze darted to the Earl.

Ravensford spoke smoothly. 'That won't be possible, Mother. The Green Room is already occupied. The Rose Room has been prepared for Annabell.' He turned to the chit. 'The colour will compliment you more than the Green Room ever could.'

Annabell giggled. 'You always were a gallant, Ravensford. I see that you have not changed.'

He made her a playful bow. 'I aim to please.'

'Well, you don't please me, Andrew.' The Countess cut across their banter. 'Have whoever is in the Green Room removed.'

Ravensford gave his parent a noncommittal look. 'No, Mother. Everything is fine the way it is.'

'Out,' the Countess said, waving her hand at everyone. When she and Ravensford were alone, she said, 'You have put that woman in there, haven't you? Well, I won't have it. She is not a proper companion to start, and even if she were, the Green Room is for important guests.'

Ravensford sauntered to the window and watched the carriage traffic on the street below. 'I believe this conversation is taking us nowhere, Mother. Miss O'Brien is staying where she is, and Annabell will be perfectly happy in the Rose Room.' He turned back to his mother before moving to the door. 'I hope you will be well enough to come down for dinner. Gaston has prepared your favourite foods, and you know how temperamental he can be.'

'Andrew—'

He walked out. Leaving his mother in a snit was not the best of things to do, but he had no intention of obeying her orders. His only worry was that she would make Mary Margaret's life miserable. He knew his mother well.

Thank goodness his parent did not know he had asked Mary Margaret to be his mistress. Any hint of that and the Countess would throw Mary Margaret into the street without a second thought.

At least he had kept away from her. He had learned early in life that there was no sense in tempting himself with something he could not have. Time cured everything—or made everything available.

A week after the Countess and Annabell's arrival, Mary Margaret donned her best gown, which had been her second best before the accident with the sea. It was dove grey wool, much like her other two dresses. Instead of dancing slippers, she wore her everyday shoes, the worn black leather doing nothing to enhance her toilet.

She turned away from the full-length mirror. She had never had more than a hand-held mirror her entire life. This one, where she could see her entire self, was an unheard-of luxury. Although right now she could do without it.

Determined to make the best of an awful situation, she carefully braided her waist-length hair and piled it atop her head. The style was a departure for her, but she knew it showed her long neck to advantage. She carefully loosened a few strands near her temples so that they curled around her eyes. Next she pulled her gold locket from underneath her bodice so that it showed like a bright spark.

Her reflection in the mirror looked like what she was—a poor companion.

Pride straightened her shoulders. She would not fare well at this ball, but there was nothing she could do. The Countess was not going so she must chaperon Annabell. Things could be worse. Annabell could be like her godmother. Instead, the girl was young, lovely and sweet.

On that uplifting thought, Mary Margaret marched from the room resolved to get through the evening ahead. At least she was not Emily, at home in Ireland wondering when Thomas would drink too much again and lose his temper.

Yes, things could be much worse.

Ravensford put Annabell's white satin-lined velvet cape around the chit's shoulders. She had been early, eager to experience her first visit to Almack's.

Ravensford heard footsteps on the landing and looked up to see Mary Margaret. She filled his senses.

''Tis a good thing my cape is securely fastened, Ravensford,' Annabell said with a touch of humour. 'Otherwise it would be on the floor from your lack of attention.'

Ravensford gave her a quick grin, but his focus returned to Mary Margaret. He watched her finish descending the stairs. She moved with the flowing grace of the cat she so reminded him of. His loins tightened.

The weeks of avoidance had done nothing to cool his ardour. Too bad she had refused his offer of *carte blanche*. Too bad she was a potential thief, he told himself, determined to stop reacting to her. It was bad enough that he desired her. Worse that he had so little control over his response to her. No other woman in his life had ever made him react as completely and physically as she did. It was an unsettling situation.

'Oh, Mary Margaret,' Annabell said, her youthful voice full of disappointment. 'Why did you not tell me you don't have a ball gown? I would have loaned you one of mine.'

'Silly child. Nothing of yours would fit me. I am just fine the way I am. A chaperon is not supposed to be fashionable, merely present.'

'But I don't want you to be a drab mouse.' Annabell's lips formed a pretty little pout.

'You are a good-hearted child,' Mary Margaret said. 'Now we must go. It might be fashionable to be late, but this is your first time. We must make sure that you have plenty of opportunity to savour the event.'

'You always think of me,' Annabell said.

Mary Margaret smiled.

Ravensford watched the byplay, free to study Mary Margaret without having her aware. Annabell was right. She looked like a drab little tabby. Anger at his mother tightened his jaw. His parent had thrown Mary Margaret into the clutches of the *ton* without a thought for the woman's wardrobe or feelings.

The thoughtlessness was typical.

To cover his unreasonable reaction, he said, 'Jones, fetch Miss O'Brien's cape. The weather will turn colder.'

Always the perfect butler, Jones turned to Mary Margaret for directions. She said calmly, too calmly, 'That will not be necessary.'

'Yes, it will.' Ravensford had had enough. He was taking charge and they were leaving. When she did not answer, he said, 'Well?'

She turned coldly to him. 'I do not have a cape.'

'Of course you do. You wore it on the trip here.'

She eyed him as though he was an exotic specimen. 'Yes, and the continual rain and mud ruined it. Now may we leave?'

He turned to Jones. 'Fetch one of the Countess's evening capes.'

The butler blanched. 'Yes, my lord.'

'Tell Jane that I order it.'

'Yes, my lord.' Looking like a man about to face his worst nightmare, Jones headed up the stairs.

'Oh, Godmother won't be happy,' Annabell said softly.

Irritation made Ravensford sharp. 'I don't care what she likes or doesn't like. Miss O'Brien requires a cape. Mother will provide.'

Annabell eyed him askance but kept any further opinions to herself. Mary Margaret turned away from him so that he could not tell how she felt. However, her shoulders were tensed and her hands clenched.

A fresh spurt of ire made him stalk away. 'I will be in the library. Notify me when the cape arrives and we can finally be on our way.'

He was being unreasonable and he knew it. His mother was always inconsiderate of others and particularly of servants and those she felt beneath her. She was the reason he had decided to champion those less fortunate than himself. He had watched his father, caught by love, flinch every time his wife slighted someone. Father had been a mild man, concerned about others. Ravensford had always thought it his father's misfortune to love a woman so completely different from him. But their marriage had been happy. They had been devoted to each other.

Now he had to contend with Mother. But he had learned young that loving someone did not necessarily mean you liked that person.

As he had expected, Jones sought him out. 'My lord, the Countess requests your presence.'

Ravensford tossed off the remainder of the whiskey he had just poured. 'Thank you, Jones.'

The butler bowed and withdrew.

Ravensford barely glanced at the two women as he passed them in the foyer. Standing up to his mother was something he rarely did. Normally he let her actions pass him by. Her being in Ireland most of the year made things much easier between them. He mounted the stairs, determination hardening his resolve to make his mother do yet another thing she would not like—and all for Mary Margaret O'Brien.

The Countess bade him enter after making him wait for several minutes outside her door. His mood was not improved.

She sat beside a dainty Chippendale table, her chair a match. A book lay open on her lap.

She turned a baleful eye on him. 'What is the meaning of this, Andrew? The chit is a servant. She has no need for one of my cloaks. Nor will I loan her one.'

Ravensford felt his teeth grinding, but he managed to keep his voice cool. 'Then give her one.'

'Andrew, you overstep yourself. Your father would never have treated me like this.'

'Nor would I if you would be generous enough to help Miss O'Brien out.'

'I pay her. Let her purchase her own clothing. And you have ensconced her in one of the best suites. That is more than sufficient.' She waved a delicate white hand as though to push the entire situation away.

Many times in his life he had been tempted to throttle his mother, but never so much as now. This anger was out of character. Another thing to lay at Mary Margaret O'Brien's feet.

Tired of arguing, he strode past her and into her dressing room. Riffling among her clothes, he grabbed the first cape he came to. Holding it in a clenched fist, he re-entered his mother's boudoir.

The Countess stood, her white hair a halo around her furious face. 'How dare you, Andrew. Put that back. Now.'

Ignoring her, he stalked to the door, opened it and left. She was too conscious of appearances to follow him. Downstairs, he flung the black velvet cape around Mary Margaret's shoulders.

'We are leaving.'

## *Chapter Eight*

Ravensford reached the front door before Jones, who rushed up and held it open. Outside, the carriage waited. A footman hurried to open the door and let down the steps, then handed Annabell and Mary Margaret inside. Ravensford followed, flinging himself down on the seat beside Annabell. He noted that Miss O'Brien had her back to the horses.

A sardonic smile curved his lips. 'I see that you know your place, Miss O'Brien.'

'As do you, my lord.'

Her sharp words were a slap in the face. He nodded ironically. 'I am out of line. Pardon me.'

'Whatever possessed you, Ravensford,' Annabell said. 'I could have loaned Mary Margaret a cape.'

'One I have no need of.'

Ravensford scowled from one to the other. 'Typical.'

He put a stop to discussion by rapping his cane against the ceiling, telling the coachman to go. The carriage lurched forward.

No one spoke for some time. As they turned down King Street where Almack's was situated, the excitement was too much for Annabell who began to chatter. Soon both women were caught up in anticipation. Ravensford, who had cut his eyeteeth on Almack's, expected an evening of boredom.

They entered to the general hubbub of dowagers sitting in chairs along the wall, couples performing a country dance, and clusters of men flirting with chits. Normal.

Ravensford scanned the room, looking for any familiar faces. He caught Mrs Drummond Burrell frowning at them. Her attention was on Mary Margaret. The Duke of Wellington had been denied admission because he was not in evening dress; Ravensford wondered if the patroness was about to come over and tell Mary Margaret she could not attend. It would be a fitting end to an awful beginning.

Just as Mrs Drummond Burrell took a step toward them, Sally Jersey caught her arm and whispered something. Both women glanced their way, Sally with a mischievous smile and Mrs Drummond Burrell with dislike. Ravensford took that to mean Sally had intervened.

He ushered his charges farther into the room and deposited them near a group of young bucks. He raised an eyebrow and one of the youths separated and came to them.

'Ravensford,' the young man said. 'Didn't expect you here. And with such lovely companions.'

Ravensford bit back a sharp retort. Potsford was always effusive where women were concerned. But the youth did not deserve the sharp edge of his tongue. It was not Potsford's fault this evening had started so abysmally and promised to continue on that way.

'Annabell, Miss O'Brien, may I present Mr Potsford. This

is my mother's goddaughter, Annabell Winston, and her chaperon, Miss O'Brien.'

'Pleased to meet you.' Always on the lookout for an heiress, Potsford lost no time. Bowing to Annabell, he said, 'May I have the pleasure of the next country dance?'

She blushed delicately. 'Please.'

'Until then, may I escort you to the refreshment table?' he asked, offering his arm.

Blushing prettily again, Annabell laid her fingers on his arm. The two headed off.

'He will be disappointed,' Ravensford said drily.

'Why ever for?' Mary Margaret asked, defence of her charge making her raspy voice catch.

'Because she is not an heiress.'

'She is a delightful young woman and will make some lucky man a wonderful wife.'

'But not Potsford.'

'You members of the aristocracy are all alike.'

'Too often,' he drawled. 'Come dance with me.'

She scowled. 'You mock me, my lord. This is a waltz. Even I know a woman cannot dance the waltz unless a patroness has approved.'

'No,' he murmured, wondering why he did such outrageous things around her. 'I don't mock you. Or are you afraid?'

She angled her chin up. 'Afraid? Of what?'

He gave her a lazy smile. 'Of what I might do—or say.'

More than that, she was scared of what she might say or do. Much as she deplored her reaction to him, he made her blood pound and her stomach churn.

'No.' Even to her own ears, her voice sounded breathy and unsure.

He laughed outright. 'Stay here.'

Mary Margaret watched him angle through the crowd. His broad shoulders, clad in a bottle-green evening coat, were an arresting sight, as were his muscular thighs in black satin casing. To her mind, he was the most attractive man here. Seeing other women follow him with their gaze, she knew her opinion of him was widely held. He was probably going to find a woman of his own station to dance with.

She turned away, her chest tight. The last thing she wanted was to see him with another woman.

She found a single chair in a corner and sat down. She did not have to be in Annabell's pocket, only make sure the girl did not dance more than twice with any one man and stayed out of dark areas. At least she could enjoy the music. She had always loved to dance and sing. Music brought her solace.

She felt a tingling awareness seconds before she heard Ravensford's voice.

'I have someone I want you to meet,' he said.

Surprised that he had come back, Mary Margaret jumped up. The woman with him was the same one she had seen earlier talking to another woman and smiling at Ravensford. She must be his latest interest, although she appeared a little old for him.

'Lady Jersey,' he said, 'I would like you to meet Miss O'Brien. She is the chaperon of my mother's goddaughter. Miss O'Brien, this is Lady Jersey, one of the patronesses.'

The woman arched one immaculate brow. 'How do you do, Miss O'Brien? Now, I would like to present the Earl of Ravensford for your consideration as a waltz partner.'

This was the last thing she had expected. There was a spark of mischief in Lady Jersey's eyes and an intense emotion in Ravensford's that she could not identify. Both waited for her answer.

She took a deep breath and gave the Earl her hand. There was nothing else she could do without drawing attention to them.

'Thank you, Sally,' Ravensford murmured.

'My pleasure,' Lady Jersey said before bubbling laughter escaped her red lips. 'I shall dine out on this for many a day. The much sought-after Earl of Ravensford needing help to get a chit to dance with him. Oh, yes, I shall enjoy telling this one.'

Ravensford winced but said nothing more.

Mary Margaret heard what Lady Jersey said, but dismissed it as a woman teasing an attractive man. She wanted to run. The last thing she wanted was for this man to hold her as intimately as the waltz required. When he slipped his arm around her waist, the dance floor tilted. She needed all her willpower not to melt against him.

Instead, she demanded, 'What do you think you are doing? I am here as a chaperon, barely one level up from a servant. I cannot dance with you. What will people say? What will your mother say?'

He drew her close. 'No more than they already are.'

She gasped and looked around. People watched them, some annoyed, others amused and more scandalised. She stiffened.

'I don't belong here.'

'You have as much right as anyone.'

'I have never waltzed.' Desperation made her voice husky.

He grinned raffishly. 'Follow me. I won't lead you astray.'

He dipped her and twirled her, making her momentarily lose her train of thought. It was hard to concentrate when a man you were inexorably drawn to held you tightly and made the world around you spin.

'I am not of your world,' she managed breathlessly. 'They know it. Lady Jersey knew it when she introduced us.'

His grip intensified until less than the proper twelve inches separated them. His face was close enough that she could see the golden striations in his green eyes. His nostrils flared.

'"My world", as you put it, is hide-bound. Too many of us are only concerned with our own entertainment.'

She stared up at him, seeing a determination that she had not realised he possessed. 'Are you a reformer?'

His mouth, those wonderful lips that she always fantasised on hers, twisted. 'I try.'

She had wondered. Too many times she had watched him reach out to those beneath him not to have pondered why he did so.

'Is that why you are so active in Parliament?'

'For the most part.'

The knowledge that he cared enough for those less fortunate than himself to stand up in Parliament and fight for their rights hit her with a jolt. Not only was he a handsome man with great wealth, but he was a caring man. The attraction she had felt for him from the beginning increased beyond anything she had thought possible.

The music swirled around them. She moved with him, their feet gliding over the floor. She felt removed from reality, caught in a dream with only him and her. He was her perfect lover.

Heaven help her. Heaven help her heart.

She swayed to a stop in his arms. The notes faded away. The other couples drifted from the floor.

He held her attention.

'Doing it too brown,' a male voice drawled.

Mary Margaret started. Behind Ravensford stood a man as dark of visage as her imagination often painted the devil. Silver wings flew from his temples and a scar ran the length of his right cheek. Dark eyes, nearly black, watched them dispassionately. His entire person was slightly dishevelled, almost disreputable, but she knew that could not be or he would not have been allowed inside. Almack's was much too proper to allow in a rogue.

'Ah, Perth,' Ravensford said without turning. 'Always in the nick of time.'

Perth shrugged. 'I do my best. But there are times when no one can help you.'

Ravensford gave a mirthless chuckle. 'Spoken like a true friend.'

He still had not released her, and Mary Margaret, realising they were creating a spectacle, tried to step away. Several young girls tittered behind their hands.

'But already too late,' Perth said, holding out his hand to Mary Margaret. 'May I introduce myself since Ravensford is remiss. I am Perth.'

'The Earl of Perth,' Ravensford added.

'Another earl,' Mary Margaret said, giving Perth her hand. He brushed her fingers with his lips.

'My pleasure. Would you care for some rataffia? Yes? Ravensford will be happy to get it.' There was a wicked gleam in his eye.

'Always in command.' Ravensford touched his brow in salute before moving away.

Mary Margaret was nonplussed. With Ravensford went her sense of warmth and security, although she would never tell him that and could barely admit it to herself. She did not have the experience to deal with a man of Perth's calibre. She slanted him a glance through lowered lashes. She had a feeling he could be as cruel as he could be kind, if he was ever kind. Yet he had put himself forward to interrupt the scene she and Ravensford had created.

He guided her to a seat. 'The old Countess hired you to play nursemaid to her goddaughter?'

She nodded, still not sure what to say to him.

'Don't pay Ravensford's mother any mind. She has been the trial of his life.'

She nodded again, knowing now that she should say nothing. The last thing a servant or employee should do was talk about her employer.

His mouth split into a grin showing white teeth. Much like a predator.

Mary Margaret cudgelled her brain for an excuse to get away. Jumping up, she said, 'I see Annabell over there with Mr Potsford. I should go to her.'

He made her an ironic bow. 'As you wish.'

She did not wait.

'You certainly scared her off,' Ravensford said. Having just arrived with the drink, he now sat on the vacated chair.

'Your inamorata is a scared tabby. I thought you more adventurous than this.' He gave Ravensford a lascivious grin. 'Especially after taking up with the "Delightful Delilah". Lord, but she led you a merry chase.'

'She did.' Ravensford smiled at remembered antics. 'I am getting too advanced in age to deal with another such as she. Too exhausting.'

'Hence the tabby?'

His friend's disparagement of Mary Margaret was oddly

irritating. 'She is no tabby. And I have not taken up with her. She is my mother's companion and Annabell's chaperon.' He cast Perth a wicked glance. 'And she has already turned down my offer.'

'Aha. That explains everything. I've never seen you dance like that with one of your mother's companions,' Perth said drily.

Determined to shake Perth from his high perch, Ravensford stated, 'She plans to steal something from my parent. I am keeping a close eye on her to see that she is unsuccessful. I thought that having her for a mistress would keep her nearby.'

'Ah...everything is clear.'

He angled to face Perth, intending to set him straight when his attention was caught by Annabell. 'Blast that chit. She can't go off with Potsford.'

'Definitely not. The puppy is as broke as shattered crockery.'

Perth's sarcasm was lost on Ravensford as he headed off. The last thing he needed was for Annabell to add another indiscretion to this evening—and hers would be much worse. Mary Margaret was not on the Marriage Mart and neither was he. Annabell was.

He caught up with the pair just as Mary Margaret gripped Annabell's arm. 'I believe Mr Potsford has taken ill and must leave, Annabell. Let us not keep him.'

Potsford looked ready to protest until he saw Ravensford over Mary Margaret's shoulder.

The Earl took Annabell's elbow in a firm hold. 'Miss O'Brien is right. It is time we left as well.'

'Quite right. Getting late,' Potsford said, edging away.

'But...but I don't want to,' Annabell said.

Ravensford stared her down. 'But you are.'

'His lordship is right, Annabell,' Mary Margaret said. 'The Countess will be wondering where we are and curious about the night.'

'I doubt that,' Annabell said rebelliously. But after an admonishing look from Mary Margaret, she acquiesced. 'I shall stop at her room if she is still awake and tell her everything. She always talks about how exciting her first Season was, she will enjoy this.'

Mary Margaret gave the girl a warm smile. 'I thought you would.'

Ravensford doubted that his mother cared about anything except her own comfort, but perhaps he judged her too harshly. She had always listened to his tales of wonder and woe. It was just when people she considered beneath her were involved that his parent could be unlikable and uncaring.

While they waited for the carriage to come around, he watched the two women. With all their differences in station and character, they seemed to genuinely like each other.

Mary Margaret O'Brien was a conundrum. She was educated, gentle and caring, yet she intended to steal from his mother. While part of him couldn't blame her, he knew the plan had been concocted in cold blood, something he would have thought the woman laughing softly with Annabell was incapable of. But he knew differently. He could still hear her wonderful voice agreeing to the deed.

The carriage arrived and they returned home with the two women discussing the evening and him watching the companion. The candles from the coach lanterns cast first shadows, then light, on the sharp angles of Mary Margaret's

face. One minute she was a tigress, all temptation and dark.
The next she was a kitten playing gently with Annabell.
   At all times she was a mystery.

# *Chapter Nine*

Mary Margaret breathed deeply of the roses that surrounded the tiny white iron gazebo. Like the Gothic folly the Countess had in Ireland, this gazebo had become her sanctuary. No one ever found her here.

She had peace and quiet to think about last evening. She had had a wonderful time. Ravensford had made the waltz seem like a part of them. For a large man he was very graceful. Even though he had held her closer than proper, she had not minded. Being close to him was too thrilling for anything else to matter.

She sighed and closed her eyes, wanting to relive the experience again.

'Miss, his lordship requires your presence in the library.'

Mary Margaret sat bolt upright. She had not heard anyone. Now a young girl stood in front of her twisting her hands.

'Susan, you startled me. I did not hear you.'

'Pardon, miss.'

Still the girl did not stop wringing her hands. 'Whatever is the matter, Susan?' Mary Margaret stood and went to the girl. She put a gentle hand on the servant's shoulder. 'Never say you are afraid of me?'

'Oh, no, niver.' The young girl sighed. 'Not you, miss. But, his lordship is in an awful hurry...'

Mary Margaret gave the maid a quizzical look. 'Then I will go upstairs and freshen up. Then I will report to him.'

'Yes, miss.'

Mary Margaret smiled at the girl who was barely more than a child. 'What are you afraid of? Surely not the Earl.'

Susan chewed her bottom lip. 'I shouldn't be talkin' to ye, miss. But...his lordship is changed since he returned from Ireland. All of us says so.'

Curiosity filled Mary Margaret. Susan was right in that Mary Margaret should not be gossiping with the servants, but then she was very nearly one herself.

'How?' she asked, hoping she only sounded mildly interested.

The girl sidled closer and her voice lowered. 'Temper, miss. He has a temper. Niver had one befores. Like he's bothered awful by somethin'.'

Mary Margaret's heart skipped a beat. It could not be because she had refused his offer to be his mistress. Nor could it be because of Thomas's plan to have her steal some of the Countess's jewellery. Ravensford knew nothing about that. Still...

'Oh.' Her voice scraped. In spite of her conviction that the Earl did not know, her nerves had still got the better of her. She started again. 'Oh? I thought he was always volatile.'

Although when she thought about it, he had not shown any impatience or anger during the discussion she had sat in on between him and his mother before they left Ireland. She would have lost patience with the Countess. The woman was as scatterbrained as she was high in the instep. Yet he was constantly losing his temper with her.

'No, niver, miss. He's ever so easy goin' and friendly. But no more.' Her shoulders drooped as though she had lost something personal.

Mary Margaret wondered at the girl's reaction. Ravensford had always seemed concerned about his people, but she had not realised how involved with him they were. He must be a good employer and landlord.

'And just now you were afraid that if I refused his summons he would be angry with you.'

'Yes, miss.'

'Don't worry, Susan. I will go. But first I must tidy up a bit.'

Mary Margaret left the girl in the kitchen and went up to her room. Alone, she went to the full-length mirror. Her hair needed straightening; pieces had come loose from the chignon and curled around her eyes like errant tendrils of thread.

Unbidden came the memory of Ravensford brushing her hair back from her face after she had nearly drowned. His warmth and concern had eased much of her panic. At the time, she had not recognised how his strength had sustained her. Realising now was like being struck by lightning—searing and surprising.

When had she come to depend on him so much? She did not know. It had just happened. She had only been in his company a month.

This was awful.

Right now, this instant, she could imagine his touch on

her, his fingers warm and sure against her skin—as they had been last night. Never in her wildest flights of imagining had she envisioned the ecstasy of being caught up in his arms, dancing the waltz. Never.

Delight suffused her. Using the hairbrush as Ravensford's hand, she began to dance. She hummed the waltz tune from last night as she twirled around the room, smiling up at her imaginary partner. Faster and faster she went, her emotions soaring.

'Umph!'

It was a rude awakening to trip against a pile of books she had stacked in the middle of the room preparatory to returning them to the Earl's library. She sat down on the floor with a thump, the brush falling from her fingers. Her foot hurt like the dickens where she had smacked it.

She sighed. This loss of control was getting her nowhere. She had to rein in her imagination and her emotions.

A knock on the door reminded her that she had to attend Ravensford. Susan was very likely worried sick that she had changed her mind and was not going downstairs.

'I am coming,' she said loudly enough for the maid to hear.

She rose and dropped the brush that had started it all on to the dresser. A quick glance in the mirror showed her hair still looking unkempt and a sheen on her face that flushed her cheeks and reddened her lips. She was a sight.

But she was already late. She wet her hands in the ewer and quickly slicked them over her hair, hoping the strands would stay in place long enough for this meeting.

Mary Margaret straightened her shoulders and headed toward the library where she knocked and waited for Ravensford's permission to enter. Silly pictures of her waltzing around her room brought a smile to her lips, lips suddenly dry. And her palms were wet. No matter how she tried to prepare herself for his presence, her reaction to him always overwhelmed her better sense. It scared her.

His baritone 'Come in' jolted her into action. She stumbled through the door as soon as the footman opened it. He shut it behind her before she even realised she was in the library.

A slight smile curved Ravensford's lips. 'Do you always make an entrance like that? If so, you should be on the stage.'

She flushed, but quickly regained her composure. 'I was woolgathering, expecting to be kept waiting longer than you did, my lord.'

'Procrastination is not one of my failings,' he said, moving from behind the large mahogany desk where he had been sitting when she entered. He bore down on her. 'How many times have I told you to call me Ravensford? After all we have been through it is more appropriate.'

She felt like he was suffocating her with his nearness. She took a step back.

'I cannot do that.'

He moved closer, frowning. 'Don't give me any of that nonsense about being a servant. You are no more a servant than I am a duke.'

She raised an eyebrow. 'Exactly, my lord. It would never have occurred to me to make the comparison you just did. That more than anything says I am a servant.'

A strange light entered his eyes. 'Did you feel like a servant last night? You didn't act like one. Not in my arms.'

His words caught her off guard. They were the last things she expected him to say. In her mind she was the one who

*The Rebel*

still thought of last night. The dance should be gone from his memory by now.

Unconsciously she raised one hand in a symbolic attempt to fend him off. His stance dared her to lie. She took a deep breath, prepared to tell him anything but the truth.

'No,' she whispered, appalled at her answer even as the word slipped out.

He was beside her in a second, his hands gripping her shoulders. 'I knew it.'

Shivers chased down her spine, followed by heat that curled in her stomach. His mouth was inches from hers and coming closer. The breath caught in her throat. Her gaze clung to his. She did not want to miss anything.

'You are supposed to close your eyes,' he said, chuckling deep in his chest.

Lethargy crept through her limbs as she did his bidding. She could feel the warmth of his breath against her skin. This was how she remembered him.

His mouth closed over hers and her heart jumped. His lips teased at hers, his tongue trailing along her flesh. His hands roamed over her back until one settled at her waist and pulled her close, so close she could feel his chest rising and falling. She swayed into him, opening her mouth to allow him to deepen the kiss.

The hand at her waist slid lower until it cupped the swell of her hip. The other hand rose to the base of her neck and angled her head to one side so he penetrated better.

Her heart pounded. The blood rushed in her ears. Her stomach rioted. Never, in her entire life, had she felt like this. Alive and tingling, ready for anything.

He broke away from her, panting. She whimpered, her hands circling his neck as she tried to pull him back.

He laughed, but it was shaky. 'Easy, sweetheart. This is not the place, much as I want to finish what we have started.'

She blinked and came to her senses. Slowly. Slowly enough that his lips brushed hers before he finally released her.

She swayed and grabbed on to the nearest object, the back of a chair. He was close enough that she could see the black of his pupils. They seemed to fill his entire eye. He looked as though he had just woken, sensual and...and something she could not explain. Excited? Hungry?

She felt bereft, his warmth no longer enfolding her.

'I will come to your room tonight,' he murmured, bending just enough for his lips to brush hers.

His mouth on hers struck sparks that she feared would start an inferno inside her. She closed her eyes and tried to control her reaction to him. He was catnip and she was a cat. Her fingers shook from the effort not to reach out to him.

'After everyone has gone to bed,' he promised, his voice like a liquid caress along the curves of her body.

'After everyone has gone to bed,' she parroted. *After everyone has gone to bed.* Her eyes snapped open. She glared at him. 'No, you will not.'

A sardonic light entered his eyes, making them sharp as facetted emeralds. 'Coming to your senses?'

'How dare you? How dare you treat me like a...a light-skirt? I won't be your mistress, and every time you ask me you insult me. You treat me like I am lower than the servant you continually say I am not.' She thrust her balled fists on her hips. 'Well, let me tell you. I would rather be the lowest of servants than your mistress.'

He stepped away, his eyes brooding, and made her a

mocking bow. 'I hear you very well, Miss O'Brien. If you are not careful, the entire household will hear you.'

She sputtered to a stop as his words penetrated her indignation. She gulped air and turned away, unable to face him. She had behaved as wantonly as a loose woman. But she was not one.

When she had finally achieved a modicum of calm, she turned back to him. 'If you will excuse me, I have much to do.'

'I don't excuse you, Miss O'Brien.'

She froze in the act of moving to the door.

He stroked the signet ring on his left hand, drawing her attention to the fine sapphire. 'I want you to go to Annabell's modiste and get yourself a wardrobe suitable for a London Season.'

She gasped. 'You jest. First you try to seduce me, then ask me to be your mistress, and now you propose to send me to a modiste I cannot afford to patronise.'

'I am deadly serious, Miss O'Brien. And I intend to pay for everything.'

'You summoned me for this? Well, my answer is no. You will not pay for anything of mine.'

'Oh, but I will,' he drawled.

'No, you will not,' she reiterated. They were at it again. He was ordering her about and she was defying him.

'This continual contest of wills is boring, Miss O'Brien,' he said, turning away and going to sit behind his desk. 'Your appointment is at three. I shall expect you down here at half past two.'

Affronted to the core, she glared at him. 'I don't need anything. While I don't have much, and none of it is up to the standards of the *ton*, it is sufficient for me.'

'But not for me,' he stated.

She bristled. 'What have you to do with my wardrobe, pray tell?'

'It offends me.'

'Offends you!' Hurt, followed rapidly by anger, suffused her. 'How shallow.'

'I can be.' He shuffled a stack of papers and lined them up perfectly. 'I have sent word to Madame Bertrice that she is to provide you with a complete wardrobe.'

'You are mistaken, my lord.' She tipped her nose in the air.

'I think not.'

She ground her teeth together. They were very close to a shouting match. Children would behave as they were. A smile tugged at her lips.

His eyes held a hint of humour. 'We are behaving as children.'

Some of the tension eased from her. Her shoulders relaxed. 'My exact thought.'

'Good. Then you will stop arguing with me and be at Madame's by three o'clock.'

Her face turned to stone. He was stubborn and used to having his own way. 'I did not say that.'

'I will have the carriage brought around by half past two.'

Mary Margaret knew a dismissal when she heard it. Just as well. She was done arguing with his lordship. She simply would not go. With barely a curtsy, she left, her ire up and her determination firmly in place.

Ravensford watched her go and knew she would disobey him—it was written in every line of her magnificent body. For the life of him, he did not understand why she brought out the stubborn streak he had worked so hard at eradicating. His father had told him once that the trait would cause him problems.

Shaking his head, he returned to his desk and re-read for the third time the Bill he intended to introduce to the Lords. His mind refused to concentrate.

Pictures of Mary Margaret O'Brien insisted on penetrating his thoughts. Her voice intruded on his dreams. She was an enigma he longed to unravel.

And that kiss. He had not intended for that to happen. After she had refused his offer of *carte blanche*, he had decided not to ask again. But kissing her had ignited a fire in him that nothing short of full possession could quench. He wanted her, and having sampled the excitement of her, he meant to have her. To hell with her plan to rob his mother.

As his mistress she would have enough jewels that she could give hers to the man who wanted her to steal his mother's. She would even have some left over. He would shower her with everything.

Now he had only to convince her that accepting his offer would be better than stealing.

That decided, he once again tried to read his Bill—and could not. As satisfying as the thought of having her for his mistress was, there was something wrong about it. He felt as though something was tarnished.

His secretary chose that moment to enter and Ravensford forced his attention to matters having nothing to do with his mother's companion.

Mary Margaret paced the confines of her room. The carriage waited for her. It would wait forever.

Part of her, the weak part, longed to have beautiful clothing. She had never had anything that was not serviceable.

Some had been attractive in a practical manner, but never designed solely to make her look good.

But she was not allowing the Earl to buy her clothes. Men of his station bought clothes and other things for their mistresses. She was not his mistress. Nor was she going to be.

The hurt that had exploded in the library was now a dull ache. With time, she would make that go away too. So what if he desired her and nothing else? She had not even dreamed that he would desire her. She was a farmer's daughter with nothing to recommend her, not even stunning looks.

She stopped and her reflection in the mirror confronted her. The grey frock made her look drab, as though she was sick. In a fit of pique, she stalked to the mirror and, using all her strength, turned it to the wall.

'There,' she muttered, dusting her hands off. 'I shan't have to look at myself any more.'

The initial satisfaction was quickly replaced by the subdued knowledge that she knew by heart what the mirror showed. She did not need to see her reflection to know her clothing did nothing for her. And how she wished it might.

That weak part of her wanted to look pretty for Ravensford. She did not want to be his mother's lowly companion who was good enough to steal a kiss from in the library when no one was around. She wanted to be the woman on his arm whom he proudly squired about town.

She wanted the moon. She was a fool. She dashed her fist across her eyes. She was not a watering pot.

A timid knock on the door, followed by Susan's hesitant, 'Miss, his lordship wants to know why you are late,' pulled Mary Margaret from her melancholy admission.

Surprise tightened her shoulders. She had not really expected Ravensford to keep track of the time and the appointment. She had thought he would be out about his business at the House of Lords, fully expecting her to do as he ordered. In her limited experience, men did not interest themselves in women's dress. Her father had never cared and nor did Thomas, whose money went on his own back.

Ravensford's persistence must come of the stubbornness she had glimpsed in him this morning. Nothing else that she could think of would explain this determination.

She crossed to the door, opened it and looked down at the maid's large brown eyes. She regretted putting the girl in the middle, but she was not going.

'Susan, please tell his lordship that I am indisposed and sorry for any inconvenience I might cause.'

The girl gulped. 'Yes, miss.'

'Oh, and would you please return this to the Countess?' Mary Margaret picked up the neatly folded black velvet cape and handed it to Susan.

After Susan took the garment, Mary Margaret closed the door behind the maid's retreating figure and crossed to the window. She looked out on the gardens, which were in full, riotous bloom. If she opened the glass, the scent of roses would fill the air. She did so and drew in a deep breath of the glorious smell. Perhaps she would be allowed to pick some of the blossoms and put them in a vase in her room. Then, perhaps not. It did not matter. She was mentally chattering, trying to keep herself from thinking of Ravensford's reaction when she did not appear as he commanded.

A second knock on the door froze her rambling mind.

'Who is it?' she rasped through stiff lips.

'Who do you think?' Ravensford asked, irritation evident in his inflection. 'I am not used to having my orders ignored.'

She closed her eyes and took a deep breath. 'I told you before. I don't need those clothes. Nor will I go to the modiste.'

Her voice was raised enough to penetrate the thick wood of the door. She belatedly wondered how many servants were listening to this clash of wills. Why was he doing this?

The door opened. He stood, elbows akimbo, and glared at her. 'You are not missing the appointment.'

She crossed her arms over her chest. 'Yes, I am.'

His eyes narrowed. 'Do you want to embarrass Annabell again?'

'Embarrassment will not adversely affect her.'

He relaxed against the door jamb. 'But your clothing might. How you are dressed impacts on how the *ton* perceives Annabell. If you look poor and provincial, then she looks the same.'

Doubt sneaked through Mary Margaret's determination. 'That is silly.'

He shrugged. 'Of course, but that does not change it.'

The last thing she wanted was to hurt Annabell's chances of a successful Season. The girl was so excited and had such high expectations.

'What about Potsford last night? He did not seem the least bit put off that Annabell was with me.'

'I introduced them. He thought she was an heiress and he is on the lookout for one. He would not have cared if she had the face of a horse and the body of a hippopotamus.'

Mary Margaret flinched at the blunt, uncomplimentary description. 'What an awful picture that creates.'

'It was meant to,' he drawled. 'Appearances are everything to society. Annabell has a moderate dowry. She needs to marry well or at least respectably.'

She sighed. She had come to care for the girl, and the last thing she wanted to do was adversely impact on Annabell's Season.

'I will go, but only if the dresses I purchase are paid for from my salary.'

He straightened. For an instant, she thought mirth flashed across his face. She must have been mistaken because, when she squinted to see better, he was solemn. There was a twitch at his mouth but nothing more.

'Hurry. The horses have been kept waiting for far too long.'

He turned and left without a backward glance, as though he expected her compliance. His arrogance raised her hackles, but she had said she would go. Very likely he was returning to whatever business her failure to show had taken him from.

As dignified as a rushing woman could be, she sped down the stairs and past the butler who held open the front door. She barrelled through the coach door the footman held and nearly into Ravensford. He grinned sardonically.

'Haste can make for some interesting seat mates.'

For what seemed like the hundredth time since she'd met him, she blushed. He constantly disconcerted her, although this last had been her own doing.

She plopped down. 'I did not think you were going. I am capable of doing this on my own.'

'But, I'm sure, not to my satisfaction.'

She drew herself straight, a set-down on the tip of her tongue, one she could not deliver. 'I am sure that nothing I can afford to buy will be to your satisfaction, my lord.'

She turned away as they set off. When he said nothing further, she tried to lose herself in the changing scenery.

London was fascinating. She had never been outside of Cashel, and that country town was not even the size of one of London's hamlets.

But it was impossible to ignore him. She was too conscious of everything that had happened to them.

It was with relief that she felt the carriage slow down and stop. A small, very discreet door sat back from the street. There was no name on the outside. Nothing that she could see to tell the customer this was a dressmaker's shop, if it was. She gave Ravensford a questioning look.

'Madame Bertrice's. She does not advertise. She does not have to.'

He got out as soon as the footman opened the door and let down the steps. Turning back, Ravensford offered his hand.

Mary Margaret eyed his fingers warily. Even covered by fashionable gloves, they looked strong and demanding. She had no doubt that his touch would sear her flesh even though she also wore gloves. After their bout of lovemaking in the library, she did not trust herself near him. He did things to her.

But she could not ignore him. It was not done.

Taking a deep breath, she put her hand into his. She was right. Heat surged up her arm and tightened her chest. She cast one disconcerted glance at him before studiously watching where she put her feet.

'I won't let you fall, Miss O'Brien,' his honey-smooth baritone mocked.

'I never thought you would,' she answered primly, refusing to look him in the face and meet his unspoken challenge.

She had spent her life trying her best to meet difficult situations without flinching, but now more than ever she felt cowardly. She had stood up to him as much as she thought herself capable of doing for one day.

The rest of the day, she was going to concentrate on not letting her desire for beautiful clothing overcome her determination to save for Emily. Soon she would be able to collect her quarterly wage. She would send it to Emily and tell her to leave Thomas. She could not get carried away here.

## *Chapter Ten*

Once she was safely on the ground, his hand slid to her elbow and guided her toward the door. He opened it without knocking, and they entered one of the most elegant rooms Mary Margaret had ever been in.

Discreet beiges and creams, with just a hint of gold, covered the chairs, settees, floor and single window. Several delicate tables held vases with a few select flowers. A light floral scent filled the air.

Mary Margaret was entranced.

A petite woman glided toward them. She wore an elegant black gown with a single row of white lace at the bodice and wrists. Her blonde, almost white, hair feathered around a face smooth as a newborn's, yet her eyes spoke of years of experience.

'My lord Count,' she murmured, calling him by his continental title and offering her hand.

Ravensford took her fingers with grace and charm. Lifting them to his lips for the briefest of touches, he murmured,

'Madame Bertrice, allow me to introduce Miss O'Brien. She is the woman I spoke to you about.'

The modiste smiled at him before turning her attention to Mary Margaret. Bright blue eyes took in everything about Mary Margaret in what seemed seconds.

'Ah, just as you said, my lord,' the woman murmured, her accent settling into a brisk mode. 'I have just the thing. It was returned by one of my clients because the colour is too strong. It will be perfection on Miss O'Brien.' She crooked a finger at Mary Margaret. 'Come this way, please. We must see what alterations the gown needs. The original owner was not as shapely as you.'

Mary Margaret missed her step. She was not used to people speaking so openly of one's proportions.

Madame winked. 'You will find, Miss O'Brien, that the aristocracy is not so delicate as others in their mode of speech.'

Mary Margaret could only nod.

She was further discommoded to have to undress in front of Madame and an assistant. Both women behaved as though nothing was out of the ordinary, which gradually eased Mary Margaret's discomfort. She knew women who had their dresses made by others always disrobed thus, but she had never had that luxury.

The gown they brought out was stunning. The colour was the deep pink of wild roses, so rich it was nearly mauve. There was no adornment. They slipped the silken folds over her head and smoothed the material down her sides. The bosom had been let out and they quickly set about sizing it. Minutes later, they finished and turned her toward the single mirror.

Surely that was someone else, she thought, even though

she knew intellectually that the reflection was hers. The deep pink put colour into her normally pale cheeks, even her lips. And the cut of the dress was masterful. She understood why Madame Bertrice did not advertise her location. Any woman seeing another in a dress like this would do anything to find out who had made it.

She looked like a long-stemmed rose, ready to sway in a passing breeze. She looked regal and beautiful. She knew, with a sinking heart, that she could never afford this dress on her salary, not even if she worked all her life.

She squeezed her eyes shut on her reflection. Temptation was something she so rarely felt—until recently. First Ravensford and now this vanity.

'It is beautiful beyond words, madame,' she said regretfully. 'But I cannot afford this dress. I am truly sorry.'

The assistant tittered, only to be swatted sharply by Madame. Mary Margaret ignored the young girl the best she could, but it was not easy. Pride was a commodity she could not afford.

'Nonsense, mademoiselle. This gown is nothing. A *bagatelle*. To me, it is worthless.' She shrugged eloquently. 'I would be much better served by having someone of your uniqueness to wear it before the *ton*.'

Hope lit Mary Margaret's face. If only…

'Come, Miss O'Brien,' the modiste pursued, 'why would I tell you something that was not true, for I can see that you doubt me?'

'I don't disbelieve you, I simply cannot see how that can be. Any woman would be delighted to have this gown.'

'Then it is settled,' Madame stated.

'But I did not say I wanted to purchase—'

'Oh, but you did. Not in so many words, but I can see the

longing you feel. Do not worry. The Count has provided me with much business in the past. The matter of this single garment is nothing. Now come along and show his lordship what miracles a fine garment can create.'

Before Mary Margaret could protest further, Madame swept from the dressing room. The maid tittered again, watching her from lowered lashes. Mary Margaret felt trapped with nowhere to go but out to Ravensford. So be it.

Head high, shoulders back, she retraced her steps to Madame's receiving room. Ravensford was in conversation with the modiste and did not look up immediately. Mary Margaret took several deep breaths, wondering if she should return to the dressing room before either of them realised she was here. Just as she decided to do so, Ravensford glanced up. An arrested look came over him. Mary Margaret flushed to the top of the gown's bodice.

Ravensford had always found her to be an exotic beauty, but now she was devastating. The thin silk accentuated her full bosom and small waist. The colour made her eyes sparkle. His loins tightened painfully.

'Superb, madame,' he said softly, never taking his gaze from Mary Margaret. 'We will definitely take that one.'

'But of course,' Madame said complacently.

'I am glad you approve,' Mary Margaret said with a tinge of sarcasm, her deep husky voice rasping. 'Now, if you are both done studying me, I will go change.'

'By all means,' Ravensford said. As soon as she was out of the room he turned to Madame. 'I want a complete wardrobe for Miss O'Brien. Expense is not a consideration.'

'But of course.'

He eyed her sharply. 'Miss O'Brien is a lady of Quality.'

'I never thought otherwise, my lord.'

'Send this gown immediately along with a cape.'

'Tomorrow, my lord.'

Mary Margaret joined them and Ravensford contented himself with the knowledge that Madame would be discreet and her clothing impeccable. He escorted Mary Margaret to the waiting coach and could not resist the temptation to rest his hand on the small of her back as she entered the vehicle. He felt her skin jump under his fingers. She was not indifferent to him. Satisfaction curved his lips.

He followed her into the closed carriage. He had chosen this vehicle in the hope that fewer people would see them. Much as he wanted her to be dressed as befitted her beauty, he did not want everyone to know that he clothed her. He had no real excuse for doing so and others would realise that. The rumour mill would soon have them an *on-dit*, and while he intended to bed her, he did not intend for the whole world to know it. He had to trust to Madame's desire for more business from him and the loyalty of his servants that no one would talk.

He settled across from her, breathing deeply of her light lavender scent. He had always thought of the flower as a way to preserve and freshen clothing and linens. But from the moment he had first heard her speaking in his mother's library, the scent had taken on a sensual connotation that he knew would stay with him for life.

'You will wear the gown at the ball in Annabell's honour.'

She looked at him from the corner of her eye. 'I will wear it when and where I choose.'

He crossed one Hessian-covered leg over the other. 'You are the most argumentative woman it has ever been my misfortune to encounter. Can't you ever do as you are told without first fighting?'

She turned away and in a tight voice said, 'I have done as others have bid me all my life. But only you have tried to make me do things that I find to be inappropriate.'

Even as she finished speaking, a furtive look crossed her face. He grinned sardonically. She must be remembering the man who had ordered her to steal his mother's jewels.

'Are you sure?' he pursued.

Her chest rose and fell and she seemed to be struggling with a strong emotion. For a moment he was contrite, but he pushed the weakness away. Now was the time for her to tell him everything. Or at least hint at it.

'Yes,' she said shortly, refusing to meet his eyes.

His jaw hardened. There was more than one way to make a cat howl.

The remainder of the journey home passed in a strained silence that Ravensford did nothing to break. Let her stew in her own lies.

Ravensford fingered the grey pearl necklace. Matching ear drops, bracelets and a ring nestled in the nearby satin-lined box. The set would go perfectly with the mauve gown Madame Bertrice was altering. Unfortunately it had not arrived for tonight's visit to the Drury Lane Theatre. It did not matter. He could no more give Miss O'Brien the set to wear than he could fly to the moon. No matter that a large part of him wanted to defy convention and his mother in order to see how the Irish woman would look dressed as befitted her exotic beauty.

He returned the jewels to their case and handed them over to Stevens, who looked scandalised. Ravensford quirked one eyebrow.

The valet sniffed. 'Please allow me to get a fresh cravat,

my lord. The one you are wearing has developed a crease where there should be none.'

Ravensford barely managed not to laugh out loud, which would have offended the valet. He should have known that Stevens cared nothing for the jewellery and everything for his master's toilet.

'Thank you, Stevens, but that won't be necessary. I realise that I am a trial to you but, as you know, I am not a dandy. I would not be happy to have you leave me for another, but I would understand.'

The valet gave his gentleman an aggrieved look. 'I could not leave. I waited years for you to hire me. You have the best shoulders and legs in all of London. You are a credit to my skills.' He sighed dramatically. 'If only I could impress upon you the importance of dress.'

Surprise stopped Ravensford from speaking for a moment. He had had no idea his valet felt so strongly about dressing him. For his part, he considered himself to be a well set-up man, but he had several friends he would describe as better physical specimens than himself. Perth was one.

Humbly, he said, 'Thank you, Stevens, for your devotion.'

The gentleman's gentleman gave his master a tight smile before handing over Ravensford's gloves and cane. Ravensford took the accessories and left. The ladies would be in the foyer shortly.

Half an hour later, Ravensford tapped his cane impatiently against his right leg and wondered why he had ever thought he should be on time. Women certainly did not consider promptness to be important.

He handed his *chapeau* to the butler. 'If the ladies come down, I will be in the library.'

He turned to leave and caught a glimpse of grey. Mary Margaret, dressed in her drab gown, and Annabell, dressed in white muslin trimmed with blue ribbons, were descending the stairs. His attention stayed on Mary Margaret. Even dressed dowdily, she aroused him.

She stood proudly, watching him. Her movements were delicate and flowing, her eyes brilliant as diamanté and her hair silky as a raven's wing. Dressed by Madame Bertrice, she would take the *ton* by storm.

She had stunned him in that pink dress. The neck had been lower than anything she ever wore, drawing his imagination to the hollow between her breasts. In many ways, it had been more erotic than her soaked chemise and pantaloons. The dress had been provocative.

He swallowed hard.

'Ravensford,' Annabell said in her high, light voice, 'you are being rude. You are putting Mary Margaret to the blush.' Her laugh filled the air.

He had to physically shake himself. His perusal had been too intense and too long. To hell with convention.

'I knew the gown would become you,' he said.

She looked nonplussed. 'This gown?'

Annabell's laughter trilled out.

Ravensford coughed to hide his own discomfiture. His mental picture of her in the pink dress had made him forget that she wore the grey. Never in all his thirty-two years had he behaved this gauche. In the end it was worth it. Her nervous laugh, low and throaty like a warm purr, filled the foyer and sent liquid desire coursing through his limbs.

'Thank you, my lord.'

'Andrew, what are we waiting for?' his mother said shrilly from where she stood on the landing, twenty feet above them. 'We will be late.'

He pulled his focus from Mary Margaret and made his parent an ironic bow. 'So we will, Mother. The coach is waiting.'

The butler showed the younger women out while Ravensford waited to assist his mother. The urge to throw convention to the wind and take Mary Margaret's arm was great, but he knew that doing so would only make matters worse for her. His parent would never condone his interest in the companion. He wondered why it mattered.

Mary Margaret kept her gaze focussed out the window of the carriage. The Countess and Annabell sat across from her, facing the driver. Ravensford sat beside her, his thigh brushing hers every time the coach lurched. She felt like a cat treading across Cook's oven, scorched and wary.

The scent of him filled her senses. He was so close that, if she turned her head, her mouth would brush his shoulder.

Memory of his kiss held her motionless. Her stomach rolled over slowly and her hands trembled. The urge to touch him, to invite his touch in return, filled her. Shivers chased sparks down her spine.

She closed her eyes and forced herself to remember why she was here, and it was not to be seduced by the Earl of Ravensford. In days her first quarter would be complete. Once her wages were in her hand, she could leave the Countess, somehow return to Ireland, and take Emily and Annie away from Thomas. That was why she was here.

She sighed with relief when the carriage finally stopped. The Countess and Annabell descended first. Ravensford followed, turned back to her and offered his hand. She stared at his gloved fingers, telling herself that allowing him to help her down would not make her breath go short and her stomach clench. She lied to herself and knew it.

Fighting to keep from trembling, she put her hand in his. His fingers closed over hers. Her eyes met his, their gazes locked. Her world narrowed to him and his touch. Nothing mattered, not her sister Emily, not her niece Annie, not the people around them.

No matter how many times he helped her from a carriage—and it seemed he did so constantly—she did not think she would ever become inured to his touch. For her, he was magical.

'Andrew,' the Countess demanded, rapping their clasped fingers with her closed fan.

He glanced at his mother and the spell broke. Mary Margaret jerked her arm back and hid her hand in the folds of her skirt.

'Mary Margaret,' the Countess said imperiously, 'see to Annabell, as you should have been doing all the time.'

Mary Margaret nodded, resisting the urge to dip a curtsy. Afraid to look at Ravensford and see his disgust at her weakness in succumbing to him yet again, she skirted away, holding her head proudly as her mother had taught her. The Countess might treat her as a nonentity, but she did not have to act downtrodden.

Annabell frowned at the situation. 'Godmother can be the most autocratic person in the world. Pay no mind to her, Mary Margaret.'

The younger girl linked her arm through Mary Margaret's and steered them to the doors where they waited for the other two. Mary Margaret could just hear the Countess's hissed words.

'Andrew, have you no pride? The chit is a servant, and barely that. Bed her if you must, but don't ogle her in public.'

Mary Margaret blanched and glanced at Annabell to see if the girl had heard. Annabell was smiling at a young man who stood nearby, her attention fully occupied. Thank goodness.

Mary Margaret could not hear Ravensford's reply but imagined it was one of indignant denial.

The Countess swept past them, Ravensford at her side. Mary Margaret and Annabell hurried to keep up. They made their way to Ravensford's reserved box and took their seats, Annabell, the Countess and Ravensford in the front. Mary Margaret sat in the back, positioned to see over the shoulders of the other two women.

The first play of the evening was nearly over. A Shakespearean tragedy that she watched with such absorption it was a shock when someone entered the box and moved in front of her.

The young man from outside had come to chat. Ravensford rose and offered his chair, which the visitor accepted with alacrity.

'Would you care for refreshment?' Ravensford asked, startling Mary Margaret further.

'No, thank you,' she murmured, glad her voice sounded calm and uninterested.

'Always composed and in control,' he murmured.

She blinked and said nothing, no riposte coming to her rescue. He gave her a searching study, his face showing nothing.

'Andrew!'

The Countess's shrill voice broke whatever had caught Ravensford's attention. Mary Margaret was not sure whether to be happy or regretful. As uncomfortable as his interest was, she also found that she enjoyed it. In all, it was a very disturbing conundrum.

The Earl made an elaborate bow in the general direction of his parent and sauntered off. Mary Margaret felt the Countess's angry gaze on her and studiously avoided looking at the woman. It would do no good. The Countess would still make her life miserable.

A flash of gold caught her eye. She looked in the direction of the gallery, squinting to better see over the distance. Bucks and dandies milled about the area just in front of the stage, many calling to the actresses.

There was the golden glint again. She leaned forward in her seat. A tall, slim man lounged against the far corner. He was impeccably dressed in evening clothes tailored to his frame. His attention was on her.

No. It could not be. He would never come all this way. Never. But…

He waved in her direction. Thomas.

Mary Margaret blanched. He had followed her here. Where were Emily and Annie? Had he left them in Ireland?

'I took the liberty of getting you some punch,' Ravensford said, his baritone seeming to come from just behind her right ear.

Her pulse jumped. She glanced back at him, hoping her countenance did not betray her unease. Had he seen her looking at Thomas? Had he seen Thomas looking at her? Surely if he had he would think it nothing but two people exchanging interested glances. He did not know Thomas.

But the Countess did.

Mary Margaret shivered.

'Here,' Ravensford murmured, setting the punch down. 'Where is your cape?'

She stared at him. His words meant nothing.

'Where is your cape?' he repeated.

She shook her head. 'I don't have one.'

'Yes, you do. I gave you my mother's,' he said patiently as though talking to a child.

She shook her head again. 'I gave it back.'

What was Thomas doing here? Was he going to contact her? Was he going to tell her to steal the jewels now? She shut her eyes.

Ravensford's hand on her shoulder brought her back to the present situation. 'That cape was yours. When I give you something, I expect you to keep it.'

She stared blindly up at him. He was making such a fuss over something so trivial. 'It was not yours to give. You cannot take something from someone else and say it is yours to give where you wish.'

His fingers tightened on her shoulder. 'Is that a philosophy you live by? Or is it just for me and that blasted cape?'

She blinked and her mouth worked, but nothing came out. He spoke almost as though he knew, but he could not. No one knew, not even Emily.

'It is a philosophy I believe in.'

Instead of replying, he moved on to his mother and Annabell. She sagged. Surreptitiously she looked back where Thomas had been. He was gone.

She chewed her bottom lip. Perhaps she had been mistaken. The lighting was not that good. It was ridiculous to think Thomas would come this far. In his mind as long as he had Emily and Annie that was more than enough to get her to do his bidding. That was it. She had been mistaken. A guilty conscience had tricked her.

She heard shuffling and noticed that the man who had occupied the Earl's seat the entire time had stood and was giving Ravensford back the chair.

'No need, Higgins,' Ravensford said. 'I am capable of standing.'

'Know you are, Ravensford, but must be moving on. Miss Annabell says I may pay m'respects tomorrow.' He bowed his way out without ever glancing in Mary Margaret's direction.

Instead of watching the young man leave, she concentrated on the activity starting on the stage. The Countess might treat her as though she did not matter, but being completely ignored was worse. She felt as though she did not exist. It was an awful sensation.

'Don't mind Higgins,' Ravensford drawled. 'He's never been known for his good manners.'

Against her better judgement, she gave the Earl a grateful smile. He always seemed to know how she felt. For a second warmth and security enveloped her, but only for a moment. Having her employer's son empathise with her was not a good thing. Especially when she had conspired with someone to rob that son's mother.

The rest of the evening passed agonisingly slowly for Mary Margaret.

Ravensford searched the gallery for the blond man who had waved at Mary Margaret. If he had not seen her blanch and look like she had been landed a facer, he would have thought the man a would-be swain. Instead he wondered if there was some connection to the man in Ireland who had been ordering her about. Far fetched, he knew, but someone had to be available for her to pass the stolen goods to.

He would have to keep an even closer eye on her. The knowledge did not make him feel better. Even knowing he was making a mistake, he had allowed himself to get involved with the woman. He had even imagined getting to know her very well.

He had been weak, something he would be careful not to be again.

## Chapter Eleven

Several days later, Mary Margaret sat in the garden behind the house while the Countess and Annabell napped. She took advantage of the quiet time to read Jane Austen's *Pride and Prejudice*. A tidy smile twisted her mouth as she lived through Mr Darcy's internal war with himself. He was high in the instep and it nearly cost him the woman he loved. She set the finished book down and stared into space. Miss Austen's book was the perfect romance of two people from different levels of society.

She had heard that even the Prince of Wales read Miss Austen's books. Knowing that made her feel less guilty that the story had taken her out of her own problems.

Every day she woke, dreading the possibility that Thomas might call or contact her. So far, he had not. That strengthened her belief that she had been mistaken that evening at Drury Lane. The Thomas she knew would have forced her to meet with him by now. Even knowing that, she still worried.

'Miss, you are needed in the foyer.'

She jerked. She had been caught in her thoughts and not heard the footman. She pushed her fear of Thomas away and made herself smile.

'Goodness, Jeremy, you startled me.' She grabbed the book and rose.

'Pardon, miss.'

She smiled at him. His face radiated anticipation, making her wonder why he had come to fetch her.

'Why am I required in the foyer?'

He grinned, showing crooked front teeth. 'A surprise, miss.'

'Hmm.'

Minutes later, she stood in shock. Footmen carried large boxes through the front door while others carried more large boxes up the stairs. A veritable treasure trove was passing by her, all headed for her room.

'What is all this?' she gasped.

'What is the meaning of this outrage?' the Countess demanded at the same time, her voice rising above the bustle. The older woman stood at the top of the stairs, her robe caught at her throat with white knuckled hands. Her eyes blazed.

All movement ceased.

'Miss O'Brien's wardrobe has arrived,' Ravensford drawled, breaking the frozen silence.

He had come into the house unnoticed while everyone apprehensively watched his mother. With nonchalance, he handed his hat, gloves and cane to the butler before moving to the farthest wall.

He appeared to find nothing out of the ordinary. Mary

Margaret knew he understood perfectly well what was going on. His bland look of interest did not fool her. Drat the man.

Both Mary Margaret and the Countess glared at him. He returned their angry looks with disregard, as though what he had done were not totally unacceptable.

'Andrew, come to my rooms immediately.' The Countess's gaze swept the assembled servants and came to rest on Mary Margaret. 'The rest of you clear this nonsense from the house. I won't have it. Return it to wherever it came from.'

Mary Margaret wanted to sink into the floor. She wanted to go up in a puff of smoke and regain consciousness in Ireland. She wished she had never succumbed to Thomas's threats and taken employment with the Countess. If only she had been stronger, but Emily had been at stake.

In spite of all that, she held her head high and met the Countess's furious look. 'I quite agree with you, my lady. None of this should be here.'

Ravensford pushed away from the wall and sauntered toward her. Mary Margaret stepped around a footman whose hands were full of boxes.

'This is my house, ladies,' he said gently, almost too gently. 'And I decide what goes on here. I also decide how members of my household will dress and present themselves to the world.' He looked at one and then the other. 'Do I make myself clear?'

Mary Margaret felt her mouth drop and quickly snapped it shut. She dared not look at the Countess. Everyone said the Earl rarely defied his mother, yet he was doing so now. Someone would pay for this and it would very likely be her.

The Countess said nothing more, turning on her heel and stalking off. There was a noticeable easing of tension.

'Continue what you were doing,' Ravensford stated. 'Miss O'Brien, come with me.'

Her hackles rose. 'I—' She stopped herself.

Everyone's attention had shifted to her. The last thing she wanted to do was make the situation worse, if that were possible, by defying Ravensford. With a supreme effort, she relaxed her rigid shoulders and followed behind him as he led the way to the library. She could feel the stares of all the servants. Her shoulders itched from tension.

Ravensford held the door for her, having gestured the butler away. She walked past him, head high, eyes focussed straight ahead. She kept moving until she had put the distance of the room between herself and the Earl's desk before stopping and turning back to face him. Somehow it did not feel far enough away.

'Feel safe?' He moved to his desk and poured a glass of the amber-coloured liquor he seemed to enjoy so much. He caught her watching him. 'Would you care for some? It will burn away whatever troubles you.'

She shook her head.

He downed it in one gulp. 'It is not every day I defy my mother,' he explained. 'Not that I am unwilling to do so, but it is generally easier not to. For everyone. She has a way of making someone pay the piper when she does not get her own way. Very likely you will suffer.'

Mary Margaret gaped at him. She had not realised he knew how his mother behaved. For some reason, she had thought him blind to the Countess's faults. Most people seemed not to see the uncomfortable in those they loved. Emily certainly could not see the evil in Thomas, or if she did she refused to admit it. Even when he hit her she made excuses. Ravensford made none for his mother.

He gave her a devilish smile that made her knees weaken.
'Please be seated, Miss O'Brien. I won't bite. I have never
bitten an unwilling woman.'

She dropped into the nearest chair, shocked by what he
had said. 'I hope not.'

He laughed wryly. 'What are you afraid of, Miss O'Brien?
That I will ask you to be my mistress again? Don't worry.
Even I understand no when it has been said to me twice.'

'You treat this with levity, but I am appalled at all you
have bought. I said the one dress, not an entire wardrobe.
What will people think?'

He poured himself another glass of liquor and downed
it in one long swallow. Putting the empty glass down, he
studied her with a reckless air. 'Who gives a damn, Miss
O'Brien? Surely you don't.'

She sputtered. How could he think that? 'Just because I
am not Quality does not mean I don't value my reputation.
In truth, I need to be more careful than one of your station.
If I become ruined, true or not, I will never be allowed to
make my living. No one will have me in their household.'

'You are right as far as it goes,' he drawled. He poured
another drink and downed it as quickly as he had the last.
'However, if I give you a letter of recommendation then
you will get work.'

'Who made you all powerful?' she demanded, incensed
by his arrogance. 'I very much doubt that a letter from the
Prince Regent would negate the rumours that will fly about
your buying me a complete wardrobe.'

He bowed to her. 'Then we shall put it to the test if need
be.'

She gaped at him. 'You would get the Prince of Wales to
write a letter about this? You are mad.'

He eyed her speculatively. 'There are moments when I have thought so. Particularly lately.'

His words nonplussed her. She had a strange feeling that he meant more than he said. It was time she was gone even if he had not dismissed her. She stood.

'I have not given you permission to leave, Miss O'Brien.' Keeping his gaze on her, he poured himself another drink and downed it just as quickly.

She frowned at him. 'I doubt you are capable, my lord. You are guzzling that vile stuff as though it were water.'

He poured another glass and saluted her with it. 'This is the finest Irish whiskey. You should be proud of your country. I brought this back when we came from my mother's. A friend first introduced me to this drink, only his is Scotch.'

He gulped the golden liquid down, his Adam's apple moving in rhythm with the whiskey. She winced. No wonder he was acting so strangely. He had to be the worse for drink.

'I will send back everything but the one dress.' She turned and made for the door. Enough was enough.

'Miss O'Brien,' he said, his voice a silky threat, 'I still have not dismissed you. Had you forgotten?'

She paused and looked back and gasped. He was right behind her; the sound of his movement had been muffled by the thick carpet. He grabbed her left wrist and held it tightly so that she could not get away without squirming. She stood like a statue.

'You are not yourself, my lord.' She hoped her voice sounded more firm to him than it did to her.

He grinned wolfishly. 'If you are implying that I am drunk, you are correct. However, I think...' he pulled her closer '... I am more myself than I have ever been around you.'

Before she realised it was happening, her body was flush

to his. His face was scant inches above hers. And his mouth was a breath away from hers. Her eyes widened as his intention became clear.

'Adding insult to injury, my lord?' she managed to say before his lips found hers.

'Pleasure to inclination,' he murmured against her flesh. 'Close your eyes, Miss O'Brien.'

Too late. She had waited too long to struggle. His arms slid around her waist, trapping her hands against his chest. She pushed but to no avail. She was held tightly and expertly.

His mouth met hers in a rush of heat that left her feeling bewildered and delighted. She tingled from her lips to her toes. His tongue slid along her skin, tickling her into a gasp. He darted in, flicking against her teeth. In her surprise, she nearly bit him.

'Ouch,' he said, drawing out and looking down at her. 'You aren't supposed to do that.'

All she could do was stare at him.

'Let's try this again,' he murmured.

'I won't. That is—'

'Hush.'

His mouth moved against hers in seductive abandon. His tongue pressed for entry, then darted in and melded with hers. He tasted of heather and smoke and something infinitely sweet. Heat, then cold, then shivers raced through her body. She felt like she was falling into an abyss from which she would never be able to escape. Her entire world exploded and then came back together with him at the centre.

His mouth broke from hers only to nuzzle the tender spot just below her ear. His hands roamed her back, stroking muscles that had tightened in delight. He moulded her to his desire. She moaned.

His lips returned to hers just as one of his hands slid to her breast and cupped it. The combination was too much. She arched into his caress. She returned his kiss as passionately as he gave it. She thought she would die if he quit. She purred.

When he broke away, she was stunned. He held her to him, but his hands dropped to her waist, his forehead rested on hers.

'I want you,' he murmured, his voice a husky rasp.

Bewilderment held her motionless in his arms. Her breathing was rapid and shallow. She felt bereft.

'Mary Margaret. Sweetheart,' he whispered against her cheek where he nuzzled her. 'You can't know how long I have wanted to do that.'

His hands shifted to rub up and down her back, fitting her against his enflamed body. She didn't know where she ended and he began. Her senses were in a daze of desire. The knowledge of his power over her was frightening, so much so that she snapped back to reality.

'Oh, no,' she moaned, appalled at what she had just done.

She pushed hard against him. This time he had not been expecting resistance and his grip failed. She stumbled from his embrace, panting as though she had run up a flight of stairs. He moved to take her back into his arms and she scrambled behind the chair where she had so recently sat.

'No! We cannot, that is I cannot, that is—'

'Cannot kiss? Make love?' He watched her with tender amusement. 'Why not?'

'You are drunk,' she gasped. 'How can you say such things?'

He sighed and ran his fingers through his hair. 'Probably. Although not so much that I don't know what I am doing.'

'What if someone came in and saw us? Especially after what you have already done.'

'Is that all you can think about—what other people will say? I have wanted to kiss and caress you since the instant I first heard your throaty purr. You excited me then and you excite me now.'

She fought back the delight his words created. To know that he had been attracted to her from the beginning was heady stuff. The interest she had felt was not all one-sided. And yet, what did this really mean? Nothing. He was treating her as he would a mistress. The momentary madness ended.

'How could you?' she demanded, fighting back the tears that threatened. He was attracted to her, desired her, but that was all this was to him. A physical liaison that any woman could satisfy.

'I could because you wanted me to.'

She gasped. 'I am not a loose woman.'

His eyes narrowed. 'I never said you were.'

She put a hand to her chest, wishing her heartbeat would return to normal. 'But you are treating me as one. The dresses and…and the kiss and…'

He took a step toward her. 'Then marry me.'

She gasped. Shame engulfed her. 'How dare you insult me? You don't mean that. I won't play your game.'

He took another step forward and reached for her. She darted to the right, narrowly escaping him.

'You play the game, Miss O'Brien. Not I. Hot, then cold, but never consistent.'

Fury made her bold. 'I think not.'

Before he could try to catch her again, she bolted for the door and through into the hall. She didn't look back and didn't slow down until she was safe in her room.

Ravensford watched her flee. What had he done, proposing to her? It was the last thing he had intended when she entered the library. But the whiskey, his pent-up desire, her ardent response to his lovemaking…everything had conspired to make him act less than judiciously.

He twisted around and went to pour another drink. In for a penny, in for a pound. He downed two more glasses of the potent liquor until he was well and truly foxed.

A knock on the door was followed by the butler's discreet entrance. 'My lord, the Earl of Perth is here.'

Ravensford turned from his vacant study of the garden. 'Send him in.'

Seconds later Perth entered, one dark brow raised. 'You look the worse for wear, old man.'

'Have a drink?'

Perth grinned. 'Is that the cause or only the solution?'

Ravensford pointedly turned his back and poured two drinks. Facing his friend again, he handed Perth one glass.

'To lust in all its forms,' Ravensford said, toasting Perth.

Perth chuckled. 'A mistress or Miss O'Brien?'

Ravensford downed his drink. 'Oh, Miss O'Brien, who else? That woman has been the bane of my existence since I met her.'

'Following in Brabourne's footsteps?' Perth drank his whiskey more slowly, amusement lightening his swarthy complexion.

'Nothing of the sort. At least, not exactly.' Ravensford sank into a chair and motioned for Perth to do the same.

'Brabourne married for love. I might do it for desire. Can't love a woman who is planning to steal from m'mother. No matter if m'mother deserves to have her jewels stolen or not.'

Perth laughed. 'Your speech is as disorganised as your mother's always is. I swear there are a few pieces of this puzzle missing.'

'Damn,' Ravensford said, appalled that he was slipping into his mother's habit. ''Tis a long story.'

'I have the time if you have more whiskey.'

'Right.'

Ravensford got the decanter and set it between them. In succinct sentences he told Perth everything.

'Don't you think marriage is a drastic solution?' Perth finally asked.

'Undoubtedly.' Ravensford tipped the decanter up only to see it was empty. 'Jones,' he bellowed.

The butler poked his head in. 'Yes, my lord?'

'More whiskey.'

Within minutes they were re-supplied.

'Blasted woman does things to my mind, not to mention my body,' Ravensford explained. 'The words were out of my mouth before I knew they were said.'

'And they cannot be taken back. You are a gentleman, unlike myself.'

Ravensford leaned over and poured Perth more whiskey, narrowly missing the table. 'You are too hard on yourself, Perth. Your code of honour is as well honed as anyone's. You just think it isn't.'

A dark look settled over Perth's features. 'So you say.' He gulped his drink. 'Come, White's beckons. I have an itch to gamble.'

Thankful to be gone from the turmoil he knew roiled

upstairs, Ravensford called for his great coat, hat and cane. Neither man cared that it was only late afternoon as they strolled from the house and made their way to Bond Street.

Upstairs, Mary Margaret was stunned by the amount of clothing Ravensford had purchased. Boxes and dresses covered her bed, the two chairs and every other inch of space. Silks, cottons, taffetas, wools—every fabric imaginable, in all the colours of the rainbow, deluged her room. Then there were shoes and bonnets for every imaginable occasion. He had spent a fortune on her. She would never be able to repay him.

Why had he done this? Anger bubbled up in her.

'Ohh, Mary Margaret,' Annabell's light voice said in awe.

Mary Margaret turned around, tamping down on her fury. There was no reason to take her anger at Ravensford out on Annabell. 'I didn't hear you enter.'

Annabell grinned. 'I knocked. When you didn't answer, I came in.' Her gaze skimmed the room. 'I can understand why you didn't hear me. If I had just received all of this, I would be oblivious to the world too.'

Mary Margaret frowned. 'It will all have to go back. I cannot afford it. I told the Earl I would take the one dress. Never this.'

'You cannot return all of this,' Annabell said, horrified. 'What will Ravensford say? What will the servants say if they see all these boxes going out?'

'What will they say if the boxes stay here?' Mary Margaret could not keep the bitterness from her words. 'I don't care what Ravensford thinks. He is too domineering by half.'

Annabell shrugged. 'He is a man and an Earl. He cannot help himself.'

'So true,' Mary Margaret said. 'So disgustingly true.'

## Chapter Twelve

Mary Margaret sat demurely in one of her old dresses and watched as the Countess and Annabell entertained Mr Finch. The Countess poured tea and dispensed sandwiches with a blithe disregard for Mary Margaret. She was not surprised. For the last three days, the Countess had been doing everything in her power to make her miserable.

She wanted to burn every piece of clothing Ravensford had foisted on her. And she would when this farce was done. Right now she was only grateful that the hateful man had not come near her since his mockery of a proposal. His absence had nearly convinced her that he regretted making such game of her, for she never doubted that the offer was made in spite over her rejection of his previous overtures.

The Countess glanced her way with a malicious smile. Mary Margaret turned her head to keep the older woman from seeing the anger and resentment in her eyes. Not even the serene beauty of the rose garden could ease her turbulent emotions. She was sorely tempted to ask permission to be excused even though she knew the Countess would refuse.

'My lady,' the butler intoned, 'the Reverend Mr Fox.'

Fear speared Mary Margaret, leaving her breathless and clammy. It *had* been him at the theatre, just as she had feared. He had come to London to spy on her, but why was he here? He could not talk to her in front of everyone, at least not about stealing the Countess's jewellery.

'Ah, Mr Fox,' the Countess said coolly. 'What brings you to London? I fear your flock will be lost without your guiding hand.'

He laughed as though at a great witticism and advanced into the room despite the lukewarm reception. 'You are always so droll, my lady. I found that I missed your intelligence and beauty.'

Mary Margaret watched in awe as the Countess began to visibly thaw. Thomas had that way with women. To her horror, Annabell gazed at her brother-in-law as though she beheld a god. Her stomach started churning.

From the corner of his eye, Thomas slid his blue gaze over her. She knew that look well, and it boded no good. She had to do something.

Surging to her feet, she said, 'Oh, Thomas, have you brought me a message from Emily?'

He gloated at her. 'She sends her love and hopes you will return soon.'

'I miss her awfully.'

That was true and there was nothing else she could say. It would only inflame the Countess more if she professed to want to return home. But she knew that Thomas was telling her to get the job done.

Dismissing her, Thomas focussed his attention on Annabell. 'Miss Winston, I trust you are enjoying your stay in London.'

Annabell beamed up at him, the dimple in her right cheek peeking out. 'Immensely.'

He bowed over her extended hand. 'I never doubted it with the Countess showing you about.'

Mary Margaret's initial fear abated as she listened to Thomas's effusive charm. She wondered why the two women did not see through him. But then, she had not at first. She, like they, had been entranced by his spectacular good looks and easy way with words.

'Very prettily done,' Ravensford's baritone said from the doorway.

He had entered while all of them had been focussed on Thomas. His cynical gaze rested on her brother-in-law, and Mary Margaret's receding fear began to return. There was something about the way Ravensford held himself that spelled danger. Perhaps his broad shoulders were a bit too straight, or his square jaw too tight. She was not sure exactly what the change was, but she knew him well enough by now to know that he did not like Thomas.

Her initial unease was increased tenfold when Ravensford's glance passed over her. Dark circles intensified the colour of his eyes. He looked debauched and deadly, as she imaged a man would look who has reached the end of his tolerance. Surely Thomas's presence had not caused this condition. She devoutly hoped it had nothing to do with their confrontation in the library either.

'Ahem... I must be leaving,' Mr Finch said, breaking into the silence.

They had all forgotten him. Now everyone concentrated

on his departure, using action to ease the discomfort caused by Ravensford's presence.

'I shall be sure and keep a dance for you,' Annabell said, referring to Finch's earlier request for a waltz at her coming-out ball.

He took her proffered hand and gushed, 'I shall hold my breath until then.'

It was all Mary Margaret could do not to laugh at his dramatisation.

'Then you will be in no shape for the dance,' Ravensford said drily.

Mr Finch looked like a balloon that the air had been let out of. 'Very practical, my lord.'

'Upon occasion I try to do the mundane.'

Mary Margaret listened to Ravensford in surprise. She had never seen him jab at someone before. Something was bothering him.

Mr Finch took his leave and hurried from the room. Ravensford settled himself comfortably in one of the chairs, his left leg over the right. His Hessians shone like mirrors.

'What brings you all the way to London, Mr Fox?'

Mary Margaret watched Thomas smile benignly at the Earl. 'My father is here for the Season and I am come to pay my respects.'

Ravensford quirked one brow.

The Countess asked point-blank, 'Is your father in trade, Mr Fox?'

Mary Margaret would have laughed if she could not see how furious Thomas was at the slight. His blue eyes were hard chips. His finely wrought mouth was a thin slash. Somehow, he managed to keep his tone level, even light.

'No, my lady. My father is Viscount Fox.' He flashed a false smile around the room. 'I am a younger son.'

A considering light entered Ravensford's eyes, turning them to the bright colour of emerald with the sun shining through. 'And went into the clergy instead of the army.'

Thomas turned to face Ravensford directly. 'My middle brother is in the army.'

'Why, I didn't know you were related to old Fox,' the Countess said. 'How delightful. You must come to Anna-bell's ball this Thursday. I am sure we sent your father an invitation.' She turned her sharp gaze on Mary Margaret. 'Didn't we?'

She nodded, remembering the name. It had struck her that it was the same as Thomas's, but she had not consid-ered that his father might be in London. What a very small world the aristocracy was.

'I—' Thomas said.

Ravensford spoke smoothly over Thomas. 'I am sure that a man of the cloth, as Mr Fox is, would find our entertaining too hedonistic.' The smile he turned on Thomas didn't reach his eyes. 'We would not want to make him uncomfortable.'

Mary Margaret enjoyed Ravensford's needling of Thomas, knowing her brother-in-law was too far from home to take his fury out on Emily. Still, part of her dreaded what he would do when he returned to Ireland. Or when he fi-nally demanded a meeting with her.

Thomas gave Ravensford a bland look. 'I should be de-lighted to attend Miss Winston's ball. I am sure she will put every other young lady in the shade.' He gave the Countess and Annabell a brilliant smile.

Mary Margaret twisted away to look anywhere but at Thomas, but not before she saw the disgust Ravensford did nothing to hide. The Countess and Annabell, however, were enchanted.

'In that case,' Ravensford drawled, rising, 'we will expect you after dinner.'

Disappointment flashed across Thomas's face and Mary Margaret realised that he had been hoping for an invitation to dinner before the ball. She breathed a sigh of relief that Ravensford had prevented that. She did not want to see Thomas any more than she had to.

To add insult to injury, Ravensford added, 'Mother, aren't you and Annabell expected at Mrs Bridges' this afternoon?'

'Goodness, I had completely forgotten.' The Countess rose and motioned to Annabell. 'We must change and be on our way.' She held a hand out to Thomas, who took it and raised it to his lips. 'We shall expect you on Thursday.'

He bowed and took his leave without even glancing at Mary Margaret. She relaxed.

'Is he the curate who introduced you to my mother? The one who is married to your sister?'

She started. In her relief at having Thomas gone, she had forgotten how acute Ravensford was. Particularly when no one else was around and he could say what he wished.

'Yes.'

'Do you know him well?'

Apprehension and guilt made their way into her thoughts. Why was he asking these questions? What did it matter to him?

'Better than I would like.'

'And why is that?'

His eyes held hers. She wondered again how much he knew. Very likely more than she wished.

She chose her words carefully. 'He is not always as charming with women as he was this afternoon.'

'How is that?'

He evinced only mild curiosity, but Mary Margaret sensed something deeper. Her shoulders tightened.

'Oh, just…just that I have seen him lose his temper upon occasion. That is all.'

Disgust at herself twisted her mouth. Now she was being like Emily and evading the real question. Why did they protect Thomas?

'I see.'

She looked sharply at him. He watched her with narrowed eyes. She could almost think he did see.

'Does he visit London often?'

She licked dry lips. 'Not that I know of.'

'Does he visit his father's estate?'

'Is this an interrogation, my lord?' She was on the defensive and knew it. What did he want from her? 'I do not keep track of Thomas's comings and goings.'

He took out his pocket watch and checked the time. 'Perhaps he is here because of you?'

'I don't see why,' she answered without thinking.

'He must be concerned about your welfare. You are his wife's sister and he did find you employment with my mother, as awful as that is.'

'Well, perhaps,' she murmured, realising belatedly that he had given her a perfectly plausible reason for Thomas being in London. Along with his family being here.

'Then he will accept an invitation to accompany us to Astley's Amphitheatre tomorrow?'

'No. That is, I mean, he surely would, but we are not

going there tomorrow. Annabell wants to see the wild animals in the Tower.'

His gaze on her was sardonic. 'Then Mr Fox will join us for a tour of the Tower. I will have my secretary send him around an invitation.'

She gulped back a retort. The last thing she wanted was to have Thomas with them. But she had no control over who Ravensford invited. She could not even stop him from buying her a complete wardrobe.

'And about the clothes you bought for me, my lord. What do you suggest I wear to the Tower?'

His eyes narrowed at the sarcasm in her voice. She was even surprised by her daring to take him to task. The surprise was quickly followed by worry as she realised that in order to be comfortable enough to berate him, however so slightly, she must be *very* used to his company.

'Wear whatever you want, Miss O'Brien. Except for Annabell's ball. Then I want you to wear the pink dress Madame Bertrice altered for you.'

She made him a mock curtsy. 'And we both know that I will do as you bid, my lord. You schooled me in obeying orders before we ever left Ireland.'

His lips parted in a white slash of teeth. 'So you say, but your actions put the lie to your words.'

Before she could think of something else to say, he rose and sauntered from the room. He was the most infuriating man.

Well, she would get the better of him. Ravensford would find out nothing about her and Thomas because she did not intend to do as Thomas ordered. As for the clothes, she would go straight up to her room and continue folding and repacking them in the boxes she had not let the footmen return to Madame Bertrice.

Mary Margaret held up an afternoon dress of the finest white muslin trimmed with emerald ribbons. Crossing to the mirror, she held the frock up to her face and could not help but admire the picture. The garment was perfect for her.

She sighed and turned away. Temptation. She was not keeping these clothes no matter how beautiful they made her look. She was not so vain as to risk her reputation further.

A knock on her door was followed by Annabell's entrance. She and the Countess must have just returned from their afternoon visit to Mrs Bridges. The girl sat on the bed and watched Mary Margaret fold the afternoon dress.

'Ravensford will be furious,' Annabell said.

'Then he should not do something as disreputable as buying his mother's companion a complete wardrobe.' In a fit of pique, she stuffed the folded garment into too small a space.

Annabell giggled, then became suddenly silent. Mary Margaret frowned at the wadded-up gown before looking at her charge. A dreamy look transformed the girl's features.

'What did you think of Mr Fox?'

Unease crept down Mary Margaret's back. The look on Annabell's face screamed trouble.

'Annabell, Thomas is married to my younger sister, Emily.'

She hoped her tone had been pragmatic with just a hint of sympathy. It was so hard to tell how one really sounded, especially to a young wom-an who had just been smitten by a very hand-some man.

'Oh,' Annabell said lightly. 'What are you doing to that beautiful dress?'

Mary Margaret scowled. 'I am trying to repack it.'

'I will send my maid in to help you,' Annabell said. 'It will take you hours to do this by yourself.'

'Thank you, but I can manage.'

Mary Margaret had no intention of getting anyone else into trouble with the Earl. When he started raving about the clothes being returned, she would be the only person responsible.

'As you wish,' Annabell said.

Mary Margaret gave the girl a considering look. Annabell was too docile. Normally she would have argued with Mary Margaret about the use of her personal maid.

The disquiet that had surfaced at Annabell's mention of Thomas returned. Mary Margaret knew only too well how devastatingly attractive her brother-in-law was to women.

The next day Mary Margaret watched anxiously as Thomas took Annabell to see the lions, who numbered among the many wild animals housed at the Tower. The girl was smitten and Thomas was doing everything in his power to keep her that way. It did not help matters that the Countess had stayed home as usual. Had she come, Thomas would have been forced to divide his charms between the two women. As it was, he could focus completely on Annabell. She had to catch up with them.

Even worried as she was, she sensed Ravensford's presence before he spoke. Her skin tingled and her senses sharpened. He did that to her.

'Is something bothering you?'

'No. Should something be?' She immediately regretted the answer. She owed it to him and to Annabell to bring her concern into the open. 'That is not true.' She sighed. 'I am worried about Annabell. I think she is more interested in Thomas than is proper.'

'He is married to your sister.'

'Yes. That is why I am so concerned about Annabell.'

'I should have thought your sister would take first priority.'

What to tell him without telling him the truth? This was so hard. She shook her head. How could Emily stand the constant lying and subterfuge needed to protect Thomas's reputation? And yet, here she was hedging. She was not strong enough to tell anyone about the beating. Nor would most people care. Under the law, Emily was Thomas's to deal with as he pleased.

Instead she implied something else. 'My sister is used to Thomas's ways.'

Ravensford watched the couple disappear around one of the buildings. 'So theirs was not a love match.'

'It was for her,' Mary Margaret said in a tiny voice.

'Ahh. I am sorry for her.'

She searched his face for the truth of his feelings. 'I believe you really are. But aren't most marriages made for convenience?'

'Most. My parents' was a love match. It just so happened that both families approved.' He shrugged. 'And sometimes arranged marriages become ones of love.'

'But that does not protect Annabell from Thomas's charms.'

He rubbed the sapphire in his signet ring, a habit she realised he had when he was troubled. 'You speak as though you expect Thomas to take advantage of her. Isn't that a rather harsh judgement to make against anyone and particularly a man of the cloth?'

Still more subterfuge, and yet Thomas did flirt with
women. She was never sure if he went further.

She shrugged. 'Perhaps. I just don't want to see Annabell hurt.'

'Then we had best catch up with them.'

She sighed in relief.

Ravensford was now positive that Thomas had been the
man threatening Mary Margaret, and his power had to do
with her sister, Emily. He watched her as they searched for
the other couple. There was a worried crease in her broad
forehead and a pinched look around her mouth. She truly
was concerned.

He saw Thomas's blond hair before he saw Annabell. Instead of going to the lions, the two had stopped to look at the
ravens. It was said that if the ravens ever left the Tower, the
monarchy would fall. A nice legend. He was more interested
in the fact that Annabell clung to Thomas, her face radiant
as she laughed at something he was saying. He began to
understand why Mary Margaret did not like this situation.

Mary Margaret picked up speed and he put out a hand to
slow her. When she looked back at him, an irritated frown
replacing the worry, he shook his head. He forced her to
saunter up with him as though they had no care in the world.

'I thought you two were going to the lions?' he drawled.

Annabell beamed. 'We are, but Thomas was just entertaining me with stories of his parish. He is so droll.'

The man could even look modest, Ravensford saw in disgust. 'How interesting.'

Thomas gave Ravensford a challenging smile. 'Miss Winston has invited me to go to Astley's Amphitheatre tomorrow, Ravensford. I hope that will be all right with you and
the Countess.'

Ravensford returned the smile. 'Of course. Perth is going so we shall be a party.' Perth did not know he was going.

For the rest of the afternoon, Ravensford kept with the couple. He had not liked Thomas Fox the first time he had seen him. There was something about the man that offended. The feeling was strengthened by the knowledge that, although Mary Margaret was careful about what she said, he knew she felt the same way. And Thomas had ordered her to steal from his mother. It would be his very great pleasure to catch the scoundrel. The problem would be to keep Mary Margaret from being implicated.

He glanced at her. She watched Thomas with an anxious look in her eyes that made him want to gather her close and tell her everything would be fine. He would protect her.

He shook his head. First he had asked her to be his mistress, then his wife. He was not in the market for either. If his luck held, she would continue to refuse him on both offers. Or so he told himself.

# Chapter Thirteen

Descending the stairs, Mary Margaret saw that Perth had already arrived and Annabell was champing at the bit to be off. The girl had been in a dither all day, picking first one gown and then discarding it in favour of another. She acted as though she were meeting a lover. The idea was enough to make Mary Margaret's blood run cold.

'I am sorry I am late.'

She did not explain that there had been a stain on her best gown so she had been forced to change at the last moment. She might not have nice clothes, but she had clean ones.

Ravensford scowled at her. She returned his look with a bland one. She knew without his saying a word that he was irritated that she was not wearing one of Madame Bertrice's gowns. Well, let him stew in his juices. She tossed her head, realising belatedly that the movement lost most of its defiance when there was no hair to swing. As usual, her hair was in a tight chignon.

'We had best be going,' Perth said, 'before Annabell here

wears a hole in her slippers with all the shuffling she is doing.' He grinned mockingly at her. 'I did not know that beautiful women riding bareback on trained horses excited you.' He cast a wicked glance at Ravensford. 'I would not have been surprised if Ravensford was the one dancing about. He has always had a penchant for exotic women.'

From the way Ravensford ignored his friend's barb, Mary Margaret decided the taunt had gone wide of the Earl only to hit her square in the heart. Just the thought of Ravensford looking longingly at another woman was enough to make her chest tighten painfully. Now it seemed she was going to have to actually see him desiring other women. She felt sick.

If she did not have to go along as Annabell's chaperon, she would plead a headache or anything to get out of this excursion. As it was, the Countess had already beaten her to the excuse.

The ride to Westminster Bridge Road, where the theatre was, seemed to last forever. She said little as Perth continued to tease Annabell and tried to goad Ravensford. Annabell rose magnificently to the occasion, while Ravensford remained a stoic.

'You are in rare form tonight, Perth,' Ravensford said. 'Is there something about this outing that you have failed to tell me?'

A gleam entered Perth's dark eyes but his voice was non-committal. 'A mild diversion, nothing more. You shall see.'

The carriage halted and the gentlemen exited. This time Perth helped Mary Margaret out. She put her hand in his, not surprised when she felt nothing but the strength of his fingers. She refused to let herself feel disappointment that Ravensford had helped Annabell. The less interaction she had with him the better for her peace of mind and body.

Thomas waited for them at the door.

As before, he was impeccably dressed. Mary Margaret marvelled that her brother-in-law could dress in the height of male fashion, yet live in a cottage no better than that of a prosperous farmer. Viscount Fox must be supplying his son.

The five of them exchanged greetings and entered the theatre. Mary Margaret had known the place would be large, but this was magnificent. Boxes went up four stories on three sides. The fourth side contained a stage and the orchestra. A huge chandelier cast enough light to make it possible to see across the rink where a scantily clad woman was standing on the back of a prancing horse and playing a tambourine.

She must have gaped for Ravensford said drily, 'It can be overwhelming the first time.'

All she could do was nod.

Ravensford led them to a box he had reserved while Perth made his way around the perimeter. Mary Margaret was entranced before they even sat down. She marvelled at the acts of equestrian daring. Beside her, Annabell clapped and joined the crowd in showing their appreciation.

'So,' Ravensford murmured under his breath.

Mary Margaret was so attuned to him that she heard even though she knew he had not meant her to. Turning to him, she saw he had a knowing smile and his attention was not on the performance, but intent on someone in a booth across the rink.

Perth—and a woman. He bowed over her hand as she smiled up at him. Even from this distance, Mary Margaret could make out hair the colour of spun silver. And she had to be wearing a king's ransom in jewels for she sparkled like the chandelier.

'Who is she?' she asked softly.

'Lady de Lisle, one of Perth's old flirts.' He frowned as Perth left the woman's side. 'What is he up to now? She broke with him many years ago and married another man. He has never forgiven her.'

'He seems to have forgiven her quite well,' Mary Margaret said with only a hint of sarcasm.

'He is up to something.'

'Perhaps he still cares for her.'

'I think not. He did not take kindly to being left at the altar while she ran away with another man.'

Mary Margaret gasped and waited for him to elaborate, but he did not. Not even when Perth joined them and sat down on the other side of Annabell. She did note that periodically Lady de Lisle glanced their way. Perth did not return the look.

At the intermission, Thomas rose and said, 'Mary Margaret, come with me for a breath of air. I have news from home.' He bowed to the others. 'If you will excuse us, this is of a personal nature.'

Apprehension made her shudder. He was going to tell her that her time was up. She rose, feeling like a prisoner going to her execution, and followed him from the theatre.

Outside he dropped the pose of solicitous brother-in-law and his voice turned hard. 'Have you got the jewels yet? I warn you, my patience is not endless.'

Her hands felt like ice even in the gloves she wore. Thank goodness he was here and Emily was in Ireland. Knowing that her sister was safe gave her the bravado she needed.

'I must have more time. Just until Annabell's ball.' She took a deep breath and rushed on. 'While everyone is busy

I will sneak up to the Countess's room and steal the jewels. No one will expect it.'

His fingers tightened cruelly on her arm. 'Be sure that you do so. I will expect you to pass them to me that night.'

'Oh, no, someone might see. 'Twould be better to meet you the next day.'

But she would not do so. The day of the ball was quarter's day and she would have her pay. She would be off for Ireland. How, she did not know, but she would manage. She knew the way Ravensford had travelled. She would take the coach and the ferry.

'Don't try to trick me, Mary Margaret. I will make you sorry if you do.'

His grip was so tight she knew she would have bruises the next day. They would be worth it for the knowledge that she had outsmarted him.

'This appears to be a very serious discussion,' Ravensford said, walking toward them.

Mary Margaret jumped, wrenching her arm painfully when Thomas did not release her. Thomas stood calmly.

He smiled smoothly. 'We are just finished, Ravensford. I fear my news was not all good. Mary Margaret's sister has an inflammation of the lungs. Fortunately, the vicar's good wife is caring for her in my absence. Still, it is never comforting to know your loved ones are in danger.'

Mary Margaret heard the implied threat, but there was nothing she could say.

'I am sorry to hear that,' Ravensford said. He took Mary Margaret's unresisting hand and pulled her from Thomas's grip. 'Would you like me to arrange for my mother's doctor to see her?'

Mary Margaret looked into his eyes and saw a strange

light in them, as though he waited expectantly for her to say something to him that he already knew. She shook herself at the fancifulness. He was being kind.

'Thank you, my lord.'

'That won't be necessary, Ravensford,' Thomas said curtly. 'My wife is well cared for.'

Ravensford gave the other man a cutting look. 'I did not ask you, Fox.'

Mary Margaret cringed and wished herself anywhere but between these two men. She did not think Emily was sick, or hoped that if she truly was Thomas would have told her before Ravensford's arrival. But then, neither of them had expected the Earl.

Concern for Emily grew. She glanced at Thomas's furious face. To defy him would only make matters worse, and yet Emily must be her first concern. While the vicar's wife was a good woman, she was not a doctor. She would ask Ravensford to send his physician when they were away from Thomas.

'Thomas is probably right, my lord. The vicar's wife is very good with the sick.'

Ravensford gave her a look of disgust. 'As you wish, Miss O'Brien.'

She wanted to cringe from his disapproval but knew that would only make him despise her cowardice more. Meekly, she allowed him to lead her back inside the theatre.

She studiously avoided looking at Ravensford for the remainder of their stay. Even after Thomas made his farewells, she kept as far from the Earl as Annabell and Perth's presence allowed. At the town house, she kept her head down and mumbled a 'thank you' when Perth helped her out of the carriage.

'My pleasure,' he murmured sardonically.

She gave him a sharp glance but said nothing. As soon as Annabell was safely tucked away she would search out Ravensford and ask him to send the doctor to Emily. In the meantime he would have to continue thinking badly of her.

Ravensford watched Mary Margaret enter the foyer behind Annabell, disgusted with the way she had let Thomas dictate to her.

'If the sky looked like your face,' Perth observed drily, 'we would be in for the storm of the century. Come to White's and tell me on the way what Miss O'Brien has done this time.'

'Good idea,' he muttered, pivoting sharply and re-entering the carriage. Inside he succinctly told Perth about the incident with Thomas and the doctor.

'Come along, old man,' Perth said as they reached White's. 'You need diversion.'

As they entered the exclusive men's club a silence fell on the room. Ravensford looked around, noting the familiar faces. Most occupants nodded; a few would not meet his gaze. A single man rose and came toward him.

'Wondered when word would reach you, Ravensford,' the lone man said. Tall and thin, he moved gracefully. Full grey hair swept back from a high forehead and black brows. Ebony eyes calmly studied Ravensford, as though the man searched for signs of agitation.

Ravensford raised one brow. 'What word was that, Chillings?'

Chillings looked at Perth. 'Do you know?'

Perth shook his head. 'We just came from Astley's Amphitheatre. Needed some normality.'

A tiny, feral smile revealed Viscount Chillings's teeth.

'Seems someone has it in for you, Ravensford. I wonder if it is the same person who wrote in the betting book about Brabourne.'

Ravensford stiffened. His and Perth's friend, the Duke of Brabourne, had found a damaging remark in White's famous betting book about the woman he was now married to. The comment had precipitated Brabourne's proposal. For the Duke it had been the best thing. He and his wife had a love match.

Without a word, Ravensford strode to where the book was kept. He opened it to the last page and read: What Earl, known for his prowess with the fairer sex, has bought his mother's companion an entire wardrobe? Beneath the damaging words was a record of the bets placed on when the companion would be leaving the Countess and moving into her own establishment, paid for by the Earl.

He had not expected this. He had told Madame Bertrice that if she valued his patronage no word would get out of who had paid for Mary Margaret's clothes. As far as the world was concerned, his mother had been the provider. This put paid to all his careful planning.

Mary Margaret was ruined, just as she had feared. With this circulating, she would not be allowed into the homes of any woman of the *ton*. Her use as a chaperon for Annabell was over.

'Easy, old man,' Perth murmured, putting a firm hand on Ravensford's stiff shoulder. 'Seems someone is out to get you the same way Brabourne was got. Although it didn't do him any harm,' he ended with a wicked smile. 'Much the contrary.'

'Brabourne was in love. I am not,' Ravensford hissed for Perth's ears only.

Chillings, his task done, rejoined his group. For a moment Ravensford wondered if the Viscount had written the damaging words. He as quickly dismissed them. He barely knew Chillings and there was no bad blood between them.

Ravensford looked slowly around the room, meeting gazes when possible. The fury that rode him abated enough that he could contemplate murder calmly. Whoever had done this would pay.

They left without a word to anyone. Outside, Ravensford pounded his cane against the ground.

'Blast it to hell! Whoever did this will pay.'

'Just as he did when this was done to Brabourne?'

Ravensford scowled at Perth. 'Brabourne never found the scoundrel, but working together he and I will now.'

They continued walking, having waved off the carriage. The cool air helped Ravensford's temper, but did not erase it.

'In the meantime,' Perth drawled, 'there are several things you can do.'

'Such as?'

'Send the chit back to Ireland or set her up in her own establishment as the mysterious writer suggests.'

'She is not my mistress,' Ravensford said through clenched teeth.

'But not for lack of interest on your part,' Perth said.

There was no answer so he gave none.

Perth left him at his town house door. 'Tell your mother that I will be at Annabell's ball tomorrow, will you? I forgot to send my acceptance.'

'You are the most irresponsible scoundrel,' Ravensford said without malice. 'Yet you are invited everywhere.'

'It must be my charm,' Perth drawled sardonically. 'It cannot be because of my title and wealth.'

'Absolutely not. Especially with Lady de Lisle. She was an heiress in her own right and old de Lisle left her very nicely provided for.' He gave his friend a knowing look which Perth ignored.

'I believe I will call in on an establishment we both know,' Perth said with an air of mild interest. 'Care to join me?'

He was fleetingly tempted. But then a face formed in his mind's eye: green eyes, ebony hair and lips he had tasted twice and wanted to taste more. No, until he was through this attraction to Mary Margaret O'Brien, no other woman interested him in the slightest. Probably he would not even be able to perform. That would make the betting book and then things would be a thousand times worse than the mess they already were.

'No,' he told Perth. 'I have much to do tomorrow. Some of us have responsibilities.'

Perth chuckled as he sauntered away.

Ravensford climbed the steps and took his key out. The door opened. Timothy, the youngest footman, stood carefully erect but his eyes were red and half-shut.

Ravensford sighed in exasperation. 'How many times must I tell Jones not to have you wait up for me? Go to bed.'

Timothy, his face now as red as his eyes, bowed before hurrying off. Ravensford instantly regretted his harsh words. He needed to speak with Jones again, not berate Timothy. The lad only did as ordered.

He took off his beaver hat and gloves, tossed them on the side table, and then propped his cane against the wall. He was exhausted and frustrated. Something had to be done about Mary Margaret, and he did not like any of his choices.

Mounting the stairs, he did not see the shadow on the second floor landing until he was upon her.

'What the—?'

'My lord. Ravensford,' Mary Margaret whispered. 'I need to speak with you.'

Her face was a luminescent oval in the golden light from the single candle he carried. Her eyes were dark pools. She still wore the dowdy dress she had worn earlier. The sight of it increased his irritation.

'My room is two doors down,' he said coldly, wondering if she would go there.

She nodded. Whatever she needed to tell him must be important. He followed her, curious in spite of himself. She slipped in ahead of him.

He closed the door and stood his ground. When she did not speak for long moments, he said, 'Well?'

Her hands clasped tightly together she said in a tiny voice, 'Will you arrange for your mother's doctor to attend my sister?'

That was the last thing he had expected. 'Braver now that Fox isn't around?'

His voice was harsh as he had meant it to be, but when she took a step back as though he had slapped her he regretted letting his anger come out. He was not in the habit of intentionally hurting others.

'What could I say? He is her husband.'

'A valid point. Does he often put your sister in jeopardy?'

He watched her closely, hoping she would trust him enough now to tell him the truth. Emotions warred across her face. She looked pinched.

'Sometimes,' she said, her voice a painful rasp.

'Is there something I can help with?'

He took a step toward her. The urge was strong to gather her close and tell her he would protect her and her loved ones from the world. He resisted, even when hope flared briefly in her eyes before dying.

'You still don't trust me,' he said bitterly.

She turned her back to him and he thought he heard a sob. He put the candle down on the nearest table and went to her.

Putting his hands gently on her shoulders, he said, 'Mary Margaret, sweetheart, look at me.'

He felt her stiffen under his touch. She sniffed and raised her head. Hope flared in him.

In a voice that shook only slightly, she said, 'Please let me go. I have told you everything.'

Disappointment speared him, followed by anger. He twirled her around. 'I am fed up with you hedging. The truth is that your brother-in-law does not treat your sister well. He may even beat her and you are afraid for her and of him. I have offered my help. Do you think that I am powerless?'

Her eyes were wide and her mouth an 'O'. 'I... Do you know how hard it is to admit that your sister is beaten whenever her husband is angry? I know it happens, but that does not make it nice.'

He pulled her to him and cupped her head to his chest. Gently he stroked her as he would a cat that had been hurt. He continued, whispering meaningless words until he felt her relax against him.

'I will take care of it,' he promised.

She wriggled her head free and looked up at him. Bewilderment knitted her brows together. 'Why? She is nothing to you. I am nothing to you.'

'How wrong you are,' he murmured. 'How very wrong.'

His kiss was gentle, as though he cherished her above all else. Mary Margaret felt her heart expand with gladness. Perhaps he did care. Perhaps he even loved her. It was a small hope that grew as he tenderly cupped her head and tasted her mouth.

She melted into him, her hands braced against his chest. She felt his heart beat through her fingers, noted that it speeded up as his kiss deepened. She sighed with pleasure.

When one of his hands covered her breast it felt natural and right. She arched her back to give him better access.

His mouth skimmed over her face and down the side of her neck to the top of her bodice. He licked lightly along the edge of material while he continued to stroke her breast. A sensation of heat and fever started in her abdomen and spread out to every part of her body.

'Turn around,' he murmured, his voice a dark, rich honey.

When she did nothing, just lying in his embrace, he shifted her himself so that the back of her hips were flush to his side. He switched his ministrations to the nape of her neck while his fingers deftly undid the many buttons that held her gown on. A rush of cold hit her as his palms skimmed down her arms, pushing the fabric down.

Slowly, so slowly that she nearly moaned in anticipation, he turned her back around. His eyes held hers captive as his hands slipped inside the bodice of her gown and slid it slowly down her bosom. His flesh burned through her chemise. Her nipples contracted into aching points.

He slid the dress further down. His palms smoothed down her hips and flanks until the gown fell to the floor. She shivered.

His gaze moved to her heaving bosom and lower. 'You are beautiful. Since you fell off the boat, I have wanted to do this. I don't know how I kept from doing this then.' A smile tugged at his lips. 'I am going to make up for all the lost time.'

She heard his words, their meaning penetrating the fog of desire he so easily created in her. This time she did not care. This time she wanted him. She thought he truly wanted her, not just her body. She smiled and moved into his embrace.

He groaned.

He lifted her and carried her to his bed where he carefully laid her on the downy comforter. Her hair had come loose and lay in ebony strands among the pillows.

The light of the candle barely reached them, but he could still see the curves and dark hollows of her body. His own responded with aching quickness. In sure, deft movements, he stripped.

The innocent in Mary Margaret told her to close her eyes. The woman in her kept her gaze focussed on him.

He took her breath away. His shoulders were broad and muscled. Auburn hair curled down his abdomen until it became a nest for the most masculine part of him. He was ready. His thighs and calves were well shaped and powerful. He was perfect in every way.

When he lay beside her, it was all she could do not to stroke and explore his body. Everything about his hard angles and dark shadows enticed her.

He undid the strings of her chemise and pantaloons, his tongue following his fingers. Delight caught her unawares and tossed her high. Contented sounds escaped her.

He chuckled deep in his chest. 'I wondered if you would purr.' He nuzzled her neck and then lower until his mouth took her breast. 'Now I know.'

He sucked and nipped. She made little gasping sounds.

Her hands circled him and her nails dug into his back. She was oblivious to everything but his mouth on her and where his fingers were going. They glided along her flesh, past her stomach and lower. She gasped in surprise when he first touched her. Her loins clenched pleasurably. His mouth returned to hers and the kiss he gave her was so deep she thought he would devour her.

Her nails raked his back as he gave her more pleasure than she had ever thought possible. When he broke from her lips, she whimpered and tried to force him back.

He laughed. 'No, sweetings. I want to watch you.'

She was beyond embarrassment. The things he was doing to her created sensations that made her body spasm and twist.

He watched her face as his hands moved gently, but firmly against and in her flesh, dipping and stroking and exciting. She strained against him. It was too much.

'Open your legs,' he murmured, his voice so husky it was more a growl than words.

She opened slumberous eyes to see him poised above her. She did as she was told. He fit between her thighs as though he belonged there. She sighed with delight as he settled himself.

'Wrap your legs around me.'

Another order, but she was happy to do as he directed. He was hot and hard against her swollen flesh. She did not know what came next, but she moved her hips against his and felt the evidence of his desire.

He gathered her to him, kissing her deeply. Her breasts pressed like hot brands against his chest. He groaned and plunged into her.

Pain lashed Mary Margaret. Her eyes started open.

He stroked the hair from her face, his eyes catching hers. 'It is all right, sweetings. The pain will go away. I promise.'

For long minutes he did not move other than to kiss her

gently and stroke her breasts and flanks. She began to relax
only to have her body start vibrating. He filled her to overflowing.

Slowly, he began to move. Sensations flowed over Mary
Margaret with each thrust of his body. He stroked her and
stoked her. A fire built in the pit of her loins. She felt tense
beyond belief.

She shifted her hands to his hips and her nails dug into
his flesh, urging him to greater speed and deeper penetra-
tion. With a groan, he obliged.

She twisted under him and pushed her hips higher. Whatever she sought was just over the next crest.

He pounded into her. She whimpered in need and pleasure—then exploded.

She gasped before a shout escaped her. His mouth fastened on hers and swallowed her sounds of release.

Seconds later, he groaned. His back arched and then he
collapsed on her.

For long moments they lay, limbs tangled, breathing hard.
When he finally rolled to her side, he pulled her to him.
His hand cupped the back of her head and brought her to
him for a tender kiss.

'Thank you,' he said softly.

She gazed at him, her body relaxed as never before. His
eyes were slumberous, and his mouth was a sensual slash
against his swarthy skin.

It came to her with a tiny shock that they had made love.
She was his mistress. She loved him. Had loved him forever, or she would never have been carried away by his
lovemaking.

He smiled at her. 'Are you ready for more?'

Unable to speak for fear she would tell him everything,

she only nodded. She did not think she could ever get enough of this closeness.

He moved over her, only this time she knew what to do.

## Chapter Fourteen

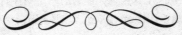

Mary Margaret overslept the next morning. She woke with a start when Annabell landed on her bed with a plop.

'Wake up, sleepyhead. I had hot chocolate and toast brought up and you cannot eat them unless you are awake.'

Dazed and still feeling Ravensford's impassioned kisses on her skin, Mary Margaret finger-combed her hair back and stretched like a satisfied cat. 'What time is it?'

'Going on eleven.' Annabell smirked. 'You must have stayed up late after we returned.'

Surely Annabell did not know about her time in the Earl's chambers. She cast a surreptitious glance at the girl, but Annabell had moved on to the breakfast tray sitting on a nearby table. By now she knew Annabell well enough to realise that if the girl really had known something she would have stayed right where she was until she had got the information out of Mary Margaret. It was with a great deal of relief that she put on her robe and joined her charge at the table.

They poured chocolate and ate several slices of toast before Annabell said archly, 'Oh, I forgot to tell you. Mr Fox is below stairs, waiting to meet with you.'

Mary Margaret choked on a piece of crust. 'Thomas is here to see me and you forgot?'

Annabell laughed. 'Someone must put your brother-in-law in his proper place. I swear the man thinks he is some sort of Greek god and that all women should swoon at his feet.'

Mary Margaret goggled even as infinite relief flowed through her like water. She took a sip of chocolate. 'I thought you were rather taken with him.'

Annabell had the grace to look slightly uncomfortable, but only for a minute. 'Oh,' she said lightly, flipping her hand as though she tossed something away. 'I was only practising my skills at flirting. After all, being married and the clergy, he should be safe.'

'Prac—' Mary Margaret put her cup down before she spilled the contents on herself. 'That is abominable. A lady would never do such a thing.' Her laugh ameliorated her words.

Annabell smiled contentedly. 'A lady certainly would. What she would not do is admit it to anyone else unless she trusted that person implicitly.'

Mary Margaret sobered immediately. 'Thank you so much, Annabell. I cannot tell you how much that means to me.'

Annabell rose and dropped to her knees beside Mary Margaret and threw her arms around her. 'Oh, I shall miss you so when this Season is over. You have become like an older sister. The one I never had.' She hugged Mary Margaret tightly and kissed her on the cheek. 'I so wish you could stay part of Godmother's family or come to mine.'

Her face lit up. 'That is it. I will beg Papa and Mama to let you come live with us. I have a younger sister who will need a chaperon. Unless I contract an acceptable alliance. Then you shall come stay with me.' She beamed with satisfaction.

Mary Margaret hugged Annabell back and fought off the tears her declaration had caused. 'My dear, that is so wonderful of you.' She carefully released the younger woman. 'But I could not live with you, your family or the Countess. Much as I would like to stay with you, I have a sister and niece who need me. I shall be returning to them when I leave here.'

'You cannot mean that.' Annabell jumped to her feet. 'Your sister is married to Mr Fox. The way he treats you he cannot want you with his family.'

Every word was true, but she could not, would not tell Annabell that. The girl did not need to know the sometimes ugly part of life. Instead she used Thomas as an excuse to end their conversation. She hugged Annabell and shooed her from the room. Minutes later she entered the drawing room where Thomas waited.

He whirled around at the sound of the door. 'It took you long enough.'

It took all of Mary Margaret's self-control not to cringe from the fury in Thomas's face. Annabell's little game of come-uppance would make this meeting nasty.

'I thought you would call tomorrow. I was asleep when I heard you were here. I am sorry it took so long.'

His words lashed out. 'See that it does not happen again.'

She nodded. How she wished she was braver and could make herself stand up to his tyranny. Somehow she managed to defy Ravensford all the time, but not Thomas.

The best she could do was ask, 'Why are you here?'

The smile he gave her was not pleasant. 'Have you heard the latest *on-dit* making the rounds of the *ton*?'

She shook her head, not liking this. He was going to tell her something awful. She could feel it.

'I thought not,' he said with satisfaction. 'You probably have not heard of White's betting book either, have you?'

Again she shook her head. She was having difficulty getting a deep breath and her fingers were starting to shake. He was enjoying this too much.

'It is a book that the premier men in London write bets in. Your name is not in it, but it mentions you.' He gloated. 'In fact, there is a bet on how long it will take Ravensford to set you up in your own establishment as his mistress. Everyone knows he bought you an entire wardrobe.'

She swayed and would have fallen but for the chair behind her. As it was, she hit the seat so hard she nearly sent it over backward.

She was ruined. Last night had been nothing to Ravensford but part of a bet.

Black spots swam before her eyes.

'An interesting bit of information, don't you think?' Thomas asked cruelly.

She could not even nod. She could barely sit upright. Her heart was slowly crumbling to pieces.

She stared at nothing. Last night had been magical and magic did not last. She knew that. But, oh, how she had wanted it to.

And did this really make any difference? Ravensford had offered her marriage—again. She had all but said yes. So what if he did not love her and was only doing it to prevent a scandal? The aristocracy did not wed for love. That was something else she knew. But she loved him.

She closed her eyes.

'What are you doing here?'

Ravensford's cold voice penetrated the haze of pain surrounding her. She had not heard him enter. She had even forgotten that Thomas was here. It was strange how her world had gone from the crystal clarity of love to the dull blur of a heart wound.

'I came to speak with my sister-in-law,' Thomas answered, his voice equally chill.

'She does not seem interested in what you have to say.'

'Oh, she was. Believe me, she was.'

Thomas's voice was slick as oil on water. Mary Margaret wanted to jump up and slap him for destroying all her dreams, however far-fetched they had been. He was the one who had put her in the position to meet Ravensford and he was the one who had told her the truth and ruined everything.

She opened her eyes and looked directly at her brother-in-law. 'Go away, Thomas.'

He looked at her as though she had grown a second head. She nearly giggled, but it was too much effort. She felt a mild sense of wonder at her bravery, quickly gone.

'I will see you tonight at the ball,' Thomas said with heavy meaning.

She ignored him. Her emotions were too battered. *Ravensford had never said he loved her*. She had been too caught up in the wonder of what they were doing and his promise to care for her and hers that she had not realised that at the time.

He came and kneeled in front or her. Taking both her hands in his, he asked, 'What did he do to make you look this way?'

'He told me about the bet.'

'Ahh.' He leaned back on his heels. 'It was stupid of me to think you would not hear about it, but I had hoped.'

'For all your knowledge of the *ton* and politics, you are not very well versed in human nature.'

He shrugged and stood. 'It does not make any difference.'

She rose and moved to the door. 'You are deluding yourself, Ravensford.'

She left before he could stop her. She needed privacy and time to sort through her feelings, time to become numb, and headed for the gazebo.

She sat quietly in the sylvan green. Roses scented the air and a light breeze kept her from getting hot. She loved it here.

*Love.* What an overused word. She loved cherries. She loved roses. She loved this gazebo. Then what did she feel for Ravensford? She cared if he was happy or hurt or angry. He was the person she thought the most about and cared the most for. She liked the way he considered others and went out of his way to help them. She liked everything about him.

Well…maybe some things irritated her, but not enough to matter.

Yes, she *loved* him. Everything else was only a like.

But what to do? He did not love her. He desired her, lusted after her. That was physical while love was emotional and spiritual. A flush warmed her as memories of last night heated her body. Perhaps there was the physical in love as well.

Marrying him would solve all her problems. He had the money and power to protect Emily and Annie from Thomas. He could give them a good life. She would be with the only man she would ever love or want to love. She would have his children. But being married to him when he did not love her would be a bitter pill.

She jumped up and paced the tiny, enclosed space. She could become his mistress. He would still provide protection for Emily and Annie. She might still bear at least one of his children—a bastard.

She stopped and buried her face in her hands. She could not do that to any child of hers.

Nor would he want to marry her if he ever found out that Thomas had placed her with the Countess in order to steal from her. It would not matter that she never intended to carry out Thomas's plan. It would be enough that she had allowed herself to go along with Thomas. Ravensford would despise her if he ever learned that. She could not bear the thought of being married to him when he found out and seeing his contempt every time he looked at her.

If he loved her, truly loved her, he might forgive her.

No, it would be better to go to the Countess and ask for her salary. It would not provide what Ravensford would, but it would be better for all of them this way. That had always been her plan.

Her decision made, Mary Margaret wondered why she did not feel at least a little better. But she did not.

She found the Countess in her suite and waited patiently until the older woman would see her. She had plenty of time to marvel at her continued bravery. In the past two hours, she had put herself forward more than she had in her entire life—except when dealing with Ravensford. She pushed that painful memory aside. There was no time to wallow in misery as the Countess's maid, Jane, had just opened the door.

'Her ladyship will see you now.' She frowned fiercely

at Mary Margaret and barely moved enough to allow the younger woman to get by.

'Thank you,' Mary Margaret said quietly.

Jane had never liked her. Having to pack her clothes for the trip from Ireland had only made the animosity worse.

'My lady.' Mary Margaret curtsied.

The Countess gave her a stony look. 'What do you want?'

Not a good start, Mary Margaret thought, but then there never was with this woman. It took all her willpower not to wring her hands. That would only give the Countess satisfaction.

'It is the end of the quarter.' Perhaps the woman would take a hint.

'So?' She looked back at the embroidery in her lap.

Mary Margaret was not surprised, but she was angry. 'My salary is due.'

The Countess turned back to Mary Margaret, her eyes hard as fine gems and her mouth a cruel line. 'Salary? You have no salary coming. It was all spent to replace my cape that you convinced my foolish son you needed.'

'What?' Mary Margaret felt as though she had taken a direct hit to the stomach. 'But I sent it back to you. It was in perfect shape. I made sure myself.'

The Countess made a tiny, derisive snort. 'Do you really think I would wear something after you had? And there are all the clothes Andrew purchased for you. You will be a long time repaying those.'

Worse and worse. Panic rose its ugly head, and it was all Mary Margaret could do to make herself breathe. This was beyond reasonable.

'Why are you doing this?' Her voice was a deep rasp of

anguish. 'I have never done anything to you. All I have ever wanted was to be a good servant and companion.'

The Countess sneered, her lovely face marred by hate. 'You have seduced my only child. Do you think I don't know what has been going on? You blanch, as you should. You are no better than the sluts who ply their wares in Covent Garden.'

Mary Margaret felt light-headed and wondered if she would further disgrace herself by fainting. She swayed but managed to stay upright.

'I have done nothing of the kind,' she said, but even to her, her voice sounded weak and false.

He had seduced her. Surely that made a difference. Didn't it? Not to this woman. Not to anyone but her.

A sly look replaced the previous fury on the Countess's countenance. 'I want you out of this house immediately. I will provide you with money to return to Ireland. If you do this, I will forget about everything else. But do not ever come near my son again.'

Blow on blow. She could get back to Ireland, but once there would have nothing to live on, let alone provide for Emily and Annie.

The small rebellious and brave part of her that seemed to be growing by the hour wanted to defy the Countess. That part wanted to marry Ravensford and be damned to the consequences. It gave her courage now.

'I need more than passage home. I need money to live on.'

She trembled at her temerity. Just days or even hours ago she would not have been able to say those things. But it was done. She kept her gaze on the other woman instead of looking away as she longed to do.

The Countess drew herself up. 'You are a bold piece. How much do you want?'

'What is due me for this last quarter worked.'

'Done,' the Countess said. 'Now get out of my sight.'

Mary Margaret did so with alacrity. She rushed out of the room, the door slamming behind her, and right into Ravensford's arms.

'Where are you going in such a hurry?'

'Home.'

The word was out of her mouth before she had time to even think. Her nerves were jangling and her mind was numb.

His face showed no emotion. 'Ireland?'

She nodded.

'Because of my mother or because of the bet?' His voice was dangerously quiet, but Mary Margaret had been through too much in the last twenty-four hours to care.

'Both.'

'I think not,' he said softly, too softly.

Before she knew what was happening, he dragged her back into his mother's room. 'Out,' he ordered Jane who stood her ground until the Countess nodded.

'You have overstepped yourself this time, Mother,' he said.

She glared down her aristocratic nose at him even though she remained seated and he towered over her. 'I am only trying to protect you from your own folly. She is nothing but an adventuress. I should have never brought her into my household.'

Ravensford still held her so Mary Margaret could not flee. She had to listen to them discuss her as though she was not present. The tiny core of rebellion growing inside her flared to life.

'I am not an object for the two of you to bicker over.'

'Keep quiet,' the Countess ordered.

'I am a human being with feelings.'

The Countess gave her a contemptuous look. 'You are little better than—'

'Mother,' Ravensford said. 'I warn you. Mary Margaret is going to marry me. What you say to her now will impact on what happens to you after we are wed.'

The Countess paled, her translucent skin looking like a ghost. Her eyes were bright flames. 'I will not allow you to do such a thing, Andrew.'

Mary Margaret twisted in his hold, but he tightened his grip. 'I did not agree,' she said softly, wondering why even now she contradicted him.

Because she wanted to marry him for love. Nor would he want to marry her if he ever found out that she had been sent here to steal from his mother.

He gazed down at her. 'Oh, you agreed. You agreed very willingly.'

She saw the fire and hunger leap into his eyes and knew exactly what he meant. By giving herself to him last night, she had, in his mind, committed to him. He was right, she had at the time.

'Things have changed,' she said, her voice deep and raspy with remembered pain. 'For me.'

'But not for me.'

'Andrew.' The Countess's tone demanded attention. 'I won't have it. If you marry her, I will do everything in my power to see that she is ostracised by Society.'

Compassion softened the angles of his face. 'That does

not matter, Mother. Not everyone cares about being accepted by the *ton*. I don't. I am sure Mary Margaret does not. And we all know that Lady Holland does not. Nor has her lack of acceptance impacted on Lord Holland's political career,' he ended with a meaningful look.

The Countess huffed. 'I was not about to suggest that Lady Holland's scandalous past has hurt Lord Holland in the least. But no decent woman will go to their house.'

Ravensford shook his head. 'I doubt it matters to them, Mother.'

'Well, it should. Just as it should matter to you.' She cast a venomous look at Mary Margaret. 'You will be sorry if you defy me. She won't make you happy.' Suddenly, like the sun peaking through clouds, a wistfulness entered her eyes. 'Not like your father and I were.'

'She is right,' Mary Margaret said. 'Ours would be a marriage of convenience. You would grow tired of me.'

A strange light turned his eyes a deeper green. 'I am going to announce our engagement tonight during the ball.'

Both women gasped.

'No,' the Countess ordered.

'You cannot,' Mary Margaret whispered, horrified.

'I can and I will.'

## Chapter Fifteen

Ravensford turned from the fire in time to see Mary Margaret framed in the drawing-room doorway. Fierce pride filled him.

After him, she was the first one down. Jones bowed himself out, leaving the two of them alone.

Madame Bertrice's gown accomplished everything he had wished for. The deep pink brought colour to her face, giving her the famous cream-and-roses complexion. Her tilted eyes glowed like green brilliants. Even the demure, almost harsh, line of her chignon appeared elegant, as though it had been specially designed to show off the gown's plunging neckline.

Mary Margaret's bosom swelled above the fine silk, drawing his eye to the dark valley that he longed to explore. Once had not been enough. He was not sure a lifetime would be enough. From the first moment he had heard the sultry purr of her voice he had desired her. Tonight she was his.

Or would be, he thought ironically, seeing the coldness in her face, once he had convinced her that marriage was best.

'You are beautiful,' he said. He picked the jewellery box up from the table beside him and opened it. 'These will complement your dress.' He took out the grey pearls.

Her gaze flicked to the necklace and back to him. 'They are not appropriate.'

There was no bending in her. 'You have gained strength since I first met you.'

'I have had to.' Her voice was lightly tinged with bitterness. 'Is your mother down?' Only now did her tone hold a hint of discomfort.

'My mother has nothing to do with this, Mary Margaret.' When she did not respond, he added, 'She will be going back to Ireland soon. You and I will stay here. Your sister and niece are being brought here.'

Mary Margaret listened to his words and wondered why he was doing all these things. He did not love her, yet he would not let her go.

After leaving his mother's suites earlier, he had told her that no matter what the Countess had said or offered to pay her, she was not leaving. Since that time, she had been a virtual prisoner in the house. The only thing that had brought her down for the evening was his vow that he had already sent for her sister. She owed him her presence that he seemed so insistent on having.

'I will not marry you,' she said yet again. 'Your mother is right.'

But how she longed to do so. If he only loved her she would take the risk. Even now, it hurt just to tell him no when she wanted so badly to tell him yes. But it would take more than lust for him to tolerate her if he ever found out that she had been sent by Thomas to rob his mother and she had not told Thomas no.

'Turn around,' he said, more gently. 'I am determined that you will wear these.'

She sighed. How much longer could she keep fighting him? She did not know. For the moment it was easier to acquiesce. After all, he had already bought her an entire wardrobe, and although she did not wear any of the clothes, the entire world knew about them. They were still packed in boxes in her room. She turned.

His fingers brushed the nape of her neck and his warm breath fanned her skin. She clenched her hands into fists to keep from turning and wrapping them into his hair. He made her blood sing and her heart thrill.

'Please hurry,' she rasped.

'Am I bothering you?' His voice was as rich as cream and as potent as the liquor he drank.

'No.'

He chuckled low in his throat. 'I'm almost done. Then there are the ear bobs and the bracelets.'

She nearly groaned. This was torture, and drat the man, he knew it. No matter how she tried, her body and soul responded to him. No matter how she strove to hide her reaction he knew.

His hands shifted to her shoulders and he turned her unresisting body so that she faced him. 'Say yes.'

She caught back a moan. How she wanted to accept him. She wanted that more than anything. If only she could. If only they could somehow make it work. If only he loved her then she would take the chance. Romantic fool that she was, she believed that love could make anything work.

She knew he watched her but she studiously looked away.

The last thing she wanted was to see the hunger in his eyes that he did nothing to hide. She wanted his love, not just his passion. He didn't love her and, foolish woman that she was, she wanted love.

'I cannot,' she whispered. 'I must not. Believe me, this is for the best.'

'Then look at me when you refuse and convince me that you speak the truth.' Anger tinged his words now and his eyes, when she looked back at him, flared.

Before she could say anything, and she did not know what to say, the door opened and Jones announced, 'The Countess of Ravensford and Miss Winston. Mr Fox.'

Mary Margaret broke from Ravensford's hold. The expression on the Countess's face as she watched them made Mary Margaret feel as though she had been caught doing something despicable. In the Countess's opinion, she had.

Thomas subjected her to a narrowed scrutiny. 'Cosy, aren't we,' he said sarcastically.

She arched one brow. 'I thought you were not invited until after dinner?' It was a low hit, but it gave her satisfaction.

He smirked. 'Your delightful charge invited me. I considered her wishes to take precedence over Ravensford's.'

Annabell came up to them and beamed. 'I see you two have finally worked everything out. I am so glad.' She hugged Mary Margaret. 'It will be wonderful having you in the family.'

Mary Margaret returned the girl's hug. 'You are so impetuous, Annabell,' she chided gently. 'The Earl and I have no agreement and nothing to arrange.'

Annabell stepped back and gave the two of them an arch look. 'I did not fall off the turnip wagon yesterday.' She laughed and moved away.

It was just as well. Jones announced more arrivals. Dinner would consume the near future. Then the ball. Mary Margaret knew the entire evening would be a crush of bodies.

And she still had to tell Thomas that she was not going to steal the Countess's jewellery tonight. Discomfort was a condition she was becoming depressingly familiar with.

'Nice pearls,' Thomas hissed. 'Make sure you take them with you.'

She jumped, not having heard him come up behind her. 'Be careful. Someone could overhear.'

He laughed. It was not a pleasant sound. She moved quickly away only to find herself caught up by Ravensford. Before she knew what he was doing, she was being introduced to everyone.

Ravensford smiled at each person as he presented her, but his eyes were hard chips until the introduction was graciously accepted. Mary Margaret realised that he was trying to present her to his Society and force them to accept her regardless of the rumours flying.

After an eternity, they went into dinner. Mary Margaret nearly fled the room when she realised she was to be seated beside Ravensford. Everyone looked at her and she did her best not to blush. The only saving grace with the arrangement was that the Countess was at the opposite end of the table.

The woman across the table eyed Mary Margaret through her lorgnette. 'Where did you say you are from, Miss O'Brien?'

'Ireland, my lady.' Old habits die hard and it was not until the form of address was out that Mary Margaret realised it was inappropriate for her current situation.

'She is from Cashel, Ireland, Lady Steele,' Ravensford cut in. 'Near my mother's estate.' He gave the woman a feral smile. 'Would you care for more turtle soup?'

'Please,' Lady Steele said, turning her attention to the gentleman on her left.

Mary Margaret's dinner partner to her right, Mr Atworthy, asked, 'How long will you be staying in Town, Miss O'Brien?'

'Quite some time,' Ravensford said smoothly before she could answer.

Mr Atworthy looked from her to the Earl, his interest obviously piqued. 'Really? Are you by any chance Miss Winston's chaperon, Miss O'Brien?'

A direct question with only one answer. 'Yes,' she said firmly before Ravensford could reply.

She was grateful that her voice had not wavered. They would dine on her like a shark on a minnow if she faltered. Ravensford gave her an approving smile.

'She was, Atworthy. No more.'

Atworthy raised one brow. 'How intriguing.'

The next course arrived and while the bowls and plates were removed Mary Margaret tried to marshal her thoughts. If she could get through dinner, she could escape while everyone was going to the ballroom and the rest of the guests were arriving. She just had to grit her teeth and bear the next hour or so.

She was nearly ready to plead sickness when the Countess stood, indicating that the ladies were to withdraw. She stood with alacrity even though she knew she had to wait for the other women to precede her from the room. All the gentlemen's gazes turned to her, watching as though she were an exotic animal and they did not know what she might do next.

A month ago she would have done her best to pretend they were not there. Even an hour ago she would have done so. But now she was tired and irritable. With a courage she had never thought she possessed, she stared each man down. The only one who refused to look away was Perth. He silently toasted her with the last of his dinner wine.

She finally swept from the room, buoyed up by Perth's silent support. Her joy was short-lived.

Two women she had previously met stood together, heads close. The first sniffed haughtily. 'So that is Ravensford's lightskirt. She isn't much. However, he has gone too far introducing her to polite society. I, for one, will never invite her anywhere.'

There it was. Even if she let herself weaken and marry Ravensford, it would be miserable. Not that she cared what the old biddy thought, but despite his earlier words, Ravensford might. And what would he and they think if they knew about Thomas's plan? It did not bear dwelling on.

Rather than continue to subject herself to such treatment, Mary Margaret decided it was time to go to her room. Later, after the dancing had started, she would come back down and seek out Thomas.

With weary relief, she entered her room and closed the door behind her. She would lie down for a few minutes and try to regain her strength.

She set the candle on the table and snuffed the flame. She stretched out on her bed with a weary sigh, careful to smooth her dress so as not to wrinkle it any more than necessary. The last thing she wanted was to get a maid to help her undress and then dress again.

* * *

Mary Margaret woke with a start. The room was too dark to see anything clearly, but she sensed she was not alone.

She sat up and swung her legs over the side of the bed until her feet touched the floor. 'Who is there?' she asked in a voice that just kept from trembling.

'Not Ravensford,' Thomas said nastily.

A kind of relief slumped her shoulders. Thomas was not someone she wanted in her bedchamber, but he would not hurt her. Or had not done so yet.

She lit the candle by the bed and carried it over to the chair beside Thomas. She sat down and placed the candle on the table.

'Why are you here?'

He snorted in disgust. 'Don't be any more stupid than you have to be. Why do you think I am here? Where are the jewels?'

The single light threw his handsome face into harsh relief. His eyes were dark sockets. Mary Margaret found that she was suddenly tense. Still, there was no sense in prolonging the inevitable.

She licked dry lips. 'I assume they are in the Countess's room. Or the Earl's safe.'

'When do you intend to get them?' he asked softly, his voice silky smooth.

She decided to get closer to the door. She stood and walked casually away, hoping he would think she was moving from nervousness caused by contemplating the theft.

'Where do you think you are going?'

He moved too fast. She broke for the door. He caught her, his fingers gripping her wrist cruelly.

'I asked you a question,' he said, tightening his hold.

Her heart beat like a drum. It was all she could do to keep herself from shouting for help. She told herself she was being silly. He might be hurting her, but still this was only Thomas. He could not reach Emily and Annie. He had no hold over her.

She took a deep breath and stared up at him. She was barely able to make out his features, but she sensed he was tense.

'I was leaving…but not to get the jewels.' She twisted her arm in a vain attempt to get free. 'I am not going to steal from the Countess.'

He tossed her against the wall. The force of contact knocked the air out of her lungs. She gasped.

'Tell me that again,' he threatened.

She forced herself to straighten up even though her chest hurt badly. She told herself she knew he would not seriously injure her, but she still feared the pain he could cause.

'Who's in there?' Ravensford's voice said from outside.

Relief flooded Mary Margaret only to be followed by dread. He would keep Thomas from doing anything more to her, but she had no doubt that Thomas would see that she paid for refusing to help him. She sighed and slumped against the wall.

'Come in,' Thomas said.

Ravensford entered and closed the door behind himself. He carried a candelabra with five candles. Light radiated out in a circle, so bright it hurt Mary Margaret's eyes after the dimness of seconds before.

'What are you doing here?' Ravensford's baritone was deep and dangerous.

Thomas smirked. 'Perhaps you should ask your *chère*

*amie.*' He gave Mary Margaret a sly look. 'Or have you already told him?'

She knew she looked guilty when Thomas laughed.

'No, you have not.' Contempt dripped from every word. 'I swear you have no spine. Just like your sister. You sleep with the man but cannot find the courage to tell him the truth about why you are working for his mother.'

Shame burned through Mary Margaret. Thomas was a cad, but he said only the truth right now.

She could not make herself look at Ravensford. She looked at a spot near his shoulder. She did not want to see the disgust on his face when she told him. She could not stand to see his eyes fill with the same contempt that shone in Thomas's.

'Tell him,' Thomas said, 'or I will.'

She cast her brother-in-law a venomous look.

'I was supposed to steal your mother's jewellery tonight. That is why Thomas is here, to pick up the gems.'

There. The awful truth was out. It was over. Now he would hate her. He would be thankful she had refused his offer of marriage. He would throw her out when he threw out Thomas.

A single tear escaped her control. Not only would she never see him again, but he would always remember her this way—as a thief and cheat and coward.

Pain such as she had never imagined possible welled up inside her. So much pain, quickly followed by anger—at herself, at Thomas.

Without thinking, propelled by the mingled pain and anger, she launched herself at Thomas's sneering face. She balled her fist and let loose. She connected and Thomas rocked back on his heels.

She glared at him. 'I hate you for what you are and what you have done to my sister and what you tried to make me do.' Tears started down her cheeks in earnest and she twisted away from his shocked face. 'But most of all I hate myself for not being strong enough to tell you no right from the start.'

She heard scuffling and the heavy thud of someone hitting the floor. Thomas sprawled on the rug, one hand on his red jaw. Ravensford towered over him.

'Get up and get out. Leave England if you know what is good for you. Don't return to Ireland. With Mary Margaret's confession I can have the magistrate waiting for you there. Once word is out about what you planned, you will be ruined. No one wants a curate like you. And don't try to find your wife and daughter. If I catch you near them, I will have you horsewhipped like the cur you are.'

Shivers raced up Mary Margaret's spine. She hoped never to see Ravensford this deadly angry again. Her heart twisted. She did not have to worry. She would never see him again at all.

Thomas turned bitter eyes on Mary Margaret. 'Don't worry about your precious sister. I never wanted her. She got pregnant and I had to marry her because of my position. All I ever wanted in life was what I deserved, what I was born to. Your refusal to steal has only delayed that. I'll find someone else with more guts than a worm.'

He strode away, pausing inches from Ravensford. 'She's not worth whatever she will cost you. Nor is her mealy-mouthed sister. You are welcome to the lot.'

Anger burned away Mary Margaret's tears. 'How dare you? How dare you speak of them like that? If Emily was pregnant before you wed, it was because you seduced her and she loved you too much to say no. You are despicable.'

'Get out now,' Ravensford said, 'before I thrash you to within an inch of your life.'

Thomas left without another word. Silence filled the room like dirt in a grave. Mary Margaret felt like her life was finished. From now on she would merely exist. But at least Emily was free of Thomas.

'Mary Margaret,' Ravensford said softly, 'come here. Please.'

She looked at him, expecting to see contempt or dislike and instead saw compassion and another emotion she did not dare name. 'I think it would be better if I left now.'

He shook his head. 'What have I been saying to you all this time?'

She stood mute. There was nothing left she could say. He knew everything about her and she knew he could not still want to marry her. He had not wanted to marry her in the first place. Only his honour had made him propose.

'Mary Margaret, if I have to come and get you I will make sure you don't get away.'

'Why?' Agony twisted her soul. 'You don't want me. You never wanted me—except in your bed. Then when the bet was made you were too much the gentleman not to propose.' She gulped air, trying to ease some of the tension tearing her apart. 'Please, Ravensford, don't do this. I can be gone immediately. You have done enough just by getting Thomas out of my sister's life. And I thank you from my heart.'

A tiny smile tugged at his mouth. 'I don't want your thanks from the heart, Mary Margaret.' He moved slowly toward her. 'I want more than that.'

She tilted back her head to see his face. His eyes were

dark, his cheeks sharp lines. If she did not know it was impossible, she would say he wanted her—still.

'I have given you everything I have,' she whispered.

He stopped when only inches separated them. 'Have
you?' A fierce predatory gleam lit his face. 'Then tell me.'

'Don't do this,' she pleaded. 'It is not fair that I love you
and you don't feel the same about me.' She buried her face
in her hands. 'There, I have told you. Once more I was not
strong enough to walk from here without doing as you bid.'

With exultation he grabbed her and cradled her against
his chest. One hand angled her reluctant head up so that
he looked down at her. The other hand burrowed into her
thick hair.

'Foolish, love. You are the strongest woman I know. You
have cared for your sister, worked for my mother and stood
up to Fox—not to mention me.'

Love. He had called her love.

Hope flared, only to die. 'I am weak or I would have
never agreed to Thomas's plan.'

He kissed her gently. 'You had no choice. I heard him
threaten you that day in my mother's library.'

'What?' She went rigid, both hands pressing against his
chest in an effort to get free. He held her closer. 'You have
known all along?'

He nodded. 'I knew you did not want to do as he said,
but that you feared for Emily. Later I learned Emily is your
sister.'

'But why did you let the charade go on? Why have you
treated me so well?' Confusion now held her still in his embrace. She did not know what to think.

He grinned ruefully. 'I was intrigued by you, by everything about you.' He stroked one finger down her jaw to her chin where the cleft was. 'I still am. I think I always will be.'

'But I am nothing.'

'Stop that.' He shook her. 'You are kind and caring. You were willing to do anything to help your sister. And Annabell adores you. The servants like and respect you.'

She was dazed. 'But you don't love me. You cannot. We are from different worlds and I have lived a lie in your home.' Every word hurt, but they had to be said. 'And I want love when I marry.'

'Ah, Mary Margaret.' He stroked her hair back from her face. 'Have I been so good at hiding my feelings? Don't you know that I love you? Can't you sense it when I touch you, when I kiss you? And when we made love, didn't you feel me worship you with my body?'

Stunned, she would have slid to the floor if he had not been holding her. 'I know you desire me. But that is not love.'

'You have so much to learn about men, my love. Making love to you is a form of loving you. Just as caring for you and caring for your sister. Men show their love through deeds, not through words.' He paused as though gathering his courage. 'Mary Margaret, I love you. I want to marry you.'

Hope began to fill her heart. Perhaps there was a chance for them. Perhaps he truly did love her.

She tried her last argument. 'What about your mother?'

'She can go to Ireland or she can accept you and stay around and watch our children grow.' He gazed lovingly at her. 'Because now that I have found you and made you admit that you love me, I am not letting you get away.'

The hope that had started filled her to overflowing. She

could no longer refuse him or herself. She loved him too much to let him go now.

'Then we will have to make this work.'

'Yes, my love, we will.'

# *Epilogue*

*One year later...*

Mary Margaret stood in the doorway to the nursery and silently watched her mother-in-law. The Countess held the future Earl of Ravensford, cooing at the infant like the besotted grandmother she was.

A large, warm hand twined around hers and pulled her away. Ravensford, her husband, smiled down at her as he guided her along the hall.

'My mother will take good care of our son, sweetings.'

She snuggled into his side. 'I know. I just like to watch the two of them together. It reassures me that there is a gentle, caring side to your mother.'

He tenderly smoothed a strand of hair from her brow. 'I know she still is not always nice to you. I am sorry for that. More than I can say.'

She went on tiptoe and kissed him lightly. 'I know. Things

are better and with time—who knows? She and I might become bosom friends.'

He shook his head in wonder. 'Your continual ability to look at the positive always amazes me.'

He caught her lips with his, deepening the kiss until she leaned against his chest in complete surrender. He was her entire world.

'Aunt,' a young, feminine voice said in shocked tones. 'You and Uncle Andrew are going to scandalise the servants.'

Another woman's warm laugh filled the area. 'Annie, leave your aunt and uncle alone. Theirs is a love match.'

Mary Margaret grinned at her niece and sister. 'I am so glad you decided to come stay with us.'

'As am I,' Ravensford seconded. 'Not only do you provide additional family for my love, but you are safer from Fox if he should decide my threat is hollow.'

All three females gazed adoringly at him, but his wife hugged him. 'Thomas would never doubt you. He ran from my room that night like a fox fleeing the hounds.'

'And just what was he doing in your room?' the Countess demanded, having come up on the group without their noticing. Baby Andrew cooed contentedly in his grandmother's arms.

Mary Margaret reached for her son. 'It is time for his feeding,' she murmured, having decided to nurse her child instead of having a wet-nurse. She cast a mischievous glance at her husband as she left him to deal with his mother.

But Ravensford was not going to be deserted. 'Excuse me, ladies. I will explain everything to you later, Mother. Right now a father's place is with his wife and son.'

Mary Margaret chuckled as she sat down in the rocker and put her baby to her breast. Baby Andrew had just settled in when Ravensford closed the nursery door. He looked at his wife and child, the boy's mouth sucking avidly at one milky-white breast.

'Your bosom is larger than before,' Ravensford murmured, taking a seat beside them.

She intended to only glance at him, but the desire he made no effort to hide caught her. A flush mounted her skin, starting where her child suckled and rising to her cheeks.

'Ravensford,' she murmured in slight protest. 'This is not the time.'

'I know,' he muttered, his voice a husk. 'But after our son has his fill I insist on having mine. He needs a little sister and I've a mind to do my best to provide him with one.'

Excitement curled in Mary Margaret's stomach. 'And I've a mind to help you, my lord.'

Ravensford leaned over and kissed her. 'I love you.'

'And I you,' she replied, meaning it with all her heart and soul.

* * * * *

# MILLS & BOON

## Book Club

Have your favourite series delivered to your door every month with a Mills & Boon subscription.

**Use code ROMANCE2021 to get 50% off the first month of your chosen subscription PLUS free delivery.**

Sign up online at
**millsandboon.com.au/subscription-2**

or call Customer Service on

AUS **1300 659 500** or NZ **0800 265 546**

**No Lock-in Contracts**

**Free Postage**

**Exclusive Offers**

For full terms and conditions go to millsandboon.com.au
Offer expires June 30, 2021

For fans of

# REGENCY ROMANCE

look in-store or online for these latest releases.

Regency now available in
a **LARGER FORMAT!**

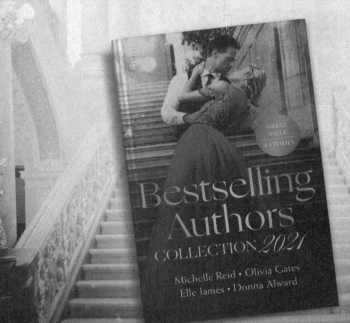

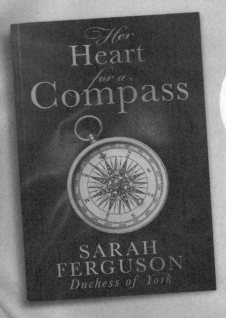

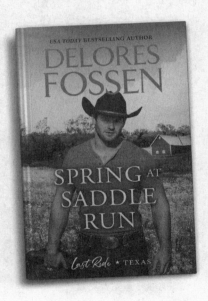

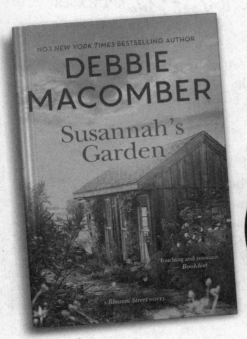

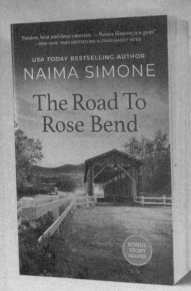

# LET'S TALK ABOUT BOOKS!

## JOIN THE CONVERSATION

MILLSANDBOON
AUSTRALIA

@MILLSANDBOONAUS

ESCAPE THE EVERY DAY AT
MILLSANDBOON.COM.AU